A CHRISTMAS CRACKER

Trisha Ashley was born in St Helens, Lancashire, and gave up her fascinating but time-consuming hobbies of house-moving and divorce a few years ago in order to settle in North Wales. She is a *Sunday Times* bestselling author.

For more information about Trisha please visit www.trishaashley.com, her Facebook fan page (Trisha Ashley Books) or her Twitter account @trishaashley.

By the same author:

Sowing Secrets
A Winter's Tale
Wedding Tiers
Chocolate Wishes
Twelve Days of Christmas
The Magic of Christmas
Chocolate Shoes and Wedding Blues
Good Husband Material
Wish Upon a Star
Finding Mr Rochester
Every Woman for Herself
Creature Comforts

TRISHA ASHLEY

A Christmas Cracker

AVON

This novel is entirely a work of fiction.
The names, characters and incidents portrayed in it are
the work of the author's imagination. Any resemblance to
actual persons, living or dead, events or localities is
entirely coincidental.

AVON

A division of HarperCollins*Publishers*
1 London Bridge Street,
London SE1 9GF

www.harpercollins.co.uk

First published in Great Britain by HarperCollins*Publishers* in 2015
1

A catalogue record for this book is
available from the British Library

ISBN-13: 978-1-84756-280-7

Set in Minion by Palimpsest Book Production Limited,
Falkirk, Stirlingshire

Printed and bound in Great Britain by
Clays Ltd, St Ives plc

MIX
Paper from responsible sources
FSC® C007454

FSC™ is a non-profit international organisation established to promote
the responsible management of the world's forests. Products carrying the
FSC label are independently certified to assure consumers that they come
from forests that are managed to meet the social, economic and
ecological needs of present and future generations,
and other controlled sources.

Find out more about HarperCollins and the environment at
www.harpercollins.co.uk/green

For Grace

Chapter 1: Bottled

'You mean you've known for ages that your boss at Champers&Chocs was passing off bottles of cheap fizz as vintage champagne, and you haven't done a single thing about it?' Kate exclaimed incredulously, her pale blue eyes wide and a cup of herbal tea the exact colour of cat pee suspended halfway to her rose-tinted lips.

Kate was my opposite in looks, being small, fair and cute, though she wasn't as cute as she thought she was, unless you were *really* fond of rabbits. And speaking of rabbits, she should long since have put her penchant for pale pink fluffy jumpers behind her, even if the angora had been ethically sourced, which I doubted.

I sighed and stirred my Americano, starting to wish I hadn't said anything about it because, after all, she and her husband were Jeremy's old friends, not mine, and she'd been less than welcoming when we'd first got engaged. But sometimes Kate and I would meet up for coffee and, that day being one of those occasions, my worries had spilled out of me the moment we'd sat down.

It wouldn't have happened if I'd been able to tell my best friend, Emma, but since she'd remarried she'd increasingly been having problems of her own with her husband, Desmond, so I hadn't wanted to burden her with mine.

Still, at least she wouldn't have gazed at me in the sad, accusing way Kate was, when I looked up.

'The idea that anything fraudulent was going on never crossed my mind until I found out by accident,' I explained. 'I mean, I don't think I'd even *seen* a real bottle of champagne, other than on the TV, until I got engaged to Jeremy.'

'No, I don't suppose there are champagne bars on every corner of council estates,' she said snidely. 'Just cheap booze shops.'

For the last years of her life, Mum and I had shared a specially adapted council bungalow on a very nice estate, but Kate always talked as if I was dragged up in a slum and had made some giant social leap by getting engaged to a member of the teaching profession.

'Oh, forget it,' I snapped.

'No, you can't just leave it there without telling me how you found out and why you didn't report it to the police,' she insisted.

'Because I thought it had stopped. It was before last Christmas, when I was packing special orders one evening and my boss and I were the only people there. There was a phone call and I walked into his office to tell him—'

'I have wondered about those late nights, just the two of you . . .' she said suggestively.

I stared at her in astonishment. 'You don't mean you thought I was having a fling with *Harry Briggs*? I mean, apart from his being twenty years older than me and not my type, I'm in love with Jeremy and wouldn't dream of cheating on him.'

'Well, you have to admit it looked a bit odd.'

'I don't see why. Harry said I had the nicest handwriting for the personal messages that went in the box with the champagne and chocolates, and I was the most careful packer for the expensive orders.'

It was a pity, I thought, that those had turned out to be the fraudulent ones.

'Jeremy said you started doing casual evening packing work there while your mother was still alive,' she said. 'Harry paid you cash in hand.'

'Yes, because luckily our lovely neighbour was always happy to sit with Mum in the evenings for a couple of hours and the money was useful. A carer's allowance doesn't go very far.'

'I suppose not,' she said disinterestedly. 'But go on, you walked into Harry's office and then . . .?'

'He was sticking labels onto bottles, which seemed odd, but he explained that sometimes they got damaged and then he had to replace them.'

'And you believed that?' she asked pityingly. 'You think it's that easy to get hold of extra labels?'

'Not when I'd thought about it a bit, especially since it was the most expensive champagne we stocked. Most of what we sell isn't actually champagne, it's Prosecco, but that's made clear on the website.'

'So, did you say anything to him at the time?'

I nodded. 'When I was going home and he came out to lock up after me, I told him I'd realised he was fraudulently passing off cheap booze as expensive stuff. He said his supplier had forgotten to label one batch and he'd had to do it himself, but he was very sorry I'd seen it—'

'I bet he was!' she interrupted.

'And he'd only started the scam when the firm was going through a rocky patch,' I finished.

'Yeah, right.'

'Well, call me naïve, but when he swore he was going to stop that very night, I believed him,' I said defensively. 'He was very contrite so in the end I said I wouldn't tell anyone if he really did mean it.'

'That was so wrong of you,' Kate said censoriously. 'I would have got my coat and gone straight to the police the moment I realised what was happening. Not that I'd have been doing a packing job at a factory anyway,' she added, unable to refrain from another dig.

'There's nothing to sneer at in doing any honest job,' I said.

'It didn't exactly turn out to be an honest job, though, did it? And I assume he didn't keep his word about stopping the fraud, either. You were very credulous to think he would.'

'I wanted to believe him. In the last couple of years when Mum was so ill, he was really good to me, letting me work as and when I could, then offering me a permanent job on the afternoon shift after she died. It wasn't like I was qualified for anything else.'

As Mum fell further and further into the grip of aggressive multiple sclerosis I'd missed a lot of school and though I'd started a graphic design degree course, I'd had to drop out of it after only a year. Of course, I didn't begrudge a moment of the time I spent with Mum, but after she'd gone I was left with no money, qualifications or even a home, since the specially adapted council bungalow was urgently needed for someone else.

So I'd gratefully accepted Harry's offer and found a tiny but cheap flat over the garage attached to Jeremy's house, which was how we'd met.

At first he hadn't been that keen on Pyewacket, my cat, but after a while he became *very* keen on me, so they learned to tolerate each other . . . just as I learned to accept Jeremy's long-standing close friendship with Kate and her husband, Luke, who not only seemed joined at the hip, but all taught at the same huge, sprawling comprehensive school. Well, I say friendship, but it was more a trio of two adorers and Kate, who they think is wonderful, though I have no idea why . . .

'When did you realise he hadn't stopped the fraud?' asked Kate, jerking me out of my reverie.

'Only recently. He'd made sure I'd seen him carrying crates of what looked like the real thing into the storeroom, but one day when I was in a smart wine merchant's shop with Jeremy they had a bottle of it – and it looked nothing at all like the ones I'd been packing. Last night I told Harry I knew.'

I shivered slightly because I'd seen a side to jovial, easy-going Harry that I hadn't even suspected existed.

'He threatened me and said if I went to the police he'd tell them it had all been my idea – and since I was the one who worked the extra shifts packing the special orders, I was implicated anyway.'

'It certainly wouldn't look good,' Kate agreed helpfully.

'But it's his company and I'm just a warehouse packer, doing a bit of overtime. I told him they wouldn't believe him but he said they would when he explained that we'd been having an affair and I'd reported the fraud out of spite because he'd ended it.'

'Gosh, it's like some low-life soap series! But it serves you right for not having gone to the police as soon as you found out,' she said righteously. 'That's what I would have done.'

'Hindsight is a wonderful thing,' I said. 'In the end I told him I wouldn't shop him, but gave him a month's notice and said I wasn't doing any more overtime. He said he didn't care, so long as I kept my mouth shut.'

'Which you haven't, because you've told me,' she pointed out.

'Only because I was so upset that I was desperate to talk it through with someone and, if you remember, you promised to keep what I was going to say secret.'

'I hadn't realised it would be something criminal, though,' she objected.

'But you *will* keep it secret, won't you?' I asked.

'I suppose so, but more because it would hurt Jeremy immensely if all this came out,' Kate agreed. 'I know you haven't told him anything, or he'd have confided in me and Luke.'

That was true, and it was what had stopped me confiding in Jeremy in the first place, but now I suddenly seemed to have blabbed it out to Kate, cutting out the middleman.

'Now you'll have to find another job,' she said.

'Well . . . maybe not. I know Jeremy doesn't think my artwork is anything other than a hobby, but I've been regularly selling designs to greetings card companies, and now I've got my first one-woman exhibition in Liverpool I really think I might be able to earn a living out of it.'

In fact, I'd have left Champers&Chocs long before, had it not been for Jeremy's insistence that I not only continue to pay rent on the flat, which I mostly used to store my things and as a studio, but also my share of the expensive meals out that he, Kate and Luke enjoyed so much.

'But you know what Jeremy's like – he thinks I should pay an equal share of everything, even though he's earning a lot more than I am.'

'Well, teachers aren't that well paid, you know,' Kate said defensively.

'They get a lot more than my minimum wages, that's for sure,' I said. 'And more holidays – plus the three of you are always going off abroad on school trips.'

'Being responsible for a coach full of adolescents is not exactly a fun holiday,' she said, tossing her smooth blond hair back in a Miss Piggy kind of way. She often streaked her hair with a bright pink when she was out of school, but I can't say it really did anything for her.

'You'd be better off training for a proper career,' she added, 'but I'll be at the exhibition, rooting for you, anyway. Luke can't come; he's off on a training course that day and won't be back till too late.'

'Thank you,' I said, surprised, because when I'd initially invited them, she'd said they couldn't make it. 'My friend Emma doesn't think she can come either, so I could do with some support. I do hope it's a success . . . and then just after that I'll have worked out my notice at Champers&Chocs and it won't be my fault if Harry gets found out.'

'Turning a blind eye doesn't exactly qualify you for sainthood, you know,' she said. 'Still, I suppose you can't do anything else now. Have you told Jeremy you've handed in your notice?'

'No, I thought I'd wait until after the *Papercuts and Beyond* exhibition, because if I sell lots of pictures, he'll be able to see that I could make a living from it.'

The owners of the small gallery had been really enthusiastic about my pictures, which had been like a light at the end of a dark tunnel after Harry's threats to implicate me. I'd been carrying a heavy burden for months, but soon I would be free and earning my living by doing work I loved . . .

'Come on,' said Kate, putting down her teacup decisively. 'Let's go and find you something to wear for this exhibition. You can't go through life dressed in black jeans and tops.'

'I don't see why not,' I said mutinously, following her out, but I did end up buying a jazzy silk tunic at her insistence, even if I did intend wearing it with narrow black trousers and flat pumps rather than the leggings and high heels she considered appropriate.

Chapter 2: Picture This

Randal

'You know, these are really good,' I said, examining the nearest pictures on the wall of the small gallery. 'The artist's taken traditional papercutting and collage techniques to a whole new level.'

'I'll take your word for it – all this arty stuff isn't my cup of tea *or* why I'm here,' Charlie Clancy replied absently, scrolling through his phone to find a photograph of the woman whose work was being exhibited and whom he hoped to meet that evening. 'I just need to get Tabitha Coombs to believe I'm interested in including Champers&Chocs in an article on successful local internet businesses, and I'll be in there.'

'But you might learn something useful, because her work is very revealing when you look beyond the flowery paper lace borders,' I suggested. 'The subjects can be quite dark – see this one?' I pointed to the nearest. 'At first glance, it's a park scene by a duck pond, with people sitting on the bench, but if you look closer, they're clearly homeless and one is drinking from a bottle.'

'Never mind the artwork,' Charlie said impatiently. His mischievous expression under his mop of dark curls was exactly the same one he'd worn when we were schoolboys and he was plotting some prank that would get us into deep trouble. Nowadays, as an investigator and presenter for the long-running TV programme *Dodgy Dealings*, it was other people he dropped into the soup. We were in a similar line of business, though generally it was the big holiday companies' shortcomings I exposed.

'There's Tabitha Coombs over by the archway through to the other room, the tallish one who looks like Cher on a bad day,' he added.

At a guess, the woman was somewhere in her mid-thirties, her waist-length cocoa-brown hair worn loose, with a fringe that framed her face and touched straight, black brows. She had high cheekbones, a narrow, aquiline nose, pale complexion and a generous mouth.

'She's quite striking, in a slightly witchy kind of way,' I said.

I was certain that the gallery was too crowded and noisy for her to have heard me, but something made her glance our way at that moment, her gaze direct from eyes of a surprisingly light, almost lilac, grey.

'Her friend Kate, my informant, is the cute blonde with pink streaks in her hair, standing next to her.'

'Hardly a friend, now she's blabbed to you?' I suggested.

'Tabitha Coombs *thinks* she is, that's why she confided in her. But Kate says she and her husband were friends with Tabitha's fiancé, Jeremy, for years before they got engaged and though they didn't much like her they just had to put up with her.'

'Generous of them,' I commented drily.

'She said Tabitha was probably cheating on her fiancé with the owner of Champers&Chocs, as well as being involved in the scam, so maybe she's got some kind of axe to grind. But I don't really care what's driving her, so long as she's willing to introduce us. Then the rest is up to me.'

Before Kate had contacted him, Charlie had already had a tip-off from a disgruntled Champers&Chocs customer about cheap fizzy wine being sold for vintage champagne, so she had given him an easy way into his investigation.

'Never look a gift-snitch in the mouth,' I said.

The two women parted company and Kate slowly drifted across in our direction in a casual sort of way, talking to one or two people *en route.*

When she reached us, Charlie introduced us.

'This is my friend Randal Hesketh – his family home is nearby, so I invited him along just for the ride. Randal, this is Kate.'

'Pleased to meet you,' Kate said, all flirty smiles and big, pale blue eyes with fluttering eyelashes. I supposed she was pretty enough, but since she wasn't in the least my type her flirting didn't have any effect on me. This seemed to disconcert her.

'Are you ready to introduce us to your friend?' Charlie asked.

She made a *moue* that looked so cutesy she'd probably practised it in the mirror a million times. 'As I've already said, she's *not* a friend, it was just that Luke and I had to tolerate her after she and Jeremy got engaged. But I always felt there was something *wrong* about her – and my instincts are usually right.'

'Then let's get on and find out the truth,' he said. 'Do you remember your story, about how we got talking and you found out I was a journalist for *Lively Lancashire* magazine, though I'd walked into the gallery by chance?'

Kate nodded. 'So I told you a bit about the artist and her day job as a packer in a warehouse, and then offered to introduce you. Got it,' she said.

She gave me another of those flirty glances. 'Are you coming, too, Randal?'

'No, I'll stay here; it's none of my business,' I said, feeling a distaste for the whole Judas situation. I may be in a similar line of work, going undercover to get film footage for the independent TV programme I work for, *Hellish Holidays*, but it's more impersonal.

'See you later,' I added to Charlie.

I took a glass of water from a passing tray, since fizz wasn't my thing, whatever it was labelled as, and surveyed the gallery. It was still crowded and buzzing, so the exhibition seemed to be a success. I noticed red 'Sold' stickers had been affixed to several picture frames too and, on impulse, bought one myself that had taken my fancy as we entered. It was of a helmeted woman in a chariot-like wheelchair, entombed in a *Sleeping Beauty* tangle of flowering briars. A figure was hacking his way in, but he looked more like the Grim Reaper than a handsome prince.

I'd just paid and arranged to have it delivered to my family home in the nearby hamlet of Godsend after the exhibition had ended, when Charlie came back looking pleased with himself.

'Got what you wanted?'

He nodded. 'She's agreed to ask her boss if I can have a

tour of Champers&Chocs and do a short interview, so I can include it in an article on local entrepreneurs. He won't be able to resist the publicity, but I could see she wasn't keen on the idea. Then the fiancé – that bloke she's talking to now – showed up and monopolised the conversation, so I left it at that. Bit of a know-it-all tosser, I'd say, too fond of his own voice.'

The man was thin and not much taller than Tabitha, with an arty lock of marmalade-coloured hair falling over his eyes in a very doomed-poet kind of way. He seemed to be lecturing her about something.

'If that's the fiancé, then your Kate was all over him like treacle when he arrived a few minutes ago,' I said. 'I assumed he was *her* husband. So, maybe he's the axe she's grinding?'

Charlie grinned. 'You could be right. She told me her husband couldn't make it tonight, but that didn't stop her flirting with you earlier, too, I noticed.'

'Do you think she's telling the truth about Tabitha's involvement?'

'No idea. The scam's certainly going on, because we've had champagne samples analysed, but I've taken what she said with a pinch of salt,' he said. 'Innocent until proven guilty. Tabby – everyone calls her that, apparently – was certainly uneasy as soon as Champers&Chocs was mentioned and suspiciously unenthusiastic about the company being featured in a magazine.'

'That's all right: it's not going to be,' I said drily. 'Though of course she may be even less keen on it appearing all over a TV programme exposing what's been going on.'

I looked over my shoulder at Tabitha Coombs as we left. The crowd had begun to thin a little and she was staring after Charlie with those startlingly light grey eyes under brows drawn together into a formidable Frida Kahlo frown. Then the fiancé said something and put a proprietorial arm around her and she looked up at him with such a loving smile that her face was quite transformed.

I felt a sudden pang: she looked like a woman in love and I found it hard to believe that she was having an affair with another man.

But, whether she was or not, if she was involved in the label-swapping scam, then she was risking her happiness for some easy money and her house of cards was about to come tumbling down.

Chapter 3: Bang to Rights

'So Harry, my boss at Champers&Chocs, told me to show the reporter the packing room and give him some information about the business, because it would be good publicity,' I told Emma, my best and, as it turned out, *only* friend. It was only my second phone call out since I'd been sent to prison and it was good to unburden myself of the whole sorry story.

I'd have rung her and told her everything the moment I was first arrested, had her husband, Des, not been back from his latest foreign contract. He'd turned into such a possessive control freak he even resented sharing Emma with her female friends.

'And I suppose the reporter snooped?' she said.

'Yes, when I had to leave him for a few minutes to go to the office to answer an urgent phone call. The line was dead when I got there and I was so naïve, it never occurred to me that this Charlie Clancy had set up the call to distract me. As soon as I was out of sight, he somehow got into the back room, even though it was usually locked when Harry wasn't there, and photographed the crates of fake champagne.'

'I do wish you'd told me about the fraud when you first found out about it, Tabby.'

‘You had enough on your plate as it was,’ I said. ‘And I’d handed in my notice when I realised Harry hadn’t stopped the fraud, so another couple of weeks and I’d have been out of there.’

‘It was a huge shock when I saw his secret film exposing the scam on that *Dodgy Dealings* programme, and there you were! And what was worse, Des was with me and he saw it, too.’

I shuddered. ‘I looked so shifty when the reporter asked me what went on in the back room and I replied that it was just an office . . . It was clear I knew what was happening.’

‘Maybe, but that doesn’t mean you were implicated in it. I feel guilty for letting Des persuade me to go on a family break with him and Marco to St Lucia before the end of the trial, even though I was sure you would be found not guilty.’

‘I thought so too, at first: I was just an employee, after all. But Harry tried to lay the blame for thinking up the scam on me and said we’d been having an affair, then Kate stood up in court and backed his story up.’

‘What a cow!’ Emma said.

I could still hear Kate’s voice as she stood there in the witness stand, all big, innocent baby-blue eyes, saying sadly, ‘Oh, yes, Tabitha told me in confidence that she’d thought up a way for Champers&Chocs to make some easy money, replacing the bottles of vintage champagne with cheap fakes. I told her it was illegal, but she just laughed and said no one would ever find out.’

‘But none of that was true,’ Emma said stoutly.

‘No, but I could see the jury didn’t believe me – and I suppose it did look bad that I hadn’t told the police, or handed in my notice as soon as I found out. Only, Harry had been kind to me in the past, letting me work hours that fitted in with caring for Mum and then offering me a permanent job later.'

'I know,' she said sympathetically. 'And things suddenly seemed to be going right for you, what with getting engaged to Jeremy and then your first solo exhibition.'

'Jeremy didn't believe I was innocent, even before Kate stood up there and lied through her teeth – we'd already had a big argument and I'd moved back into the flat,' I said. 'I was found guilty of involvement in the fraud and the judge said he was going to make an example of me and send me to prison, and though my solicitor had warned me the day before to pack a small bag just in case, it was still a huge shock when I got an eight-month custodial sentence.'

'I couldn't believe it when I got back from the holiday and found out you were in a prison in Cheshire! I wanted to visit you, but Des was still home and . . . well, he's worse than ever. Wants to know what I'm doing every minute of every day. But at least I managed to write to you and tell you when he'd gone off again. Was the prison horrendous?'

'It passed in a bit of a blur, to be honest. I was totally stunned when I heard the sentence, though someone said to me, "You'll be out by the spring," as I was led down to the cells below the court, which I think was meant to cheer me up. Prison – especially over Christmas – was like a strange nightmare I kept thinking I'd wake up from. I was so scared that I retreated right into myself, but then in the New Year I got moved here, to the open prison.'

'Is it much better?'

'Yes, it's in a lovely old building in the countryside, and though of course we're still prisoners, with strict rules and regulations to obey, it's more relaxed. I've got a library job and help clear after dinner, too, so I keep myself occupied.'

'Perhaps you'll be able to do your papercuts and collages again?' she suggested.

'I haven't got any art materials with me and I'm not sure even open prisons would be that keen on my having sharp craft knives,' I said. 'I'm only hoping the greetings card firms I've sold designs to in the past didn't see that TV programme and realise it was me, so I can carry on working with them when I get out.'

'Probably not,' Emma said optimistically. 'And even if they saw it, people aren't that quick at putting two and two together.'

'That's true,' I said, feeling a slight flicker of hope.

'I'm afraid it's too far away for me to come and visit,' she said apologetically, though I hadn't expected her to, since her little boy, Marco, was only six and in addition to being a mum she was doing some supply teaching in the reception class at his infants' school.

'It's lovely just to talk to someone,' I said. 'The only other person I've rung is Jeremy, because I was desperate to know how Pye is. Even though the engagement was off, I'd begged him to look after Pye if I got sent to prison and he said he would, though I'm sure he didn't believe that would happen any more than I did.'

'So, how is Pye? You were so inseparable, you must be missing each other terribly.'

'I am, and I'm so worried about him, Emma!' I told her. 'The minute Jeremy heard my voice he put the phone down, and when I wrote he didn't answer, so I don't know what's happening.'

'Look, don't worry, I'll drive over there tomorrow after

school with Marco and see how Pye is,' she promised. 'I can't take him home with me, because Des would have a hissy fit when he gets back, but I'll make sure he's OK.'

'If you would,' I said gratefully. Emma had only met Jeremy a couple of times, but she was less than twenty minutes' drive away. Thank God Des was working abroad again and she was, for the moment, a relatively free agent.

'Do you need anything?' she asked. 'I could send it in a parcel if so?'

'That would be wonderful, because I seem to have packed all the wrong things. I need more clothes and maybe my sketchbooks . . .'

I told her what I needed and where they would be found.

'What about money?' she asked.

'I'm actually all right for cash, because when the solicitor warned me the night before the verdict that I might get a custodial sentence, I drew out a month's rent for the flat to give to Jeremy and then forgot and wrote him a cheque, so I've got quite a bit of credit for my phone calls and anything I need. On release, they deduct it from the money you brought in with you.'

'He was so mean, making you carry on paying rent for the flat after you got engaged!'

'He is a bit tight, but I spent quite a lot of time there working on my pictures. I was going to keep it on as my studio when we finally got married . . .'

If we'd ever got married, because Jeremy had proved really reluctant to name a year, let alone a date!

I was on tenterhooks, wondering how Pye was and hoping for good news, but Emma sounded troubled when we spoke again.

'Jeremy wasn't pleased to see me at all, and didn't even invite me and Marco into the house. And I'm afraid Pye wasn't there, Tabby – Jeremy said that he couldn't cope with the constant yowling after you'd gone, so he'd found him a good home, but he wouldn't tell me where, or who with.'

Cold dread seized my heart, for not only did I adore Pye, but he was the last living link to my mother, who had also loved him.

'You don't think he's just saying that and he's had him put to sleep?'

'No, I'm sure he hasn't,' she reassured me. 'When I told him he shouldn't have rehomed Pye without your permission, he said you'd abandoned him by committing a crime, so it was your own fault, but I was to assure you the cat was perfectly all right.'

'I hope so . . . and thank you for trying to find where he was,' I said, but inwardly I was thinking of Pye – my awkward, demanding, adorable Pye – out there somewhere living with strangers . . . Was he happy and safe? A slow tear slid coldly down my face.

'The other thing is, Tabby, that your belongings weren't in the flat any more, but in boxes piled at the back of the garage. Jeremy said since obviously you and he didn't have any kind of future together and your rent had run out, he was going to let the flat again. I can't *believe* how mean and horrible he's turned out to be!'

I didn't feel that surprised after our final argument . . . and anyway, it paled into insignificance compared with his arbitrary rehoming of Pye.

'He let me go and rummage through the boxes and I

found most of the things you wanted. He says he'd be grateful if you'd have them removed at the first opportunity,' she added.

'He'll have to wait then, because I can't do anything till I get out – and even then I'll have nowhere to live, no job and a criminal record.'

'Jeremy's such a pompous, self-satisfied prig, though I couldn't say so when you were in love with him. And I should know, because I married one myself,' she said wearily.

'Is Des being just as difficult?' I asked sympathetically.

'He gets worse every time he gets back from a contract and wants every second of my time accounted for. And the least thing that isn't quite the way he likes it, or the way his mother used to do it, and he flies right off the handle. Even when Marco was a toddler, he didn't have tantrums like that!'

'He isn't violent, is he?'

'No, it's all verbal bullying. I'd be straight out of there if he tried anything else. And I know I should stand up to him more, but I don't want Marco to hear us arguing *all* the time. I could do with your sharp tongue to cut him down to size occasionally.'

'My sarcastic tongue frequently gets me into trouble,' I said ruefully. 'I don't think one or two of my smart answers to stupid questions went down well in court.'

Emma was still following her own thoughts. 'Sometimes he's really sweet, just like he was when we were first going out. It's since he started working away on longer contracts that he's really changed.' She sighed. 'It seems to me we're both in prison, in a way.'

'I'll get out in a couple of months, if I don't blot my copybook.'

'And Des is going to be back for only a couple of days and then he's off for six weeks to Dubai,' Emma said, then added, to my puzzlement, 'And thank you for not saying it.'

'What?'

'"I told you so." Remember when Des and I decided to get married only a couple of months after we met and you suggested I didn't rush into it? I told you he was wonderful and I knew it was the right thing for me and Marco. But you were quite right.'

I'd worried that it was too soon after she'd been widowed, even though I could understand her longing to be loved again and to give Marco a father. I hadn't been sure that Desmond was the right man for her, either.

'I'm a fine one to talk about making mistakes – I didn't exactly choose wisely with Jeremy, did I?' I pointed out.

'We're both poor pickers,' she agreed. 'I'll catch up with you whenever I can and when I can't phone you, I'll write.'

'That would be wonderful. I can't tell you how nice it is to get good, old-fashioned letters!'

I wished Jeremy felt the same way about letters but, not unexpectedly, I had no answer to the one I wrote to him, telling him I would pay him back for storing my belongings when I was released and asking him to give me the name and address of Pye's new owners, so I could write to them, too, and make sure he was all right. Not getting a reply made me want to escape and go to find him – but I knew if I did that I'd be sent back to a stricter prison again and it would be even longer before we could be reunited. I had to bide my time and count the days until my release. But at least I now had a link to the outside world in Emma.

Until the happy day that I met Cedric Lathom, I think she was the only person in the whole wide world who was prepared to believe I was innocent.

Chapter 4: The Prisoner's Friend

Ceddie, as he asked me to call him during his first visit, described himself as a Prisoner's Friend but he was also, as it turned out, a Quaker Friend, too.

When it had been suggested to me that since I had no visitors of my own, I might like him to visit me, I'd thought, well, why not?

This proved to be one of the best decisions I'd ever made, because not only did it give me access to the visitors' rooms in a small separate building, where I could indulge in coffee, hot chocolate, fruit juice and even biscuits, but Ceddie was the most wonderful person.

He was a tiny, elderly man with a pointed face, a mop of silvery curls and large, innocent grey-blue eyes – though perhaps the word 'innocent' implies a trusting simplicity, which he didn't have. It was more an unshakeable belief that there was inner good in everyone.

Over several visits I found myself pouring out my life story to him. I'd never had a significant male figure in my life, father or grandfather, but if I had I'd have wanted him to be just like Ceddie.

'Looking back, my life seems to have been a bit sad, only

it didn't feel like that at the time,' I said ruefully one day towards the end of my sentence, while I was drinking the cup of hot chocolate he'd bought me as usual.

'Your mother sounds such an interesting and loving person that giving up everything to care for her was clearly something you did from love, not duty,' he agreed.

'When she was first diagnosed with MS we hoped that it might be the slow kind, but she deteriorated very quickly . . . But she was never a burden and I had the support of my best friend, Emma, and my childhood sweetheart, Robbie, so I didn't feel totally alone.'

'Ah, yes, I remember you mentioning Robbie before,' he said, smiling at me benignly.

'He went straight into the army from school and we were too young to get engaged really, especially since I'd never have left Mum, but he understood that. He was a really nice boy.'

'You said he was badly wounded and married one of the nurses who'd looked after him?'

'Yes, they just fell in love. I hadn't been able to get down to see him much, because of leaving Mum, so I didn't blame him in the least. In fact, I wished them both well.'

'That shows a warm and generous heart, my dear,' he said.

'I think our engagement lasted only as long as it did because mostly we were able just to write to each other,' I confessed. 'But by the time he got married I was fully occupied anyway, what with my casual packing job at Champers&Chocs, when my neighbour could pop in and sit with Mum, and my art work, especially when I started to sell designs to greetings card companies.'

'I'm very impressed with your papercuts, Tabby,' he said. 'I think you have great talent.'

I'd recently given him one depicting the prison as seen through the rose arch, the thorns like a circlet of barbed wire and inmates standing in every window, looking out.

'Thank you – I get my arty side from Mum. She was a costume assistant and dresser at a Liverpool theatre until she got too ill to work. My father was an actor who was part of a touring production, but when Mum discovered she was expecting me, she found out he was married with a young family, so she never told him.'

'I think she should at least have given him the opportunity to provide for you,' he said, 'but I can see that she wouldn't want to upset his wife and family with such a disclosure.'

I looked at him fondly, quite used by now to the somewhat Victorian flourishes of his conversation.

'I checked him on the internet out of curiosity once, and I don't think he'd have been much of an asset as a father. Anyway, we moved in with Granny and then later, after she died and Mum's condition had deteriorated, the council gave us a specially adapted bungalow, so we were all right.'

'When one door shuts, another opens,' he said.

'One thing does seem to lead to another,' I agreed, 'just not always fortunately. Once Mum passed away I had to give up the bungalow and started working regular shifts at Champers&Chocs, so I could pay the rent on Jeremy's flat . . . which led to us getting engaged.'

'Which should have made a happy ending, at last.'

'I did feel as if I was on the brink of it, just before I was arrested. I'd had a successful small solo exhibition at a gallery in Liverpool and I was hoping to make a living from my artwork. I'd handed in my notice once I realised Harry, my boss, was still defrauding the customers, but the only thing I was guilty of was not reporting what I found out immediately.'

I smiled and added, 'Practically everyone I've met in prison has protested their innocence of the crime they were charged with, but I really didn't do it!'

'I am certain in my heart that you are innocent of any crime,' Ceddie assured me.

'Thank you – and I wasn't even guilty of having an affair with Harry Briggs. I was engaged to Jeremy and, other than Robbie, my childhood sweetheart, I'd never even been out with anyone else.'

'God always knows the truth,' Ceddie told me, but I wished the judge had, too.

'I will be away visiting relatives next week, but a friend of mine would like to come here in my stead, if you approve of the idea,' said Cedric Lathom, on his next visit.

My heart sank and I realised just how much I had come to depend on seeing him.

'A friend as in Quaker Friend?' I asked. I'd been reading up about the Quakers since Ceddie's first visit had piqued my curiosity.

He nodded, silvery curls bobbing. 'She's called Mercy Marwood. Her benevolence, like that of all the Marwoods, has always taken a practical turn. For many years she's been sourcing and renovating old sewing machines to take out to Malawi, where she has also taught needlework. She's just returned from her final trip there, for she feels that now she has turned eighty, it's time to attend to affairs closer to home.'

I'd grown used to Ceddie rambling on as if he'd escaped from between the covers of a Charles Dickens novel, but I thought that if Mercy Marwood had been teaching in Malawi into her eighties, she must be a tough old bird!

'I hope you don't mind, but I've told her a little about you,' he added, slightly anxiously.

'No, not at all,' I replied. 'I imagine you can read the whole story of my life online, by clicking on the newspaper reports of the trial.'

'I doubt the affair made the national headlines and, in any case, they would reveal little about the real Tabitha Coombs, who is a very fine person,' he said, with one of his warm smiles.

'Thank you. Somehow, after your visits I always feel better . . . and when they release me, I'll miss you.'

'I will always remain your friend,' Ceddie said. 'Had you any thought about where you might go and what you might do after your release?'

'I have to wear a tag for two months and be under a sort of night-time house arrest – assuming I have a house to live in, of course,' I said. 'With no relatives, little money and a criminal record added to my lack of qualifications, I don't see much chance of getting a job and renting somewhere, and anyway, they need an address before they'll even release me. But I'm told they can find me a temporary place in a hostel somewhere, till I get back on my feet,' I added, trying to sound more positive than I felt.

'Well, my dear, Mercy has a proposition to put before you that may change that.'

'A proposition?' I echoed. 'Do you mean . . . a job?'

'The possibility of a fresh start, with somewhere to live, at least,' he said. 'But I'll let her tell you all about it herself.'

'But surely she won't want to employ an ex-con?'

'I have every reason to believe that she will and I think you'll suit each other very well,' he reassured me.

He wouldn't say any more about it and I wondered if his friend was returning because she was now so decrepit she needed a carer. After all, I had been my mum's sole carer for years, so I was certainly experienced at looking after an invalid.

It would mean my life had gone round in a circle again . . . but then, beggars and people with criminal records can't be choosers.

Chapter 5: Engagements

Randal

Charlie Clancy and I were having a catch-up session over a few beers at my flat between assignments. Being more or less in the same line of business, we were seldom in London at the same time.

'I haven't seen you since we bumped into each other in the street after you got back from that cruise. You looked like crap – and you don't look much better now,' Charlie said, with the frankness of an old friend. 'How much weight have you lost?'

'Too much: I wouldn't recommend a toxic tummy bug to anyone as a diet aid,' I said. 'You don't expect amazing luxury from a cut-price cruise company, but Kharisma sucked. So many passengers and even crew went down with it that if there hadn't been a mutiny off Mexico it would have been like the *Mary Celeste* and running on autopilot round and round the Caribbean.'

'That bad, was it?' Charlie said sympathetically.

'You'll see the horrible details when the programme comes out,' I said. 'It was even worse than we'd been told, mainly due to a lack of deep cleaning between cruises and poor food preparation practice. I bribed my way into the kitchens for a look and, believe me, I pretty much lived on bottled water and biscuits after that. And when half the toilets weren't functioning . . . well, you can imagine. It spread like wildfire. The stewards were paid so little, it's not surprising they weren't keen to tackle sick passengers' cabins.'

'But you caught it anyway, despite all the precautions.'

'I was careful, but I suppose it was inevitable, and at least we'd all been taken off the ship at Cancún by that point. It was a week before the medical authorities would let me fly home and I'm still sticking to eating bland stuff for the time being. This is the first alcohol I've tasted in weeks.'

'I have to say, you still look gaunt. I can't believe they sent you to Greece on another assignment so soon after you got back.'

I shrugged. 'That's how it goes. I'm off to investigate gap-year black spots worldwide next for a special programme, with some back-to-back filming for the ordinary series thrown in. South America first.'

'Back to Mexico?'

I shuddered. 'Luckily no, because I'm always going to associate the place with feeling like death. I'm off to Peru first.'

'I've always wanted to go to Machu Picchu,' Charlie said enviously.

'So have I, but not on the cheapest and dodgiest tour and staying in the worst backpackers' hostels. I only hope my digestion is up to a series of new challenges by the time I get there.'

'At least you visit exotic locations, while I just endlessly circle the dodgy dealers and rip-off merchants of the UK,' he pointed out.

I looked around the living room of the tiny flat that was my London base and thought how happy I'd be just to stay there. 'The sense of excitement I used to get at the start of each new assignment has long since worn off,' I said. 'I think I'm getting too old for this game. What have you been up to?'

'Got back yesterday after following a lead about horse-race fixing, but it was a bust.' He took another swig from his beer. 'But do you remember going with me to that small art gallery in Liverpool early last year, when I was following a lead about fake champagne?'

I nodded, a brief vision of a woman with long, dark brown hair and unusual light lilac-grey eyes sliding into my mind. 'The artist did brilliant papercuts, but also worked for that firm you wanted to investigate . . . what was it called?'

'Champers&Chocs. I'd already had a tip-off from a disgruntled customer that they were selling cheap fizz relabelled as expensive bubbly, when by sheer good luck, I got a lead on Tabitha Coombs.'

'It's all coming back to me – her "friend" dropped her right in it, didn't she? So, *was* she involved in the racket?'

'Up to the eyes, as well as having an affair with the owner. It all came out at the trial before Christmas.'

'Really?' I felt vaguely surprised. 'Her papercuts and collage pictures were really clever, so I wouldn't have thought she'd need to work somewhere like that, let alone be involved in a fraud.'

And now I came to think of it, I'd actually *bought* one of her pictures and arranged for it to be sent to my family home, Mote Farm, so presumably it had long since arrived and been stored away somewhere. I'd have to look next time I was up there.

'Her boss, Harry Briggs, said the scam had been her idea in the first place and they always packed the special orders up after the others had gone home in the evening, then had a bit of how's-your-father,' Charlie told me.

'I'm not sure I entirely believe that last bit – wasn't she engaged to someone? I seem to remember a fiancé.'

'Well, an affair isn't illegal anyway, but Kate, her "friend", got up and gave the court the same story, so it told against her. I don't think the judge was convinced she was the instigator of the fraud, though, because Briggs got a five-year stretch, but he still sent her to prison.'

'Really? If she hadn't committed any crime before, I'd have expected a suspended sentence, or community service, or something,' I exclaimed.

'So would I, but the judge said he was going to make an example of her. She's the reserved, sarcastic type, and I don't think he took to her.'

'Well, being reserved or sarky isn't a hanging offence,' I said mildly.

'She *looked* guilty – but not half as shifty and guilty as she did on that secret film I shot inside Champers&Chocs, when she was showing me the packing room! I had someone pretend to phone her with an urgent message and then sneaked into the backroom – it was locked, but any baby could have opened it with a bit of bent plastic – and found a stash of fake champagne.'

'How long a sentence did she get?'

'Eight months' custodial, so she'll probably be released

before too long. I don't suppose the fiancé stood by her; he didn't look the type to forgive and forget. But she was attractive in a witchy kind of way, wasn't she?'

I considered. 'She was striking, I suppose – it's not a face you'd forget easily.'

'Maybe she's your type?' he suggested. 'You could offer her a shoulder to cry on when she's released.'

'You're way out, because I've just got engaged to Lacey Bucknall.'

'What, the daughter of the All Thrills sex shops Bucknalls?' Charlie exclaimed. 'I didn't even know you were going out with her!'

'It was a bit of a whirlwind romance.'

'Lucky you. I've seen her about in nightclubs,' he said. 'Stunning redhead, legs up to her armpits, slim as a model but with curves in all the right places . . .'

'Yes, that's Lacey, but she's no airhead. In fact, she's a businesswoman to the core.'

'Still, you'll be all right there. She's probably got her own set of fluffy handcuffs and maybe a naughty nurse costume?' he teased.

I sighed. 'You know, I'm getting tired of that sort of comment, and Lacey's fed up with men who assume she's up for anything, just because her parents own a chain of sex shops. She's not like that at all.'

In fact, she'd shown a distinct lack of enthusiasm for that aspect of our relationship, so I suspected the whole subject bored her rigid, which I suppose wasn't surprising, given her background . . . I hoped to change her mind about that. And anyway, we shared a desire to settle down and start a family, and there was only one way to do that.

'Sorry,' said Charlie. 'I'm sure she's really nice.'

'She sees the family business as like any other, just filling a gap in the market and making money. She's recently set up her own mail-order company and it's starting to take off.'

'Selling what?' he asked. 'Tell me it's not the same line as her parents!'

'Not far off,' I admitted reluctantly. 'Instant Orgy. It's party supplies, basically . . . for adult parties.'

'Right . . .' Charlie said slowly, though a glint of devilment appeared in his dark eyes. 'That's going to go down a storm with your aunt Mercy, isn't it?'

'It's not going to be easy,' I agreed, because my elderly aunt by marriage, Mercy Marwood, came from a long line of Quakers, as had my late uncle. My mother had married out and lapsed, but I was aware enough of the Quaker outlook to know that Mercy might take a dim view of my fiancée's business interests. 'I'm hoping she gets to know Lacey first, before she finds out.'

'How *is* Mercy?' Charlie asked. We'd often spent part of our school holidays at Mote Farm and he was fond of her. And I was, too, even though by rights the family estate should have come directly to me after my uncle died, rather than have been left to my aunt to pass on. 'Is she still out in Malawi, teaching needlework and stuff?'

'She was, but she'll be flying back soon and says this time it's for good, though she'll still be sourcing and sending out sewing machines. I'll have to visit her after my next trip.'

I took a swig of my beer. 'I had some plans drawn up to redevelop the factory complex at Godsend and sent them out to her a while back, so I think we'll have a lot to discuss.'

'What, the old Friendship Mill site?'

'That's it: Mote Farm will be mine one day, after all, and Aunt Mercy's always encouraged me to see it as my home, so she should be happy I'm taking an interest and want to settle down there when I'm married.'

'But your uncle left everything to her, didn't he? He told her that he wanted you to inherit after she'd gone, but it wasn't in writing.'

'He did, but he trusted her to do what he wanted and she will,' I said confidently. 'She's got money of her own, after all, though now she's guardian to the daughter of an old Malawian friend, I expect she'll want to provide for her from that. I don't think you've met Liz yet, have you? She's a nice girl – Mercy sent her to that Quaker boarding school near Pontefract, but she's often at the farm in the holidays.'

'No, but it's typical of Mercy to take in waifs and strays. Look at all those so-called employees she has living in the cottages!'

'True, and they're all well past retirement age. The cracker factory in Friendship Mill should have closed long ago, because it's losing money hand over fist and at this rate there's going to be nothing left by the time I inherit.'

'So, what were the plans?'

'I propose to immediately retire the workforce, close the cracker factory down and then redevelop the mill complex as a tourist venue, with a café, craft workshops and a farm shop, that kind of thing. I'd invest some of the money I inherited from my parents into it and manage the place, so I'd expect to be a shareholder and director.'

Charlie whistled. 'How did that go down with Mercy?'

'I think it was a bit of a shock, really. She emailed saying she'd looked at my interesting proposals, but since she hadn't realised things weren't doing well at the cracker factory she'd consider what I had to say more fully when she was home and had had chance to look into everything. And that's where it stands at the moment.'

'Maybe your plans were the tipping point that made her come home for good, then?' Charlie suggested.

'Perhaps. I think she put too much trust in her brother to keep any eye on things while she was away, because apart from paying out the wages, Uncle Silas barely goes down there. I know he's got health problems, but he's hardly a total invalid.'

'Silas is a funny old codger, practically a recluse,' Charlie said. 'But Mercy seems fond of him.'

'Mercy's fond of everyone,' I said, which was only a slight exaggeration. 'I'm sure she'll see sense about the mill, when she's had time to think about it. After all, I'm not proposing we throw the workforce out of the cottages after they're retired, or anything like that . . . though as soon as the cottages do become free, they could be renovated and let as holiday rentals.'

'I see you've given it a lot of thought.'

'I had a lot of time to think in Mexico, before I was fit to fly home,' I said ruefully.

'Are you going to tell her about Lacey when you go up there after your next assignment, or take her with you?'

'I'll tell Mercy I've got engaged, but take Lacey to meet the family later, after I've talked her round about the mill,' I said confidently.

And when I did take Lacey there, I'd have to try to persuade her to keep quiet on the subject of what she and her parents sold for a living, until Mercy had grown to know and love her, which I was sure she soon would. And anyway, once Lacey had visited the place, I might even be able to persuade her to give up her own business entirely and help me instead . . .

Charlie popped another can and raised it in salute: 'Here's to success in all you do!' he said, twinkling. 'But I feel you might be in for a rocky ride!'

Chapter 6: The Quality of Mercy

I was expecting Mercy Marwood to be a frail, elderly woman, but I was in for a big surprise for, although she was small and skinny, I'd never seen anyone so crackling with energy. I think she probably burned off calories as fast as she ate them.

Her white hair was cut into a pudding-bowl style and she was dressed in a bold blue and white patterned cotton caftan top with wide sleeves, worn over khaki linen trousers that sagged at the seat and knees. She had children's trainers on her tiny feet and they lit up when she walked.

She shook my hand firmly, scanned me with warm brown eyes set in delicate origami folds of tanned skin, and then smiled. 'My dear, you are just as Ceddie described to me – but so thin! Still, we'll soon put some flesh back on those bones once you're at Mote Farm.'

She sank down into a chair with a pleased expression. 'I've been staying with the friend who collected me from the airport – I only got back from Malawi the day before yesterday – but I borrowed her kitchen and baked you a cake. I'm sure the people here will let you have it, once they've finished examining it for handsaws, or rope ladders, or whatever it is they think I might have hidden inside it.'

'Probably more likely to be drugs, these days,' I said, slightly dazed by all this energy and information. 'And since I hope to be released in just over a fortnight, if a hostel place has been found for me, absconding would be pointless.'

'I've visited women's prisons many times in the past,' said my visitor chattily, 'but not an open one. How do you find it?'

'A hundred times better than the one in Cheshire, where I was initially taken,' I said. 'I didn't really believe I'd get a prison sentence until it happened, so I wasn't prepared in the least.'

'Poor thing! And Ceddie tells me you were there over Christmas too, which must have made it extra hard.'

'It did make me think of Christmases with my mum and miss her so much that my throat closed up every time I tried to eat anything,' I admitted. 'It was only the kindness of some of the other prisoners and the staff that made it bearable, but it's surprising how quickly you adjust to the routine.'

'There is so much good in people everywhere,' Mercy said, sounding rather like Ceddie. 'I hope you are now eating properly?'

'I'm trying to, though I seem to have got out of the habit of feeling hungry.'

'Once I have you at Mote Farm, we'll get you back into it,' she said firmly.

'It . . . sounds as if you intend to offer me some kind of employment,' I said tentatively. 'But how can you be sure you can trust me? Has Ceddie told you what I was imprisoned for?'

'Oh, yes, and very unfortunate it all was, too.'

'I didn't actually do it, though I'm guilty in so far as I

knew about the fraud and didn't report it. But of course, I could be just saying that, couldn't I?'

'It doesn't matter to me, dear, so long as you're ready to put the past behind you and take on a challenge and a new beginning.'

'A challenge?' I echoed blankly. I'd long since abandoned the idea that Mercy Marwood could have any use for a carer – if anything, it seemed likely that the boot would be on the other foot! But what on earth could she want me to do?

'Oh, of course – Ceddie told me he would leave it all to me to explain, so you don't know a thing about why I need your help, do you?' she said, smiting her forehead with one small, clenched fist. 'What an idiot! We'd better get down to it straight away, because Job's collecting me when I leave and he wants to drive me back home before it gets dark.'

'Job?'

'I'll explain about Job in a minute. We have to get back to West Lancashire, so it's quite a long drive.'

'Is that where you live?' I asked, hopefully.

'Yes, my home is called Mote Farm and it's in the hamlet of Godsend, near Little Mumming. Do you know it? Ceddie said you were brought up in the Formby area, near Southport.'

'I – yes,' I stammered. 'It's right over to the east of Ormskirk, beyond the M6, where it starts to get hilly, isn't it? In fact Snowehill Beacon, above Little Mumming, was one of my mother's favourite places while she was still mobile enough to get there,' I added, rocked by the coincidence – for following her wishes, the beautiful hillside, carved with the figure of a red horse and topped with a small tower, had also been where I had scattered her ashes . . .

'Then I think that's a sign from God that you should

return there, don't you?' she said, beaming at me. 'Now, I'll get us both a cup of that hot chocolate Ceddie told me about, and put you in the picture.'

'Right, explanation time.' Mercy settled back into the chair as if it was infinitely more comfortable than it could possibly be. 'I was born a Fell, which is a very old Quaker family, and I married into another, the Marwoods, and moved to Mote Farm.'

'I'm afraid I don't know anything about farming,' I said doubtfully.

'Oh, the Marwoods haven't farmed anything for centuries, dear,' she assured me, 'or the family before them, who rebuilt the original thirteenth-century farmhouse. You can still see traces of that in the central hall and we think the oak front door and the moat are of that period, too.'

'*Moat?*'

'Just a small one. The house looks as if it's sitting on a grassy cushion, rather sweet.'

'Right,' I said, trying to picture this.

'It's not at all grand, or by any means a stately home, but it was further extended in Tudor times with two wings and a central porch, then the whole wattle-and-daub construction faced in bricks,' she said. 'It's quite quaint.'

I didn't know about quaint, it sounded very grand to me, but I didn't say so, only nodded as if I had the faintest idea what she was telling me all this for.

'My husband died many years ago and so Mote Farm came to me, but on the understanding that, in turn, I would leave the estate to the son of his sister, which of course I intend to do. For several years I've been away from home for extended periods, since I felt called to go out to Malawi.'

'Yes, Ceddie told me, but that you are now home for good.'

'Everything has its season, and I feel that mine for working in Malawi has come to an end, though of course I will still continue with the work of finding sewing machines and other materials to send out there.'

I suddenly wondered if that was the job I would be helping her with. But before I could ask she continued, 'I was so busy that I seem to have neglected what was happening at home and once you take your eye off the ball, there's no telling where it will go.'

'True,' I agreed, still baffled.

'I've always encouraged my nephew, Randal, to make his home at Mote Farm, since it will one day be his, so he's a frequent visitor, though of course his work means he spends most of his time either abroad or at his flat in London.'

'So Mote Farm has been empty a lot?'

'By no means: my older brother, Silas, who is somewhat crippled by rheumatism and a reclusive nature, has lived there since I married. Whenever I was abroad, I charged him to make sure all ran smoothly at the factory, but he hasn't taken the interest in it that I hoped he would.'

'*Factory?*'

'The cracker factory in the mill, dear. The house itself is well run in my absence, for Job looks after Silas, and his wife, Freda, lets the cleaners in each week, sorts the laundry, reports anything that needs ordering or repairing and generally acts as housekeeper. Of course, when I'm home I do all the cooking – I do love to cook.'

I was starting to feel much as I had done on my arrival

at prison, that I was trapped in some strange dream . . . or nightmare.

'What is this factory you mentioned? Did you say . . . crackers?'

I had a vision of those thin, crispy biscuits for cheese, which was instantly dispelled when she replied, 'Marwood's Magical Christmas Crackers.'

'Oh, yes – we had those when my grandmother was alive,' I said, enlightened. 'She loved everything traditional.'

'I fear that may be part of the problem,' mused Mercy absently. 'We have not moved with the times.'

'So, is the factory near Mote Farm?'

'Just across the valley and it's actually the Friendship Mill, for the Marwoods were originally engaged in the cotton manufacturing process and harnessed the power of the stream. But in Victorian times the building was turned over to the production of fancy goods, which eventually dwindled to just crackers.'

'Right,' I said, slightly dazed by this further onslaught of strange information. 'So really, now it's a cracker-making workshop in an old cotton mill?'

'That's it,' she nodded. 'And so it remains, with a much diminished workforce. They live in a little row of terraced cottages below the mill, and Job and Freda have the first one. Then . . .' she ticked off on her fingers, 'there's Dorrie in number two, then Bradley, Lillian and Joy . . . and Phil, who is a widower, in number six. I suppose they must all be the wrong side of seventy – how time does fly!'

She looked at me bright-eyed, her head tilted to one side like a bird.

'But my nephew informs me that the outgoings of the

cracker-making business are about to exceed the profits and, while I'm glad to see that the boy has taken some interest in what will one day be his inheritance, his ideas for rectifying this are a little too arbitrary. He wants to invest in developing the mill site and has even had plans drawn up and sent out to me in Malawi.'

'You mean, he wants to turn the cracker business around?'

'No, he wants to close it down entirely and use the mill as some kind of shopping and café venue for day-trippers. He seems to think the workforce should all be ready to retire, though I'm sure they are no such thing. But I can see that they must overcome their resistance to change if the firm is to continue. And this is where *you* come in, Tabitha – as my right-hand woman.'

'Do call me Tabby – and do you mean you need a PA?'

'Of sorts. I need someone with artistic flair, youthful energy and vision, who can breathe new life into the cracker business.'

'But I don't know anything about running a business; I only packed things in boxes,' I said blankly. 'Or about crackers . . . except that sometimes, when we hadn't much money, Mum and I made our own.'

'Well, the principle is much the same. And I don't need someone to run the business, because I'm quite capable of doing that now I'm home, I need . . . an artistic director and someone to back me up when my nephew comes to discuss the way forward.'

She sat back and beamed at me. 'What do you say? I'm sure with your input we can turn things round by Christmas and Randal will have to accept that any plans he has for the rest of the site must include cracker making at its heart. And after that, if you should want to stay on with us, we will earmark a studio for you when the outbuildings are redeveloped, so you can pursue your own artistic ambitions.'

'I – it all sounds fascinating,' I confessed. 'Where would I live?'

'Since the cottages are all currently occupied, I thought you might have the former cook-housekeeper's apartments behind the kitchen in the west wing. There's just a small bedroom and a tiny sitting room, but it would be all your own.'

The thought of space in which I could be entirely alone and unobserved was bliss.

'I'll do it,' I said, 'if you really think I'll be useful.'

'I'm certain you will. There, that's settled,' she added, looking pleased. 'We'll expect you once you're released. Cedric has explained to me that you will have to wear some kind of electronic tag for a few weeks and be confined to the house at night – not that there is anywhere to go to in the evenings in Godsend, anyway.'

'Yes, and I'll have to give them your address before they'll release me. Then all my things are at my ex-fiancé's house, so I'll need to collect those at some point, too. He's packed them up and put them in his garage.'

'I hope it isn't damp,' she said, tutting disapprovingly. 'Give me the address and phone number and I'll have Job drive me over to collect them in a day or two – it will make you feel more at home if your own things are waiting for you at Mote Farm, won't it?'

'Well . . . yes, though he lives near Formby.'

'That's no distance,' she assured me.

'And he's likely to present you with a bill for storing them!'

'Don't worry, I'll take care of it.'

'That's so kind of you,' I said, 'but I don't think I'll have enough money to pay you back straight away.'

'Oh, don't worry, it can come out of your wages eventually. I'm afraid they won't be substantial, but as you'll be living in and eating with the family, that will save you expense.'

'It sounds wonderful,' I said.

'Then that's settled and you'll come to us as soon as you're released. I'll look forward to it. I'm sure Ceddie was guided to tell me about you, because you're just the person I need.'

'I hope so,' I said.

'You are bright, artistically talented and practical – those are all the qualities I require,' she said cheerily, then asked if I had enough money to travel to Lancashire on my release. I assured her I had and declined her offer to send the long-suffering-sounding Job down again to collect me.

I didn't tell Mercy I intended making an illicit detour to Formby in search of Pye, because I needed to know exactly where he was and if he was happy. I was pretty sure the authorities would expect me to go straight from the prison to the known address, but with a bit of luck they'd never know and I'd still arrive at Mote Farm in time to be ringed like a pigeon that afternoon.

I tried to identify the strange feeling stirring in my heart, and eventually decided it was the pale wraith of optimism.

Chapter 7: Life of Pye

Q: What happened to the man who stole an Advent calendar?
A: He got twenty-four days!

By my release day I'd started to wonder if I might have become so institutionalised that I'd soon be looking back longingly at the safe familiarity of the open prison.

The final formalities were completed and I learned that even though I had a long journey ahead of me, I still needed to be at Mote Farm by five, so that I could be tagged there the same day.

When I got into the waiting taxi to be driven to the nearest station I had with me the small suitcase and handbag I'd gone to prison with (though with less money, since my phone calls had been deducted from what I'd had) but also a black bin bag, since Emma had sent me that big parcel of clothes and art materials and I'd had to put the overflow into *something*. It was not a good look.

Still, at least I now had access to the small amount of cash in my bank account . . . enough to buy a train ticket and a bit over. When I changed trains in London I purchased a cheap nylon holdall from a shop on the concourse and shoved the whole bin bag into it. I felt less as if I had 'newly released prisoner' stamped on my forehead after that.

My heart lifted with every mile that passed on my long journey home to Lancashire, though I was worried that when I got to Formby, either Jeremy wouldn't be home, or he would refuse to tell me where Pye was. I didn't have a lot of time to spare before I had to be at Mote Farm for the electronic tag to be fitted, so though I was desperate to discover how – not to mention *where* – Pye was, I knew if there were any problems I'd have to dash off and come back another day.

Unless the timetable had been changed, Jeremy had no school music lessons after two on Mondays and was always home by three.

And luckily, when yet another expensive taxi dropped me off there (depleting my fast-dwindling reserve of cash), I saw his car on the drive – but unfortunately, so too was Kate's familiar white Polo.

I wondered why she had come back with him – and also if I could restrain my natural urge to take her by her scrawny throat and shake her till she explained why she'd stood up in court and told all those lies about me. I knew she'd initially resented me when I'd got engaged to Jeremy and the three of them became four, but I'd thought she'd got over that when she saw that Jeremy still adored her. If anything, it should have been *me* who resented *her*!

But following my natural urge to throttle her would lead me straight back to prison and, more importantly, delay my finding out what had happened to Pye, so I took a deep breath and rang the doorbell.

I thought no one was going to answer, but finally the key

rattled in the lock and Kate opened it – pink, flustered and tucking her blouse into her skirt.

'You!' she gasped, looking like a frightened rabbit, as well she might, given the circumstances. 'Have they let you out already?'

'No, I avoided the searchlights and vicious guard dogs and climbed over the barbed wire, using a rope ladder that came in a cake,' I snapped, wedging my nylon holdall in the door as she attempted to shut it.

Her mouth dropped open, before sanity set in and she realised I was being sarcastic. 'I suppose they *must* have let you out, but what on earth are you doing here?'

'I might ask you the same,' I replied.

'I came back with Jeremy, so we could sort out the arrangements for the school trip to Paris, though Luke had to stay at school to take detention, so he'll be joining us later,' she said, recovering her composure slightly. 'Not that it's any of your business.'

'Who is it?' Jeremy's voice demanded as he came down the stairs, fastening the cord of a blue velour dressing gown that was as familiar to me as my own. The scenario I'd interrupted was plain as a picture.

'Oh, *right*, I understand everything now, Kate!' I said. '*This* is what all the lies were about – you wanted Jeremy to yourself.'

'Tabby? What the hell are you doing here?' Jeremy said angrily, pushing Kate out of the way like the gentleman he wasn't. 'I told you we were through.'

'She wants to make trouble, that's what,' Kate said. 'Go away, Tabby, or we'll ring the police and have you arrested for harassment.'

‘I’m not harassing anyone,’ I said, with more calm than I actually felt, because I knew from the other girls that putting a single foot wrong once I was let out could well mean being sent back to prison to serve the whole sentence.

‘In fact, I don’t give a damn about either of you. All I want to know is, what have you done with Pye?’

‘All this is about a stupid *cat*?’ Kate said incredulously.

‘He’s not just any cat, he’s *my* cat,’ I said fiercely, ‘and I love him.’

‘I’ve already told you that he went to a good home,’ Jeremy snapped. ‘There was no point in you coming here.’

‘Then tell me the name of the people you rehomed him with. I need to see for myself that he’s all right and that he’s settled with them. What’s the name and address?’

He avoided my eyes. ‘I can’t give it to you.’

‘Look, this is my cat we’re talking about and he’s microchipped as belonging to me, so it wasn’t even legal to give him away without my permission.’

‘I don’t think that will wash, because in effect, you abandoned him through your illegal actions,’ he said smugly.

‘Listen, you pompous prig, I’m not going until you tell me where Pye is,’ I insisted.

‘Shall I call the police?’ asked Kate helpfully.

‘Yes, why not?’ I said, throwing caution to the winds. ‘Perhaps you’d rather explain to them what you’ve done with my cat?’

Jeremy ran his fingers through his dark marmalade-coloured hair. There seemed suddenly to be a lot more forehead and a lot less hair than I remembered . . .

‘Oh, just tell her so she’ll go away,’ said Kate impatiently.

‘The Leafy Lane Pet Rescue Centre,’ he replied defiantly.

'You mean, you put Pye in a *cats' home*?' I said, stunned.

'It's a good home, I told you.'

'But . . . you let me think you'd rehomed him with nice people! If no one adopted him, he could have been put down by now!' I exclaimed, panicking, for although Pye was very dear to me, I was aware he wouldn't be the easiest cat to rehome.

'They said they never put a healthy animal down, so he'll be OK,' Jeremy said. 'You're making a fuss about nothing.'

'How *could* you? And how was it that I used to think you were so kind and wonderful, when really you're callous and cruel?'

'There's no need for insults. You've got what you wanted, so why don't you go away?' Kate suggested.

'I can see *you* got what you wanted, too, Kate,' I said, then added to Jeremy, 'You deserve each other, you poor, credulous mutt!'

Then I hefted my bags and walked off down the drive, feeling glad I'd bought a belt at the station when I'd got the holdall, because losing my jeans halfway down the drive wouldn't have done a lot for the dignity of my departure.

I knew where the cats' home was: a good couple of miles away. I managed to balance my bag on top of the wheeled suitcase and drag them both together, but I was still exhausted by the time I'd walked there.

The girl behind the desk had a doughy face and scarlet-tipped black hair exploding out of a high knot, and I could see from her guarded expression that she'd recognised me the moment I walked in. I suppose the case had been a seven-day wonder locally.

I pretended I hadn't noticed and explained the situation anyway: that I'd been away and my cat, Pye, had been brought there without my permission, so now I needed to know what had happened to him.

'Oh yes . . . Pye,' she said uneasily. 'We renamed him Pip because it sounded more friendly, though he isn't, is he?'

'Not to strangers, no.'

'You must be Tabitha Coombs.'

'Give the girl a coconut,' I said shortly. It had been a long and stressful day already and the tension was slowly building inside me. 'I'm the person his identity chip is registered to, if you checked it?'

'Yes, but he was brought in by a man living at the same address as that on his chip, so—'

'My ex-fiancé. We shared the same address, but not the same name. Pye is *my* cat.'

'He told us he couldn't keep him and you'd agreed that he should be brought to us for rehoming.'

'Well, I didn't – and he told me he'd found Pye a good home, he just didn't tell me it was a cat rescue one. So . . . *have* you rehomed him? You didn't . . . put him down?'

'No, of course not! He was healthy enough to go straight onto the rehoming wing of the cattery, though actually, black cats are the most difficult to rehome, especially adult ones with odd eyes and . . .' she paused, wondering how to put it tactfully, '. . . difficult temperaments,' she finished.

'He does have his little ways and he's very vocal,' I conceded, and then, like music to my ears, a far-away, familiar wailing noise began to slowly work towards what I knew would be an ear-splitting crescendo.

'Pye? He's – still here?' I demanded.

'I— yes, but I'm not sure where we stand about . . .' she began, but I was already heading for the inner door.

She moved quickly to block me. 'I'm afraid that visiting time for future rehomers has finished for the day, but if you could come back tomorrow, when I've had a chance to discuss the matter with the manager—'

I faced her. 'I'm going to see my cat *now*,' I stated, and I expect I was giving off a powerful vibe that I was prepared to knock her down and trample over her to do so, if necessary, because she backed away a little.

'Please,' I added, attempting an ingratiating smile that was probably scarier than my previous expression. 'I've missed him so much.'

'Oh, well . . .' she said, giving in suddenly and ushering me through the swinging door to the cattery. 'Let's see if he recognises you.'

We walked down a short corridor and then along a row of cages, the unusual wailing noise now rising and falling like some kind of demonic lullaby.

In the very last pen, thin, angry and bristling with displeasure, was a very large black cat. He stopped wailing and stared at me coldly from mismatched eyes, one blue, one green.

'Pye?' I whispered tremulously.

He turned his back disdainfully and sat down.

'He doesn't exactly seem pleased to see you,' the girl commented.

'He's just angry with me because he thinks I abandoned him,' I explained. 'Pye? I came back as soon as I could.'

Pye, his back still turned, began to wash one paw, as if he wasn't listening.

'You are sure this is your cat?'

'Yes, of course it's my cat! Could you let me inside the pen?'

'Sooner you than me,' she said, unlocking it so I could step in. 'And I wouldn't touch him, because he's all claws and teeth and . . .'

Pye, when I picked him up, made a weird snarl and then went limp and heavy. I held him in my arms and a fat tear dropped onto his sharp, furry face. 'Oh, Pye, I'm so sorry!' I told him.

He gave a galvanic jerk, painfully rabbit-kicking me, before scrambling up and attaching himself like a burr to my neck, where he butted my chin so that my teeth clicked together. There was more angry grumbling.

I turned, holding him and laughing. 'That's my Pye!'

'Well, he wouldn't be everyone's cup of tea, but he certainly seems glad to see you, in his way,' she conceded.

'Come on, Pye, let's spring you,' I said, carrying him out into the corridor. 'This is the day we both get out of prison!'

'But I'm afraid that's impossible,' the girl said. 'Since he was signed over to us for rehoming, he'll have to stay here while we go through that process – you know, inspect your house and suitability as an owner and—'

'Don't be daft,' I said shortly. 'I lost my home and fiancé when I went to prison and I've only just got out.'

She flinched. 'But we have to make sure they go to suitable homes.'

'Look, the cat is mine, he's microchipped in my name and was given away illegally and without my permission. And anyway, if you think you can detach him from me, go ahead and try!'

She accepted defeat.

'I suppose in the circumstances . . . though we'll have to go and do some paperwork and I'll need an address.'

'I have a job with living accommodation, so he'll be fine,' I assured her, though not in the least certain how Mercy Marwood felt about cats, especially cats like Pye.

But I filled in the form with my new address and had to pay her some money before she would sign him over to me. My cash was fast running out, but I also purchased a cardboard pet carrier into which, with extreme difficulty, I inserted Pye.

It was now four o'clock and I needed to be at Mote Farm by five, to be tagged, and while it was only about twenty miles away, I suspected it would be a long and convoluted journey by train and bus – and Pye was already working on shredding the box. I counted what was left of my money and then got the receptionist to call me a taxi.

Due to the miracles of satnav I was dropped off at dusk, at the bottom of a narrow tarmac road which apparently led to Mote Farm, my destination.

Paying the taxi took every last penny I had and then I trudged wearily off up the road, trundling my laden suitcase and weighed down by the cat carrier. The hills enclosing the narrow valley cast a dark shadow over it, but the lights were lit behind the curtains of the short terrace of workers' cottages that Mercy told me about.

The shape of the mill loomed up, closed and silent, and I turned to cross a stone bridge towards the drive that led up to the distant house, the cat seeming to get heavier with every step.

I had to keep stopping to rest, and Pye was getting crosser and crosser. But at last I trudged over another stone bridge that spanned a narrow moat, mocked by the quacking of ducks beneath. The house stretched out on either side of the porch with the glimmer of light showing the edges of inner wooden shutters.

I put Pye down again and pulled at a ring in the huge ancient door that pealed a distant bell. It swung open so quickly that Mercy Marwood must have been standing right behind it.

'My dear, there you are!' she cried, as if she'd been expecting my arrival at that exact moment. 'Come in, come in. Welcome to Mote Farm.'

I stepped into a long, paved entrance hall lined with flickering electric candles in old iron brackets and immediately put down the cat box and luggage again. I swear my arms had stretched at least six inches during the walk up the hill.

The pet carrier began to move about, growling, like a strange, rectangular and very vocal giant jumping bean and Mercy looked down at it with surprise.

'Now, what's this?' she said.

'I'm afraid I had to bring my cat,' I began to explain nervously.

'Of course you did!' she agreed. 'Come into the drawing room and we'll let the poor creature out – he really doesn't like being in there, does he?'

'To be honest, he doesn't like most things,' I warned her.

'He and my brother, Silas, are clearly destined to be soulmates, then,' she said with a giggle, hoisting the cat carrier with amazing ease. 'Come on, let's introduce them!'

Chapter 8: Clouded Mirrors

Q: What do you call a cat that falls down a chimney?
A: Santa Claws!

I followed my new employer into a large, flagged inner hallway, from which a wide staircase ascended into darkness. We went through a door to the left into a huge and rather splendid room, wood-panelled to dado height and with an intricately moulded ceiling.

For all Mercy's assurances that Mote Farm was not a grand house, it seemed pretty impressive to me. An immense, dimly hued carpet covered most of the floor, and old sofas, chairs and tables were randomly grouped around, like early guests at a party.

There was a larger cluster around the flickering fire, which as I drew nearer proved to be a realistic gas log one. The room resembled a surreal filmset and I began to feel somewhat swimmy-headed with tiredness and the stress and emotions of the day.

'Now, Silas,' Mercy said loudly, advancing on a small elderly man who was peacefully dozing in a high-backed chair before the fire. 'Here's Tabitha come to join us.'

He started awake and bestowed a look of acute loathing on both his sister and myself, before struggling painfully to his feet.

'Please don't get up!' I begged him, but he ignored me, tottering forward to shake my hand, using only his sandpaper-dry fingertips.

'One must do these things, however agonising it is. Rheumatism is a dreadful thing and bouts of sciatica even worse,' he said, in a martyred way that seemed to cheer him up. Then, relieved from the burden of good manners, he subsided back into his chair.

'Mercy says you've come to help with the cracker factory at the mill. It was too much for me. I'm a sad invalid, you know.'

'You're a sad, grumpy old malingerer,' Mercy said. 'You just couldn't be bothered, I know.'

He glowered at her. Then his eye fell on the jumping and increasingly shredded cardboard pet carrier. Pye had been quiet for some minutes, but now emitted a bloodcurdling scream.

'Tabitha's brought her sweet little pussycat with her,' Mercy told him. 'I was going to get a cat now I was home again, so that has saved me the trouble. I think he'd like to get out, Tabby.'

'I'm afraid he's very far from being a sweet little pussycat,' I began to warn her, but before I could leap forward and stop her, she'd popped open the carrier and out shot Pyewacket, all snarl and claws.

His first view of the strange, vast room stopped him dead in his tracks, his odd-coloured eyes wide. If he'd been able to raise his eyebrows, he'd have done it.

He sat down, in order to take it all in and better consider his options, his tail lashing from side to side like a slow metronome.

'Pye,' I warned him, 'behave yourself!'

'Mmmrow!' he said crossly, expressing his indignation that first I'd abandoned him for weeks on end, then closed him up in a box for a couple of hours. He decided to show me how far from favour I'd fallen by getting up and advancing in a friendly way on Mercy, who made much of him. Then he turned his attention to Silas, even going so far as to jump on his lap and sit looking triumphantly at me.

'This place is more like it!' he seemed to be saying.

'He must know that Silas and I are fond of cats,' Mercy said. 'What a clever, handsome creature he is!'

'Speak for yourself. Unless they catch mice, I've no use for the creatures,' Silas snapped, though his thin hand, knobbed with rheumatic joints, was slowly stroking Pye's black fur. 'Are we never to have any dinner?' he added, obviously feeling the civilities had been completed.

'Of course, but it's still so early that you've not long since had your tea! I'll just show Tabitha her rooms and then call you into the kitchen when dinner's ready to dish out. There's no point in setting the dining table just for the three of us.'

I picked up my bags again and followed Mercy through another door into a small dining parlour and on into a big kitchen with an outside door equipped with a cat-flap. Pye, who had elected to follow us, was a large cat and looked at it dubiously before sticking his head through to see whether what was on the other side was worth the effort.

'Should you let him go out right away?' asked Mercy.

'Perhaps we should keep him in for a day or two, so that he knows this is his new home? Or put butter on his paws?'

'Please, don't even *attempt* that,' I begged her. 'And he won't go far from me, because we're sort of joined at the hip, even though he's mad at me right now because he thinks I abandoned him.'

'Well, if you're sure,' she said doubtfully as the rest of Pye squeezed out into the night like black ectoplasm. 'Come on, let's just put your bags in your room and then you can unpack and settle in properly later.'

'Yes, the tagging people could turn up at any minute, too. They said they'd be here between five and seven and it's well past five now.'

From the back of the kitchen a short passage led past a pantry, scullery and a cloakroom to a tiny, square parlour furnished and decorated in Victorian style, except for a new electric fire in the grate. The boxes containing my worldly belongings – and, I hoped, Pye's litter tray, bowls and other necessities – were piled against one wall, along with the small yellow velvet nursing chair that was the one piece of furniture I'd not parted with after Mum died.

'The chair looks very well in here, doesn't it?' said Mercy. 'We managed to squeeze all your belongings into the back of the car quite comfortably. And through here is the bedroom – not palatial, but in the days when the family had a cook-housekeeper, having her own plumbed washbasin was the pinnacle of luxury. I'm told she was the envy even of the housekeepers in the local big houses.'

It was indeed a small room, containing a single brass bedstead covered in a fluffy modern duvet, a chest of drawers with a clouded mirror on top and a narrow wardrobe. The walls had been papered in a leafy William Morris design and an oval braided rag rug sat like a faded Technicolor island on the green lino.

'All Victorian mod cons, as you see,' Mercy said, indicating the solid washbasin in the corner. 'And the cloakroom is just down the passage, too. I hope you'll be comfortable here – the central heating does run this far, but it's not terribly efficient,' she added. Then she opened what I'd thought to be a cupboard door in the passage right outside the parlour, revealing a small spiral stone staircase.

'This takes you up to the west wing, where the door directly ahead is a bathroom. My room is further along the landing, in the central part of the house, and Silas has a small suite downstairs in the east wing, behind the library, so he doesn't have to tackle the stairs.'

'Right,' I said, wondering if her energy ever flagged, because mine certainly had!

I think she noticed I was tiring, because she said, 'Not to worry, I'll give you the guided tour in the morning, when you're rested – and here comes Pussy again.'

Pye stalked down the passage towards us and then head-butted my legs meaningfully.

'I think he's hungry.'

'Like Silas,' she said.

'I hope there are some tins of catfood in one of those boxes along with his dishes and stuff,' I said.

'No matter for tonight, for I'm sure I can find a tin of tuna in the cupboard, if he would like that, and I have lots of odd saucers he can use until you find his own crockery.'

She made it sound as if he always travelled with a complete Minton dinner service, but I agreed that he would love tuna.

'Did you say he was called Pie?'

'Yes, but spelled P-Y-E, short for Pyewacket. It's from an old film called *Bell, Book and Candle*, which my mother loved.'

Too late, I thought that perhaps Quakers might not be that keen on films about witchcraft, but she said cheerfully enough, 'Oh, I remember that one – hokum, but amusing. I used to be very fond of going to the cinema when I was a young thing. Now, come along with me, Pye, while Tabitha freshens up. Join us in the drawing room when you're ready, dear. I'll pop the nice hotpot I made earlier in a slow oven to reheat and we can have dinner as soon as these Tag People have been.'

She made them sound like a tribe.

When I arrived back at the drawing room, it was to find two strangers there and Mercy explaining to Silas what they were going to do.

'I did tell you earlier, Silas,' she pointed out. 'I knew you weren't listening.'

'I'd have heard if you'd told me someone was going to come and put a tag on the new girl's leg, as if she was a pigeon,' he said testily. 'Load of nonsense.'

'It's so they know if Tabitha has left the house at night,' Mercy said.

'Yes, I can't leave between seven at night and seven in the morning, until the tag is removed in a couple of months – isn't that right?' I turned for corroboration from the newcomers, a man and a woman, and they said it was.

The tagging was soon done, but the layout of the house gave them problems, it being very much wider than it was deep. My tag must allow me to walk from one end to the other – but then, it would also allow me to leave the house and walk a short way. But when Mercy pointed out that I still couldn't get beyond the moat, they thought that would be acceptable.

Mercy invited them to stay to dinner and seemed genuinely disappointed when they said they couldn't, even waving them off from the front door as if they had been old friends she hadn't wanted to part with. I deduced that she extended this amicable spirit to most people she met, because although the taggers (whose names I hadn't managed to catch) were nice, they weren't *that* nice. I mean, I've never indulged in an ankle bracelet because I think they're naff, and now I had a super-naff semi-permanent plastic one.

In our absence, Silas had hobbled through to the kitchen and was now seated at one end of the long pine table, with a checked napkin tucked into his blue lambswool jumper. Pye was sitting on a Windsor chair by the big Aga stove, though I noticed there was a utilitarian electric one nearby, too.

It was a strangely homely meal. Mercy dished out bowls of rich brown casserole in which bobbed dumplings and chunks of beef and carrots, served along with a basket of warm and floury soft bread rolls, and we set to. I discovered I was hungry. I'd forgotten what that felt like.

We followed that with cheese and biscuits and the remains of a big sherry trifle, into which I nearly slumped, since by then I was so dazed with food and exhaustion my backbone seemed to be wilting.

'Here, take the coffee tray through to the drawing room, Tabby, and sit with Silas, while I pop everything in the dishwasher,' Mercy suggested.

'I'll help you first,' I said.

'No, no, you're too tired tonight. Go and pour the coffee and I'll be with you in a minute. We keep early hours here, so you can get off to bed as soon as we've had it.'

'I'll be off to my bed straight after the coffee, too,' Silas agreed.

'I know you like to watch the news on the TV first,' Mercy said, then explained to me, 'I'm afraid Silas has the only TV in the house. I don't bother, because I like to listen to the radio. But I could get a little one for your room, if you missed it.'

'No, I don't mind in the least. I like to read, or work on my papercuts, in the evening.'

Pye came into the drawing room with us and continued to make much of Silas, who seemed to like him more than he did me, for he still glowered at me from time to time. But then, that might just be his natural expression. His nose and chin appeared to be attempting to join forces and his eyes were sunken under amazingly bushy eyebrows, which didn't help.

Silas went to his rooms the moment he had had his coffee, and I told Mercy I would, too.

'Yes, do go, dear. I'll lock up and follow suit. Of course, when I'm away Job makes sure that the house is secured for the night before he leaves, after serving Silas his dinner. Silas has those frozen ready meals delivered that you just heat up in the microwave – he loves them – but when I'm home I cook the dinner with a little preparation beforehand by Freda, Job's wife, and we eat together. Then, in the morning, do help yourself to breakfast in the kitchen if I'm not there, and give Pye anything he wants.'

I nodded, taking in only half of this through crashing tidal waves of tiredness. Mercy seemed to produce a running commentary to her life, but I thought perhaps if I missed something it would come round again . . . and probably again after that, too.

'It will be such fun, showing you over the house and mill tomorrow!' she said, before kissing me warmly and with such kindness to someone who was not only a stranger but, for all she knew, a criminal, that it brought tears to my eyes.

'I hope you'll be very happy here,' she said. 'Good night, my dear.'

Pye, following me back into the kitchen wing, made brief use of the cat-flap again, before joining me in my quarters and watching with interest as I unpacked the basic necessities before getting into bed. It was soft, lavender-scented and warm, and felt as if it was undulating . . . perhaps it was and I was floating away on the moat among the quacking ducks . . .

I half woke as four furry feet landed next to me with a heavy thump.

'Good night, Pye,' I said, wondering, as I fell asleep, at the astonishing turn my life had taken.

Chapter 9: Rumbled

Q: Who delivers presents to cats?
A: Santa Paws!

I'd slept deeply and dreamlessly and woke feeling the heaviness and warmth of Pye hogging most of the bed. For a moment I thought it was some kind of lovely dream and I was still in my room at the open prison. But then Pye rabbit-kicked me a couple of times with his back legs before leaping off the bed and I was wide awake, seeing the unfamiliar shapes of the furniture in the small room and remembering where I was. I could feel the tag around my ankle, too.

I switched on the bedside lamp, for it was only just starting to get light, and looked at my watch. It was five and the rest of the house was, naturally, still silent.

Pye indicated he wanted to go out and so I opened the doors through to the kitchen so he could use the cat-flap. Then I tiptoed up the spiral stone staircase with my spongebag, in search of the bathroom.

There was a dim light burning in a wall bracket in the passage at the top, and lots of closed doors, but I opened the one directly opposite the stair head, as I'd been instructed, and, after some fumbling in the dark, found a light switch on a cord.

It illuminated a scene of Victorian splendour: the room was palatial, with a black and white chequered lino floor, on which stood a claw-footed cast-iron bath, a throne-like toilet with a metal chain running down from a water cistern balanced overhead on metal brackets, and a washbasin large enough to bath a baby in.

The only incongruous note was struck by the large and roomy modern corner shower, but I was very glad to see it, because the radiators were as cold as stone and I'd probably have frozen to death by the time I'd run a bath.

There were fluffy fresh towels on a rack and also some wrapped French rose soaps in a bowl. I thought the latter were probably intended for guests, but I couldn't resist taking one into the shower with me.

I wouldn't say there was a great deal of water pressure, but at least it was hot, though the way the water pipes clanked made me guiltily hope I hadn't woken anyone up.

I washed the prison off my outer self, shampooed my hair with a bottle of something that looked even more expensive than the soap, then stepped out feeling if not like a new woman, then at least one ready to take on the world again.

I went back downstairs in a cloud-soft towelling robe that was hanging on the back of the door – that too looked new – and untangled my hair. Then, while I was making a cup of coffee in the quiet kitchen, Pye materialised through the cat-flap and I went to rummage for his bowls in the boxes piled in my sitting room. I discovered them quite easily, along with a few tins of his favourite food, half a bag of dried mix, some kitty litter and his tray, because Jeremy, a teacher to the last, had not been able to resist labelling the cartons with things like: 'Cat: Equipment for the Maintenance Of' and 'Kitchen: Sundry Utensils'. He must have got bored after a while, though, because there were an awful lot of 'Miscellaneous' and two that weren't labelled at all.

I fed Pye, who indignantly expressed strong disappointment that it wasn't a tin of tuna like last night.

'Don't get ideas above your station,' I warned him. 'Silas thinks you ought to catch mice for your living.'

'Pfft!' he said, with a scathing look.

After I'd filled his water bowl I scalded out the saucers Mercy had put down for him last night, before setting up the litter tray in one of the many unused rooms, little more than a cupboard, off the passage. Pye gave it a cursory glance, but though he much preferred to go out, he also hated heavy rain, so it was as well to be prepared.

Taking another mug of coffee through into the sitting room, I started to sort out the boxes. Most of my clothes were in the small tin trunk that had belonged to Mum, who'd kept her materials in there when she'd worked as a dresser and costume assistant. Her old Singer sewing machine, a black and inlaid mother-of-pearl thing of beauty in its own right, was sitting on the floor in its carrying case, and I put it on the wide windowledge before rummaging for clean clothes.

It was odd to picture Jeremy, who I'd once thought the love of my life, unable to resist folding everything neatly before putting it in there. He so hated untidiness and mess . . .

I felt better when I was dressed head to foot in new clothes – black jeans, a T-shirt and sweatshirt, socks and old baseball boots. My slippers must have been Miscellaneous, because they were nowhere to be seen.

Any garment that had been in prison with me was going straight into the washing machine and then on to the nearest charity shop, because the tag on my ankle was reminder enough. There was a laundry basket in the scullery and I tossed everything in there.

I began unpacking and my clothes and shoes were soon stowed away in the bedroom, with my balding teddy bear sitting on the chest of drawers alongside the locked box of my small treasures . . . the key was still on my ring.

Books, photograph albums and a few ornaments went into a small, empty bookcase or on the mantelpiece, and once I'd pulled the yellow velvet chair in front of the electric fire and hung a framed theatre poster on a vacant picture hook, the little room started to look very much more like home.

I left the two unlabelled boxes for later – things just seemed to have been randomly tossed into them in a most un-Jeremy way – and repacked anything I wouldn't need into two cartons, which I stowed with the unopened kitchen ones in another of the small flagged rooms off the passage, which didn't seem to be being used for anything. It had stone-slabbed shelves along one side, so had probably been another larder.

My freshly washed hair was now dry and hung straight and thick almost to my waist. It could do with a trim and so could my fringe, which was practically in my eyes, but it would have to wait. I twisted my hair into a practical plait, the end secured with an elastic band, and felt ready for anything: I was determined to earn my place here, and Mercy Marwood's trust.

And since I could now hear her moving about in the kitchen, clashing pots and pans and clinking china, I went through to offer my help with breakfast with a cheery 'good morning!' on my lips . . . only to discover two total strangers there, instead.

One was a tall, cadaverous elderly man with suspiciously boot-black hair parted in the middle, dressed in a dark suit with a deep red tie. He returned my greeting in a fruity, mellow Noël Coward voice, and made a kind of strange half-bow.

'Ah, you must be Miss Coombs,' he intoned. 'Madam told us you were taking up residence here. I am Job Carpenter, Mr Silas Fell's personal servant, and this is my wife, Freda, who helps Mrs Marwood with the housekeeping.'

'I don't know why you're being so formal, when she's one of us,' said his wife in a broad Yorkshire accent. She was a comfortably plump woman with a wild shock of permed white-gold hair and was dressed in a dark purple fun-fur coat under which stumpy legs were clad in pink leggings and blue and white spotted wellies.

'What shall we call you, love?' she asked me. 'Tabitha or Tabby?'

'Tabby is fine,' I said.

'Then Tabby it is,' she agreed. 'So, what were you in for, then?'

Chapter 10: Crumbs!

Q: What do snowmen eat for breakfast?
A: Ice Krispies!

I stared at her, shocked, and then glanced down my leg to see if my tag was visible.

'*In for?*' I repeated blankly. Had Mercy told everyone I was fresh out of prison, or did I have 'ex-con' written all over me, so that it was totally obvious at first glance?

'Now, Freda, you know Madam wanted us to put all that behind us when we made a fresh start here, and I'm sure it's just the same for Tabby,' chided Job, picking up a tray containing a rack of toast and a boiled egg in a pottery cup shaped like a chicken. 'I'd best get this to Mr Silas while the egg's still hot.'

Freda pulled a face at her husband's departing back. 'Like we all had our memories wiped when we got here! But you can tell me what you were doing time for, because you must already know we're all ex-cons in Hope Terrace.'

'I – you are?' I stammered. 'No, Mercy didn't tell me that.'

'Oh, yes, the whole family are benevolent Quakers so they've always employed ex-cons in the factory when they could. But there's only the seven of us left now and we've all been here a long time, so you were a bit of a surprise, like.'

'Oh, right,' I said, relaxing a bit. No wonder Ceddie had thought of me! 'I was convicted of helping to run a scam, selling fake vintage champagne,' I explained.

'Classy!' she commented, seemingly without sarcasm. 'I was done for persistent shoplifting and I met my Job in a hostel when I came out. He was a proper butler to a titled family till drink got the better of him and he absconded with the silver. But he took the pledge when Mercy offered him a job here and he's been sober as a judge ever since.'

'That's wonderful,' I said.

'And there's nowhere here to shoplift, unless you drive into a town, so that knocked that habit on the head,' she added chattily. 'There's the village shop, up in Little Mumming, of course, but that Oriel Comfort what owns it has eyes like a hawk, even if I was tempted by her stock, which I'm not.'

'No, I suppose it isn't likely to be very exciting,' I agreed.

'At first, Job and me worked in the cracker factory, but now we're semi-retired and work in the house, though we do lend a hand with packing the boxes if there's a rush order on.'

'Does that often happen?' I asked curiously, in the light of what Mercy had told me about the business running down like an unwound clock.

'Practically never lately, now I come to think about it,' she said, looking vaguely surprised. 'Job looks after Mr Silas – gets his breakfast and a bit of lunch and dinner, though when Mercy's home, he comes out of his rooms and has afternoon tea and dinner with her. I get in any shopping needed and let the cleaners in Wednesdays, and bag up the laundry, that kind of thing.'

The cat-flap rattled and Pye oozed in, stopped dead at the sight of a stranger and stared hard at her.

'Is this yours?' Freda said, surprised. 'He's a strange-looking cat and no mistake, with those funny eyes.'

'Yes, he's called Pye.'

Pye continued to stare at her and then said something that was probably uncomplimentary, if you understood cat.

'He doesn't exactly look nice as pie, does he?' she said, returning the stare assessingly.

'He can be a little . . . *tricky*, till he gets used to new people,' I conceded, 'and he's very vocal, so he certainly makes his presence felt.'

'I remember when Mercy had a big Siamese cat – that was noisy too; yowled like a banshee sometimes.'

'She did say she liked cats.'

'There are two down at the factory, to take care of any mice trying to get into the place,' Freda said. 'Bing and Ginger. It's to be hoped if they meet yours that they don't fight, though those two rarely stray from the factory side of the bridge.'

'I'm sure they'll all get on fine together,' I assured her, which I was – so long as the two resident cats accepted their sudden demotion to the bottom of the pecking order. 'Did you say there were seven former prisoners working at the cracker factory?'

'Only five, if you don't count me and Job, and the others are all a bit long in the tooth. They work ten to four on weekdays, from February to November and manage the orders all right, but there used to be a lot more workers when business was brisker.'

'Yes, that's what Mercy told me.'

'Well, she told *me* she was bringing in someone young and artistic to come up with new ideas for the crackers. Not that everyone's that keen on new ideas . . .' she mused. 'But I suppose you'll get to meet them soon, and you can size each other up.'

That sounded ominous. I wondered what the others had been to prison for, but I was about to be enlightened.

'Me and Job live in the first cottage and Dorrie Bird in number two – her daughter Arlene's married with a family and lives in Great Mumming, but she comes and works in the factory office three mornings a week. Dorrie was done for running a house of ill repute,' she added conversationally. 'But she said she never did, it was just the flat was in her name and she let her friends rent rooms there. It wasn't her fault if they brought their boyfriends back.'

'Unlucky,' I said, fascinated.

'At number three is Bradley Dudge. He drives the delivery van when needed, keeps the garden here tidy and likes to tinker with his old car, but mostly he keeps himself to himself and gets fits of depression when he remembers what he did.'

'What did he do?' I asked, without meaning to.

'Killed his wife, though they brought it in as manslaughter. Heard a noise upstairs where she was with her lover and thought it was a burglar. He was holding a heavy golf trophy in one hand he'd just won . . .'

'He hit her with it?'

'No, he threw it at her, but don't worry, he's never remarried, so he's not going to make a habit of it,' she assured me.

'Then there's Lillian in number four and Joy in five, both the wrong side of seventy. We all are, come to think of it,' she said. 'Still, I expect seventy is the new fifty, isn't it?'

'So they say,' I agreed.

'Lillian swindled thousands out of the benefits system and blew it on holidays, horses and men, and Joy used to stay in posh hotels, passing herself off as a toff, and then abscond without paying.'

'Enterprising,' I commented, riveted.

'They've always been pally, though they fell out a few years back when Phil, in number six, was widowed, but he told them he wasn't in the market for a new wife so it simmered down again. Ex-navy, he is, and must have been a firebrand when he was younger, because he killed someone in a fight. But there, we've all mellowed now and we often meet up of a Friday or Saturday evening for a drink and a game of dominoes in the Auld Christmas.'

'The Auld Christmas?'

'The pub in Little Mumming. With your young legs you can get to it up the footpath behind the factory in about fifteen minutes, but we oldies need to drive round by the road. Job can use the big estate car whenever he likes and Bradley, he's got a car too. Phil's more of a motorbike man and Lillian's always glad to get her arms round a bloke, so when the weather's fine she goes pillion.'

'I won't be going anywhere in the evening for a couple of months, because I've been tagged,' I told her.

'Well, it beats having to report to a probation officer every five minutes,' she consoled me.

Mercy came in and looked pleased to find us both there, chatting.

'Oh good, you're getting to know each other already.'

'That's right,' agreed Freda comfortably. 'Tabby says she's going to help you make some changes at the factory.'

I didn't remember saying anything of the kind, but Mercy nodded and beamed.

'She's my Girl Friday and very artistic, so I hope she's going to come up with some great ideas to liven up Marwood's crackers. I'll be taking her down to the mill after breakfast and introducing her to everybody.'

Freda shook her head. 'The others aren't likely to take to being livened up.'

'Oh, I'm sure you're wrong,' Mercy said briskly. 'I'll call a meeting as soon as Tabby's had time to think things over, and I'll want you and Job to be there, too.'

'Wild horses wouldn't keep me away,' Freda declared. 'Right, I'm off to the supermarket for a few things and I've got the list off the fridge. Was there anything else you was wanting?'

'Did I put crumpets on there? You can't get a crumpet in Malawi,' Mercy explained to me. 'One of the things I most missed, along with a bit of fried bacon and a potato cake.'

Freda took the list and went. Our conversation had certainly been illuminating. I was also starting to understand some of the problems Mercy might face in making changes, when everything had been the same for so long.

My new employer was now getting out eggs and bacon and a frying pan. 'I thought we'd have a good cooked breakfast this morning, to set us up before we start,' she said, tying on a tartan pinny.

She wouldn't let me help her cook it, but effortlessly produced eggs, bacon, and potato cakes cooked in the fat, with half a grilled tomato, which was delicious.

While we were eating, I confessed I'd used the expensive French soap in the shower, plus the robe and towels.

'Well, of course you did, dear – I put them there for your use,' she said. 'Consider yourself as part of the family while you're under my roof. And I constantly get soaps for Christmas, but there are only so many bars one person can get through in a lifetime.'

'You are so kind,' I told her, tears coming to my eyes.

'Not at all – you'll be doing me a kindness, and it's so lovely to have a young person under my roof again.'

'I'm not *that* young,' I said. 'I've just turned thirty-seven.'

'So has my nephew, Randal – what a coincidence! My goddaughter, Liz – short for Liziuzayani, did I tell you about her? – usually stays here in the school holidays and it will be so nice for her to have some younger company.'

'How old is she?'

'Sixteen, and I have her at a very nice Quaker boarding school near Pontefract. She wants to be a doctor and is a very serious kind of girl. Other than that, our only other regular visitor is my nephew and he's back now from wherever it was he went – I forget – and wants to come and discuss his plans with me next week. I expect we'll have all kinds of suggestions of our own to make by then, won't we?'

She beamed, obviously relishing the challenge.

'First, a quick tour of the house,' she said, when we'd stacked our crockery in the capacious dishwasher. 'It won't take long because, as I told you, it's not huge.'

'It seems very big to me.'

Pye, who'd been hanging around in the hope of sharing our breakfast, elected to accompany us.

'Now, you've seen this wing, though you may not have noticed that that door there in the passage isn't another cupboard or storeroom, but leads down to the cellars – there's electric light down there and the boiler . . .' She shut the door again. 'And you've been upstairs to the bathroom, so you could see that all the bedrooms and two more bathrooms are off it. At the far end, past the top of the main stairs, you come to my nephew's rooms in the east wing. When my husband died, I thought it fitting to give them over to Randal, since all would one day be his. Mine is the Rose Room – there's a little plaque on all the doors of the main bedrooms – should you need me in the night.'

We went through the dining room, where Mercy opened a door in the panelling to let me peep into a small parlour that looked out at the back.

'The ladies of the house used to like to sit here in the mornings, I'm told, but it isn't much used now unless I'm doing some sewing and want to be out of the way. I store any old sewing machines in there as I collect them, too, until I have enough to send out to Malawi.'

In the drawing room, the dark, shadowed corners had been dispelled by the bright rays of sunshine that were falling through the mullioned windows and warming the muted but lovely colours of the carpet.

'Now, as you saw last night, this passage with the stairway leads from front to back of the house – we think it's the oldest part, because that was the way the houses were built then, with the family in one side and the animals in the other. But you can explore the garden later. Bradley keeps it tidy, he's keen on gardening, but it's not extensive.'

She opened yet another door. 'This is the library, which

my nephew seems to favour quite a bit. Are you a great reader?'

'Yes – in fact, I got most of my education by working my way through the small branch library near my home as a child, because I had to miss quite a bit of school and we didn't have much money to buy books.'

'The public libraries are a great asset that should be cherished,' she said. 'Silas's apartment is down that corridor, but we won't disturb him. He has a small sitting room, bedroom and a tiny kitchenette, where he can make himself a hot drink or a snack, if he can be bothered. And there are the usual offices – the wing was extended at the back in the days when listed buildings were not beset by all these silly rules.'

'What does he do all day?' I asked curiously.

'He's compiling a genealogy of our family, the Fells, and also the Marwoods. The internet has speeded up that kind of research remarkably in the last few years.'

'You can get on the internet here?'

'Yes, though it's far from fast. In fact, Freda usually does the main weekly supermarket shop via the internet and it's all delivered – so convenient, just like when I was a little girl and the tradesmen brought what you ordered round in a van.'

'I suppose it is,' I agreed, thinking how wrong I'd been to equate age with a lack of computer skills. I suspected I was in for a surprise, and so it was.

'Job went on an evening course for beginning computing and passed on what he learned to Silas, and Freda seems to have a natural bent for it. But there, I picked it all up from young colleagues out in Malawi, so it's not at all difficult.

When my ward, Liz, is home she keeps me up to date on all the latest technology.'

'I think you're probably more up to date than me, then,' I said ruefully. 'Jeremy – my ex fiancé – had an old laptop he gave me, but I notice it wasn't packed up with the rest of my things, so he must have kept it. And my phone's just a basic pay-as-you go one.'

'You can use the desktop in the library – the password is stuck to a piece of paper under the mouse,' she offered.

'Thank you,' I said, though I didn't know who I might email, other than Emma, if horrible Desmond was away and not likely to be looking over her shoulder.

'The phone signals are another thing – the hill behind the house seems to block them, so you need to walk down to the main road before it becomes really reliable. I rely on the landline, but when I go further afield there are always a million missed calls and text messages on my mobile.'

She laughed merrily. I had clearly fallen into a nest of silver surfers and techno babes.

'I must dig out my charger, my mobile is dead as a dodo,' I said. 'But I can see I don't need to rush.'

'No, and you can make free use of the landline, dear. There,' she added, 'that's the whole place, bar the orangery, which is really just a glassed conservatory, at the side here. It should be full of plants, but with my being away so much I don't bother. When Liz brings a school friend to stay, they often go in there – like a den, I suppose. There's an old sofa and some wicker garden furniture. But do explore the whole house at your leisure later,' she added.

'Thank you,' I said. 'It is lovely – quite big, but somehow friendly and homely, too.'

'I'm glad you feel that. Now, let's put on our coats and go down to the factory,' she said inexhaustibly. 'You must meet the workforce and get a feel for the lie of the land and the business, so that when I show you my nephew's plans after lunch, we can have a jolly good think.'

'Wonderful,' I said faintly.

Pye followed us into the hall, watching us put on our coats without comment or, it appeared, undue worry.

I think he was starting to forgive me for abandoning him, and also to understand that this was where we both lived now and I wasn't suddenly going to vanish again.

Mercy handed me a piece of dry bread from the pocket of her baggy moss-green corduroy trousers.

'For the ducks. Come along!' she said, and trotted off, the lights in her trainer heels flickering like fireflies.

Chapter 11: Cat Flight

Q: What do you get if you cross Santa with a duck?
A: A Christmas quacker!

We went out by the huge front door into a perfect early spring day, though there was as yet no warmth in the bright sunshine and a chilly breeze was stirring a nearby stand of sheltering trees. My coat was a short wool one, the vivid scarlet of holly berries, and Mercy complimented me on the colour.

'I've only seen you wearing black before, but that is such a nice, cheerful shade and it suits you.'

'It was Mum's. She liked a pop of strong colour. I do wear a lot of black, but it's from laziness really, so I don't have to think about what goes with what. I brighten it up with a T-shirt or scarf or something when I remember.'

As we crossed the bridge over the moat the ducks instantly appeared from underneath it and we threw them the scraps of bread before walking on down the drive.

'This was originally a stable block, but it's now garages, where we keep the estate car and my small hatchback,' Mercy said as we passed some ancient brick outbuildings and a sweep of gravel. 'Do you drive?' she added.

'I can, because we used to have a little car when Mum could still get in and out of it. She liked Southport, where I could park overlooking the beach, and I think I mentioned that she loved to go up to the top of Snowehill Beacon, before she became too ill.'

'You did, and it's such a coincidence that you should know the village.'

'We didn't go into the shop or pub because we always took a picnic to save money. It's years since I've been there now,' I said, and my mind went back to the chilly autumn day when I'd fulfilled Mum's last wish, the sad grey clouds scurrying away, as if they'd wanted no part of it . . .

'You must go on a pilgrimage to the top then, one fine day, and remember all the happy times,' she suggested.

'Actually, if you don't mind, I thought I might do that this weekend on Mothering Sunday.'

'Of course not – the weekends are your own to do with as you wish. Silas and I will be going to the Friends' meeting in Great Mumming on Sunday morning, of course, and you and any of the workers who want to come with us will always be sure of a warm welcome.'

'Do many of them go?'

'Not regularly, but some are occasional attenders, especially Freda, Job, Joy and Bradley.'

'I'd like to go another time, because Ceddie told me so much about the Quakers,' I said, and she beamed at me.

'I'm sure you'll find it will give your thoughts a new turn,' she said.

'I haven't actually driven for years, because my old car failed its MOT after I moved into Jeremy's flat and I couldn't afford to replace it.'

'I'll put you on my insurance, dear, and then when I'm not using the car, you can borrow it.'

'That's very kind of you, but I'm so out of practice I'd be nervous about it.'

'It comes back to you very quickly. I never drive in Malawi and yet as soon as I get home and back behind the wheel, I'm fine,' she assured me. 'The drive all the way down to the road at the bottom of the hill is private, so you could take a little practice spin up and down to get used to it again.'

'I think that's a good idea,' I agreed.

'I expect I'll be sending you on all kinds of errands, so it will be very useful. You can take either car, though of course Job considers the estate as his own and it's his pride and joy, so while he drives Silas and me around in it quite happily, he gets terribly grumpy if I take it out myself.'

'Right,' I said thoughtfully, because I certainly didn't want to get on anyone's wrong side, especially five minutes after I'd arrived. Anyway, I'd never driven anything that big in my life.

'Come along,' she said, setting off again down the drive to where a second and more substantial bridge spanned the stream on sturdy stone piers. 'Silas tells me there was originally just a ford here, then stone slabs on piers, until it was rebuilt as you see it now, in the eighteenth century, or thereabouts. Job painted the inside of the walls white, after one of my friends accidentally grazed it on their way home in the dark.'

I followed her across it but Pye, who had appeared from some shrubbery and was trailing us, didn't. Instead, he jumped onto the low wall and watched. I felt he'd probably already marked the area on that side as his own territory and he'd never been a cat who strayed far away from home.

‘We’ll be back soon, Pye,’ I assured him.

‘Mrrow!’ he said, in a scathing tone, though I don’t know what I’d done to deserve that.

‘Now, from this side you can see the whole lay of the land,’ Mercy said, with a sweeping gesture of her arm that encompassed the mellow redbrick house we’d just left, sitting on its raised green cushion above the moat, with a backdrop of trees and hillside, as well as the other side of the valley, where the mill building stood higher up the stream with, below them, the curved terraced houses.

On the B road at the bottom of the valley, occasional cars slid past like beads along a waxed string.

‘This, and a couple of farms along the road, makes up all of Godsend – it really is a tiny hamlet, not even a village. It’s marked in the Domesday Book, though.’

‘Perhaps there were more people here then?’ I suggested.

‘I think it was more likely because there was already a house on the site of Mote Farm,’ she said. ‘One of my husband’s ancestors built the mill, then in Victorian times it was changed from some aspect of cotton manufacture to the production of fancy goods. The cottages were specially built to house the workers.’

‘Did the family always employ ex-prisoners in the mill?’ I asked curiously.

‘There’s certainly a long tradition of it, though we haven’t taken on anyone new for many years: the workforce has naturally dwindled, but none of them wanted to retire. But now, if Marwood’s Magical Crackers is to survive, we must move with the times and embrace change.’

‘Or close, as your nephew, Randal, would like,’ I commented. What Freda had said earlier about the elderly workers not liking change very readily had made me wonder if they were up to the challenge.

'Oh, I'm quite sure you can come up with an alternative plan,' Mercy said, with more faith in me than I felt myself at this point. 'In fact, we *must*, because I feel I've let my husband down by not taking more interest in things. But my mission in Malawi seemed to do so much good . . .' She sighed, but then her natural cheerfulness and energy returned and she said, 'Still, I'm back now and we'll see what can be done. Come along!'

We were now almost at the mill, which, since it lacked a chimney, grime and urban setting, was not at all darkly satanic, or even Lowry. Mercy pointed out the extensive attached outbuildings, the roomy parking area and more garages, where they kept a delivery van and Bradley's small car.

'Phil, who has the last house in the terrace, keeps his motorbike in one of the garages, too – men do seem to like taking machines apart and putting them back together again, don't they?'

'Yes. My ex fiancé used to spend a lot of time polishing his car and tinkering with it.'

'Do you miss him, dear?' she asked suddenly, with her acute, bright-eyed gaze.

'No, not at all,' I replied, surprised into frankness. 'I think I must have been in love with a mirage. Perhaps we both were, because he can't have known me, or he'd have realised I was telling the truth about the fraud. *And* he sent my cat to a rescue centre without telling me.'

'That was not an act of great kindness, but he probably meant it for the best.'

'Yes: *his* best. I'm sure Pye thought it was a cat prison and he was being punished for something, but I've got him back now, that's the main thing,' I said. 'We can both have a fresh start together.'

'Once you've found your bearings, you can register him at the vet's practice in Great Mumming – turn left onto the road at the bottom of the hill. You already know the way to Little Mumming, but you can get to it by means of a track behind the factory, too, if you don't mind a bit of a climb.'

She led the way into the main building, which had 'Friendship Mill' carved into the stone over the entrance, with, below it, a faded royal-purple board proclaiming, in worn gilt lettering, 'Marwood's Magical Crackers'.

Inside was one of those large, anonymous lobbies, with washroom facilities, a coffee table and worn tweed-effect chairs. An office was partitioned off from it with glass windows, like an aquarium for secretary fish. It was in darkness today: no piscine inhabitants lurked in its depths.

'Arlene, Dorrie Bird's daughter, works part-time in the office and the rest of the week at the bank in Great Mumming, but this isn't one of her days,' Mercy explained, pushing open double doors at the far end of the lobby with a flourish. 'And here we are: the cracker factory!'

The interior was surprisingly large and well-lit, both by a series of long windows down one side and a double row of large suspended green-shaded lights. A staircase ran away to the right to a mezzanine floor.

Only one side of the space seemed to be in use and most of the workforce were seated there at benches. They looked up curiously as we entered.

'Hello, everyone, I've come to show Tabby, my new

assistant, around,' called out Mercy. 'Do carry on and I'll introduce you individually as we get to you.'

They continued to suspend operations and stare, but Mercy didn't seem to notice, just led me across to a slender black lady with striking short silver hair. She had on a flowing dress in a bright yellow daisy pattern, an Arran cardigan with big wooden buttons and red leather clogs. My initial impression that she looked as serious and stately as an elderly Maya Angelou was dispelled the moment she spoke.

'Pleased to meet you, luv,' she said in a strong Liverpool accent along with a puckish grin. 'My daughter, Arlene, will be, too. She works in the office a couple of mornings a week, but she won't be in till tomorrow.'

'I'll look forward to meeting her then,' I said. She was sitting at one of a row of workstations, with drawers and trays at the back, and a small unit on casters next to her.

'We've got everything we need to make the crackers right to hand,' she explained. 'We lay out the novelties ready, according to what kind it is, though we only produce two different ones now, unless we get a special order.'

'Do you all make the complete crackers from start to finish?' I asked. 'I thought it might be sort of an assembly line, with each of you doing different parts.'

'We can all make them, but Bradley and Phil do other jobs, too. Brad makes sure each workstation is stocked with the right paper, jokes, novelties, hats and decorations, while Phil rolls and glues the central tubes and gets the snaps out of the storeroom as needed.'

'Don't you need those to hand, too?'

'Yes, but you don't want a lot of them together, because

they're a fire hazard,' she said. 'They're in a reinforced fire-proof bin in the back room.'

'Silver fulminate,' said Mercy. 'When the snap is pulled apart, the friction makes the small explosive sound.'

'Joy and Lillian usually pack the crackers in the display boxes and the boys carton them up for delivery. But as I say, if we're busy we can all do anything.'

It didn't look as if they'd been busy in a very long time but it did remind me very much of Santa's workshop, what with the half-open drawers and trays full of novelties, spools of bright ribbon and half-made colourful crackers in crinkled crepe paper.

As I watched, one of the other women rolled a tartan-edged green paper rectangle round the central tube, secured it with a dab of glue and dexterously gathered and tied off the ends with red ribbon.

'Them glue guns we got last year were good, once we got the hang of them,' Dorrie said. 'That was our Arlene's idea.'

'Brilliant,' Mercy said. 'I'm sure she and Tabby will come up with all kinds of other things too, once they put their heads together.'

She introduced me to the others one by one, who eyed me with a wary speculation that I recognised from prison. I only hoped I wasn't permanently wearing the same expression.

Bradley was a pale, slender man with thin, pepper-and-salt hair, freckles and watery grey eyes behind severe glasses. He seemed morose and didn't look directly at me when he shook hands, barely touching my fingertips before dropping them.

Phil, on the other hand, was a burly, cheerful, bald-headed man with no discernible neck, and tattoos up both arms.

The mermaids would have looked at home in the aquarium office.

The other two women were totally unlike each other. Lillian's improbably bronze curls were lacquered into an upswept nest and she had outlined her lips – or at least where she thought they should be – in a dark pencil before sloppily filling in the generous shape like a child who had trouble staying between the lines in a colouring book.

Joy, who I remembered had passed herself off as a member of the upper classes at hotels and then absconded without paying, was small, quiet, well-spoken and pleasant. The word that best described her was grey: grey hair, grey clothes and grey eyes.

I wanted to linger over the dusty racks of card and crepe, old-fashioned paper scraps of Santas and cheeky cherubs; the foil stickers, tinsel edging and curling festoons of ribbon.

It all looked a lot more exciting than the finished boxes, which were, it has to be said, rather cheap and tacky-looking and old-fashioned in a bad, not retro, way.

'There are three large storage rooms here at the back,' Mercy said, remorselessly detaching me from a box of old scraps I was rummaging in and urging me on. 'Apart from the first one, which has the doors to the loading area at the back, I can't say they're really used any more, and goodness knows what's in them. They could do with a good clear-out.'

She switched on a dim light, revealing a trio of adjoining rooms running right across the back of the building, full of racks and shelves jam-packed with shapes so furred with dust it was impossible to see what they were.

'We've always kept a few boxes of each kind of cracker we've produced – there were lots of varieties at one time.

But now we only have two, Happy Family crackers and the Marwood's Magical ones. The latter have little harmless jokes and tricks in them.'

'Mmm . . .' I said non-committally, because the ones I'd seen out in the workshop hadn't looked terribly exciting.

'So, that's the extent of the operation now,' Mercy said finally, taking me out of the further room onto the mill floor again, though this area under the mezzanine level was entirely empty.

We looked into the extensive attached outbuildings, the rooms bare except from a sifting of soft dust and the occasional packing case, apart from one that was fitted out as a sort of staff room, with a kettle, small fridge and more of the tweedy armchairs like the ones in the reception area. One of the side doors was fitted with a new-looking cat-flap.

'I don't know where the cats have gone,' Mercy said, but the two resident moggies silently appeared as we began to retrace our steps into the mill.

'This is Ginger, obviously,' she said, stooping to stroke them, 'and here's Bing. Lillian feeds them, because she's very fond of cats.'

The cats, perhaps bored and in need of a diversion, trailed us as we said our goodbyes and headed back towards the house . . . only to stop dead when we got to the bridge and they spotted the large, dark and menacing form of Pye, still sitting on the far end like a monstrous gargoyle, awaiting our return.

There was a confrontation of silent stares. With his strange, odd-coloured eyes, Pye did staring *very* well. It seemed to unnerve the other two, at any rate, but the final straw came when he slowly rose, puffed himself out hugely and began a slow advance.

They backed away, one paw at a time . . . then suddenly, their nerve broke and they turned and fled back towards the mill.

'You big bully,' I chided him, but he just made his strange 'Pfft!' noise and stalked regally past me towards home.

'Funny old pussycat,' Mercy said to him fondly. Then she added, with her usual sunny optimism, 'I'm sure they will all soon be the best of friends! Come along: I think we've earned our lunch.'

Time had flown by and suddenly I realised what the strange feeling in my stomach was: hunger!

Chapter 12: Christmas Lists

Q: What do you get if you eat Christmas decorations?
A: Tinselitis!

Mercy had a few calls to make and emails to send and told me to help myself to whatever I fancied for lunch in the kitchen and she would make herself something when she'd finished.

'Breakfast and lunch are always whatever comes to hand, and Silas won't join us – he has become addicted to meals from a service that brings frozen food and Job will have popped one into the microwave in his kitchenette, though he's perfectly capable of doing it himself. Truth to be told, I think he prefers his ready meals to my home cooking!'

'There's no accounting for taste,' I said.

'No, but a family should eat together at least once a day, that's *so* important. Besides, I can't let him turn into a complete hermit.'

I made myself a cheese sandwich and followed it with a crunchy apple from the fruit bowl, and Mercy, when she came down again, opened a tin of pea and ham soup.

'Well, we'd better go and look at Randal's proposals, hadn't we?' she said with her inexhaustible energy, once she'd finished chasing the last bit of soup round the bowl with a hunk of bread. 'Do you feel any ideas of your own are forming yet, now you've seen the lay of the land, as it were?' she asked hopefully.

'I do, actually,' I said. 'I was thinking about it while I ate my sandwich.'

'There, I knew your clever, artistic mind would come up with something!'

We went through to the library where Mercy opened a drawer in a mahogany desk and pulled out a large manila envelope.

'These are the original plans Randal had drawn up. He emailed me copies to Malawi.'

She spread the papers and plans out on the desk top and I studied them. They were much as she'd already described, but with more detail.

'Hmm . . . I think he was right about opening the mill to the public and his idea of a café on the mezzanine floor is inspired,' I said.

'I don't see why anyone would come to an old mill,' Mercy objected.

'But in the last few years lots of old mills have opened as tourist attractions, usually with craft workshops and that kind of thing,' I told her. 'People will go anywhere for a day out, especially if there's a café.'

'So, you consider his ideas have some merit?'

'Definitely, though I think he'd be missing a trick by replacing the cracker factory with more craft units or shops, because it could be the central attraction. Visitors would love to watch them being made and then have the opportunity to buy them right afterwards.'

'But surely crackers are just a Christmas thing and visitors would be seasonal?'

'Not at all – they'd come all the year round, especially if there was one of those Christmas shops too, selling not only the crackers but everything from baubles to fake trees.'

'Well, I never!' she said. 'Christmas all year!'

'The cracker factory hardly takes up half the mill floor, leaving plenty of room for a Christmas shop. And the customers could see down into the workshop from the café, if it's on the mezzanine.'

I sketched out a rough plan on a piece of notepaper. 'See – the visitors come through the front door into the lobby, where they can pick up a free leaflet giving them information about the attractions on offer. You might have to upgrade the loos there; I don't know what they're like,' I added. 'You'll certainly need a disabled one somewhere and a ramp up to the front door.'

Mercy nodded, jotting it down. She'd pulled out a reporter's notebook and appeared to have started a list.

'While we're on the subject of access, a small lift could be fitted to take customers up to the café, too – climbing all those stairs isn't going to be for everybody.'

'Very true, dear,' she said, making another note. 'Carry on.'

'They enter the main floor of the mill down a central walkway, with the Christmas shop to the right, and the cracker factory to the left, which will be divided off by some kind of partition, either waist-high or with viewing windows, to keep the visitors from getting underfoot.'

'Good thinking. Health and Safety would probably have something to say about that.'

'Health and Safety are likely to have a lot to say on all kinds of things,' I said. 'Anyway, they walk down past the cracker making, and then enter the middle of the storeroom through doors at the back.'

I drew a quick sketch. 'See, the first storeroom's door can be blocked off, so it's only accessible from the cracker workshop. Then I suggest you turn the other two into a museum dedicated to the history of Marwood's Magical Crackers, including the Quaker connection and any bits of interesting family history.'

'A *museum*?' Mercy exclaimed. 'Well, that sounds very exciting, and Silas would be a great help with the research.'

'I'm sure there'll be lots of interesting things in the stockrooms to go on display, but we'll need information boards and perhaps blown-up photographs of the family and the mill.'

She nodded, making another note. 'What do we do with our visitors next?'

'They'll exit the museum *here*,' I explained, making a cross on my sketch, 'which takes them right into the big Christmas shop. They'll need to go through it to get to the café and other attractions, giving them lots of opportunity to spend some money on the way.'

'Brilliant!' she enthused. 'And it looks as if the ground floor shouldn't be too difficult to arrange, so that Randal can busy himself with the more difficult task of creating the café and developing the rest of the buildings as craft workshops. And of course, one of those will be reserved for you, if you should like it,' she added kindly.

'I'd love a workshop of my own,' I agreed, though clearly this was not going to happen overnight.

She pored over my rough plan for a moment. 'So, except that they would lose part of the old storage area, which actually they never seem to use, things wouldn't be much different for the staff?'

'Not in terms of the layout,' I agreed. 'But there would have to be some major change in what they produce. They're currently making only two kinds of cheap crackers, when the market has changed, grown and become way more sophisticated. Crackers have now become a luxury *essential* and a plastic joke nose or bracelet wrapped in a tissue paper hat isn't going to cut the mustard any more.'

'I'll have to take your word for it, because clearly I haven't kept my eye on the market as I should have,' Mercy confessed. 'I do always celebrate Christmas in the traditional fashion, because my husband's family did, even though many Quakers don't go in for all the trimmings.'

'I think you could look at some of the ancient crackers in the storeroom for inspiration and do a retro luxury range not that dissimilar to the family crackers they're making now, but much improved in quality, especially the gifts. You could call them Victoriana Crackers and charge a lot. In fact, the key thing we need to do is improve the quality all round and charge much more. Take the Magical Crackers – it's a great idea, it just needs updating for the modern market.'

'Improve the quality and charge much more? But won't we sell less?'

'I don't see how you *could* sell much less,' I said frankly. 'People expect to pay quite a bit for unusual or luxury crackers these days, even though it's such an ephemeral thing.'

'If you say so – but getting the workers to understand that might be a challenge,' Mercy said.

'For it to work they'd need to be totally onside. And once we'd got them brought up to speed, there's a whole new area of cracker making to explore, for weddings and Easter, for example.'

'Crackers at weddings? Really?' Mercy's brown eyes opened wide. 'How surprising! But if being willing to adapt to new ideas means that the factory will stay open and they can keep their jobs, I expect they'll come round to it.'

'I think they'd not only keep their jobs, but you might end up having to employ more cracker makers.'

'I knew you were just the person to come up with the fresh new ideas we needed,' she said, patting my arm as if I'd been a really good dog.

'I hope your nephew thinks so, too,' I said wryly.

'I don't see why he shouldn't, because you've retained most of his suggestions about the craft workshops and the café.'

'Yes, and there can still be a gallery selling the craftwork made in the workshops in the second phase of the development.'

'Including yours, my dear. You will have to choose which workshop you'd like when you've had time to have a better look around.'

'I've always managed so far with just a cutting mat and a sharp knife, but it would be lovely to have more room. Sometimes I have bigger ideas . . .' I added. In my head, my papercuts often spilled out of their frames and took three-dimensional forms.

I don't think Mercy had been listening for she was studying her list and my plan.

'I think if we all worked really hard, we could complete

the ground floor conversion of the mill and even open the café long before Christmas,' she said.

'I'm sure you could, providing you get the necessary permissions for change of use and everything else. I've no idea what you need to open a café,' I added.

'Well, that would be Randal's baby,' she said cheerfully. 'He said he wanted to resign from his job as soon as possible and manage the mill complex full time, so it would give him a challenge.'

She pondered for a minute. 'I know you said people would buy crackers and Christmas decorations all year round, but it's bound to boom just before Christmas itself, isn't it? That would show Randal we were on to a winner!'

'Definitely. But the mill would be open every day, all year round.'

'I don't think it should open on Sundays,' she said dubiously. 'And with everyone in the cracker factory used to working from February to November, weekdays only, I'm not sure what they'll make of that idea.'

'All those details can be worked out later,' I suggested. 'Perhaps at weekends there could just be a couple of demonstration cracker-making sessions. We can find ways around things.'

'I've just remembered something else, too: all my employees spend Christmas and New Year in a hotel in Blackpool together,' she said. 'It's an annual tradition that I pay for and they love it. They usually go the day before Christmas Eve.'

'That shouldn't be a problem, because the mill could close from lunchtime that day till the New Year.'

'As long as everyone's happy,' she said. 'Could you put your suggestions on the computer for me and print them out? I'll call a meeting of everyone tomorrow at ten in the morning at the mill and we'll tell them all about it. Dorrie's daughter, Arlene, will be there then, too.'

Time had sneaked silently past us again. We discovered Silas in the great hall, the gas logs lit, fast asleep with the newspaper spread over his stomach and his rimless glasses down his nose. Pye was sitting on the chair opposite, his tail neatly disposed around his feet and his eyes tracking something on the other side of the room, though when I turned to see what it was, there was nothing there . . .

Weird.

'Must be time for tea,' Mercy said, and together we made sandwiches and cut a fruitcake. Silas woke up when Mercy dragged a Benares brass table near him and put his teacup down on it with a rattle.

While we ate, Mercy told him at length about our ideas.

'You've more sense than you look like you have,' he said to me with cautious approval after she'd finished. 'If you can get the workforce on-side and that boy to change his ideas, it could work.'

'I don't think you can call Randal a boy any more, Silas, he must be thirty-seven by now,' Mercy objected.

'He looked sick as a dog after that cruise he'd been on, when he got food poisoning. But he was off somewhere else exotic almost straight away.'

'Yes, he's constantly being sent abroad – it's the nature of his job – but he hopes to be able to visit us next week to discuss his plans . . . and now we'll have some of our own to counter with!' she said gaily. 'Now, Silas, Tabby will need lots of help with the history of the Marwoods, the mill and the crackers.'

'"The Marwoods, the Mill and the Crackers" would make a really good name for the museum,' I suggested.

'I'll see what I can do,' Silas said grudgingly, but I could see he was interested in the idea.

I only hoped Mercy was right about this unknown nephew, too, especially since he seemed to be thinking of packing in his job in London and moving here permanently. If he turned out to be the Grinch, we'd be in deep trouble!

Chapter 13: Sleeping Beauty

Q: What do snowmen wear on their heads?
A: Ice caps!

After tea, Silas retreated to his rooms and I went into the library to type up my ideas on the computer. Then I checked my emails, which was something I hadn't done since before I went to prison.

It was all spam of one kind or another, except for a very sweet email from Robbie and his wife, dating back to last December and saying they'd just found out what was happening and where was I? Was I all right? Could they help in any way? There was a picture of the new baby, too.

I really should get engaged again, so I could be jilted a third time and make it a hat trick . . .

I answered that one, thanking them and saying I was fine and settling into a new home and job, but I kept it short and didn't give them my address – I don't want to be the old hanger-on at the coat-tails of their marital happiness.

Then I emailed Emma, giving her the Mote Farm phone number and saying I could ring her if it was OK, meaning of course if Dismal Desmond had gone away again.

She emailed right back to say it *was* OK, so I rang her on the library extension.

'Des has gone back to Dubai already – they seem to like him over there, for some reason. I'm glad someone does, because I've had quite enough of him,' she said.

'Like that, is it?'

'He's talking about us all going with him if he can get a longer contract, but I don't want to. Having him home even for a week or two is bad enough, because he wants to know practically every breath I take when I'm out of the house and I even found him snooping in my phone bills. I think he needs a psychiatrist, but he flew off the handle when I suggested it. Still, never mind me for the moment: how was the journey there and what are the place and the job like?'

I told her how I'd rescued Pye and that I seemed to have caught Jeremy and Kate in a compromising situation. 'I definitely interrupted something, but whether they were having an affair all along, or it's only just started, I don't know.'

'Well, if she wanted Jeremy for herself that explains why she told that investigator about you, and lied at the trial,' Emma said.

'It was a pretty nasty way to go about it, though. When Jeremy and I got together she wasn't very friendly, because she was used to being the centre of both his and Luke's attention – they always seemed to think she was wonderful, though I could never understand why. But they still carried on adoring her, so she learned to suffer me. In fact, I thought she quite liked me, but evidently not.'

'Two-faced cow,' said Emma. I'd once invited her and

Desmond (before he got jealous of even her female friends), and Luke and Kate to have dinner with me and Jeremy, and though it had been all right, it hadn't been so much fun that we'd been tempted to repeat it. Mind you, since Emma was a qualified nursery teacher, at least they hadn't been able to sneer at her lack of higher education, like they tried to do with me.

'So, what's the set-up like there?' she asked.

'Weird. I'm officially Mercy's PA, though I think I'll be more of a Girl Friday, and I've got a sweet little bedroom and tiny sitting room suite behind the kitchen in one wing, where the housekeeper used to live in Victorian times.'

'One of the *wings*?' Emma repeated. 'How many are there? Didn't she tell you it wasn't a big house?'

'I think her idea of a big house is different from mine, though it's not a huge stately home like Chatsworth or somewhere. But it's large enough to have two wings and a ton of bedrooms, a huge drawing room, a library, an orangery . . . And it's on a sort of little island, surrounded by the moat, with ducks.'

'Oh, yes, that sounds just like your average two-bed semi next door,' she said sarcastically.

'It's quite homely, really, and I've got the run of the house, just like I was a member of the family. I can't leave the place between seven at night and seven in the morning, though, because of the tag. I'm a sort of part-time Sleeping Beauty.'

'I'd forgotten about the tag,' she admitted. 'How do they know where you are?'

'I've no idea, but I'm certainly not going to test it out, because I'd get sent straight back to prison to serve the rest of my sentence.'

'No, it's definitely not worth it. Tell me more about the house and the job.'

'Mercy's older brother, Silas, lives in the other wing. He's a bit reclusive and dour, but he's going to help me with some research I have to do. And there's a nephew who comes to stay when he wants to – which is probably going to be some time next week.'

'Have you seen this cracker factory she wanted you to help with yet?'

'Yes, and it's really a small cracker workshop in a big, empty old mill. There are only a handful of elderly people working there now, making the most boring, old-fashioned cheap crackers you've ever seen – and guess what, it turns out they're all ex-prisoners, like me.'

'Really? How odd!'

'I think employing ex-cons is something the Quakers have traditionally done, but these were the last ones and have all stayed on, even though they're the wrong side of seventy. They only work from ten till four on weekdays and live in little grace-and-favour terraced houses, so I can see why they were happy to keep going indefinitely.'

'But you said Mercy wanted you to come up with some new ideas for the factory?'

'Yes, because Randal, the nephew, had plans to transform the mill into a tourist venue and shut down the cracker making.'

'I take it your employer wasn't too keen on that idea?'

'No, though his plans did have some good points, like a café and craft workshops in the outbuilding. But I could see straight away that opening the cracker making to the public, with a museum about its history and a Christmas shop, would really pull visitors in. I do love Christmas shops.'

'So do I, and it all sounds fascinating,' Emma said. 'Perhaps a bit later, when you've settled in, I could come over and see it?'

'I'm sure Mercy wouldn't mind. She's putting me on her insurance so I can borrow her car, so I might be able to drive somewhere to meet you and Marco for a day out, too. I don't want to presume too much, too soon, though, and also I need some practice first, because I haven't driven for ages.'

'It'll soon come back to you and you might be able to buy a car of your own eventually, when you get paid.'

'I don't think I'm getting that much, because I'm living in. Mercy would have let me have one of the terraced cottages, but they're all occupied. And Jeremy made her pay for storing my boxes while I was inside when she collected them, so I have to refund that before I do anything else.'

'What a cheapskate!' she said, then added, 'But it would be nice to have a place of your own, wouldn't it? Perhaps one of those cottages will come free soon.'

'I don't think I want one of the oldies to pop their clogs just so I can get their cottage,' I said. 'I'm OK where I am for the present, and Pye is happy as a pig in clover. Mercy's going to give me one of the craft workshops when the mill's been developed, though, but I'll have free time to do my own work till then. I'm going to start sending stuff out to the greetings card manufacturers again.'

'I think it all sounds riveting and it makes me wish Marco and I could have a fresh start somewhere else, too, without Des. Who'd have thought he'd have turned out like this? And if he thinks I'm now going to be interrogated on Skype every night, he's got another thing coming!'

'How long did you say he'd gone for this time?'

'Three months, and I can't even go out to visit, because luckily he's staying in a house with a lot of other single men. I've decided to give him an ultimatum when he gets back: either he comes with me to Relate and gets help for his jealousy and anger issues, or I want a divorce.'

'I can't say I'm surprised, but I'm very sorry it's come to this.'

'My own fault for rushing into marrying him. I was in a bad place, but it was still stupid. But I'm entitled to a life of my own, to see my friends . . . or the ones he hasn't managed to alienate.'

'I'm not going anywhere, any more than you abandoned me when all the fraud stuff blew up.'

'He told me you were a criminal and I should have nothing more to do with you, so I said if you were a criminal, I was Titania, Queen of the Fairies.'

'You're small, but not that small,' I said. 'No wings, either.'

'I'm so glad you're out of prison and living nearby again,' she said. 'And there's a chance I might be offered a full-time job at Marco's school after summer, since, with the supply teaching I've been doing there, I've got my hand back in.'

'That's great,' I said. 'You'd be totally independent then.'

'Yes, that's what I thought, just in case we do split up. I'd better go now,' she added. 'Marco went straight from school to a friend's birthday party and it's almost time to pick him up.'

'You can email me here or ring this number. My mobile

won't work unless I walk down the hill a bit, but I'll try and do that once a day to check for messages.'

I set out my art materials on the small, sturdy table under the window in my sitting room, while Pye got into his furry igloo and snored.

Already I was feeling settled, as if there was some magic in the little valley to soothe and heal. I could see why the residents of the cottages had stayed put all these years and I might well end up doing the same!

When I finally emerged from my work and went to see if I could help with dinner, Mercy was there in the kitchen and said that Freda had been in to prepare vegetables and put a fat chicken to roast in the oven, so all she had to do was make gravy.

'I can cook a bit, mostly thrifty meals like casseroles,' I said, 'but I've never really done much baking.'

'I can show you, later on, when you've settled in. I love to cook and bake and I'm sure you'd enjoy it, too,' she offered kindly. 'By the way, did I tell you that I have some old friends coming for dinner?'

'No, but I'd be happy to serve it and then eat in here so—'

'Oh, no, dear,' she interrupted. 'We'll all eat together – it's the Quaker way. You'll like the Brownes, they're a lovely couple.'

They were, too, and interested in our plans when Mercy told them what we intended. Silas had already printed out a short history of the factory and said he would look out for old photographs, too, and start to think what would make a good display in the museum. I got the feeling he felt bad that he hadn't had more input into the ailing cracker factory while Mercy was occupied with her overseas work and was making up for it now.

Mrs Browne, though fascinated with all this, was almost deaf, so her husband had to relay everything loudly into her ear. This made the conversation somewhat long-winded.

By the end of the meal, the second long day began to catch up with me, though Mercy still showed no sign of flagging.

Later, lying in bed with Pye a weight on the end of the duvet, I looked out at the slender moon through the drawn-back curtains of the window and listened to a silence broken only by the occasional mocking quack of a duck out in the darkness. I felt quite tranquil.

Chapter 14: Cat-Flap

Q: What do you get if you cross a sheep with a kangaroo?
A: A woolly jumper!

Mercy remarked, while drinking tea and watching me eat cereal and toast, that it was as well to be out of the house on a Wednesday morning in any case, because a team of cleaners from an agency called Dolly Mops went through it like a dose of salts on that day every week.

'Normally Silas gets Job to drive him into St Helens and he goes to the library, to be out of the way, but today he's coming to the meeting instead. I'm so glad he's showing such an interest, it will take him out of himself.'

'He's obviously going to be vital when it comes to the information boards and displays in the museum,' I agreed. 'He had some great ideas at dinner yesterday and he's got all the knowledge about the Marwood family history at his fingertips.'

'It might inspire him to actually finish writing the Marwood and Fell family histories, too, and if so we could even have copies printed to sell in the mill,' Mercy suggested.

'What was he intending doing with them?' I asked.

'Nothing at all, apart from preserving them as family memoirs, though I told him he could put them on the internet as e-books. Other genealogists and those interested in Quaker history would find them of interest.'

'Yes, that kind of specialised area is where self-published e-books are really useful.'

Pye elected to accompany us when we set out to walk down to the mill and Job appeared from the east wing, pushing Silas in a wheelchair.

'I could walk, but it would take me so long you'd probably be coming back before I got there,' he explained.

'I really should have noticed how bad your rheumatism has become lately, Silas,' Mercy said remorsefully.

'It's not always this bad, and anyway, I could have told you, couldn't I?'

'True,' she said. 'Job, this is very kind of you, but we could have managed the wheelchair ourselves, had we known.'

'That's all right, madam,' Job said in his plummy, deeply mournful tones. I noticed that even the stiff March breeze wasn't disturbing his centre-parted black hair, which lay as flat and glossy as patent leather. 'The exercise of pushing Mr Silas down and, especially, back up will do me a world of good. Or so Freda informed me earlier.'

'Well, I suppose she's quite right in a way, because once you get older, it's either use it or lose it,' Mercy agreed.

'I'm not sure I ever had it in the first place,' Silas said gloomily. 'Shall we get on? This wind is coming straight from the polar ice cap, from the feel of it.'

Pye probably felt the same, because he didn't cross the bridge over the stream with us and I suspected would be back through the cat-flap into the warm kitchen in minutes.

Ten in the morning was the normal time for the cracker makers to start work, so they were all there waiting for us when we arrived. They'd arranged a miscellaneous collection of stools and chairs in a half-circle near the door and stood about like an audience awaiting a call for the first act of a play.

'Good timing, I've just made a brew,' Freda told us. She was presiding over a tray, on which reposed a giant, mottled brown teapot, a carton of milk and a collection of mugs, which Dorrie was distributing as fast as they were filled.

'Lovely – two sugars for me,' Mercy said, but Silas and I turned down the offer. I was already feeling nervous at being, if not the centre of attention, then at least a satellite to Mercy's planet, and I thought I'd probably spill it, or drop the cup, or something.

I remembered that the thin, pale man with the glasses and pepper-and-salt hair was Bradley, while Phil was the burly, tattooed one, but for a moment I went blank on which of the two remaining older women was Lillian and which Joy. Then it came back to me: Joy, dressed in fifty shades of grey, looked the least joyful, while Lillian had drawn herself a pair of even larger, smiling, sugarplum-pink lips than yesterday's.

Dorrie introduced me to the tall woman of about my own age standing next to her, though I'd already guessed who it was.

'This is my Arlene, who works part time here and in a bank in Great Mumming.'

'Job share at the bank, but they're closing the branch down soon,' Arlene explained, shaking hands in a businesslike manner. She had skin the colour of dark coffee, black, spiky hair in an urchin cut and was wearing a burgundy leather pencil skirt, cashmere jumper and stilettos, so she looked about ten times more elegant than the rest of us put together.

'How lovely to see you again, dear,' Mercy said, kissing her. 'It seems ages since I was last home. I hope your family are all well?'

'Yes, thanks – Jon finished retraining as a paramedic and he loves it, and the boys are sports mad, so that keeps them out of trouble.'

'And little Lucille?'

'Worried she's going to grow too tall to be the next Darcey Bussell.'

The tea and biscuits distributed, they all sat down and Mercy outlined the reason for the meeting as though they'd no idea what it was about, though I was pretty sure Freda would have brought them up to speed by now. Or Job, who seemed to flit about the house like a shade at all kinds of odd hours, so probably knew everything going on.

'Being away so much, I'd managed to overlook the fact that the cracker business has been declining over the last few years, until my nephew drew my attention to it and suggested it should be shut down,' Mercy said, and there was an angry mutter from the room.

'He was poking round the mill for ages a while back with some strange bloke,' Phil said. 'We wondered what he was up to.'

'That must have been the architect Randal employed to draw up some interesting plans for the redevelopment of the whole mill complex.'

'But without the cracker factory?' said Dorrie acutely.

'Yes, indeed. But naturally that was not at all what *I* wanted, so I've employed Tabitha here to come up with some fresh, alternative ideas for rejuvenating the cracker factory. But before we discuss them, I must first ask if you all wish to carry on working. Of course, you can continue living in Hope Terrace, whatever your decision.'

There was a buzzing, like bees stirred up with a stick.

'I don't know what we'd all do with ourselves if you closed the factory down and we weren't coming here every day,' Lillian said, and there was a murmur of agreement.

'It's not like it's hard physical work anyway, is it?' said Phil. 'Though there's nothing wrong with me – I can still haul boxes about with the best of them,' he added, flexing the impressive tattoos revealed by a short-sleeved black T-shirt.

'Seventy is middle-aged these days,' agreed Joy, though I suspected she – and probably Job, too – were nearer eighty.

'I think you can take it that none of us want to retire,' Bradley said.

'And I don't want to lose my job here either, because when my branch of the bank closes down they've offered to relocate me to another branch so far away that the commute would make family life impossible,' Arlene said.

'I'm so sorry to hear that, Arlene. But I'm glad everyone would like to carry on,' Mercy said, 'because I'd hate to see the end of Marwood's Magical Crackers after all these years – and on my watch! My poor husband would have been so disappointed in me for letting it get to this pretty pass. Still, now I'm home for good and raring for action.'

She beamed around them impartially. 'You have all grasped that regenerating the business means things will have to change, haven't you?'

'What kind of change?' asked Bradley suspiciously.

'Well, I think it's perhaps best if I first outline what Randal proposed, and then Tabby can tell you her ideas for modifying his plans to include the cracker making – and more besides.'

She quickly summed up Randal's plans to transform the site and then open it to the public, including his intention to quit his job eventually and manage the mill.

Then it was my turn and I nervously explained how I thought we could retain and revitalise the cracker factory, producing an extended and expensive range of both traditional and new designs, made in quality materials and with much improved novelties. 'No more cheap crackers,' I finished.

'I thought the advice was always to "pile them high and sell them cheap",' Dorrie said.

'Not where crackers are concerned,' I told her. 'People are prepared to pay for good quality ones, especially if they have unusual contents. And they aren't just for Christmas these days, either. You can now buy them for weddings and birthdays and even Hallowe'en and Easter.'

'Well I never!' Lillian said. 'Still, I expect we'd all be up for the challenge – especially if there's no alternative.'

'What about Randal and his plans for opening the place to the public, with all these craft shops and so on?' asked Freda.

'Some of his ideas were really good,' I said. 'We'd still open to the public, have a café on the mezzanine floor—'

'What's a mezzanine, when it's at home?' interrupted Lillian.

'It's that upstairs floor over half the mill, you daft ha'porth,' Freda told her.

'Yes, so they could look down on the cracker factory while they were eating. And in the second phase of the development, there'd be a gallery and craft workshops in the attached outbuildings.'

'So *we'd* carry on as usual where we are?' asked Bradley.

'More or less,' I agreed. 'But you'd lose two of the storerooms to the museum and the right-hand side of the floor space, though you don't appear to be using that anyway.'

'What's this about a museum?' asked Joy.

Silas, who had been a silent onlooker so far, said, 'A most fascinating display about the Marwood family and the history of cracker making.'

'Right,' Phil said doubtfully. 'That sounds riveting, then.'

'Oh, it will be!' Mercy exclaimed, then enthusiastically described how the space would be divided up, so that the visitors would be able to see the cracker making, walk through a small museum area and then on into a Christmas shop.

There was a short pause while the workers digested this.

'I'm not sure I'm keen on the idea of being watched by a lot of visitors, like something in a zoo,' Phil said at last.

'But it won't feel like that, because there'll be a partition with viewing windows between you,' I said quickly.

'I saw something similar in a clog factory once and it worked very well. I love the idea of an all-year-round Christmas shop, too,' Arlene said. 'I think it could be a real visitor attraction. But would you still want me to work here if Randal was managing it full time?'

'Of course, we'll always need you,' Mercy said, 'and anyway, he won't be giving up his job straight away. Even when he does he'll be involved in the creation of the café and the craft workshops and will have his hands full. In fact, we'll probably need you full time, as well as eventually employing extra staff for the café and shop.'

Arlene looked pleased and said that that would be perfect and her mother-in-law was always happy to look after the children in the holidays.

After that we had a lot of general discussion. Most of the employees would really have liked things to stay exactly the same as they were for ever, but Dorrie and Lillian were up for a change.

'What about our working hours?' asked Bradley. 'We work ten till four weekdays, with a bit of overtime if we have a lot of orders, but if the mill's open to visitors, they'll probably mostly come weekends, except in the school holidays, won't they?'

'We still have to decide the finer details like that,' Mercy said. 'I'm certainly not keen on anyone being forced to work longer hours against their will, or on a Sunday . . .'

'If the cracker factory isn't open at weekends, I thought perhaps some of you might like to demonstrate cracker making to the visitors at set times instead. But as Mercy says, we can sort all that out later.'

'We'd aim to get the ground floor of the mill up and running by the end of the summer,' Mercy announced, taking me by surprise, because I thought she was being optimistic, given that we'd need planning permission and probably have all kinds of other hoops to jump through first.

'Then we'd make a big killing on the run-up to Christmas!' she finished, rocking to and fro on her heels like an excited child, so that the lights in her shoes flashed.

You could tell she came from generations of businesspeople. I was only surprised she'd taken her eye off the ball for so long. But she was certainly making up for it now!

'The factory is usually shut in December and January,' said Freda. 'And we always go to Blackpool for Christmas and New Year. Would we have to give that up?'

'Not at all,' Mercy assured them. 'We'd want the mill to stay open in the run-up to Christmas, obviously, but Tabby thought it could close before Christmas Eve and reopen after the New Year, when you've returned.'

'That's not so bad, then,' said Lillian.

'It doesn't seem to me as though we've got any alternative but to go with what you want, though we're old dogs to learn new tricks,' Joy said.

'Speak for yourself,' Freda told her.

'I really need you all onside to make this work – and also, to convince Randal that it will, when he visits next week,' Mercy told them.

'Right you are, then, we'll back you up: and you set Tabby onto that Randal when he comes home; she'll sort him,' Dorrie said, seeming to speak for all of them. I had no idea why they thought I'd be able to deal with this unknown nephew!

But Freda was nodding her agreement. 'That's right,' she said. 'Now, anyone want another brew, before you start work? The morning's half gone and not a cracker made yet!'

We left them to it and went into the office with Arlene, where I told her some of my initial ideas for new boxes of crackers.

'Arlene, you and Tabby can start sourcing new materials and novelties online – we get most things from China, these days, Tabby – and perhaps find somewhere that can create fresh artwork for the boxes,' Mercy said.

‘I’ll enjoy that,’ she replied. ‘It gets boring, putting in the same orders over and over.’

‘Meanwhile, I’ll press on with getting the plans for the mill changed and the necessary permissions applied for,’ Mercy said. ‘The whole thing shouldn’t be too disruptive, if done in stages.’

‘Who’s going to tell Randal there’s been a bit of a change to his plans?’ asked Silas.

‘I will,’ Mercy said happily. ‘I’m sure the dear boy will see they’re an improvement.’

I much preferred the idea of her telling him to Dorrie’s suggestion that she should set me onto him!

We’d just popped back into the mill to say goodbye to everyone – finding them still grouped round the tray of fresh tea on an extended workers’ playtime – when there was a sudden scuffling, hissing and yowling, followed by the arrival of Pye from the direction of the outbuildings. Presumably he had discovered the cat-flap.

He stalked majestically in and fixed one blue and one green eye on the assembly. Ginger and Bing slunk in after him, looking resentful but cowed.

‘This is my cat, Pye,’ I explained. ‘I didn’t think he’d follow us all the way down here. Still, it looks as if the cats are all getting on together, doesn’t it?’ I added hopefully.

‘Mrrow!’ growled Pye in agreement, while poor Bing and Ginger pulled desperate, silent faces behind him.

Then he climbed onto Silas’s lap and remained there, while Job pushed the chair all the way back up the hill.

Chapter 15: Ghost Mice

Q: What song do snowmen like to sing?
A: There's no business like snowbusiness!

Pye and I settled in as if we'd always lived at Mote Farm and I spent most of the next two days at the mill, getting to know everyone better and some idea of how things worked.

First off, I learned the two most important skills: how to make large pots of darkly stewed tea and Christmas crackers. Bradley set up one of the unused workstations for me, with some old stock paper and contents, and Lillian gave me a lesson in the basics.

They said it could take weeks of practice before I turned them out to saleable quality, which I thought was absurd: how hard could it be? But after only one session with a glue gun and some crinkled crepe, *I* looked more like a Christmas cracker than the misshapen objects I was creating.

It gave me a greater respect for the professional way the others could just sit there and neatly produce identical ones, at least twenty or thirty in an hour, depending on which they were making. And it started to spark ideas for the type we should be producing . . .

Arlene researched on the internet what crackers were currently bestsellers and we compared notes and ideas, not only for the designs but for the novelties they would contain. I'd noticed from the expensive crackers that Jeremy had always insisted on (colour coded to match the Christmas decorations) that it was only the exteriors that ever differed: the basic range of items inside remained much the same.

Arlene showed me some of the sites in China from where they usually ordered paper, card, ribbon, embellishments and novelties and I was astonished at the range . . . and even more inspired.

Meanwhile Mercy, with her usual energy, threw herself into the whole business and the three of us had lots of exciting discussions.

'I thought, if you agreed, I'd start cleaning and stocktaking in the back rooms on Monday, and I'm sure I'll find an early design we can reproduce for our retro Victoriana range,' I said.

'Will that be popular, dear?' asked Mercy doubtfully.

'Oh, yes, everyone loves retro stuff these days,' Arlene assured her. 'So we're thinking about a much more luxurious version of the traditional family crackers we make now, an updated version of Marwood's Magical Crackers . . .'

'More magical tricks, less plastic joke items,' I said.

'And small tree crackers in modern colourways, like black and silver, or purple, as well as pastel shades, with just a motto, snap and tiny charm of some kind in them,' Arlene continued. 'And the Victoriana one.'

'That's enough to think about to start with,' Mercy agreed.

* * *

Mercy got the man who had drawn up the original mill redevelopment plans for Randal to come out, and she showed him how she would like them altered.

From bits I overheard as she took him around the mill, explaining the new layout, he initially tried to fight Randal's corner (they seemed to have been at school together), before totally capitulating.

'There we are, Josh's promised to work right over the weekend, if need be, to alter the plans so we can have them back next week, before Randal gets here,' she said, coming back from waving the dazed designer away. 'Then he's going to submit them for planning permission, so we can get them approved very quickly and start the work. Though actually, since the building isn't listed, we can make a start on altering the mill interior right away.'

'I've no idea how long planning permission for this kind of thing usually takes,' I said.

'I haven't either. Perhaps two or three months at the most?' she suggested, though I thought that might be optimistic. 'I expect the café will take longer, because there are bound to be many food, hygiene and health and safety criteria it will have to meet, but I hope Randal will take all that on.'

If he approved of the idea, I thought, but refrained from saying. The unknown nephew could well throw both a hissy fit and a spanner in the works!

On Friday afternoon, encouraged by Mercy and watched gloomily by Job, who was lovingly polishing the chrome on the estate car, I drove the small hatchback down the drive to the main road and back several times until my confidence returned.

Then I did a few three-point turns in the mill car park, and by the time I returned, Mercy was talking to a sturdy, elderly lady on a brown cob.

I managed to insert the car back into its narrow garage, watched critically by Job, and when I came out Mercy introduced her friend as Becca Martland.

'Pleased to meet you,' she said, transferring the reins to one hand and reaching down to shake mine. 'But I won't keep Nutkin standing any longer in this cold wind – you should get in out of it too, Mercy; you'll catch your death.'

'Oh, not me,' Mercy declared. 'This old duffel coat's as warm as toast.'

When her friend had ridden off, she explained that the Marwoods from Godsend and Martlands from Little Mumming had always been friends.

'Liz calls us the M&Ms,' she added, 'after some kind of sweets, apparently.'

'Are they Quakers, too?'

'No, dear, but good friends for all that, especially Noël and his wife, Tilda, who live at the lodge and Becca, who has her own house, New Place, in Little Mumming. Jude Martland, Noël and Becca's nephew, was at the same school as Randal.'

'Not another one,' I said, and she looked puzzled.

'He wasn't in the same year, because he is a little older. He inherited the family home, Old Place, a couple of years ago and then married the sweetest girl, called Holly. Now, Becca tells me, they have a little baby boy, just when they'd given up all hope of a family – I'm so delighted.'

'Will that be all, madam?' intoned Job gloomily, appearing at her elbow like the Ghost of Christmas Past. 'Mr Silas said earlier that he wouldn't need me any more today and I have a barber's appointment.'

'Of course! I thought you were just watching Tabby drive out of interest, to see how she got on,' Mercy told him.

I thought it was probably more out of fear that I would be an appalling driver and she'd let me loose on his beloved estate car!

'Funny old thing,' she said affectionately as he walked off, tall, stiff-backed and melancholy. 'I'm forever telling him to call me and Silas by our first names, but he never will. But he's very good with Silas, which is the important thing.'

The next day, being Saturday, was theoretically my first day off, but Mercy suggested I drive her to Neatslake, a village over towards Ormskirk, for the practice.

She was hot in pursuit of a sewing machine that was being given away, which she had heard about through the Friends, and on our arrival we found that a neighbour had donated another, so Mercy was highly delighted. They both looked in need of a little TLC to me, but Mercy assured me that Phil was a dab hand at renovating them before they were shipped out.

I drove back, too, and I found I was enjoying it.

We unloaded the sewing machines by the front door and I carried them through to join half a dozen others in the small parlour.

'There,' she said, surveying her hoard with satisfaction. 'Let's go and have something to eat!'

I was still stuffed from the coffee, cake and scones the Friend we'd visited had pressed on us. I was starting to equate being a Quaker with generous hospitality, for the woman had seemed genuinely disappointed that we wouldn't stay for lunch, too, but Mercy had clearly already burned off the calories and was hungry as a hunter.

We had Welsh rarebit, followed by apple pie and ice cream, and we'd no sooner finished than she said she fancied a Lancashire hotpot for her dinner and would cook up a batch of individual ones with shortcrust pastry tops that very afternoon.

I stayed to learn how to make those and the chocolate sponge cake she whipped up afterwards, before finally going off to my rooms to do a bit of artwork.

Pye decided to hang out with Mercy, provider of treats and unbounded admiration. I think she might have partly exorcised him, because when he was with her he gave every appearance of being the sweet-natured pussycat she believed him to be . . .

And that thought gave me an idea for a papercut . . . perhaps even a Puss-in-Boots inspired one. I'd already had lots of ideas in prison, once my brain had started functioning properly again, and even more since I'd come to this romantic-looking moated house on the edge of the Lancashire moors.

But before I could explore any of my weirder flights of fancy, I needed to produce some commercial designs intended for one of the greetings card companies who used to take my work and pay quite well for it.

I used the house and moat as a backdrop with, in the foreground, two swans (artistic licence, since we only had ducks), their necks entwined into the shape of a loving heart. I believe swans mate for life, which is more than most humans seem to manage these days.

And then, when I was putting the partly cut design in one of my small portfolios, I spotted a large card envelope – and inside were two designs I'd finished and packed up ready to send before I'd been arrested last year! The shock of it all had sent them right out of my head.

They needed only a new letter to accompany them and I could pop out and post them on Monday.

Dinner at Mote Farm seemed to be a flexible feast that took place anywhere from six onwards, but I forgot all about time until Mercy tapped on the door to tell me it would be served in ten minutes.

Silas was already seated at the kitchen table, with Pye twining affectionately around his ankles, purring throatily, but as soon as he saw me he went and looked pointedly at his dinner bowl.

'You old fraud,' Mercy told him, laughing. 'I fed you hours ago, because you pestered me so much!'

'Oh, thank you, I was so lost in work that I lost track of the time,' I confessed. 'Mind you, Pye usually comes and tells me in no uncertain terms if I miss putting his food down!'

'He's still a bit thin, as are you, so a little extra feeding up won't do either of you any harm,' she said, putting one of the hotpot pies we'd made earlier onto each dinner plate and then passing round the vegetables. 'It's a pity you missed tea, because the most interesting man joined us.'

'Door to door salesman,' Silas explained. 'Household goods.'

'They travel about so much and it can be very disheartening when doors are so often closed in their faces,' Mercy said. 'He used to be an alcoholic, but saw the light and turned his life around. He was interested to learn we were a temperance household.'

Now she came to mention it, I realised I hadn't seen or been offered anything alcoholic to drink since I arrived, apart for a small bottle of brandy in the kitchen cupboard, which presumably didn't count because it was for cooking purposes. But I'm not really much of a drinker, so I hadn't missed it.

'I noticed that splendid pottery frog by the sink when I came in – did you buy that from him?' I asked tactfully, because actually it was a lurid green and hideous, with a wide gaping mouth.

She nodded. 'I felt I had to buy *something*, and the frog holds a wire pan-scrub so it does have a purpose.'

'Rubbishy thing,' scoffed Silas.

'I think it's cute and *you* bought that ingenious stick with a crocodile-shaped head for picking things up from the floor without bending,' she reminded him.

'That's practical,' he said, then asked for another hotpot. For a skinny elderly gentleman, he could certainly put away his food – and faster than even Mercy did.

'Randal emailed to say that he was back again and will come and stay next Thursday night – he has a lot of business to attend to first and then he needs to go away again – to Peru, I think he said.'

'Like Paddington Bear, in reverse?' I suggested.

'Where did he say he'd been last time?' asked Silas.

'Greece, I think. He does get about the world on his assignments. And he *can* be a bit of a bear, Tabby, though of course he isn't short and fat. Or furry,' she added, and I nearly choked on my hotpot.

She patted me on the back.

'As well as wanting to discuss the mill plans with us, he says he has some good news,' she continued, when I'd stopped coughing.

'Assignments?' I echoed, taking in the first part of this.

'He works in travel, he's always going abroad – didn't I say?' she said, surprised.

'I don't think so. I just sort of assumed he was dead rich and took lots of holidays.'

'His parents did leave him well provided for, but of course, he's always worked,' she said. 'I think he proposes to invest some of that inheritance into the mill redevelopment, in return for shares and perhaps being made a director. But of course, that is all to be thrashed out with the company accountant and the solicitor at some future point. I'm so glad he's taking an interest in the family business, even if it was a little misdirected at first.'

I thought they might also have to thrash out a compromise plan, unless the unknown Randal was more amenable to keeping the cracker factory going than he'd sounded, but time would tell. And I couldn't see Mercy relinquishing total control of the mill for a long time to come, either, so there would probably be a few battles . . .

'I wonder what Randal's good news is?' she mused. 'Perhaps he's going to get married at last!'

'Does he have a girlfriend?'

'I don't know, dear. He's had several lady friends, though he's brought few of them here. But perhaps he's ready to marry and settle down and that's why he showed a sudden interest in running the mill?'

It sounded quite possible to me and, though I quite

dreaded his arrival in case he made difficulties, I was also becoming curious to meet him at last.

While we were having coffee in the drawing room afterwards, Pye seemed to be tracking something invisible from one side of the room to the other again, which was a little disconcerting. I asked Silas if the house was haunted and he said there were a few stories about a White Lady, but she was supposed to be benign.

'Not that we believe in such things,' Mercy said. 'I'm sure Pye is just playing.'

'I expect you're right,' I said. 'He looked as if he was chasing invisible mice yesterday.'

Pye was now sitting staring fixedly at a section of panelling where there was no door, as if he was expecting someone to pop out and say *Boo!* I wouldn't have put it past him to do it on purpose, just to unnerve me.

Chapter 16: To the Point

Q: What did the stamp say to the Christmas card?
A: Stick with me and we'll go places!

It was a strange twist of fate that had brought me to Godsend, so near to Mum's beloved Snowehill and the place where I'd scattered her ashes, but I had to slightly adapt my plan to spend Mothering Sunday making a kind of pilgrimage by taking the track behind the mill and walking all the way up to the summit.

Some of the cracker factory workers asked me to go to the Auld Christmas in Little Mumming with them for one of Nancy Dagger's famous Yorkshire pudding lunches and since I'd already had to turn down their invitation to join them there on a Friday or Saturday evening, because of my tag and the curfew, I didn't want to seem stand-offish.

And after all, I could start my hike from the village afterwards and then make my own way home by the track.

Mercy drove Silas off to Great Mumming in the hatchback for the Quaker meeting, which she'd told me was today going to be followed by a Thrift Lunch, when everyone ate soup and bread and donated the money they would have spent on their normal lunch to a good cause.

Mercy seemed to be looking forward to it and had made a giant pot of soup, which she decanted into two large lidded plastic boxes. I'd carried them out to the garage for her and wedged them in the boot, so they wouldn't slide about.

'Load of nonsense – could have opened a couple of tins!' grumbled Silas in his usual way as he manoeuvred himself, in a crablike, sideways manner, into the passenger seat.

'I expect some of the others *will* bring tins,' Mercy said, 'and bread rolls, too. But I like making lentil soup and I had all the ingredients I needed, including some nice chicken stock from the freezer. But you don't have to eat any of it, if you don't want to, Silas.'

'Now you want me to starve to death?' he complained grumpily, fastening his seatbelt, not without some difficulty. I refrained from offering to do it for him; I didn't think he'd take it well in his current mood.

I waved them off and then set out for the mill, carrying my small flowered canvas rucksack, containing a flask, sketchbook and pencils for later. Everyone but Dorrie, who always spent Sundays at Arlene's house, would be going to the pub and I was to be given a lift in Bradley the-wife-murderer's car.

Job was already sitting in the front passenger seat when I got there, so I was crammed into the back with Freda and Joy. It being a clement spring day, apparently Lillian had already set out pillion on the back of Phil's motorbike.

On the way up to Little Mumming, Joy and Freda pointed out the gates to New Place, Becca Martland's house, and told me about some of the other local characters and also the annual Twelfth Night Revels.

'The villagers like to keep the Revels to themselves,' Joy

explained. 'I think Godsend folk are welcome, but of course we're always in Blackpool when it's going on, so we haven't seen it.'

'We've heard about it, though,' Freda said. 'There's play-acting, morris dancing and a special free hot toddy called wassail. I'd quite like to go, but I prefer the entertainments they lay on in the hotel in Blackpool.'

The Auld Christmas was an ancient and cosy pub, with an open fire scenting the room with wood smoke and fir cones. Lillian was loudly flirting with an elderly gentleman who was seated in a chair pulled up close to the hearth.

Phil, his burly form tightly encased in scuffed, studded and zippered leather, was at the bar lining up the drinks – they seemed to have a system of taking it in turns to buy a round. When he asked me what my poison was, I asked for a half-pint of Guinness, because I thought I might need something sustaining to get me up that hill – and said I'd get the next round in. I hoped my purse could stand it, after that taxi out to Godsend the other night, but luckily I'd found a ten-pound note tucked into the inner pocket of my rucksack from the last time I'd used it.

Phil had reserved a table and benches for us by laying his and Lillian's helmets and gauntlets along them, which was just as well, because the pub was filling up fast.

'That's old Nick Dagger Lillian's flirting with,' Joy told me primly. 'She'll flirt with anything male, that one. Nick's son runs the pub now with his wife, Nancy.'

I only caught a brief glimpse of Nancy, because she was in the kitchen producing wonderful plate-sized Yorkshire puddings, filled with vegetables, roast beef and gravy. No wonder the place was popular!

Job, in his plummy, sepulchral voice, told me that most of the customers were locals. 'That's why there are so many oldies, like us: they live a long time up here, what with the clean air and Nancy's cooking.'

When we'd demolished the food (my appetite had returned with a vengeance) and I'd ordered another round of drinks, Bradley got out a battered wooden box of dominoes and we settled down to a game, though I told them I hadn't played it since I was a little girl and matched ladybirds and butterflies on giant cards, rather than spots on wood.

They obviously took the game seriously, because there was much concentrated slapping down of tiles and bickering. After the first game, Bradley went to buy in another round (I was on to lemonade by now, not wanting to stagger up Snowehill) and as he was at the bar, a slight, dark, handsome man of around my own age came in. He was carrying two bottles of sherry. It seemed an unlikely choice.

'That's Guy Martland. He must have been buying sherry in the snug to take up to Old Place,' Lillian told me, following the direction of my gaze. 'He's the younger brother of Jude, who's the head of the family now. They had a bit of a falling-out a couple of years ago but they seem to have made it up and he sometimes comes back from London for weekends.'

'He's got one of those huge Chelsea tractors,' Freda put in. 'I don't know why townies think they need to clog the streets up with those.'

Guy, catching my eye, smiled at me and I blushed at having been caught staring. He said something to Bradley then, leaving his sherry on the bar, helped him carry some of the freshly refilled glasses over.

'Hi, everyone – but *especially* the luscious Lillian,' he said, with a wink at her. 'And here's another lovely face that I don't know.'

'This is Mrs Marwood's new personal assistant,' Job said. 'Tabitha Coombs – Guy Martland.'

'Delighted to meet you,' he said with a winning smile. 'I wish I could stay and get to know you better, but I've been dispatched on an emergency mission to get sherry for the Ancient Ones up at Old Place. Apparently, the food will turn to dust and ashes in their mouths without it. Still, I'll hope to see more of you in future,' he added, and sauntered off to collect his sherry.

I seemed to have a thing about handsome, slightly built men not much taller than me, so he was very much my type, and I have to say I was a bit flattered by his evident interest. But even if I'd been in the market for a new love interest, which I most definitely wasn't, there had been just a hint of the slick and untrustworthy about him . . .

Lillian, who appeared to be much more experienced in such matters, confirmed my opinion. 'He's a smooth operator, that one,' she murmured admiringly.

'So are snakes,' I said, and she laughed.

Time flew by and I set out for Snowehill very much later than I'd intended, though the sun seemed amazingly bright after the gloomy pub.

I walked across the green and past the village shop with its attached, closed Merry Kettle tearoom, which Freda had told me opened from Easter to late autumn. I remembered once stopping the car so we could admire the small, ancient church and the quaint row of almshouses . . .

But standing dreaming of the past wouldn't get me up

the hill, so I crossed the hump-backed bridge and followed the familiar, narrow, single-track lane signposted to Snowehill and Great Mumming.

It was a steep, but pleasant, walk and I didn't see another soul, unless you counted the birds and occasional small, brown rabbit. I passed the gate to Old Place and remembered Mercy telling me her old friends Noël and Tilda Martland lived in the lodge just inside it. There was no sign of life: I expect they were part of the lunch party up at the big house.

Further along the road was a parking area near the track that led up to the beacon and there were one or two cars there.

I leaned on the stile and took a picture on my phone of the distant small tower, with its pointy roof like a witch's hat. There was movement in the gorse below it, but more sheep than people – in fact, I think the only visitors to the place were the ones that passed me heading down as I was climbing up.

You could climb steps up onto a square stone viewing platform where, on a clear day, you could see the next beacon hills in the distance.

The last time I'd brought Mum here she'd been in her wheelchair and we hadn't expected to be able to get further than the car park. But a local farmer was offering rides to the summit in a tractor-drawn trailer and he'd picked her up and put her in without a moment's hesitation, while I folded the chair and followed. He made her laugh, too, by saying she was a bonny lass, and left us up at the top with a promise to take us back down again in an hour, which he had.

It was a happy memory, so I don't know why it made me cry . . .

After a little while I got my act together and sat on the steps to drink my flask of not terribly hot coffee. Then I did some sketches before packing everything up and wandering down to the red horse that was carved from the sandstone below. It was a bit untidy and in need of an edge cut, which I expect they did a couple of times a year, or it would lose its shape. I wondered, as I had before, if it was really ancient or relatively new.

As I stood in the horse's ear looking down towards Little Mumming, I could see a large house, which I now knew to be Old Place, with the white shape of a real pony in the paddock.

I was just thinking it looked a bit like a toy farm play-set when my phone burst into noisy life, startling me.

'When you said in yesterday's email that you were going to walk up a hill, I thought I'd just try your phone and see if it worked,' Emma explained. 'I got distracted, though, so it's later than I intended and I thought you might have gone home.'

'No, I'm still at the top of the hill, because I went to the pub first with some of the cracker factory workers and it made me late setting out . . .'

Suddenly I noticed the long shadows and checked my watch. 'Look at the time! It's just as well you did ring me, because it's nearly six – I must have been up here for *hours*!'

'It's easy to lose track of the time and I expect you were thinking of your mum,' she said sympathetically, since she'd known why I was there today.

'I was, but in a good way,' I said. Still talking, I began to take a shortcut from the horse across the rough ground towards the track. 'Mercy will have been wondering where

I've got to, because dinner's usually about seven – and so is my curfew!'

'Oh God, I'd forgotten about that!' she exclaimed. 'Can you get back in time?'

'I think so, because it's all downhill. If I walk quickly I should make it easily,' I began – and then the phone flew from my grasp as my right foot was swallowed by a hidden rabbit hole, wrenching my ankle.

'Yow!' I exclaimed, subsiding onto the grass, while the mobile quacked urgently next to me.

When I finally picked it up Emma was shouting, 'Tabby? Are you there? What's happened? Speak to me!'

'I fell down a huge rabbit hole, like Alice, but not quite as far,' I said. 'My ankle feels a bit painful, so I think I've wrenched it slightly.' I tried standing up and putting some weight on it. 'Oof! Sore, but nothing broken.'

'Is there anyone about? How remote *are* you?' she demanded. 'Shall I get help?'

'It's not that remote – I'm nearly back on the road already – and I can see a farm and a house from here,' I assured her. 'Anyway, I can already hobble and I'm sure my ankle will ease up as I go. I'd better get on with it, or I'll be late back and get banged up in prison again.'

I assured her I'd let her know when I was back at Mote Farm, then switched off the phone and stowed it in my pocket, before making my painful progress back over the stile and down the narrow lane.

Luckily, after a bit, I found a sturdy branch to use as a walking stick, but it was still slow work and time was ticking inexorably on. When I stopped for a rest just past the drive to Old Place, wondering if I should call Mercy while my mobile still had a signal and beg her to come in the car and rescue me, I heard the welcome sound of an engine behind me.

I turned round waving my arms and a monstrous four-wheel-drive truck stopped right beside me, with a squeal of brakes.

'I thought it was you,' said Guy Martland, winding his window down and smiling dazzlingly at me. His teeth had been polished so white, they looked radioactive. 'Going my way?'

'. . . So then Guy helped me into his car and brought me all the way home. He was on his way back to London, so that was lucky,' I told Emma, when I called later to tell her I was safe. 'Though when I first got in, he kept insisting we call back at the pub on the way so I could have a stiff drink for the shock. I had to explain about the tag and curfew before he got the message it was urgent I was back before seven.'

'Was he surprised?'

'Not really – in fact, he seemed to think it was funny! But he was very kind really,' I added. 'He helped me into the house when we got back and then Mercy invited him to stay for dinner.'

'So you had a chance to get to know your rescuing hero better?'

'No, because although I think he wanted to stay, his aunt Becca was already there and she told him he'd do much better to get off to London. She's going to bring me some horse liniment tomorrow, for my fetlock,' I added.

'Neigh, never!' whinnied Emma, and I groaned. 'How is your ankle feeling now?'

'OK. As soon as Guy had gone, Mercy put an elastic bandage on it and it barely twinges,' I assured her. 'It was only a little sprain. I'd have phoned you earlier, but by the time Guy had gone and Mercy had done her first-aid bit, dinner was ready. The others are all drinking tea in the drawing room and I'll have to go back in a minute, because they're going to teach me how to play mah-jong. There seems to be a local passion for it.'

'It sounds as if you might be developing a local passion of your own,' Emma suggested.

'Not if you mean Guy Martland. Lillian and even his aunt Becca have warned me that he's the black sheep of the family, and I can take a hint.'

'Now he sounds even more exciting,' she said, laughing.

'I think learning to play mah-jong is all the excitement I can cope with these days,' I said, and went off to sedately sip tea and have the game's arcane mysteries explained.

Chapter 17: Reanimated

Randal

Lacey knew I was in line to inherit the family home and business eventually, but I hadn't wanted to tell her about my future plans for the mill until I'd had some feedback from Mercy.

But now that Mercy had emailed, sounding really eager to discuss it all with me when I made my flying visit the following week, this seemed to be the right moment.

We were heading for her favourite nightclub. I wasn't a great one for clubs, but she was younger than me and liked the lively atmosphere, so I went along with it.

'I've hardly seen anything of you since we got engaged,' she complained, 'and you're off again at the end of next week! I could have come to Greece with you – I've never been there; it might have been fun.'

'I was there for work, not a holiday,' I pointed out. 'You wouldn't have liked to stay in any of the places I did, either. But never mind, we can go somewhere exotic together after I've stopped working for *Hellish Holidays* – maybe for our honeymoon?'

I put my arm around her and she turned a startled, beautiful face up to me.

'You're going to leave your job?' she exclaimed.

'I hope so, because these last few months I've literally had a bellyful of it and it's definitely time to settle down and do something different.'

'Like what?' she demanded. 'Unless you've had another TV offer – perhaps presenting your own programme?'

'No, nothing like that. I mean, I'm not really a TV front man, as you know, just an undercover researcher. The most you ever see of me is when I'm talking to my own camera in a gloomy hotel room.'

She looked disappointed. 'People still recognise you from the programme anyway, and I don't think you should give your job up. You just need a break. You never really had time to recover from that terrible bug you picked up on the cruise before they sent you off again.'

'True, and that was the last straw. It used to be fun when I was younger, travelling about the world looking into death-trap nightclubs, dodgy tourist trips and unsanitary hotels, but the novelty has definitely worn off. And anyway, now we're getting married I want to settle down and do something else – maybe something we could *both* get involved in.'

'Like what?' she demanded. 'I mean, I've already got my own business and it's going from strength to strength. I've just added "Fifty Shades of Bondage" to my Instant Orgy range and it's very popular.'

'I know you're making a big success of it,' I said, thinking how beautiful she was – and how matter-of-fact and businesslike about what she did for a living. Come to that, she was matter-of-fact and businesslike about *me*, too . . .

I'd understood when Lacey had played hard to get at first, because so many men had seen her as the embodiment of the sex fantasies her parents peddled in their All Thrills shops, as if she'd been a doll created for their amusement. But even after we were engaged, she still seemed to tolerate my gestures of affection rather than welcome them, so I was starting to think either she was uninterested in sex from anything but a business point of view . . . or that I was a *really* unexciting lover.

In fact, now I came to think of it, the only time she'd spontaneously embraced me with enthusiasm was after I let her choose her own huge, flashy, engagement ring . . .

She shrugged off my arm, but instead took my hand and looked up at me with her delightful, transforming smile. 'So, what is this new job you've been offered? Is it exciting?'

'It's more a case of creating my own job,' I explained. 'You know that one day I'll inherit the family home and business in Lancashire?'

She nodded. 'Your aunt lives there now, but when she's dead, you get it.'

'Succinctly put,' I said. 'I'll take you to meet Aunt Mercy after the next assignment, because next week I'm going to dash up there for one night, to discuss the plans and get the ball rolling.'

'Plans? I don't understand what you're talking about.'

'You remember I explained that Mote Farm wasn't entailed and though my uncle told Mercy that he'd like it to come to me eventually, he left her everything outright?'

'Yes, but you said she encouraged you to see the place as your home and you were sure she'd do what your uncle wanted.'

'Yes, but while she's alive, she still has control of everything, including the old mill, where they make Christmas crackers – unless I can persuade her otherwise. I'd like to redevelop the site as a tourist venue, with attractions like craft workers, shops and a café. I'd put some of my own money into it and become manager.'

'If you invest your own money in the place, then you ought to be a director of the company,' she said shrewdly.

'That's one of the things I need to discuss. I do already have a few non-voting shares in the cracker factory part of it, and get a dividend . . . or I did when it made a profit, which it hasn't done for a long time.'

We'd arrived at the club by now and, since it was still early and quiet, we took our drinks to a table and I expanded on my plans for shutting down the cracker factory and developing the rest of the buildings.

'That could work,' Lacey conceded, her business head on. 'Cut your losses with the crackers, retire the old employees, and replace the unit with something more profitable.'

'*If* Mercy goes for the idea, and she sounds keen to discuss it. If she does, then I'll hand in my resignation as soon as I've finished the current series and the one-off *Gap Year Hells* programme, so I can oversee the project full time.'

She frowned. 'You mean . . . you'd be living up there?'

'Of course – after we're married we both would be. Mote Farm isn't a huge stately home, but it's certainly big enough for all of us to share – and our children, when they come along. I probably wouldn't be able to take a salary from it till next year, but—'

'Live in *Lancashire*?' she said, as though I'd invited her to share a yurt in Outer Mongolia. 'I mean, I thought we'd spend weekends there but not move there permanently!'

I smiled. 'Don't sound so horrified: I don't think you've ever been further north than the Cotswolds, but there's some lovely countryside up there and if you missed the bright lights, we'd still be near big cities, like Liverpool and Manchester.'

Lacey's huge blue eyes gazed at me blankly. 'Country houses are all right for weekends and holidays,' she said finally, 'but I'm a London girl at heart and my business is based here.'

'I've sprung it on you and you haven't had enough time to think about it,' I said ruefully. 'I should have discussed it with you before – but you did say when we got engaged you were ready to settle down and wanted a family.'

'Yes, but not instantly, and certainly not in the middle of nowhere, miles from all my friends!'

'But one of your friends married a footballer and lives in Knutsford, doesn't she? That's only a short drive away from Godsend.'

The thought didn't seem to mollify her, but I was convinced that once she saw Mote Farm she'd love it as much as I did.

'Wait till you visit, you'll be surprised,' I said. 'And you'll understand what I mean about the mill development, too. You could even relocate your mail-order business there,' I told her, though what Mercy would say to that idea when she found out what my fiancée was selling was a moot point. Still, Quakers did tend to be very tolerant and all-embracing . . .

'I've got everything running fine from my warehouse in

Hammersmith – a good manager, the right staff and everything,' she said.

'Once you've seen the scale of the redevelopment project up in Godsend, I thought you might even want to work together with me on that, instead,' I said wistfully. 'It's a really exciting challenge and I think we'd make a great team.'

'What, give up my own business? Never,' she said positively. 'And I'm not giving up my flat, either. Mummy and Daddy bought it for me for my twenty-first birthday.'

'I'll sell mine, but of course we could still have a London *pied-à-terre*, if you wanted to.'

'I've already got one,' she snapped, frowning again. 'You said this Mote Farm wasn't really a farm at all, but a decent-sized house? How many bedrooms does it have?'

'Bedrooms? I don't know, I've never counted them.' I tried to reckon up. 'Maybe around ten . . . and then there's the nursery and some other rooms on the upper floor that were once for servants.'

She looked slightly impressed. 'And it's got a moat and everything?'

'I don't know about *everything*,' I said, smiling down at her, glad she was taking an interest, 'but it's certainly got a moat with ducks on it, and a terrace and knot garden behind the house. The interior has a lot of dark wood panelling, Tudor plaster ceilings and a thirteenth-century oak front door. It's a complete mishmash, like a lot of big old houses.'

But Lacey, her lovely face suddenly more animated than it had been so far that evening, was waving at a noisy, boisterous group of her friends who had come in and was no longer listening.

Chapter 18: Potent

Q: Why don't penguins fly?
A: Because they're not tall enough to be pilots!

Before going to bed that night, I'd soaked my sore ankle in an old white china footbath that had been unearthed by Mercy from one of the storerooms off the kitchen passage. She'd filled it, and then cast a handful of something I think she said were Epsom salts into the steaming water. Whatever it was, by morning things were much improved and I could hardly see any swelling, just a bit of a bruise coming out.

I was dressed and wondering whether to put the elastic bandage back on or not, when there was a knock on the sitting-room door. When I opened it, Job bowed and presented me with a tarnished silver tray, on which reposed a small plastic whisky bottle of the kind you get on planes, full of a greenish solution.

'Miss Becca rode down early and left this for you,' he said with deep gloom, then retreated to the kitchen, now holding the tray as if he was about to hit a tennis ball with it.

He was a little strange in his ways, quite the opposite of his wife, whom I'd already got to know quite well, since she was constantly popping in and out of the house, preparing food for Mercy to cook for dinner, collecting shopping lists, taking in the upmarket frozen ready meals that Silas so loved and stowing them in one of the two large freezers, letting in the cleaning service and the laundry . . . her list of duties was impressively long.

Becca had stuck a handwritten label on the bottle that said: 'Horse liniment, rub in three times daily'. It smelled vile, but since she'd gone to all that trouble, I rubbed some in anyway and then replaced the bandage.

My foot barely twinged when I walked after that, but maybe I'd find my ankle had turned into a hairy fetlock later?

Trot on, Tabitha . . .

Pye kept wrinkling his nose whenever I was near him and saying 'Pfft!' in disgusted tones, but I expected the smell would keep the flies off. And maybe vampires . . . and if Guy Martland came back, I could try it on him.

My sore ankle didn't stop me gathering everything I'd need to clean and catalogue the stockrooms after breakfast and making a start – in fact, I was *dying* to get in there and see what there was – and I did little else for the next few days, unless called on by Mercy or Arlene for an opinion about something, or, at Joy's insistence, try my hand at making another misshapen cracker.

'Practice makes perfect,' she kept saying, but so far her theory wasn't working.

Arlene was already putting in extra hours sourcing new materials and sending for samples, especially for the revamped traditional crackers, which we hoped would soon be taking the place of the current ones, but we had lots of ideas for other kinds, too.

Mercy, meanwhile, had extracted the revised mill plans from the unfortunate architect and had also submitted a set to the planning department. She didn't hang about.

But the pull of the stockrooms always lured me back, and as soon as I set foot over the threshold I tended to lose track of time, it was so interesting.

I'd started in the first room, which would remain a stockroom, since it had the loading bay at the back so the cartons of crackers could be trundled through. Going by the amount of dust on everything in there, apart from the large fire-proof storage bin in which the cracker snaps were stored, they hadn't been using it for anything else for years. Phil said they packed the boxes of crackers into cardboard cartons at the back of the workshop.

My plan was to clear, clean and catalogue what was worth keeping on the shelves in the first room. This should create a lot of space to temporarily store items as I cleared the other two, which were much more tightly packed.

I had so far found boxes of mottoes and jokes, a bag of small plastic cowboy and Indian figures, a dozen penny whistles fixed to a display card with elastic, and about a mile of faded and filthy festive ribbon. It was all so fascinating I'd probably have forgotten to eat and drink, had Mercy not put sandwiches and flasks of soup under my nose from time to time.

The cracker workers brought me strong tea and biscuits when they were having a break, too. Despite his reserve and general melancholy, Bradley proved to be the most thoughtful in remembering I was there, even offering his assistance to move heavy items when I came to them, like the small press in the second storeroom that had once been used to emboss seasonal designs onto circular foil cracker embellishments. That one would probably be included in the museum.

Each evening I'd return to the house tired but happy, though black as a sweep from dust and grime, which I showered off with deliciously scented French soap, before giving Mercy a hand with dinner. She didn't really *need* any help, but she was expanding my cooking repertoire and, anyway, I enjoyed it.

Then I retired to bed totally exhausted each night – but looking forward to the next morning, like a child on Christmas Eve . . . and strangely, though in the prison I'd dreamed of being at home with Mum at Christmastime, now I often woke hearing the echoes of my fellow prisoners belting out 'Jingle Bells' and other seasonal favourites . . .

On the evening before her nephew was to visit, I found that Mercy had already baked his favourite chocolate cake and made mountains of cheese scones, to which he was also apparently partial. Since she'd been whirling in and out of the mill all day, trainer heels flashing, like a small, self-illuminating dervish, I don't know when she'd had the time to fit it in, but she seemed to produce food effortlessly.

When I said so, she replied, 'I've always enjoyed cooking – it's something I share with my friend Tilda, who is married to Noël Martland and lives at the Old Place lodge.'

'Oh, yes, I remember you mentioning them and I passed the lodge when I walked up to Snowehill.'

'Tilda was one of the very first TV cooks, you know. But unfortunately, she was ousted by Fanny Cradock and found the disappointment very hard to bear. But she still had great success with her cookery books, right up until the eighties.

Pretty Party Titbits was a bestseller of its day.' She smiled. 'One magazine called her "The Queen of Canapés" and she loved that. She's older than me and very frail now, but they still sometimes come here for dinner.'

'I'll have to look up her books online.'

'You'll find several of them on the cookery-book shelf,' Mercy said, indicating the tomes ranged in an impressive row above a large spice rack. 'She's given me signed copies, so do borrow them if you want to.'

She finished preparing pork tenderloin and popped it into the hot oven. 'There, I'll make a little apple sauce now, because Silas is very partial to it, and then there are just the vegetables to put on later, which Freda has prepared.'

I volunteered to peel and core the cooking apples and then we decided to have baked apples stuffed with dried fruit and sugar for dessert, so I did three more.

'Soon Liz will be coming home for Easter, Tabby,' Mercy told me as she stirred the apple sauce. 'She'll most likely stay for a day or two with her best friend first, whose family live nearer to the school. I must remember to get her an Easter egg and make a Simnel cake – she does love all the British traditions.'

'I don't think I've ever eaten a Simnel cake, let alone made one,' I confessed.

'I'll show you; they're very easy. I do a lot of traditional baking at Christmas too – puddings, the cake and mince pies, turkey and all the trimmings . . . A lot of Friends don't celebrate Christmas at all, they simply gather together to reflect on the true meaning of the occasion. But the Marwoods were big Christmas celebrators and it was my husband's favourite time of the year.'

For a moment, her round face under its pudding-bowl circle of silvery hair was sad, and I thought she must miss him very much, even after all these years.

'I always loved Christmas with Mum,' I said. 'We never had much money, but we always managed a few treats and often her old friends from the theatre days would pop in with gifts of food or drink.'

'You don't need money for happiness, just warm, loving hearts,' Mercy agreed.

'Jeremy, my ex-fiancé, didn't really celebrate the same way, which was a bit disappointing. In fact, he liked to go out for a meal with friends on Christmas Day, which wasn't at all the same. And then, of course, last Christmas I was in prison . . . though I think I was still in a state of shock, because I don't actually remember what the Christmas dinner was like.'

'Well, now we must look to the future and hope that our new scheme for the cracker factory will be a huge success, so that we've something extra to celebrate by next Christmas.'

I wondered if this unknown nephew would have moved in and be ruling the roost by then. And if so, whether I would still be here.

So much depended on what he was like . . . and I'd find out the next day, when he arrived.

He might be just like Mercy'd described him – her dear boy – but given what I'd already learned about him and her propensity to view everyone through rose-tinted spectacles, I wasn't holding my breath.

Chapter 19: Brief Encounters

Q: What's black, white and red all over?
A: A newspaper!

Mercy stayed at the house next morning to await Randal's arrival, for he'd been intending to set out at the crack of dawn, so as to be well on his way before the morning rush hour started.

She suggested I wait with her, but I said I'd rather get on with my work and set off for the mill, because not only was I thoroughly enjoying myself sorting out the old stockrooms, but I thought it would be a good idea if Mercy first showed Randal her revised plans on her own. While I'd made lots of suggestions, I was just another employee, after all, so he might not take well to my being present at the discussion.

I'd finished clearing the shelves on the left-hand side of the room, with what was retained occupying a fraction of the space, and began slowly working my way back down the other side – *and* back in time, it seemed, from what I was finding.

By now I'd developed a method, tackling one section of shelf at a time, starting with the top of the stack. First I took everything off and put it on the floor, before cleaning the shelf and the festoons of cobwebs behind it. Sometimes this disturbed large spiders, so I was always glad when Pye or the two resident cats were there to pounce on these unexpected and juicy snacks.

Then I cleaned the grime of years from what had been on it, revealing all kinds of treasures. I was starting to find complete boxes of discontinued lines of crackers, but also the empty display boxes, some with interesting graphics, and box after box of old-fashioned plastic moulded charms, metal puzzles, spinning tops, pencil sharpeners, rings, hats, scraps, mottoes, embossed foil stickers . . . and lots and lots of rubbish, like filthy rolls of crepe paper and ribbon. Several things had been wrapped in yellowed and crumbling newspaper, which gave me some idea of when they had been stored.

After my first day's work in there, I'd asked Mercy if I could have some cardboard filing boxes to sort things into and she'd dispatched Job in the car to buy a supply, along with rolls of white adhesive address labels and big black marker pens. Once things were sorted into the fresh new boxes and labelled with the contents, the rows I'd already finished looked neat and workmanlike. It would make it easier to decide on and find what we wanted to display in the museum, too, when we got to that stage.

I'd also learned by experience that enveloping myself in an old, faded, flowered cotton overall, loaned to me by Freda, and completely covering my hair with a scarf, saved me an awful lot of time in the shower.

I was writing down everything I found on a clipboard as I went, and the paper was so grubby, I had to type it up on the computer each evening.

On the morning of Randal's arrival, I'd worked away methodically for a couple of hours, before giving in to the temptation to treat myself to a quick dip into the contents of the second room, where presumably even older things were stored . . .

Taking my stepladder, I chose at random a top shelf in the middle row and saw that it wasn't so much a layer of dust up there, as it was furred with the stuff. I brushed it in the direction away from myself with the feather duster, to prevent a choking fit, then peeked inside a pasteboard box to find it crammed full of wonderful old Christmas scraps. The next one contained a tangle of tarnished tinsel.

Then I spotted something tightly rolled up right behind it, at the back of the shelf . . . The rickety steps teetered as I shifted and reached out for it, then heavy footsteps crossed the wooden floorboards and the ladder was quickly steadied by a large and firm pair of hands.

'Thanks, Bradley,' I said. 'I thought I was going to end up clinging to the shelf and have to climb down like a monkey.'

'It's not Bradley,' rasped an unfamiliar, deep voice. Startled, I stepped backwards into thin air, so that he had to let go of the ladder, which fell over with a clatter, in order to grab me.

His hands inadvertently rested in places they shouldn't be and he dropped me on the floor like a hot potato, snatching them away as if they'd been burned.

'Thank you – I think,' I said, feeling my face go hot as I turned round to see my rescuer. 'Though I wouldn't have fallen off if you hadn't startled me like that.'

'You need a better stepladder than that old thing,' he snapped, frowning down at me, and I found myself staring at him in surprise. Assuming this was Randal, he wasn't remotely the way I'd imagined him!

In fact, apart from being dressed in jeans and a sweatshirt, he looked like a Victorian factory owner in a TV melodrama. He was tall and well built, with honey-blond hair that wanted to curl but was cut too short, and a pair of surprisingly dark hazel eyes, set in a lean, craggy – but not unattractive – trouble-at-t'mill face.

You could picture him dressed in riding boots and breeches, leaning against the mantel at Mote Farm, kicking logs back into place and frowning . . . much like he was still doing at me.

'I'm Randal,' he said. 'Mercy sent me down with some sandwiches, because she said you'd forgotten lunch – but since she's spent the entire morning going on and on about all your brilliant ideas, I thought I'd come and see what you were like and—'

He broke off as I pulled the scarf from my hair and used it to wipe off some of the dust on my face – or, more probably, just smear it about a bit. My fringe, which still needed cutting, immediately fell into my eyes.

'I've met you before,' he said slowly, examining me with those sharp, hazel eyes with their fascinating green flecks.

'No, you haven't,' I said positively, sure the only reason he looked vaguely familiar was because I'd seen his type on TV or the cover of romantic saga novels. My dark brown hair, quickly unravelling from its loose plait, swung back around my face like half-drawn curtains.

He gave an exclamation. 'Got it! You're the artist – she was called Tabitha something and Mercy kept referring to you as Tabby.'

'I'm Tabitha Coombs,' I admitted, 'but I'm still sure we haven't—'

'I went to your exhibition in Liverpool last year with a friend. We didn't speak, but I remember you.'

And then it all came back to me in an unwelcome rush, for his friend was the reporter who'd ruthlessly used me to get access to Champers&Chocs and I'd seen him talking with this man at the gallery. It didn't exactly endear him to me. In fact, I glared at him.

'I remember now – you were with that horrible man from the *Dodgy Dealings* programme, who pretended he was a journalist,' I said coldly.

'Charlie's not horrible, he's just good at his job,' he said, equally frigidly, and we eyed each other with mutual antipathy.

'Trust Mercy to find a fraudster to help her with her business!' he said at last. 'She's taken rescuing lame dogs too far this time, but if you thought you were going to wangle your way into her good graces and swindle her in some way, then you can think again, because you'll have *me* to deal with.'

'You're completely mistaken. Mercy is an *angel* and I'd do anything to help her,' I said hotly. 'Even work with *you*, if I have to!'

His mouth, already inclined to be straight and firm-lipped, tightened into a thin line and he swung round on his heel and strode off without another word.

Trouble at t'mill, indeed.

I was still sitting on the bottom rung of the stepladder, recovering from this encounter, when Dorrie came in a few minutes later with a cup of tea, though really she was just an envoy sent by the others, who'd heard the raised voices and wanted to see if Randal had murdered me.

‘He’s always seemed a nice enough lad,’ she said, ‘but he likes his own way. And since he came back so poorly from a cruise last year, he seems to have got a really short fuse.’

‘That could turn out to be a bit dangerous in a cracker factory,’ I said and then we both giggled, the tension broken.

Chapter 20: Fishy

Q: What do you get if you cross a bell with a skunk?
A: Jingle smells!

Later, Arlene came to see how I was getting on and told me Mercy had rung down to make sure I was intending to get back for tea. 'I think she wants you to back her up over her plans,' she added. 'Randal went past the office earlier looking like a thundercloud on legs, and Lillian said you'd had a bit of a set-to.'

'Just a little,' I agreed wryly.

'He can be abrupt, but he was nice to me earlier, when he arrived – asked why I was still there in the afternoon and commiserated with me about my bank branch closing. Not that I don't prefer working here, if there are enough hours,' she added.

'I don't know why Mercy thinks he'll listen to me, but I suppose I'd better get back to the house,' I said reluctantly, because it was almost teatime and if I had to meet the horrible Randal again, then I was determined to shower off the filth first.

I managed to get into the house without bumping into

the Young Master, by sneaking in the side kitchen door, where I found Pye watching with huge interest as Mercy cut smoked salmon sandwiches into neat triangles.

'Oh, there you are, Tabby! I'm just about to take tea through, so do join us in the drawing room when you've tidied up.'

'I think I need more than a tidy up – I'd better have a quick shower. I'll only be half an hour,' I promised. 'I'll make myself some coffee when I get down and bring it through.'

'We'll save you some sandwiches, scone and cake,' she promised, and then I heard a heavy male tread approaching that was definitely *not* Job, who flitted about like a shade, so I fled.

I felt better once I was clean, though, with my hair loose and brushed, a bit of make-up and clean clothes. There was no sign of Pye in the kitchen when I made my mug of coffee, but I filled his food bowl for the moment when he realised no one wanted to share the smoked salmon with him.

The others had already eaten their fill, going by the crumb-littered tea plates and empty cups, and I was only just in time to glimpse the back of Silas's stooped figure as he tottered back to his rooms. Randal was standing in front of the lit fake logs in much the same pose I'd envisaged for him earlier. He looked up at me sombrely from under his strongly marked brows, but said nothing.

Pye was sitting bolt upright, staring very hard at the remaining two smoked salmon sandwiches, as if he could magic them off the plate and into his mouth.

'Ah, Tabby! Let me give you something to eat,' Mercy offered, but I said I wasn't very hungry.

'I'll save up for dinner,' I said. 'It was late when I ate the lovely lunch you sent down.'

'Well, if you're sure, then bring your coffee and we'll go through into the library to look at the plans again,' she suggested and, with looks of mutual antipathy, Randal and I fell in behind her.

It appeared that Randal, however reluctantly, had already given in to Mercy's amendments, but with the proviso that if the cracker factory hadn't gone into profit by Christmas, they'd think again about closing it.

'I'm sure it will, providing we can start to produce some of the new lines of crackers quickly enough,' Mercy told him. 'And Tabby says that the cracker factory and the museum will be the focal point that will draw the visitors in.'

'Does she, indeed?' he said in that water-running-over-gravel voice.

'It's a unique attraction and the history of the development of cracker making and the Quaker connection will fascinate the visitors,' I said defensively. I hoped I was right.

'So clever of dear Tabby to think of it! Silas agrees with me and has promised to help with the museum. In fact, he's already well advanced in planning out the information display boards.'

'Silas is not a businessman,' Randal said disagreeably.

'He doesn't need to be. Instead, like Tabby, he has his own useful talents.'

'Yeah, right,' he said with another darkling look at me.

'We're all born with talents,' I said. 'Yours seems to lie in prejudging people.'

'I think we know where *yours* lie,' he replied.

Luckily Mercy was studying the plans again and this exchange had gone over her head.

'So, Randal, we're agreed in principle, aren't we? And I'm sure we'll get planning permission, so I'll make a start on some of the changes to the mill interior as soon as possible,' she said. 'The development of the café, and the workshops and gallery in the outbuildings will be your particular concern, though one studio will be earmarked for Tabby. I want her to have her pick. Did I say she was a very talented artist?'

'I already knew it. In fact, I went to her first exhibition in a gallery in Liverpool last year.'

'What a coincidence!' Mercy said, beaming.

'Not really: it was so his friend could sneakily meet me to wangle his way into the firm where I worked and expose the champagne scam.'

'I was there with Charlie Clancy,' Randal explained to his aunt. 'But you know Charlie – he goes after the truth like a fox after a rabbit and, after all, you can only expose fraud and deception where it exists.'

Mercy looked in a troubled way from one to the other of us. 'Oh dear – perhaps that was not the best start to what I hope will be a good working relationship. But you know very well, Randal, that everyone who works at Marwoods makes a fresh start and is judged on what they do, not what they once did.'

'Or didn't do,' I amended.

Randal didn't say anything to this, but gloomily shook my hand when Mercy insisted on it. If you've ever put your hand in a mangle, you'll have some idea what *that* felt like, but I was only glad she hadn't suggested we kiss and make up.

'There, all friends together,' she said happily. 'Now, Randal, we'll have to arrange a meeting with the accountants when you have more time. Since you'll be investing your own money in the company, you must have shares and a say in things. It will be a *joint* venture – and how happy your uncle would be to know you were joining the family business.'

'Or what's left of it,' he said.

'I know it wandered off course when I took my hand off the tiller,' Mercy said ruefully, 'but now I'm back, all that will change.'

She turned to me. 'Randal has had quite enough of gallivanting about the world for his work and is ready to settle down here at Mote Farm.' She patted his arm affectionately. 'He's got so thin since he was ill that I'll be glad to have him under my roof where I can feed him up again with good home cooking.'

'That shouldn't take long: I'm sure I've put on pounds already,' I said.

'He has to fulfil his obligations by completing this current series—'

'Two, really, but I'm investigating some of them back to back on the same trips,' he said. 'As well as the usual *Hellish Holidays* episodes, I'm gathering material for a one-off *Gap Year Hells* special. I'm off to South America next.'

'As soon as those are finished, Randal, I hope you'll resign and move down here permanently. We'll certainly need your input, if we're to have everything finished and open before Christmas.'

'I'll have to keep my flat on for a while after I've resigned to give me a London base, because – well, I'm engaged, and my fiancée lives in London,' he said, abruptly breaking the welcome news to her.

Mercy clapped her hands together. 'Oh, how wonderful! When you said you had something to tell me, I did hope it might be that. Who is she?'

'I'll go and leave you both together,' I suggested tactfully, turning for the door.

But Mercy said quickly, 'Oh, no, do stay, Tabby, because you're quite one of the family now.'

Randal looked as if he was about to put her right about this notion, then thought better of it.

'Do tell us who she is.'

'She's called Lacey Bucknall. Her family have a chain of shops selling . . . fancy goods,' he added, and I wondered at the slight pause. 'Fancy goods' could be almost anything.

'Bucknall?' she mused. 'I don't think I know the family.'

'Lacey runs her own mail-order business . . . party supplies.'

Again that almost imperceptible pause. I was starting to feel curious.

'How enterprising of her! Will she carry on with it, once you're married?'

'We haven't worked that one out yet,' Randal said, looking a bit tight-lipped again, though this time presumably with the absent fiancée, rather than me.

'I'm sure we could find her enough space in one of the outbuildings, if she wanted to relocate it up here?' Mercy suggested.

'That's very kind of you,' he said. 'But there's time enough to talk about that when she's seen her future home and met my family.'

‘I can’t wait,’ Mercy told him. ‘Do tell her how much I’m looking forward to meeting her.’

‘I’ll bring her as soon as I get back from my next trip,’ he promised.

When we went back into the drawing room, the last two sandwiches had magically disappeared, and so had Pye.

Dinner was not the liveliest of meals, though Mercy, as always, chattered away enough for all of us. Since I seemed to rub Randal up the wrong way, I tried to keep quiet and efface myself as much as possible but I think Silas’s rheumatism must have been playing him up again, because he was very morose.

Afterwards, Randal had arranged to meet his friend Jude Martland up at the Auld Christmas and Silas took himself off, so Mercy and I had a quiet evening watching Pye chase ghosts around the room.

It was the first night there that I hadn’t gone out like a light once my head hit the pillow, for Randal had not only stirred up memories I was attempting to forget, but his evident belief in my dishonesty was patent.

I woke from a nightmare later in which he and his friend were trying to bodily force me into a kind of large birdcage, and if Pye hadn’t been comfortingly curled up next to me I might not have slept again that night.

I’d hoped to escape to the mill before Randal came down next morning, but I found him eating breakfast with Mercy, since he wanted to set off early for London.

It quite put me off my bacon and eggs, which I had to eat because Mercy cooked them specially. I think she’d already begun trying to fatten up Randal, as well as me.

Pye ignored me – he was staring fixedly at Randal, which seemed to disconcert him.

'Mercy, I thought your last cat was weird, but it's got nothing on this one,' he said uneasily. 'Why is he staring at me like that?'

'He's not mine, dear, he's Tabby's.'

'That explains it,' he said. 'It's the witch's cat.'

'He wants your bacon rind,' I said.

'Mrrow,' agreed Pye.

Randal managed to get me alone for a moment before he left, in order to warn me not to try anything in his absence.

Then, before I had a chance to angrily rebut this idea, he added, 'Jude told me you and his brother had met up and had such a good time you nearly missed your seven o'clock curfew. Maybe you should concentrate on your work and paying Mercy back for her kindness, rather than getting yourself rearrested and upsetting her.'

'I was *not* out with Guy Martland—' I began furiously, but he ignored me.

'On second thoughts, *get* rearrested. At least then you'll be out of our hair for good.'

He turned on his heel and left, leaving me fuming and wishing I'd had the chance to say exactly what I thought of him.

I thought I'd found Paradise in Godsend, and instead a very wormy apple had just fallen on me.

Chapter 21: Well Spiced

Randal

I rang Charlie's mobile when I got back to London, though when he answered there was so much background noise that I thought he might be in a zoo. Maybe the gorillas were passing off fake bananas as the real thing?

'Charlie, can you hear me? What's all that racket? Where are you?'

'I'm in The Spice of Life restaurant in Bradford. I was in the area following a lead and I couldn't resist the chance of having a really good curry. It's packed out in here. I was lucky to get a table.'

I felt envious. I loved spicy food and I was fed up with eating bland meals since my illness. Maybe it was time to slowly reintroduce a bit of variety?

'Did you want me for anything in particular?' he asked, crunching what sounded like a poppadom in my ear. 'I thought you were in Godsend.'

'I was, I got back earlier. And you'll never guess who Mercy's new PA is – and who persuaded her to change all my plans for the mill.'

'No, I won't,' he agreed. 'Just tell me.'

'Tabitha Coombs. Quite a coincidence, when we were only talking about her the other day.'

He whistled. 'Well, that's a turn-up for the books. Does Mercy know she was in prison?'

'She not only knows, she visited her there, in order to offer her the job,' I said bitterly. 'Now the woman's living in the house like one of the family and she and Mercy are thick as thieves.'

'Now I come to think of it, all Mercy's employees are ex-cons, aren't they?' he said reasonably. 'So I don't know why you're getting het up about this one.'

'But *they're* all elderly and they've been around for years. They're not living in the house, either, getting their feet under the table.'

'Anyone can get their feet under Mercy's table,' he pointed out fairly. 'All you have to do is turn up at her door looking hungry. But she's no fool, Randal, so I wouldn't worry about her.'

'I'm not, now I've warned Tabitha Coombs that I've got my eye on her! If she puts a foot out of line, she'll be back behind bars.'

'Why do I get the feeling you didn't take to her very much?' he said, sounding amused. 'And maybe she just wants a fresh start and will turn out to be as much of a success as Mercy's other old lags.'

'I don't think so. In fact, I think she's just using her. But you can be sure that as soon as I move in, Tabitha Coombs will be packing her bags and leaving. And she can take her familiar with her,' I added, remembering the cat's unexpected assault.

'Familiar what?' Charlie asked. 'Oh – never mind, here comes my lamb rogan josh, so I'll catch up with you later.'

He rang off, but I swear I could smell that curry all the way from Bradford.

Chapter 22: Thin Air

Q: What athlete is warmest in winter?
A: A long jumper!

As soon as Randal had taken his odious self off, I went down to the mill and threw myself back into my cleaning and clearing with renewed vigour, determined that by the time he returned, the museum would at least be taking shape. Pye came with me, a certain swagger in his step, as if he'd slain a giant. He might have done, too – a giant ego.

And speaking of giant egos, when I finally remembered to walk down to the road and check for messages on my mobile, there were several from Guy Martland!

After he'd brought me home from Snowehill Guy had refused to go away until I gave him my number, but I hadn't thought he'd actually *ring* it . . .

He still wanted to see more of me and I had a sneaking suspicion I knew which bits.

That evening, Mercy rang her dear boy at his London flat to make sure he'd got home safely, though presumably someone would have informed her by now if he hadn't, and to wish him *bon voyage* for his South American trip.

She'd left the library door wide open, so I heard her end of the conversation. I was obviously still preying on Randal's mind, because I heard her say firmly, 'Don't be silly, Randal! You've quite misjudged Tabitha, who's the sweetest girl and *so* helpful. Besides, what on earth do you think she could get up to here, even if she wasn't? Pass off cheap crackers as luxury ones, perhaps?'

The quality of Mercy is never strained.

'I'd love to see South America, especially Peru – the Andes and Machu Picchu in particular,' she told me wistfully when she came back. 'I think I've left it a little too late in life to go to extreme altitudes, though, so Randal will just have to tell me all about it, instead. Unfortunately, he has to use an unreliable and unsatisfactory tour guide company, because of that *Gap Year Hells* programme he's researching, but I expect he'll enjoy the experience anyway.'

'I don't know that exposing student gap year dangers on TV is such a great idea,' I said doubtfully. 'I mean, they're going to choose all the dodgy cut-price options and put themselves in danger anyway, aren't they? So the programme will just terrify their poor parents even more.'

'Very true, dear, I hadn't thought of that. But perhaps it *will* make those young people who haven't yet set off more cautious?' she suggested.

'I doubt it,' I said, because my optimism thermostat had been stuck on a low setting ever since I was imprisoned and was clearly going to take a long time to warm up.

'Poor Randal says he'll have to sleep in terrible hostels and backpackers' dives, too,' she added, though I wasn't entirely sure she knew what he meant by 'backpackers' dives'.

'What a shame,' I said insincerely.

'Yes, isn't it? But then afterwards they're sending him back to Mexico, to investigate complaints about a supposedly luxury hotel for his usual series, before he comes home.'

'Well, whatever the faults with that one, I expect it'll seem like Paradise after cheap hostels.'

'I hope the food will be good and wholesome, at least . . . though, actually, I'm not sure what they eat in Mexico,' she confessed.

'Nor me, though I think it involves refried beans and tortillas.'

'Really? I can't imagine wanting to fry beans *once*, let alone twice,' she said, puzzled, so we went back into the library and explored the wonderful (and varied) world of Mexican cuisine.

When Freda popped in later to drop off a bit of shopping, she told us the supermarkets stocked taco-making kits, if we wanted to go all Mexican she'd get one sent in the next order.

The introduction of tacos into Silas's diet was unlikely to do his digestion or temper any good, because he did like his plain, traditional food, but Mercy always seemed up for any culinary challenge.

Saturday morning was dry and bright, so I took my sketchbook out and went to look for inspiration. I drew the house from the other side of the moat and the bridge over the stream, before walking up the Little Mumming track through the woodland behind the mill, stopping to sketch mossy, fallen trees, a fairy ring of toadstools and anything else that took my eye.

I was sitting on a log drawing a pale, semi-circular fungi

that reminded me of a coral reef, when Becca rode past me on her brown cob, Nutkin. The sound of his hoofs was deadened by the thick carpet of pine needles, so that she was there before I knew it. Pye, who was seated next to me, looking over my shoulder like an art critic, alerted me with a growl.

She reined in and called cheerily, 'Morning! You look just like a young witch, sitting there in that black jacket with your cat.'

'It certainly feels like a magical spot just here,' I said, then thanked her for the horse liniment. 'It totally healed my ankle almost instantly.'

'I knew it would do the trick,' she said, looking pleased. Then she said she had something in her saddlebag for Mercy, and rode on downwards.

Pye got up, stretched and then prepared to follow her.

'She didn't say it was fish, Pye,' I pointed out. 'In fact, I'm fairly certain she's *not* riding about with fish in her saddlebag.'

But he just gave me a look, then sauntered off and was quickly lost in the black shadows.

Mercy was in the kitchen when I returned, lunching on Welsh rarebit, with a disgruntled-looking Pye sitting on a wheelback chair and keeping her company.

'I take it Becca wasn't carrying fish?' I said to him. 'Told you so.'

'Fish? No,' said Mercy looking up. 'She *does* sometimes bring me gifts of fish and game, but today she only wanted to unload some of Tilda's cheese straws. She makes huge quantities and gives them away very generously, but they never taste of anything much.'

'I like them when they're really cheesy,' I said.

'So do I, but luckily Silas seems to quite like Tilda's and, I find if I put anything edible in the biscuit tin at the mill Phil and Bradley will gobble it up.'

She looked at my sketches admiringly, while I made a ham and tomato sandwich, then she asked me if I intended spending the afternoon on my artwork, too.

'Only someone in Merchester has an old but reliable electric sewing machine they would like to donate and didn't you tell me your best friend lived there? I thought you might like to call on her and then I could pick you up on my way home.'

'That would be lovely,' I said, and gave Emma a quick ring to make sure she'd be in.

Mercy dropped me outside Emma's lovely little old terraced stone cottage near the botanical gardens and it was wonderful to see her again, even though we only had a little time before she had to go and collect Marco from a birthday party.

'Mercy says you and Marco must come over and see Mote Farm,' I told her. 'She's very hospitable and she loves children. In fact, she seems to love everyone, including her horrible nephew, Randal!'

'Is he really horrible?' she asked, so I told her all about Randal's visit and the ghastly coincidence of his being best buddies with Charlie Clancy, the man who had duped me into letting him into Champers&Chocs.

'Pity,' she said, pushing the pink-spotted teapot and the plate of gingernut biscuits in my direction across the kitchen table. 'If this was a novel, he'd turn out to be a romantic hero, who would clear your name, then sweep you into his arms and tell you he'd adore you for ever.'

'Well, that's not going to happen because I think he's more likely to push me in the moat,' I said. 'He told his auntie he'd just got engaged, too, and his eyes went all glazed when he mentioned his fiancée, so I'm assuming she's a stunner.'

My phone bleeped and when I took it out of my bag, yet another spate of messages popped into the inbox: they sometimes seemed to arrive hours after they've been sent.

'Guy Martland again,' I sighed.

'Oh, that man who rescued you when you hurt your ankle? Is he texting you?' she asked interestedly, though you'd think after her disastrous experiences with Desmond she'd give up trying to marry me off.

'Whenever I go far enough away from the house to get a signal on my phone, there are loads of them.'

'But you must have given him your number?'

'Yes, but I didn't really expect him to contact me.'

'Does he fancy you? Is he asking you out?'

'He says he wants to see more of me when he next comes up to stay in Little Mumming, but I haven't answered him yet,' I said. 'I only noticed the messages late Friday and I don't really know what to say.'

'Don't you like him?'

'He's very attractive and probably lots of fun, if you're looking for a good time, but he's got "unreliable" stamped all over him. And anyway, I'm not looking for another relationship. I've decided to work towards being a mad old spinster with a cat. I'm halfway there already.'

'If Des doesn't buck his ideas up, I might just join you,' she said darkly.

'You'd have to be a mad old single mother,' I pointed out, 'but you could share my cat.'

'OK,' she agreed. 'Now, what are you going to reply to this Guy? You'd better say *something*.'

'Thanks, but no thanks?' I suggested.

'Be serious,' she said and eventually we fixed on the innocuous, '*Thank you so much for coming to my rescue and I do hope we bump into each other again sometime*', and I added a smiley emoticon.

The next morning I went to the Sunday Quaker meeting for the first time with Silas and Mercy. Job, Freda and Joy were there too, having driven over in the big estate car.

I'd read all about the Friends after meeting Ceddie at the open prison and I was very drawn to their beliefs. Historically, they had a long tradition of equality between the sexes, as well as being at the forefront of anti-slavery and many other issues – in fact, wherever compassion and humanity was needed, Quakers seemed to have been involved. It was fascinating.

The Victorian factory-owning Quakers like the Marwoods showed benevolence towards their workers, too, housing them comfortably and treating them well, which I expect is where Mercy got her interest in employing former criminals from.

The meeting house in Great Mumming was a small, ancient, black and white timber building, set back behind a walled garden, just off the main street. A new brick annexe had been added behind, but the meeting itself took place in a sunny, peaceful room in the old part.

I knew what to expect from my reading, so I wasn't surprised when about twelve of us sat in a square, facing each other, in total silence, apart from a bit of breathing.

I tried to clear my mind of all thoughts, as if I was meditating, which I suppose I was in a way, and it was all strangely soothing and tranquil.

After about twenty minutes of this, a tall, elderly woman stood up and remarked in a conversational voice that she was shocked to hear about the prevalence of female genital mutilation in this country and had been giving it a lot of thought. Then she sat down again and there was more silence, until finally a couple of the elders rose, indicating that the meeting was over.

There was tea, coffee and iced buns in the annexe, where the FGM lady handed out leaflets for a focus group she was thinking of setting up, after which I hitched a lift home with Job and the others, because Mercy and Silas were going to lunch with friends.

Going by his surprised and slightly grumpy expression, I don't think Silas had been consulted about this plan, but now Mercy was home he'd just have to get used to having a social life imposed on him, because she seemed very gregarious.

Job, Freda and Joy were calling at the Auld Christmas for lunch on the way back and invited me to join them, but I felt like going home and doing some more work on the latest picture, so I said I'd like the walk down, and set off. The track descended the hill from just behind the pub in a series of zigzags, imprinted with lots of large hoof-prints, probably from Becca's Nutkin.

Pye awaited me on the bridge, though I have no idea how he knew when I was coming. He jumped onto my shoulder as soon as I was within leaping distance and clung there like a large prickly burr. Perhaps he'd just wanted a lift home.

Chapter 23: Fine-Tuned

Knock, knock.
Who's there?
Holly.
Holly who?
Holly-days are here again!

I put Randal and any doubts about what would happen in the future, when he would be around all the time, to the back of my mind and settled back to work again. Soon I'd practically cleared the first stockroom.

It was quite amazing how little space everything took up, once it was cleaned, sorted and packed into a fresh box, though I was discarding a lot of rubbish, too.

I red-stickered anything that might be interesting to display in the museum. Silas and I had already been discussing the layout and what might go on the information boards.

One evening after dinner, he got out a lot of ancient photograph albums and we pored over them. There were several posed pictures of the family and the workers seated in rows in front of the mill, one of everyone setting off in an ancient charabanc for a picnic and some soupy interior shots of the cracker making, which was all quite fascinating. We made a list of the ones that would best illustrate the story of the Marwoods and the mill, and Silas was to write the narrative to go with them.

'There used to be a work's annual picnic to a beauty spot in a valley to the west, above a village called Halfhidden,' he said, pointing to the charabanc surrounded by a lot of happy workers in what looked like their Sunday best. I expect you got dressed up for picnics in those days.

'But one year, some of the young girls went for a walk up to the falls and one of them vanished,' Mercy put in.

'Oh?' I said, interested. 'Like *Picnic at Hanging Rock*?'

'I don't know, dear,' she said puzzled.

'It was a film about some girls in Australia, who vanished after a picnic and were never seen again.'

'Oh, then it's not quite the same, because they did see Florence again. After hours of searching, her young man finally thought to tell them that they'd had an argument just before she disappeared and they picked her up on the way back, trudging along the road. I expect they were very cross with her, because it must have quite spoiled the day for everyone.'

'I can imagine,' I said. 'Is there still an annual picnic?'

'No, they gave it up after that. And now, of course, they have their annual Christmas and New Year holiday in Blackpool.'

'They really do seem to look forward to that,' I said. Then I told them that a greetings card company who used to buy my work had just accepted two of my designs.

'I finished them just before I was arrested, but of course

then they never got sent. So I posted them as soon as I found them.'

'That's excellent news,' Mercy said, beaming.

'Yes, and they said they'd like to see more, so I'm back in with them again. There's another card firm who used to buy my work too, so I'll try some new ones with them when they're ready. I'd still love to work on bigger and less commercial pieces one day, though,' I added wistfully.

'And so you shall,' Mercy said, like a kindly fairy godmother. 'Once the first phase of the mill has opened, you can spread your wings in one of the workshops and your time will be your own.'

'Thank you, but I'll always still be there if you need my help with anything,' I said gratefully, though I was becoming slightly distracted by Pye's fixed stare as he appeared to track some invisible creature across the room.

'Just think, dear Liz will be here tomorrow, too – what fun,' Mercy said, for her Malawian ward was coming home for Easter. Her room was made up ready and Mercy had bought and hidden away a large Easter egg. 'We will be four for dinner.'

I didn't point out that we quite often seemed to be four or five for dinner, due to her habit of inviting friends, or even, it appeared, random strangers, to share the meal with us.

'She calls me Grandmother,' Mercy said. 'It's a mark of respect, because I'm so *very* old.'

'I'm looking forward to meeting her,' I said, and Mercy looked pleased. I'm sure she thinks of us both as young things, but sixteen-year-old Liz is likely to think I'm almost as ancient as her godmother!

* * *

Arlene, who was now officially working the same hours as the other cracker workers, called me in on Friday morning, as I passed the glass-fronted office in the lobby, to show me some more foil and paper samples that had just arrived. Things seemed to be arriving by every post, some all the way from China, and we were quite excited.

That day's cracker papers were a more refined version of the crinkled crepe Mum and I used to make our own out of, in white, holly-berry red or ivy green. There were pre-cut tartan paper-foil lace edgings, too, samples of tartan or plain red ribbon and Scottie-dog die-stamped stickers.

We tried the effect of the tartan foil trim against the various coloured papers and decided the tartan ribbon was a step too far.

'I'm expecting more samples of alternative cracker fillers soon,' Arlene told me, 'but the miniature musical instruments were delivered earlier. There were kazoos, ocarinas, penny whistles and a mouth organ, though Phil has got that one and won't give it back.'

When I walked through the workshop on my way to the stockroom, he was sitting at his workstation, sucking and blowing at it in a monotonous manner, though I expect that was due to his not being able to use his hands, which were engaged in cracker making.

I stopped at my bench briefly and constructed another cracker. I was getting better – at least this one didn't look like a badly stuffed sausage.

Liz was dropped off at the house by her friend's mother later the same day and Mercy was quite right about her being a serious girl: she was sixteen going on forty.

She was tall, slim and dark-skinned, with short, glossy black curls and large, intelligent chocolate-brown eyes behind heavy-rimmed glasses.

She shook my hand and said how pleased she was to meet me, then went upstairs to unpack. When she'd gone, Mercy said she'd like her to lighten up a bit and have more fun appropriate to her age, but her mind was entirely set on her aim of becoming a doctor.

'Which is, of course, very estimable. But since she tells me she's grown out of her casual clothes, perhaps being younger and more in touch with fashion, you wouldn't mind taking her shopping to buy new ones?' she appealed to me.

'I'm not really in touch with fashion, either,' I confessed. 'That's why I generally stick to black jeans, T-shirts and sweatshirts. And I like to be comfortable, rather than teeter round in high heels and a skirt so short you have to think before sitting down, so I'm not a girly girl at all.'

'I think you can be feminine without losing your dignity,' Mercy said, and when Liz came down she explained her plan.

'Liz, Tabby will take you to find some new clothes – and I'll give you your first month's salary, Tabby, so you can get something new and nice, too.'

'Actually, I've just been paid for those greetings card designs I've sold – the money went straight into my bank account, because I've done several for them before. So now I'll be able to pay you back out of my salary for Jeremy's storage charge and we'll be all straight.'

'I'll deduct it from your wages – it wasn't much,' she assured me, though so far I haven't managed to get the exact figure out of her.

'Where would you like to go shopping, Liz?' I asked.

'I like a bargain,' Liz said, thinking it over. 'So I'd rather go to the open market in Ormskirk than any of the big shopping centres, and the market will be on tomorrow.'

'Really? Mum used to love going there before she got so ill,' I said.

'Liz needs to get away from navy and grey,' Mercy said. 'She looks so pretty in bright colours, when she's wearing her Malawian dress.'

'Somehow those bright colours only seem right in Malawi,' Liz said.

'What's Malawian national dress like?' I asked, interested.

'The women wear a huge sarong called a *chitenge*, generally in a bold pattern and often with a matching blouse and headdress. I wear mine with a T-shirt, though.'

'It sounds lovely and I do like pretty things, it's just that I feel I'm not the frilly type,' I said ruefully. 'My features are too bold and my hair's so thick and straight, I can't do a thing with it.'

'I think you'd suit Malawian dress very well,' she said, considering me. 'And I can never do anything with *my* hair, either, so I keep it quite short, like Dorrie Bird. Last summer her daughter, Arlene, styled my hair in two bunches, like Mickey Mouse ears and I liked it so much I left it like that until I went back to school.'

The unexpected smile that accompanied this revelation showed that the teenager was not that far beneath the surface!

'I think I hide behind my hair most of the time,' I confessed.

'But it suits you the way you have it – I like the way your fringe graduates into your hair at the sides, so it's not just straight across,' she said, examining me with her serious, big brown eyes.

After dinner, once Silas had retreated to his rooms, Liz invited me up to her bedroom to try on *chitenges* and when we went downstairs again to show Mercy, she said we looked like two beautiful tropical flowers.

'Mmmrow!' said Pye, looking at me in astonishment. 'Pfft!'

'Your cat talks!' Liz said, giggling.

'I think he was saying how nice you look,' I said tactfully, but you never knew with Pye.

It was actually fun shopping in Ormskirk with Liz: it was not like being trapped in an enormous mall, which to me is the stuff of nightmares, because the stalls were laid out along two streets, open to the sky and the weather.

The university on the outskirts of the town had expanded hugely since I'd last been and so the shops and some of the stalls stocked the kind of clothes students liked.

Liz lightened up as instructed and bought blue denim jeans and a retro-looking full skirt with a flowered pattern, which she said was for Sunday Quaker meetings. Then we had to find a jumper that went with one of the colours in the flowers, new tights and trainers.

I bought a long green cotton jumper and a layered lace tunic top in a deep and wonderful purple-blue, which Liz assured me would make a great go-anywhere top.

'Since I got this electronic tag on my leg, I don't actually go anywhere,' I said. 'You know I've been in prison?'

'Oh, yes, Grandmother told me,' she said. 'And I saw your tag last night, when we were trying on the *chitenges*, but I didn't mention it because I was being tactful.'

Mercy had given Liz money to take us both out to lunch and she picked Subway, another surprisingly teenage choice, so I didn't think Mercy had anything to worry about.

While we ate, she said, 'Grandmother's always told me not to ask any of the mill staff what crime they committed, but they told me themselves anyway. And as Mercy says, now you can see that the good in them has become stronger and the bad weak and helpless.'

'I was sent to prison over a scam selling cheap fizzy wine as vintage champagne,' I said. 'My boss got a lot longer sentence.'

'That doesn't seem as bad a thing as some of the others have done,' she observed. 'And it was right that your boss should take most of the blame, even if you were helping him.'

'The court believed that I'd thought up the idea, as well as being involved in it,' I said. 'But it wasn't true.'

'You didn't think of it, or you weren't involved?' she asked with interest.

'I didn't think of it – I didn't even suspect my boss was doing it until I found out accidentally. Then he told me he'd stopped . . . but he hadn't, so I resigned. I *was* guilty of not reporting him when I first found out about it, but I felt a misguided sense of loyalty, because he'd been kind to me in the past.'

'And then it was found out?'

'Unfortunately I'd confided in a person I'd thought was a friend and she told a TV programme that investigated scams. Once they'd exposed what was happening, the police got involved and my boss implicated me – not to mention saying we'd been having an affair.'

It was odd to find myself telling all this to someone so young, but Liz was very mature. She nodded understandingly.

'You weren't doing that, either?' she guessed.

'No, I was happily engaged to someone else.'

'But the court didn't believe you and sent you to prison? That seems very harsh.'

'It was certainly a shock . . . but in the end Mercy came to the rescue and offered me this job when I was released.'

'What happened to the fiancé?'

'He believed the woman I'd confided in, who I'd thought was my friend, so that was the end of that. But I do have one true friend, called Emma, who lives in Merchester.'

'I'm so glad,' she said warmly. 'I also have my good friend Maisie, who I often stay with during the holidays. We tell each other *everything*.'

'I didn't tell Emma about the champagne scam because I didn't want to burden her when she had troubles of her own – a difficult husband,' I explained.

'*I* don't intend having a husband,' she stated. 'It seems, from my experience, that most of them are trouble, or want their own way in everything, and when I'm qualified and have a house of my own, I'll want *my* own way.'

'I must say, I feel the same now, and all I want out of life is to one day have my own little home with Pye and support myself with my artwork. Mercy's promised me one of the new workshops in the mill buildings, but I can't live up at Mote Farm for ever, especially when Randal gets married.'

'Oh, yes, Mercy told me he was engaged, though even if they live in the house, it's big enough for everyone, surely?

When I first came here I'd never seen such a huge home, but Maisie's parents have a bigger one so now I see it's not that enormous at all.'

'It's big enough,' I said. 'Still cosy, though, and it has a welcoming atmosphere.'

'Mercy will be happy for you to live there for as long as you want to. And now, as well as Emma, you have a friend in me.'

'Thank you and it's lovely to be with people who believe in your innocence,' I said gratefully.

'It's obvious to me that you're telling the truth, and though perhaps you should have told the police what was happening, you're certainly not a criminal.'

'I only wish your uncle Randal thought so,' I said darkly, and then explained about the unfortunate coincidence of it having been Randal's friend who exposed Champers&Chocs, and me with them, and how he'd recognised me from the gallery.

'He's probably been swayed by what his friend Charlie's told him, and also, Mercy said he was a little cross that his ideas for the mill were changed because of your suggestions. I expect he'll come round eventually,' she said sagely.

'I'm not that sure, especially if I'm still living in the house and under his nose when he moves back here,' I said. 'He'll be wearing that grim "trouble at t'mill" look all the time.'

She giggled. 'I know just what you mean! Maisie's father's mad about old ships and often plays DVDs of an ancient TV series called *The Onedin Line* and there's a captain in it who looks and sounds very much like Randal. He's very rough and bossy, but his heart is kind, like Randal's.'

I hoped she was right about that, but I hadn't seen much evidence of it so far.

We returned home firm friends and later we found a few clips from *The Onedin Line* series on YouTube. She was quite right: Randal *was* just like Captain Onedin!

Mercy found us giggling over it, but when we explained, even she had to agree to the likeness.

Chapter 24: The House of Mirth

Q: What's the difference between a buffalo and a bison?
A: You can't wash your hands in a buffalo.

Liz, looking pretty in her new skirt and top, went to the meeting with Silas and Mercy next morning but I stayed home, partly because I thought it would be nice for them to be on their own together, but also to work, because my mind was bubbling over with new papercut ideas.

They'd all been invited to family lunch up at Old Place afterwards, too. Apparently Liz is quite friendly with Jess, a girl a year or so older, who was also there for the holidays, though I hadn't yet worked out what relation she was to the others. There were way too many Martlands, though Guy seemed determined to imprint himself on my memory with a succession of flirty texts.

I went to the Auld Christmas with some of the cracker workers for my Sunday lunch again when they asked me, and very good it was, too.

When Liz returned, she said Guy had been at Old Place – along with Becca, Noël, Tilda and Jess (who it turned out was Jude Martland's niece) – and he'd seemed disappointed I wasn't there.

'I can't imagine why he thought I would be,' I said, surprised. Mercy had said that Jude Martland's wife, Holly, would always be pleased to include me in any invitation, but I assumed she was just projecting her own conviction that the more total strangers you crammed round a dinner table, the better.

'Well, he did, and he sent you a message, too. I was to tell you that you were cruel not answering his texts, but he'd definitely come and winkle you out, next time he was up. "Winkle" is a funny word,' she added.

'Oh dear,' I said. 'I haven't checked my recent messages, or I'd have told him I wasn't going to be there and I didn't want to meet him. In fact, charming though he is, I just wish he'd leave me alone, because I'm not the flirting type.'

She nodded gravely. 'That's what Mercy told him, and Becca said he should leave the poor lass alone – that's you – because he'd only love you and leave you, like all his other girlfriends.'

'If that's what even his family think of him, it's just as well I didn't take him seriously, isn't it?' I said. 'And I'm not his girlfriend – I've only met him twice, once in the pub when he introduced himself, and then later the same day when he gave me a lift home from the village after I hurt my ankle.'

'It's because you're so beautiful,' she said, and I laughed.

'No one could possibly call *me* beautiful! My nose and mouth are both too big, and short of shaving my eyebrows off and drawing them in with a pencil, there's no way they're ever going to arch.'

'You are,' she insisted, and then appealed to Mercy, who was just coming into the kitchen, for support.

'Of course she is – and a kind and loving heart lends loveliness to every human vessel, so we're all beautiful in the sight of God.'

I felt like a ship – a brightly lit one – heading straight for a Randal-shaped iceberg.

Mercy's natural energy and impatience to get on with things led her to decide that she wouldn't wait for the planning permission before starting to remodel the interior of the mill.

'After all,' she said, 'it belongs to me and it isn't a listed building, so I may do what I like with it. We'll start by dividing up the mill floor and upgrading the toilet facilities off the lobby.'

Then she handed me a long list of bathroom fitters, builders and the like to ring up. I think she must have been surfing the web for hours in the night. 'We want as many estimates as possible before we pick the firms to do the work,' she told me. 'And warn Arlene that tradesmen will be coming in to do them.'

That took a large chunk of the Monday morning, but I got back to my stockroom sorting as soon as I could and, over the next few days, discovered that having Liz at home was a huge advantage. She threw herself with Mercy-like enthusiasm not only into helping me, but also into the office with Arlene, poring over the internet for unusual cracker fillers and thinking up new corny jokes, which she proved surprisingly good at.

It fell to Mercy's lot to show around any officials, like the people from the planning department, but Arlene deputed Liz to deal with the hordes of tradesmen who descended on us and soon Mercy had handfuls of quotes from which to take her pick.

She didn't drag her feet, either, and the initial work was to start right after the Easter break.

Liz and Mercy were out quite a bit over the Easter weekend and spent Saturday visiting Malawian friends who were staying in Liverpool.

They invited me, but I said I was otherwise engaged – which I was, first trimming my fringe and then soaking myself in the huge claw-footed bath upstairs. By then I was totally accustomed to the naff plastic bracelet that warmly clasped my ankle like a strange parasite, but I could never quite forget it was there. I hoped it might drown in the bath and drop off, but it must have been able to breathe underwater.

When I'd soaked myself scented and crinkly, I indulged in a bit more me-time, playing with Pye, chatting on the phone with Emma and working on my pictures.

My table was set in front of the window and from time to time I looked up from my work and caught a glimpse of Bradley, bent double in the garden. He appeared to be trimming the box hedges round the knots with a pair of very small scissors.

Pye was sitting on the end of the table watching him too, and after a while his curiosity got the better of him and he went out to investigate. I spotted him a few moments later, pacing up and down behind Bradley and pulling silent faces, like a ham actor.

Whenever an unnerved-looking Bradley glanced over his shoulder, Pye stopped still and looked innocent.

Mercy and Liz returned in good time for dinner, which was a huge homemade shepherd's pie from the freezer that just needed heating up, and vegetables that I'd prepared ready.

There had been no sign of Silas all day, but he shuffled into the kitchen in his scuffed leather slippers the moment the delicious smell of cooking wafted from the kitchens.

'I'm going Pace-egging in Little Mumming tomorrow afternoon,' Liz told me, passing the vegetables. 'Do you want to come? It's not just for children; everyone does it. Jess said she might be there.'

'Pace-egging?' I echoed.

'Yes, it's an old British tradition. You hard-boil eggs and roll them down a hill, and the first one to the bottom is the winner. You have to dye your eggs, or mark them with your name, so you know which is which.'

A thought struck me. 'Will Guy Martland be there, by any chance?'

'Oh, no, he had to go back to London early this morning, didn't I say?' Liz said. 'That's why he sent you the message.'

'In that case, I'd like to come,' I said. 'We could walk up – I was thinking of doing that anyway, if the weather is nice. We'd better boil our eggs tonight, I suppose.'

'When I was a little girl, I seem to recall that we used to wrap the eggs in onion skins tied on with cotton thread before we boiled them, to make them go golden yellow,' Mercy said. 'And goodness knows, we have more than enough onions, since Freda seems to be under the impression that I live on them when I'm home.'

'I only like them with lamb's liver, fried till they're just a little bit crispy at the edges,' Silas said, distracted from chasing the last bit of cottage pie round his plate.

'We were talking about using them to colour boiled eggs, Silas, for the Pace-egging,' Mercy told him.

'We'll give it a try,' I said. 'I've got marker pens that should stay on the shell, too.'

Luckily the box of mixed free-range eggs contained some white ones, which we thought would take the dye better. We wrapped four in onion skins after we'd finished dinner and boiled them and they did indeed come out quite yellow.

We left them to go cold and I said I'd put them in the fridge when I went to bed.

'But I'd better make sure they're in a different place from the others, or Job might give one to Silas in the morning for breakfast,' I said with a grin. 'It would be as hard as rubber and he does seem to like them soft boiled.'

Liz giggled. 'You should give him one on April the first,' she suggested, and Mercy, who was making coffee to take through to the drawing room, smiled indulgently at us both and said it was lovely to hear laughter in the house again.

Liz was duly presented with her large chocolate egg the following morning after she, Mercy and Silas had returned from the meeting and she said she would break it up and share it out after dinner, to avoid getting the zits to end all zits. I don't think I'd been that generous with my chocolate, even at sixteen.

Then later we decorated our golden boiled eggs with black marker pens, mine striped and Liz's like leopard spots, before walking up to Little Mumming.

The Pace-egging races were held on a slope near the back of the Auld Christmas and everyone seemed to take it very seriously. We didn't win, but I have to admit it was fun.

Liz introduced me to Jess Martland, who was a tall, skinny teenager with black hair, but there were also lots of people there that I recognised from the Auld Christmas, or the village shop when Mercy sent me on errands.

'Look at Aunt Becca go!' Jess said admiringly – and go she did, despite her age, bounding down the hill after her Pace-egg like a mountain goat.

'There are loads more oldies in the village who aren't here, but most of them don't come out till spring. They're hibernating,' Jess said. Then she added, qualifying that statement, 'Well, they come out for the Revels after Christmas, but then they have braziers and rugs and wassail to keep their insides warm.'

'Wassail?' Liz asked.

'Hot spiced toddy. Jude says I'm not allowed it yet,' Jess said darkly, and I could see this was a sore topic.

'I haven't even seen the Revels yet,' Liz said regretfully. 'Randal's usually here for Christmas, but he's gone by then and Grandmother won't let me go up the track on my own in the evening. She and Silas say they would find it too chilly.'

'It's something to do with fertility anyway, according to my grandpa Noël, so they're probably a bit past that,' Jess told her. 'He knows these things, because he's written a whole book about the history and tradition of Christmas.'

'Really?' I said, interested. 'Maybe we could stock that in our Christmas shop in the mill.'

'Pace-egging is about fertility too. Oh, look,' she added, 'it's the last race and this time it's for everyone who's still got an egg in one piece.'

'That rules me out,' I said, and if it was true that it was all about fertility, then I'm not sure that the way my egg exploded first time out of the starting gate boded very well.

Chapter 25: Going Spiral

Q: What do you get if you cross an elephant with a mouse?
A: Great big holes in your skirting board!

Next day, it being Easter Monday, the mill was shut and the workforce amusing themselves in their own various ways, but Liz and I decided to carry on clearing the stockrooms anyway.

I'd now moved into the second one and I think Liz thought I'd find treasures in there, which actually I did, all the time, only not the kind she hoped for.

I was methodically sorting the first row of shelves in the way I'd found worked best – one shelf at a time, starting at the top and moving downwards – but every so often, one of us couldn't resist taking a lucky dip into the last room, which I don't think anyone else had even looked into for at least half a century. We weren't just moving back through the rooms as we worked, but back through time, too.

The cobwebs were phenomenal, like festoons of tattered, dirty lace curtains, so I hated to think how big the spiders might be . . .

Not bigger than Pye, Bing or Ginger, I hoped, who were usually hanging around hoping for a tasty tarantula snack.

I was the first to weaken today and discovered a whole pasteboard box of moulded papier mâché Father Christmas tree-toppers, with hand-painted robes and beards. Liz followed me in and found a hoard of glass tree ornaments shaped like bunches of purple grapes, lemons and oranges, of a type I'd never seen before. I put the Santa box back where I found it for the moment, but Liz wanted to take the baubles up to the house, so I just made a note of where they'd been found.

'Grandmother lets me decorate the Christmas tree and there are lots of lovely old decorations,' she said. 'These should join them, because they're very pretty.'

'I think both the Santas and the glass baubles are late nineteenth century,' I said. 'The mill switched from cotton to making fancy goods well before that, but they weren't producing crackers at first. They might have made the Santas themselves, but I don't know what the glass ornaments are doing in here.'

'Is late in the nineteenth century still Victorian? I forget,' she asked.

'I think so,' I said, and then just at that moment Silas appeared, so we could show him our finds and ask him.

He'd commandeered Job to push him down in the wheelchair, so he could see how we were getting on and get some preliminary ideas about where the information boards and the display cabinets would go, so as to create a story.

'I thought in this first room we could lead the visitors through the early days of the mill, when it was for cotton production, and also relate the history of the Marwood family, with their Quaker connections and interest in the welfare of their workforce,' he said.

'Yes, illustrated with some of those wonderful photographs you found and perhaps one or two mementoes of the family,' I enthused.

'Then there will be the decline in the cotton trade and the subsequent switch to the manufacture of fancy goods, leading eventually to Marwood's Magical Crackers. The second room can then be dedicated to the history of the cracker itself and the various types of scraps and other ephemera the Marwoods also produced,' he finished.

'I thought a large glass case in the middle of the second room to display boxes of Marwood's crackers through history would look good,' I suggested. 'I've just started finding wartime boxes now and I'm sure there are all kinds of weird and wonderful ones further back.'

'When I first came to live here, they made at least twelve different varieties of cracker, priced to suit all pockets, from inexpensive to luxury special-edition ones,' Job put in, his deeply mournful voice startling us, since I'm sure we'd all forgotten he was still there. 'Of course, that was a long time ago now,' he added lugubriously.

'I expect Tabby's already found samples of those in the first room, if you want to go on a nostalgia trip,' said Liz, but he shook his head and told her it was always better to move forward.

'Well, speaking of moving forward, Liz and I will push Silas back up the hill for lunch, Job, if you'd like to get off,' I suggested, and he said he would, since in a rash moment he'd offered to drive Freda, Joy and Lillian to some huge shopping mall.

Dorrie was in Great Mumming, spending the weekend

with Arlene and spoiling her grandchildren with a dragon's hoard of gold-wrapped Easter eggs.

'I hate those big shopping places, but I'll sit in the car and read a good book,' he intoned gloomily.

'Have you *got* a good book?' I asked, interested.

'I've got a murder on the go: *Death Comes to Pendle*.'

'Isn't that *Pemberley*?'

'No, you're thinking of some other book,' he said, and went off, leaving us to wheel Silas back up the hill. We were escorted by a trio of cats, though Bing and Ginger stopped on the mill side of the bridge. Pye leaped onto Silas's lap for the last steep bit up to the house: he's not stupid.

Mercy had made a stack of sandwiches and heated some soup, so we all lunched together, before going our separate ways for the rest of the day.

I had a papercut to finish and beams of golden sunshine were lying invitingly across my worktable. Out of my little sitting-room window I again caught glimpses of Bradley, trimming away with what looked like the same tiny pair of metal snippers. This time he was working on one of the four spiral bushes at the corners of a knot and it could be Christmas by the time he'd finished it.

Enjoyment comes in many strange forms.

The second that Easter was behind us, work started on the mill interior, with the main floor about to be partitioned off with the cracker factory on one side and the Christmas shop on the other.

And out in the foyer, the toilets were getting a total makeover, including turning a large walk-in windowless storage cupboard opposite the office into a disabled loo.

The ladies' convenience was to be the first for revamping, and when Dorrie, Joy and Lillian heard that they would have to share the gents for at least a week, followed by the men having to share their toilets once they were completed, they voted as one woman to just go home when the call of nature struck.

Soon, whenever I emerged from the stockroom, there seemed to be people everywhere, walking round with notebooks, measuring, drilling, hammering, trundling wheelbarrows of broken tiles though the lobby to a skip outside . . .

As Mercy said cheerfully, it would have to get worse before it got better.

'The sooner they've installed this screen with the glazed viewing windows down the middle of the mill floor, the better,' Phil said.

'Yes, at least that might shut us off from some of the rumpus,' grumbled Bradley.

'Just wait till they start building a café on the mezzanine floor and putting the lift in,' I told them.

Then, that having really made me think about it, I went to find Mercy to tell her that when they made the café, they'd have to put a temporary ceiling of draped plastic sheeting over the cracker factory area, or the dust would get everywhere.

But this was just one of many things that cropped up as we went on, and as fast as Mercy crossed one thing off her list, twenty more took its place.

But she seemed to be positively thriving on the pressure; she was everywhere, the lights in her trainer heels sparkling firefly bright.

* * *

Liz had been such a huge help, as well as good company, that I was sorry to see her leave to spend the last few days of the holidays at her best friend Maisie's house.

I was starting to suspect Maisie's parents were loaded, because when I asked Liz what they got up to there, she replied that there were dogs to walk, ponies to ride – though personally she'd *much* rather walk – an indoor swimming pool and tennis courts. Then she asked me to email her and keep her up to date with what was happening, before getting into the back of the car with Mercy. Job was driving them, wearing an incongruous peaked hat on his glossy, flat black hair.

Thunderbirds were go.

'I had an email from dear Randal this morning,' Mercy told me at breakfast next day. 'Of course, I've been updating him with our progress at the mill, because even though he's so far away, I still want him to feel involved. It's a pity he couldn't resign his job immediately, but I do understand that he feels he must first complete his current obligations.'

'I bet he told you to keep an eye on me again,' I said ruefully. 'He really doesn't trust me – in fact, he told me before he left to watch my step, because he was onto me!'

'He's got entirely the wrong idea of your character,' she agreed. 'But you're quite right: he suggested I check the books, the petty cash in the office – not that we keep more than enough to buy stamps – and watch my handbag.'

'I was prosecuted for fraud, not for being a common thief,' I said indignantly. 'And even if I had done it, why would he think I'd now be going in for a spot of petty larceny?'

'Goodness knows. I don't know what's got into the boy. Perhaps you've just got off on the wrong foot. He was perhaps a *little* peeved that we changed his wonderful plans,' she added indulgently.

'Yes, I noticed that.'

'But I reminded him that none of my workers has ever relapsed . . . or not totally. There may have been a little backsliding at first when temptation was too much, like the occasion Dorrie picked up a sales rep in a pub in Great Mumming. But Arlene was the result and, once she arrived, Dorrie put her past behind her and was a model mother.'

'I can't imagine Dorrie picking up men in pubs – she's so dignified!'

'I think she missed the bright lights of the city when she moved here – she was born and brought up in Liverpool, you know.'

'She only has to open her mouth to make that clear,' I said.

'But as I say, once Arlene arrived she settled down, and of course she'd never have brought the man back to her cottage because my late husband was very clear that the terrace should only be occupied by married couples or single people, and they've respected that.'

Now I'd got to know the workers much better, I suspected that there had probably been some rather complicated flings in the cottages between Bradley, Phil (after he was widowed) and Dorrie, Lillian and Joy. But of course I didn't say so, because now the occupants of Hope Terrace seemed to have settled into a tightly knit, if strange, community.

I reverted to the original subject, still feeling aggrieved. 'I wasn't part of the fake champagne scam and I certainly didn't have an affair with my boss, but I don't suppose Randal would believe me if I told him.'

'I know you didn't, for I'm a great judge of character, and so I told him,' Mercy assured me.

'You're kinder to me than I deserve,' I said.

'But you're such a good investment, dear,' she said with a smile. 'Only look how hard you work for your modest salary. And you have brilliant ideas.'

'So does Arlene,' I said. 'Oh, I do hope it's all a great success after this, or I'll feel so guilty!' I sighed.

'There's no reason why you should, since bringing you here was my doing. But I'm convinced it *will* be a big success and then you'll be able to work full time on your lovely paper pictures instead.'

'That would be my idea of heaven on earth,' I said.

I'd decided which of the proposed workshops I'd like when the second phase of the redevelopment begun. It was a large, airy space with windows onto the woods at the back of the mill, directly under what would become the gallery.

'Perhaps by then I can find a little cottage of my own to rent.'

'I suppose one of the cottages in Hope Terrace might come free eventually, though we know that would mean a sad event, unless Dorrie decided to live with Arlene and her family,' she said. 'But you know that you're very welcome to make your home with us for as long as you wish.'

Not if Randal has anything to do with it, I thought.

'Where is Randal now?' I asked. 'Is he still in darkest Peru, pursuing the last, elusive and endangered Paddington Bears?'

She smiled. 'You are so amusing, dear! And I'm afraid I entirely forgot to ask, so he may have arrived in Mexico, or wherever they were sending him next. I don't know why he can't travel from one country to the next in a logical manner, but no, they must send him hither and thither randomly.'

'Random Randal,' I said, but she didn't hear me, having given in to Pye's blandishments, and was busy presenting him with the last snippets of smoked salmon from her savoury scrambled eggs.

Guy had gone quiet for a couple of days and I thought he'd given up on me, but no, when I drove over to Great Mumming to collect a sewing machine for Mercy, a whole flurry of texts dropped into my message box.

He said he would be back in Little Mumming later that day and hoped I'd be in the Auld Christmas, but if he didn't see me, he suggested he pick me up tomorrow morning. He didn't say for what.

I was a little bit flattered by his refusal to take no for an answer, but that's what I sent him again, though wrapped up politely.

'*Sorry – I'll be otherwise engaged this weekend*,' I texted.

And I was otherwise engaged, too: I had a lovely morning with Pye and my art work, then walked up the track through the woods to the Auld Christmas for lunch with Lillian and a couple of the others. She told me Guy had been in briefly the evening before, looking for me and I wasn't altogether surprised when he turned up now.

'The elusive Tabitha Coombs,' he said, bringing his drink over. 'You said you were doing something today?'

I laid my knife and fork neatly on the empty plate –

another Nancy special had hit the spot – and said, 'I am doing something, as you see.'

'I meant to come over to Mote Farm earlier and winkle you out, but my brother's cutting up rough. He's gone all Patriarch of the Family and says he's tired of me treating Old Place like a hotel, and if I'm not there for the Gathering of the Ancients at lunch, I can kiss my weekends in Little Mumming goodbye.'

'Then shouldn't you be there and not here?' I asked.

'I made a temporary escape by offering to collect the old family nanny and the retired vicar from the almshouses over the road,' he said. 'I'll have to go and get them in a minute, or Old Nan will be getting agitated. Henry doesn't know what day of the week it is most of the time, so he'll have forgotten he's going.'

'Then you'd better get off. Have a nice lunch – mine was wonderful and I've just ordered dessert,' I said brightly.

'I suppose I had better go,' he said, looking at me in a dissatisfied kind of way. Then he leaned close. 'But listen, I've got an idea: I'll tell them I've got to leave earlier this afternoon than I thought I would, and then I can pick you up and we can go somewhere quiet away from here, where we can get to know each other better. I've been thinking about you ever since we met.'

His aftershave was intoxicating and his handsome face only inches from mine, his dark eyes intent . . . but on what? I strongly suspected the chase was the excitement and the more disinterested I seemed, the keener he was.

I mean, I might float some men's boats, but I was hardly the face that launched a thousand ships.

'No, thanks,' I said resolutely, and he looked at me in a

baffled sort of way, before putting down his empty glass and getting up to go.

'Well, I do love the thrill of the chase,' he said, confirming my fears. 'One day I'll get you on your own,' he added, with a fetching smile.

'I think we know what he wants to do with you if he does,' Joy remarked primly as we watched him go.

'Tempting, isn't he?' Lillian said with a grin. She was sitting next to me and, like Joy, had been eavesdropping shamelessly. 'Pulled out all the stops for you.'

'He might have done, but I'm convinced he'd lose interest five minutes after I said yes,' I said.

'Funny you should say that, because he's got past form. He sneaked off with his brother's fiancée a few Christmases ago and then he dumped her after they got engaged.'

'I'm surprised his brother still has him in the house then!'

'After Jude met his wife, I think he felt grateful he hadn't married the other girl,' Joy said.

Chapter 26: Lukewarm

Q: How do snowmen get around?
A: They ride icicles.

On Monday I worked on for an hour or so after the others had left, letting myself out of the empty building around five and locking the door carefully after me. I was certain Randal would have been horrified to know I had a key – but then, he probably didn't realise that practically everyone else had one, too!

I supposed eventually security would be tightened and new locks and burglar alarms installed, but for the moment, no one was likely to break into the mill to steal a carton of crackers.

Pye had been with me earlier but had long since gone back to the house, probably hoping it would be smoked salmon sandwiches again for tea, though never having been used to regularly eating halfway through the afternoon, on the whole I'd rather save space for my dinner.

The late afternoon shadows cast by the hill lay in darkest-violet pools over the valley as I walked down to the road to stretch my legs, get some air and check my phone, though

I didn't expect anything except junk calls . . . including Guy's.

I headed for a big, rectangular block of smooth grey stone a little way along, half sunk into the grassy verge, which was handy to sit on. I didn't know what it was doing there, unless it had fallen off a passing wagon years ago, and they couldn't lift it back.

There were six missed calls, all from a number I now recognised as Guy's, but I ignored those and had a little chat with Emma, instead. Then Marco insisted on coming on the line and informed me gravely that he couldn't speak to me for long, because today he was an Arctic explorer and had to go and drag his wooden boat over the frozen wastes. I can't imagine where he got that idea from and he put the phone down, so I couldn't ask Emma.

Before I could ring her back, my mobile jingled into life again. I never set it to play 'Things Can Only Get Better'; it must have done that itself.

'Tabby?' demanded a voice from my previous life, which now seemed so long in the past that it took me a moment or two to recall who it belonged to. 'Are you there? It's me, Luke.'

'Hi, Luke, this is a surprise! How did you get my number?'

'Kate had written it in the address book, though it's been unavailable for the last couple of days.'

'That's because there's no reception here, unless I'm away from the valley, and even then I don't always remember to turn my phone on. Were you trying to get hold of me for any particular reason?'

I mentally added, 'Like maybe apologising for having a lying cow for a wife?'

However, it appeared the boot was on the other foot, because what he was burning to tell me was that I was the cause of a breach between him and the fragrant Kate.

'Ever since you were exposed on that programme and then arrested, we've done nothing but argue and we used to be perfectly happy together,' he said accusingly. 'It's all *your* fault.'

'*Mine?*'

He ignored my interjection. 'I realise that she's such a truthful little soul that she simply *had* to tell someone about the scam, once she found out, but she really should have discussed it with me first, and not gone running to that TV guy. And then, I found it hard to believe you'd been having an affair with that old bloke from Champers&Chocs.'

'That's because I wasn't,' I told him crisply, but he clearly just wanted to unload, because he wasn't taking in a single thing I said.

'Kate accused me of calling her a liar and insisted everything she'd said about you was true.'

'No, Luke, it was the opposite of true.'

'Now she says we need some space apart, so she's moved into Jeremy's granny flat and though it's very kind of him to let her stay there, it makes it a bit awkward, since the three of us have been friends for so long. I mean, we still see each other every day in the staff room at school, but she won't speak to me. Jeremy says she just needs a bit of time to forgive me for doubting her.'

'My heart bleeds for you,' I said sarcastically.

'I still don't understand why she had to go to that programme if she felt so strongly about it and not the police – and it would have been even better if she'd just told Jeremy what she knew and let him deal with it.'

'What, and given me a chance to defend myself against her fairy tales? That was *never* going to happen,' I said. 'Luke, have you ever even considered whether she really *was* telling the truth?'

That did seem to get through at last. 'What, about you having an affair with that man? Well, as I said, it seemed odd, when you—'

'With the *scam*, numbskull,' I interrupted. 'The only thing I was actually guilty of was not reporting Harry Briggs when I found out what he was doing, and being naïve enough to believe him when he said he'd stopped. And no one in their right mind would think I was having an affair with a short, fat man, old enough to be my father, when I thought the sun rose and set out of Jeremy.'

'That's what puzzled me, but then your boss said so too, and that he'd sent you home with wads of cash after those late nights you spent at the warehouse.'

'I was packing special orders and he'd always paid me in cash when I was doing casual work for him while Mum was alive, so I didn't think twice about it. And it wasn't wads of cash, it was the minimum wage plus a bonus for working late. Both he and Kate lied in court.'

'But Kate's the most truthful person in the world,' he insisted. 'Why would she lie about you?'

'*You* tell *me*,' I said.

'Even Jeremy was convinced you were guilty,' he pointed out, as if that was the clincher.

'He obviously never really knew me at all, and I was so blinded by love that I didn't realise quite how credulous and stupid he was,' I said bitterly. 'Did you know that as soon as I was sent to prison he cut off all contact? He didn't even answer my calls and letters, and if my friend Emma hadn't stood by me I'd have been totally abandoned, isolated and alone. I didn't even know what had happened to my cat.'

There was a short pause in which I hoped he might finally be attempting to look at things from a point of view other than his own for a change.

Really, I was starting to think you must have been able to get onto teacher training courses at the time he did simply by signing your name on the application form!

At last he said slowly, 'I knew your mother was dead, but surely you had other relations to visit you and—'

'I've no other relatives,' I said. 'I had no visitors and no outside contact other than Emma, until an elderly prison visitor kindly took pity on me. He was the one who arranged this job for me, or I'd either be still at the open prison, or living in a hostel.'

'But the sentence was quite lenient, really. They said you'd be out in a couple of months.'

'Oh, yes, very lenient, especially since I didn't commit the crime in the first place! First I was locked up in a prison over Christmas, unable to contact anyone and desperate with worry about Pye, and then I was moved to an open prison at the other end of the country, so even Emma couldn't visit me. Yes, that was lenient all right,' I said sarcastically.

'But I didn't know . . . I mean, I didn't think about it,' he confessed. 'Still – you're already out, so you weren't in there long.'

'I have an electronic tag on my leg. They don't just open the door and release you, they ring you like a pigeon and put you under nightly house arrest,' I snarled. 'And all this happened because your wife lied right down the line about something I'd told her in confidence.'

'But Kate can't have lied,' he reiterated. 'I mean, she liked you and she said how that made it hard to tell anyone what you'd been doing.'

'Did she? Magnanimous of her,' I said.

'I suppose she *might* have misunderstood what you told her and you weren't quite as involved as it seemed . . .' he conceded grudgingly.

But I could see he was struggling and I was tired of trying to convince him to take off the rosy-tinted specs, so I cut him off short.

'Luke, I don't really *care* what any of you think any more. Why don't you just go and tell Kate you'll never doubt another word she says? Then she'll come back to you and you can all three live happily ever after in each other's pockets, just the way you were before I came along,' I said, then turned the phone off.

I suspected Kate was having a fling with Jeremy now, under the guise of 'time out from the marriage', but for all I knew, she could have been conducting the affair under Luke's nose for years.

The conversation brought back all the feelings of betrayal and abandonment I'd felt at the time, especially Jeremy's. Now he was sleeping with the enemy, too . . . On reflection, however, I thought they probably deserved each other.

Trudging back up the hill I was so lost in thought that it was only when Dorrie Bird called to me that I noticed she was standing at her cottage door. She invited me in for a coffee and a nip of her home-made sloe gin.

'Though we won't tell Mercy about it, because she's convinced we're all as temperance as she is. I don't know what she thinks we drink up at the Auld Christmas – lemonade, perhaps?'

Her cottage sitting room was tiny, bright and cosy, cluttered with rugs, ornaments, candles and throws. It was all very *Out of Africa* by way of Ikea.

Over slices of violent pink- and yellow-squared Battenburg cake, I found myself telling her about the call. I suspect this was due to inadvertently drinking too much sloe gin, but I was out of the habit and, in any case, had never had much of a head for spirits.

'That Jeremy doesn't sound much of a man to me,' she said disparagingly. 'Guy Martland now, he's a proper man – and a proper scoundrel, too!'

'I think I've grasped that,' I said.

'He'd be good for a quick fling, if you were in the mood, luv,' she said, in her warm Liverpool accent. 'But the first hint of you getting serious and off he'd fly.'

'I'm not a fling sort of girl,' I said. 'In fact, I think I'm a settling-down-into-a-mad-old-spinster-with-my-cat one, so I'll leave trying to clip Guy Martland's wings to someone else.'

She pressed on me another glass of gin and a slice of Battenberg and then told me a few things about her deprived but jolly-sounding childhood in Liverpool, where there was a shortage of everything except love.

It still struck me as odd that she could look so like Maya Angelou, yet sound purest Cilla Black.

Luckily I got back into the house and to my rooms without seeing anyone other than Pye in the kitchen, and by the time I was called for dinner (fortunately running a little late tonight), I'd splashed my face with lots of cold water and could pass for sober.

I went into the library later to type up some notes, but first rang Emma back to tell her all about Luke's phone call.

Then I relayed an invitation from Mercy to bring Marco over for the day on 13 April, a Saturday.

'If the weather's nice, I thought we could walk up to the village,' I suggested, and then described how Mercy was pressing on with alterations to the inside of the mill, despite not yet having planning permission for the redevelopment.

'She seems certain she'll get permission to open it, so I hope she's right! But the cracker factory regeneration can go on anyway and we've already made up some trial crackers to new designs,' I said, and added proudly, 'I can now make a cracker good enough to sell! Only it takes me five times as long as any of the others.'

'Are you managing to do any of your own art work?'

'I'm aiming to keep sending out designs to the greetings card companies, because it's so lucrative, but there's not that much time to do any, even though I'm bubbling with ideas – Godsend seems to have totally inspired me! I expect when the Lord and Master is here as full-time manager, he won't need my help, but until then, I have to do everything I can to make the regeneration scheme a success.'

'Where *is* the Lord and Master?' she asked.

'In Peru, or Mexico, or possibly somewhere else by now, sending Mercy emails telling her not to trust me further than she can throw me!'

I smiled reluctantly when she giggled.

'You know,' I said, a sudden thought occurring to me, 'everyone keeps telling me how bad Guy Martland is – so maybe *he's* not as bad as he's painted, either!'

Chapter 27: Queen for the Day

Q: Why couldn't the elves lift Santa's sack onto the sleigh?
A: Elf and Safety!

By the time Emma drove over to Mote Farm with Marco the following Saturday, I was more than ready for a rest, for the mill now resembled an ant's nest that had been stirred with a stick.

Workmen were everywhere and Mercy had added electricians to their number, so that strange bunches of cables now hung from freshly excavated caverns in the walls, or from the ceilings.

There had been a near-mutiny in the cracker workshop, until Mercy got the builders to concentrate first on finishing the wall that divided her workers from the rest of the mayhem and put up a draped ceiling of translucent polythene, but it was still touch and go until the viewing windows had been fitted.

I was getting along well with the second storeroom, though by the time the builders had filled in the opening between that and the first room (leaving space for an emergency fire door, since there was access to the outside in the cracker factory stockroom, via the loading bay), I had to dust off all the boxes again.

I was totally ready for a bit of time off.

'I'm so glad you're here,' I told Emma, meeting them at the garages near the house. 'I was half afraid Desmond would come home early for some reason and scupper our plans!'

'No, he's still in Dubai until the end of the month,' she said, opening the back door and letting Marco out, trailing a blue velvet cloak.

'You look very fine today, Marco,' I said admiringly.

'I'm a monarch,' he explained. 'Where's Pye? I've brought him a catnip toy. Mummy bought it; she says he'll like it.'

'He will and he's in the house waiting for you with Mercy, the lady I'm working for. Let's go in and say hello, before we decide what to do after that,' I suggested.

Job opened the door with a flourish as we approached – he'd been polishing Silas's shoes in the scullery earlier, so actually I think he was just on the point of leaving.

He bowed. 'Welcome to Mote Farm. Madam is awaiting you in the drawing room,' he intoned sepulchrally.

'Thanks, Job,' I said, and my guess was right, because after we passed him he shut himself on the other side of the door.

Marco was round-eyed.

'A *butler*?' whispered Emma. 'And where's he gone?'

'He was a former butler but now he just helps Silas, Mercy's brother, and lives in one of those cottages near the mill. He slips back into the role all the time – it's like being in a P. G. Wodehouse novel!'

Mercy had made coffee and brought it through, together with a plate of iced fairy cakes. Silas, who seemed to have come out in search of yesterday's newspaper, was half-poised for flight back to his rooms. He rearranged his features from a scowl at being caught by visitors, into a politer expression.

'This is my friend Emma,' I said, making the introduction, 'and this is her son, Marco.'

'As in Polo?' Silas said.

'Polo is a game with horses and sticks, everyone knows that,' Marco said, fixing him with the dark eyes that were so much like his late father's.

'Well, Mr Smarty-pants, *Marco* Polo was a famous explorer.'

'That's very interesting, I'll find out about him,' Marco said seriously.

Silas, as if his knees had suddenly given up, tottered back and sank down into his usual chair near the fireplace.

'Yes, do stay for coffee, Silas,' Mercy said warmly. 'That will be lovely!'

'Huh!' Silas said, then added, 'Why is the boy wearing a ruff?'

'I'm Queen Elizabeth the First,' Marco said seriously, and then, spotting Pye, who was stalking invisible mice in a dark corner of the room, went over to pay his respects and hand over the catnip toy, which seemed to be well received. They'd always got on well.

'What a fertile imagination your little boy has,' said Mercy admiringly, pouring out a glass of orange juice for him, while I began to dispense the coffee and pass round the cakes. 'How old is he, did you say?'

'Nearly seven,' Emma told her, with slight despair. 'A neighbour gave him a box of old Ladybird history books recently and I made him the ruff when he wanted to be Shakespeare. But today . . .'

'He'll probably be Marco Polo next time,' I said.

Marco came back and asked, 'Is there a man inside that suit of armour?'

'There wasn't the last time I looked,' Silas said, 'but you never know, someone might have sneaked in.' Then he laughed at his own witticism, hauled himself to his feet and took his coffee cup off to his rooms. He only remembered to hobble when he was halfway across, so I deduced his rheumatism wasn't too painful today.

After coffee, Mercy returned to the little parlour, where Phil, who was good at anything mechanical, was tinkering and oiling the most recently donated sewing machines. There were now about a dozen of them, ready to be dispatched to Malawi.

Pye had gone back to the non-existent rodent extermination and showed no sign of wanting to come with us when we went out.

I'd taken some bread to feed the ducks in the moat and Marco leaned over the low stone wall to toss it to them. The wind whipped his dark, silky-straight hair about, the ruff flapped and the folds of his blue velvet cloak, worn over his anorak, undulated. He could have stepped out of another century.

Then he ran off down the hill towards the second bridge and hung over that parapet, too. 'Oh, I hope he doesn't fall in!' Emma exclaimed.

'He'll be OK even if he does, because we haven't had much rain lately and it's really low,' I assured her.

'You can see Marco's getting even more eccentric in his ways,' she said, as we followed him down. 'He was always bright and *I* don't mind what flights of fancy his imagination takes him on, but Des doesn't understand. He thinks I'm turning him soft by letting him dress up and act things out all the time and I should be making him go to football and rugby, not taking him to theatre club and modern dance classes. But at least he decided quickly that ballet wasn't for him,' she added, 'because it gets very expensive paying for all these things.'

'I think he's going to become a great actor,' I said encouragingly. 'Remember when he was four and decided he'd be a dog? He kept it up for a whole day.'

She grinned. 'Yes, that was quite funny, especially when he ate his dinner from a dish on the floor and barked to go in the garden.'

'He's always tried on various roles, that's why I think he's destined for an acting career,' I said. 'And there's nothing soft about him – he's just focused on what he's doing.'

'Des seemed to find his ways amusing before we were married, but perhaps he thought all small children were like that and grew out of it. Now he's so critical all the time that Marco steers clear of him. And he said the other day that he liked it much better when Des wasn't there, because he shouts at me so much and makes me cry.'

'Oh, Emma, that's not good!' I said. 'He seems to have changed so much from the man you married. We all liked him then and he seemed to adore you.'

'I know you all thought I'd remarried much too quickly after Ricky died – and you were quite right. I think I was just grasping for the love I'd lost and he came along.'

'You were happy enough at first,' I said.

'It was OK then, it was only when he started working

abroad so much that he slowly became more jealous about what I was doing and who I was seeing while he was away.'

'And checking up on you, or trying to.'

'Yes, the supply teaching gives me my own income and independence, but he snoops around my phone bills and bank statements when he's home. Last time he even asked Marco who Mummy had been talking to lately. Marco clammed up and said he didn't know, but I was really furious when I found out.'

'Emma, if he's not even nice to Marco any more, maybe it's time to cut and run?'

'Don't think I haven't thought about it, because I'm starting to wish we'd never married. If we'd just lived together I could have asked him to move out, because it's my house, but if we divorce, he might have a claim on it.'

'I know you love your home,' I said. 'Perhaps you need to chat to a solicitor and really see where you stand.'

'I thought I'd give Des a chance first, by suggesting to him that we go to Relate together when he's home, but I can tell you that's not a conversation I'm looking forward to.'

'I suppose it's worth trying, but at least if the worst comes to the worst and you divorce, he's never officially adopted Marco, so he can't apply for custody or anything like that.'

'Marco wouldn't want to see him anyway and I expect he'd tell the judge so, in no uncertain terms!' She sighed. 'It's hard to recall why I loved Des so much . . . or thought I did.'

'Well, just look at me: I was madly in love with Jeremy and now I simply can't understand what I saw in the miserable little twerp.'

'He is handsome, even though he isn't very tall.'

'Small, handsome and wearing a permanently peeved expression,' I said with a grin. 'Guy Martland, that man who keeps texting me, is smallish, dark and handsome. I seem to have a type.'

We caught up with Marco, who was engaged in an imaginary sword fight with an invisible opponent, and walked up the track behind the factory, where there were lots of exciting fallen trees and rocky outcrops to explore on the way to the village.

As we strolled, I told Emma I'd had another card design accepted and been able to pay Mercy back for the storage charge horrible Jeremy had levied.

'He's such a cheap man, and I'm sure Kate has only moved into the flat so they can carry on their affair more easily, whatever tale she spun to Luke about them just needing some time apart.'

'Well, it's not your problem any more,' she said. 'You're free of them all and as soon as that tag comes off your leg, you can put the past behind you and move on.'

'I'm going to begin saving up for a little car of my own, and maybe our book will be a huge success one of these days, too,' I added, for we had started planning a joint venture, where Emma would write a story for a pop-up book and I would do the graphics and paper engineering.

'Only if we stop talking about it and actually get on with it,' she pointed out. 'But I think it's definitely time for a really good new children's pop-up book and I don't see why we shouldn't be the ones to produce it.'

By the time we got to the village, the Merry Kettle tearoom next to the village shop was open, so we had lunch there, before carrying on up to the summit of Snowehill and showing Marco the magical red horse cut in the hill.

This time I didn't do an Alice and fall down a rabbit burrow, which is just as well, because Marco got tired on the way home and we took it in turns to carry him piggy-back for the last part of it. Luckily he's very light; a good gust of wind would blow him away.

We were back at the house in time for tea, as arranged, and Silas was not only there again, but had picked out a Victorian children's book about explorers and inventors with a lovely embossed and gilded cover. He presented Marco with this, so the little boy must have gone down very well.

Marco was quieter now, though, tired after the long walk and the fresh air, but his manners were very good and a credit to Emma.

When they left, Mercy invited them to come over any time they wanted to.

'Thank you so much,' Emma said. 'I'd love to see the cracker factory next time.'

'Yes, there wasn't time today. Emma is quite arty, too,' I said.

'I do craftwork, really. I like to knit and sew,' Emma said. 'I haven't got Tabby's artistic flair. But I'm trying to write for children – I'm a nursery teacher by profession, though I've just been doing supply teaching since I had Marco.'

'Then come during the next school holiday and you can see the crackers being made and how much progress we've achieved on the mill conversion,' Mercy said.

'Yes, do: some of the dust may have settled by then,' I said drily.

Chapter 28: Winding Up

Q: What do snowmen eat for lunch?
A: Iceburgers!

I went with Mercy and Silas to another Quaker meeting, since the last one had seemed to have a tranquillising and calming effect on me, and goodness knows, what with Luke stirring the past up again and Randal still warning his aunt that I was a snake in her bosom, I needed it.

This time no one got up and said anything for an entire hour, but although I tried to empty my mind in order to let in any Higher Thoughts that God might direct my way, as the instruction booklet for new attenders suggested, ideas for a whole series of three-dimensional papercuts filled it right up again.

I could visualise what I wanted to create quite clearly against the soft white walls of the meeting house: at the heart of each picture would be books – spilling their words out in cascades onto the floor, bursting out like a cuckoo from a clock, or with characters leaping out and escaping . . . I felt very excited.

I knew I'd need more time and also my large workshop

space to explore what I wanted to do – not to mention the gallery, when it was opened, to sell my work from.

I confessed to Mercy and Silas on the way home that instead of thinking selfless thoughts about bigger issues, I'd been filled with ideas for new pictures, but Mercy said not to worry, because God moved in mysterious ways.

Then Silas remarked that it sounded like my pictures might do much the same if they were spilling right out of their frames, and gave the odd, sealion bark of amusement that had both amazed and enthralled Marco.

I'd taken to walking down and checking my phone occasionally and had now embarked on a desultory (on my side) conversation with Guy, conducted entirely by text.

It had started when he'd changed tactics, stopped pestering me for a date, and asked me what my idea of fun was.

I'd replied, '*Talking to my cat. Cutting holes in paper. Walking in the woods, or on a beach. Eating out, though nowhere fancy.*' (Until I met Jeremy, my idea of classy was fish and chips at Harry Ramsden's.)

'*Can do the last two,*' he replied, '*learning to talk Cat might take a little longer. Grateful for any pointers you can give me.*'

This made me laugh and warm to him a bit, but not to the extent that I lay down and rolled over, even metaphorically speaking.

There was only one message from him today which read, '*How is my little Tabby cat this afternoon?*'

That was a good one, seeing as he was only a couple of inches taller than me! Wouldn't it be fun if the next time I saw Guy, I could fluff myself out to twice my size like Pye did when he wanted to look scary?

I was debating whether to bother answering this missive or not, when four delayed messages from another caller tumbled into the inbox.

Jeremy.

They said, in order: '*Call me.*' '*Call me.*' '*Call me.*' '*Don't you ever answer your damned phone?*'

It was only just the time of day when teachers emerge blinking into the light, so he must have sent them off in a five-minute salvo the moment he got home – and he rang again, even as I was thinking he couldn't possibly be calling for any good reason and my fingers were itching to press Delete.

'Tabby, is that you at last?' he snapped.

'Hello, voice of my past,' I said. 'I'd sincerely hoped never to hear from you again.'

'Then perhaps you shouldn't have contacted Luke, stirring him up with all your lies about being innocent and casting poor Kate as a liar and meddler.'

'Don't be stupider than you can help,' I said, astonished. '*He* rang *me.* He said I was to blame for his breach with dear, sweet, innocent Kate.'

'I don't know what you said to him, but he came round and told Kate he thought she'd got it wrong about your having an affair with your boss at Champers&Chocs and it had made him wonder about the rest of it.'

'Wonders will never cease,' I said sarkily. 'I thought you both just echoed what Kate said, like a pair of Midwich Cuckoos.'

'Kate would never lie, but the whole situation is very difficult.'

'I bet it is,' I agreed.

'I think I've smoothed him down now, so if you butt out and leave us alone, things will soon go back to being the way they always were.'

'Before I came along?' I finished for him. 'But I've no interest in any of you, and the boot is on the other foot, because I wish you would all butt out and leave *me* alone. So goodbye, Jeremy – I hope for ever, this time,' I said, and turned off the phone.

It's true what they say: there's nowt so queer as folk.

The following day Mercy announced that there had been an indication that planning permission for the mill site to be altered and opened to the public would be granted, though I wasn't sure how she knew this: perhaps the town hall flag was hoisted partway, or the smoke from the chimney turned a different colour.

However, this news seemed to embolden her to press on even harder with the work. The following week the car park in front of the mill was to be gravelled. I even caught Mercy and Arlene in the office, picking out picnic tables on a website for the flat, grassy area just above it, which I told them was putting the cart before the horse.

'I'm thinking of the redevelopment as a whole, or the first phase of it, at any rate,' Mercy explained. 'I'd like everything finished and open to the public at the same time. Then we can crack on with the second phase, converting the attached buildings to workspaces for craftspeople and a gallery shop.'

'And we'll get a special deal if we order all the signage to the mill from the road and the site map board for the car park at the same time as the display boards for the museum,' put in Arlene. 'It makes sense.'

'So many things are falling into place already and soon Randal will be home again and we can discuss the café with him then, since that will be his special preserve,' Mercy said. 'I'm so looking forward to meeting his fiancée at last, too.'

'When *will* he be back?' I asked. I mean: pretend I care.

'I think he said early next week, though I expect he has business to attend to before he can think of coming here. And now we've got half a dozen types of sample crackers made up and designs for the display boxes, it will be good to have his opinion before we go into production.'

Since he'd been the one determined to shut the cracker factory down, I didn't really think his opinion was either here or there, so I just made a non-committal noise.

Then Mercy said she'd come with me to look at my latest discovery in the last stockroom: a hand-printing press of great antiquity, with a set of plates for old-fashioned Christmas card scenes depicting horse-drawn coaches in the snow. It was destined to be cleaned up by Bradley and become a central point of the museum display.

Dorrie asked me when my tag was coming off, so I could go to the pub with them on a Friday or Saturday evening, whenever I felt like it.

'You're a young thing, so you must miss going out and a bit of life.'

'I'm not *that* young,' I said, 'and I've never been much of a one for discos and nightclubs. My ex-fiancé was a champagne bar and fancy restaurant kind of guy and so were his friends. It was OK, but on the whole I'd rather curl up at home with Pye and a good book.'

'It takes all sorts,' said Dorrie, shaking her head. 'You'd be surprised what I used to get up to at your age.'

I didn't think I would, now I'd got to know her better and heard some of her stories, but I didn't encourage her to give me the lurid details.

'They're supposed to come and remove the tag at the end of this month,' I said. 'I've sort of got used to it now, though I never forget it's there even for an instant, and I'm counting down the days till I can get rid of it. It would be wonderful just to be able to go for a walk in the evenings now it's staying light later, maybe stroll up to the woods . . .'

Walking, especially in the early dusk, had always given me great pleasure, and now that I was actually living in the country the prospect was even more enticing.

Randal had returned to the UK and, typically, he has chosen to bring his fiancée to stay at Mote Farm on the same day my tag was to be removed.

'It will be humiliating if they arrive just as they're untagging me,' I said to Mercy. 'It's supposed to happen between three and seven.'

'I don't think there'll be any need to hide away then, dear, because Randal said they were leaving London late and having dinner on the way, so we weren't to wait for them.'

'Oh, good,' I said, relieved. 'I'm hoping the tagging people come earlier rather than later. And, of course, after dinner I'll go to my rooms and leave you to greet your future niece-in-law with Silas, anyway.'

I was naturally curious to see the woman who had captured the bluff (and admittedly, even though underweight at the moment, *buff*) Randal's heart, but it could wait. Mercy was still convinced she must be the sweetest girl in the world and I sincerely hoped she was right.

'Oh, no, you must wait with us, because you're quite one of the family now and it would look very odd if you weren't around in the evening . . . unless, of course, you have things you wanted to do?'

Actually, what I'd have liked to do was go to the pub with the others once my tag was removed, but the tag people might be late . . . or even not turn up at all until another day. I'd been told one or two cautionary stories while I was in prison.

'I thought perhaps you might see Lacey to her room for me, while I made coffee,' Mercy suggested. 'They're bound to want refreshments after such a long drive.'

I didn't want to seem churlish in the face of her generosity so, even though I was quite sure that neither Randal nor his bride-to-be would either expect or welcome my presence on their arrival, I agreed I'd happily do that. I still intended taking myself off at the first opportunity afterwards, though.

We'd done a final check on the room that was to be Randal's fiancée's earlier, and either modern manners had not invaded Mercy's consciousness, or more likely, she disapproved of sex before marriage, because it was in the west wing and about as far as she could put her from Randal, with herself in the middle. But the bedroom allotted to Lacey was a very pretty one, done in a blue and white French paper with toile de Jouy curtains and a matching coverlet on the bed.

There was a sort of wooden shelf, shaped like half a royal crown, sticking out over the head of the bed, from which hung matching drapes, held back by blue silken ropes.

Mercy, thoughtful as ever, had added a blue Delft bulb pot full of hyacinths to scent the air and when I told her everything was perfect, she was pleased.

'I want her to feel very welcome in what will soon be her home,' she said and I, like a cuckoo in the nest, felt a sudden pang. One day, *I'd* be the one pushed out of the nest by the newcomer . . . or maybe Randal, I could feel it in my bones.

I woke with a strangely Christmas-morning feeling on the Thursday and told Pye, who, having nudged me to the edge, was lying in an abandoned way across the centre of the bed, that my tag was to be removed later that day.

'Just imagine what it would feel like if I made you wear a collar all the time,' I suggested. 'One without any elastic, so you could never take it off.'

'Ppfft!' said Pye, which translated as, 'Just you try it!'

Mercy and even Freda seemed more excited by the prospect of seeing Randal's fiancée than in my imminent freedom, but I was in such a fever of anticipation that I was back from the mill long before the earliest possible time the untaggers might arrive.

And after all that and a lot of floor pacing, they arrived only minutes before dinner, though the deed was quickly done. There was no time just then to savour my freedom alone, but I vowed that the very second I'd done my duty to the visitors, I was slipping off to the kitchen wing and then right out of the door with Pye, to roam freely in the gloaming!

Chapter 29: Thrown

Randal

On the long drive up to Lancashire, I tried to impress on Lacey the need for tact during this first visit to Mote Farm . . . or at least, I did once she'd stopped sulking because I'd been cross about her not telling me she was bringing her overweight, wheezing little pug dog with her.

'Why wouldn't I?' she'd said. 'He goes everywhere with me.'

It was a pity he didn't *walk* everywhere with her, instead of being carried, so the poor thing might not be so out of condition.

'Not quite everywhere – you're always leaving him with your housekeeper,' I pointed out, because she had a long-suffering Latvian lady who cooked, cleaned and mopped up after the not always continent Pugsie.

'Maid, not housekeeper,' she corrected me. 'And she's not so good that I wouldn't get rid of her, if it wasn't impossible to get decent staff these days.'

'I suppose it doesn't matter really and Mercy does like animals,' I conceded. 'It would just have been good to ask her if it was OK first.'

'He's an ickle doggie that everyone will love,' she said, kissing the top of the pug's head with an enthusiasm I wished she'd expend on me occasionally.

Once we were getting closer to Godsend, I reverted to the subject most on my mind. 'Just give Mercy a chance to get to know you on this first visit – don't go into any details about what your mail-order firm actually sells,' I suggested, because her upbringing had made Lacey totally matter-of-fact on the subject of sex, which to her was just another business opportunity.

She looked astonished. 'You think she might disapprove? But that's so old-fashioned and puritanical!'

'Actually, Mercy's pretty broad-minded on the whole, most Quakers are, but I'm not sure how she's going to take it – and my uncle was really strait-laced, so he would have been horrified by the idea of something like Instant Orgy being run from Friendship Mill.'

'Well, now I've had more time to think about it, *I'm* not sure that I want to relocate my business to the sticks,' she snapped. 'For a start, I hadn't realised it took so long to get all the way up here! But anyway, if you invest your own money in the redevelopment and you're a director and shareholder, you can do what you like.'

'Not quite: Mercy will be investing some of her own money in the mill redevelopment and I'm sure will remain the majority shareholder.'

'She's got money of her own, not just what you're uncle left her?'

'Yes, she was an heiress and she's still loaded, even though she's given away a fortune to charities, especially those working in Malawi.'

'And she's no children of her own to leave it to?'

I could see where she was heading with this. 'She's guardian to her Malawian goddaughter, Liz, who calls her "Grandmother" and she's very fond of her. I'm sure she'll support her through school and university and leave her well provided for, and I should think her pet charity projects will get some hefty sums of money, too.'

I glanced across at Lacey and saw her beautiful, pensive face, chin still resting on top of Pugsie's head.

'So you see, darling, I'd like her to get to know and love you before you go into details about your business – and when you've seen the scale of the mill project, you might even want to help me with that, instead. It would be fun to work together, wouldn't it? We'd make a great team.'

'What, give up Instant Orgy? You must be joking,' she said. 'And when we're married she'll have to get used to what I do for a living, wherever it's based, so better sooner than later. I'm not ashamed of it.'

'No, of course not,' I agreed quickly, and gave up with a sigh. Maybe she'd think it over and see that tact in the first instance would be a very good idea . . . or perhaps Mercy just wouldn't be as shocked as I thought she would be.

Pugsie began to make unmistakable retching noises. 'God, he's going to throw up. I told you not to give him what was left of your dinner,' I exclaimed. 'Hold his head over something, quickly.'

'Like what?' she demanded, holding him away from her.

'Your handbag – that's more than big enough,' I suggested.

'It's a Bayswater – you're *mad*!'

But luckily I'd just turned off the motorway and pulled into a lay-by with a squealing of brakes. Lacey opened the door just in time to let Pugsie empty the contents of his stomach into the long grass, but relations all round were still a bit strained by the time we reached Mote Farm.

Chapter 30: Unfettered and Free

Q: What do you call a penguin in the Sahara?
A: Lost!

After dinner I cleared away and stacked the dishwasher, then set out the tray for coffee, before going back through. It was weird, not feeling the clasp of the tag around my ankle.

Silas was half asleep in his armchair with Pye curled up on his lap, but Mercy was bobbing up and down, eagerly listening for the sounds of arrival. As soon as the bell pealed, she was off into the hall like a whippet.

'Silas,' I hissed, 'I think they're here!'

'What?' he exclaimed, giving a galvanic jerk that startled Pye into jumping off and stalking away in high dudgeon. 'I wasn't asleep, I just closed my eyes for a second.'

'Of course – but I think your nephew and his fiancée have arrived. Mercy's gone to let them in.'

'Load of nonsense!' he uttered in tones of disgust. 'Another damned stranger in the house.'

I didn't take that personally, because he'd got used to me now, but if Mercy'd heard him swear, she'd have washed his mouth out with soap and water.

She was back now, herding the visitors before her like an over-eager sheepdog. Randal didn't look to be in a good temper, though with that thin, straight mouth and square jaw, it's hard to tell. But after one glance at him I just *stared* at Lacey Bucknall in amazement: she was the most stunningly beautiful woman I'd ever set eyes on.

She was a little taller than me, slender, but also curvy in the right places. Her skin was palest alabaster, lit from within, her eyes huge periwinkle-blue pools with lashes that fluttered like black butterflies . . . though I expect she darkened them, since her cloud of silken hair was a vibrant bronze-red.

'Here we are – and a warm welcome to your future home, my dear,' said Mercy, kissing the newcomer, a salute that was received rather than reciprocated. Lacey was clutching a fat fur muff with both hands, rather like a comfort blanket, which I thought must be a current fashion trend.

She cast a rather disparaging glance around the dark-panelled room with its intricate moulded Tudor ceiling, and said, 'Well, as to that, we'll see, won't we? It's very old,' she added, though not as if that was a good thing.

Mercy took this at face value. 'It is indeed very old and I'll show you round tomorrow, unless Randal would like to. But at the moment I expect you'd like to see your room and then have a drink and something to eat. But first, let me introduce you to my brother, Silas, and Tabby.'

Silas held out his hand, as one duty bound, and before shaking it she bent and put the grey-brown muff on the floor. It sneezed and turned two bright, black button eyes on the assembly.

'Oh – it's a pug!' I said. 'Is he—' But my enquiry as to

whether he was used to cats died on my lips as he and Pye spotted each other at the same moment.

Pye immediately fluffed himself up to twice his size and a less brave, or possibly more *intelligent,* dog would have backed off with due meekness at this point. Instead, the small creature hurled himself into battle, yapping and snarling.

Astonished and affronted, Pye held his ground and dealt the intruder a sharp smack across the nose, claws out, which sent him bowling across the room like a furry football.

'Oh dear,' said Mercy. 'I was just about to tell you that Lacey had brought her little doggie with her, but I'd quite forgotten about Pye.'

'Pugsie!' exclaimed Lacey, with more animation than she'd so far shown and Randal scooped up the little dog and handed it to her.

'I forgot about the cat, too,' he said. 'It's Tabby's. It was here last time I came.'

'His poor little nose is bleeding,' Lacey said, examining the panting pug, whose eyes were bulging alarmingly as she clutched him to her bosom. 'You vicious, nasty creature!' she said to Pye.

Pye had sat down again and was washing the contaminated paw he'd swiped Pugsie with. He stopped and gave her a look and she recoiled.

'What's the matter with his eyes?'

'Nothing, he's just got one milky blue one, and one green, that's all,' I said. 'And I'm so sorry he hurt your dog, but he did attack first, and Pye was only defending himself. If dogs ignore him, he doesn't take any notice of them.'

In fact, I think Pye considers the disgusting creatures

totally below his notice, so had Pugsie abased himself from the start, he'd have been tolerated.

Pye now turned his mismatched eyes on the dog and said warningly, 'Mrrow!'

'Put the dog on the floor and let them sort it out between them,' Silas suggested, sitting down in his chair and clearly feeling he'd done all that good manners could expect of him. 'I don't think he'll make the same mistake twice.'

'He's not hurt really, Lacey,' Randal assured her. 'It's just a little scratch on his nose. But I don't see why Tabby's cat should have the whole run of the house. He could stay in the kitchens while we're here.'

'You explain that to Pye, then,' I told him, and he gave me a cold look from those hazel eyes.

'We like having him about and I'm sure they'll get used to each other,' Mercy said optimistically. 'Do let Tabby take you upstairs and show you your room now, Lacey, while I go and make the coffee. I expect Pye will come with me – he always hopes for a little titbit, don't you, pussums?' she said fondly to him.

'I don't know about coffee, I could do with a stiff drink after that,' Lacey said. 'Vodka and soda, if you've got it.'

'I'm afraid we're a temperance household, dear,' said Mercy.

Lacey looked blank. 'A what?'

'They don't drink, or even have alcohol in the house,' explained Randal.

'Bloody hell, it's like the Dark Ages up here,' she muttered, but luckily I don't think either Silas or Mercy caught that.

'Get my case from the hall, will you?' she said to me tersely, clearly thinking I was the home help.

'Get it yourself,' I said, startled into rudeness.

'I'll bring it up,' Randal said, a hint of amusement in his voice. 'You go ahead with Tabby, darling. Mercy, where have you put her?'

'The French bedroom, Randal.'

'Come on, then,' I said to Lacey, who was still gazing at me as if no one had ever been rude to her in her life before, which maybe they hadn't.

Still carrying Pugsie, she followed me upstairs and along the passage to the west wing, where I opened the door and ushered her into her charming room.

'Here we are,' I said. 'Pretty, isn't it?'

Lacey surveyed the draped and crowned bed and then remarked, 'It looks like a set from a bad porn film.'

'I'll have to take your word for that, I haven't seen *any* kind of porn film,' I said, glad that Mercy had sent me to show her up to her room, rather than take her herself!

'The bathroom is just across the passage, though I use that one too, so if it's occupied just go along to the right a bit and you'll find another.'

'What's that dreadful smell?' She was sniffing the air with her perfect little retroussé nose.

I sniffed experimentally with my great big hooter. Ever since I set eyes on Lacey I'd felt oversized and remarkably plain.

'There isn't one. All I can smell is hyacinths.'

'Then that's what it is. They're vile and you'll have to take them away.'

'Randal, darling,' she said, turning to him as he appeared in the doorway with her case, 'someone's put stinking flowers in my room!'

'I'll remove them,' I said quickly, and picking up the pottery trough of offending blooms, made a hasty retreat down the backstairs to the kitchen.

Mercy had just made a pot of coffee and put it on the tray when I went in and she looked surprised to see me carrying the hyacinths.

'Lacey loved them, but flowers give her hay fever,' I said tactfully.

'Silly me, not to have thought of that,' she said. 'Do put them in your sitting room if you'd like them, dear. Now, are you joining us for coffee?'

'If you don't mind, I think Pye and I will stay in here now,' I said. 'If we close the kitchen door, he and Pugsie won't have another confrontation tonight and perhaps we can introduce them carefully to each other in the morning.'

'It hasn't been the best start,' Mercy commented. 'She seems a reserved kind of girl, doesn't she?'

'I expect she's just tired and it's always a bit of an ordeal facing a room full of strangers, isn't it?' I suggested.

'You're right, that will be it!' Mercy said, looking more cheerful.

When she'd gone, I opened the kitchen door and Pye and I went out into the herb garden at the side of the house, which had been out of bounds to me at night since I'd arrived.

We followed the path round the edge of the moat to the foot of the terraces behind the house. The shutters hadn't been closed over the mullioned windows of the drawing room and a tall, broad-shouldered and unmistakable figure passed one of them, then stopped and looked out.

I didn't think he could see us in the dusk and there was no reason why we shouldn't have been in the garden, but I felt like an intruder. We carried on, circumnavigating our little island and then retreating back to our rooms.

In bed, there was no weighty tag to tether me to my past, and my dreams that night were unfettered and free.

Chapter 31: Four-Legged Friends

Q: Why did the skeleton go to the New Year's Eve party on his own?
A: Because he had no body to go with!

I woke early as usual next morning and though the sky was still a translucent dusky cerulean blue, the birds were already singing.

I opened the doors through to the kitchen so Pye could go out and then tiptoed upstairs for a shower. There was no sound of anyone else stirring yet, though I knew Mercy wouldn't be far behind me.

I left the bathroom as pristine as I'd found it, ready for Lacey when she made an appearance, and I was just coming out when I heard a muffled yapping from the direction of the French Room. Then a door opened and closed and Pugsie hurtled towards me down the landing, like a fur-covered bullet.

I recoiled, but his intentions were apparently friendly, for when he reached me he wriggled his whole body and would have wagged his tail, had he had enough of one. He yelped again, meaningfully.

'You want to go out, don't you?' I said, resignedly scooping him up and carrying him down the steep stone back stairs and into the kitchen, where Pye greeted us with a disgusted-sounding 'Pfft!'

'Right, you two: best manners, OK?' I warned, putting the pug down. But I needn't have worried, because Pugsie had learned his lesson. He lay down and rolled over submissively and Pye sighed, got up in disgust and oozed out through the cat-flap into the garden.

Pugsie watched him go, seemingly astonished by this feat, so I had to open the door and take him outside, where he peed for quite ten minutes on the box hedge.

'You realise if Bradley spots you doing that to his garden, he's likely to turn you into a small pair of mittens, don't you?' I asked him, and he grinned, his tongue lolling out. He was overweight and rather grotesque, but quite endearing for all that.

He followed me back inside, where we found Mercy had started cooking bacon and eggs, and Pugsie immediately transferred his attention to her.

'I expect he's hungry,' I said. 'He'd better have those saucers you used for Pye when he first arrived, because Lacey probably hasn't brought his dishes with her,' I suggested. 'I hope she remembered to bring some food, though.'

'I'll ask Randal when he comes down – he's usually an early riser. But what about Pye, have they met again yet?'

I told her they had, and that I thought Pye would tolerate the intruder, as long as he kept to his place. Then I put my share of the bacon in a bun to take with me and made my escape to the mill.

A couple of quiet hours working in the old stockrooms

before everyone else arrived was infinitely more attractive than the prospect of sharing the breakfast table with Randal!

At last I'd finished all the clearing, cleaning and sorting, and everything destined for the museum was stacked up in the middle of one room and covered with dustsheets.

I'd volunteered to paint the walls with a neutral undercoat, while Mercy and Silas debated the final colour, so I got on with that next. Painting was soothing and I wasn't conscious of time passing until Dorrie Bird appeared with a cup of tea, a slice of marble cake and some gossip.

'Randal's here, showing that fiancée of his over the mill. She's a beauty and no mistake, luv,' she told me, putting the cup and plate down on the top rung of the ladder.

'Yes, she's stunning,' I agreed.

'Still, beauty is as beauty does, and her manners aren't so pretty,' Dorrie said darkly. 'When Randal was showing her the cracker workshop I overheard her say, "God, all the people here are so old – and those crackers are such total crap I'm surprised you sell *any*."'

'Age is immaterial – and just wait till she sees our wonderful new range of crackers!' I said. 'Have they gone, now?'

'Only into the other buildings. She said she'd got some kind of business she might relocate here when they're married – or at least, he seems to think she will, but she didn't sound that enthusiastic to me.'

'I *think* it's mail-order party supplies, and there'd be plenty of room to accommodate that. Did she have a little pug dog with her?'

'No dog at all that I saw, unless you count Randal,' Dorrie

said, grinning. 'He was panting after her, all right. But then, I expect most men do.'

'Lacey of Troy, the face that launched a thousand ships,' I said absently, thinking that Lacey must have left Pugsie at the house, so I only hoped Pye didn't forget himself and eat the poor little morsel.

'Hey up,' Dorrie warned me as Lacey and Randal walked into the first of the museum rooms, then she gave me a conspiratorial grimace and sidled out past them.

'These rooms look huge when they're almost empty,' Randal said, 'but you don't have to paint the walls yourself, Tabby. We'll get the decorators in.'

'Actually I quite like doing it, and it's just the undercoat to freshen it up. The electricians are going to change the lighting and put some more sockets in later, so I'll probably have to retouch it before the final coat goes on and the new flooring's laid.'

Lacey spun on her stiletto heel and looked into the other room through the big archway. 'There's lots of space in here,' she said assessingly. 'Light, too, with those long windows.'

'The new layout will channel the visitors past the cracker workshop and through the museum displays in these two rooms, before they exit by way of a big Christmas shop.'

'But I agree with Randal that the workshop and museum are a total waste of valuable retail space,' she said.

'Mercy wants the cracker factory to remain the focus of the visitor experience and I think she's quite right,' I said firmly.

'Well, you would, wouldn't you? For an ex-con you seem to have landed yourself a cushy little number,' she said tartly.

I gave Randal a glare, since I couldn't think who else would have revealed my past. I expect he'd told her *everything*, too. He shifted uncomfortably and looked away.

'I'm working very hard for my pay, and Mercy's happy with what I'm doing, which is the important thing,' I said evenly. 'But as soon as the mill is open and she doesn't need my help any more, I'll be earning my own living, working from one of the new studios. I make papercut pictures.'

'Oh, you're an *artist*,' she said, as if it was a dirty word. 'So presumably you'll be moving out of the house then, too? The fewer hangers-on cluttering the place, like you and the old man, the better.'

'I don't see Uncle Silas as a hanger-on. I'm fond of him and Mote Farm is his home now, too,' Randal said, frowning.

'But he's only your aunt's brother,' she said, staring at him, wide-eyed and appealing. 'He's not really related to you at all, so I don't know what he's even doing there.' She shrugged. 'Still, we'll see. I don't really like old houses – I'd prefer to knock it down and build something fresh and new.'

'Mote Farm is a listed building so that wouldn't be an option even if I wanted to do it,' Randal said, looking startled. 'I'm not even sure we'd get permission to build a new house on the estate. Probably not.'

'Oh, I expect I can do something with the interior,' she said. 'Make it lighter, more open plan.'

She clearly wasn't familiar with the intricacies of the Listed Building regulations, but Randal was.

'I don't think Mercy would take to that idea,' he said.

'Blast, I'd forgotten that she'll have control over what we can and can't do to the house,' Lacey said.

'But it's beautiful as it is, Lacey,' he told her. 'You just haven't had a really good look round in daylight yet. Come on, it's just about lunchtime, let's go back.'

My tea had gone as cold as Lacey's heart, but I ate the slice of cake Dorrie had brought me, before I started painting again.

I wasn't sure a tour of Mote Farm was likely to change Lacey's mind. Although it seemed grand to me, it sounded as if she'd be unimpressed by anything less than a Chatsworth.

Since I hadn't appeared for lunch, Mercy sent Job down later with a fifties picnic basket, containing cheese and pickle rolls, an apple, a flask of soup and another of coffee.

Pye strolled into the stockroom in mid-afternoon with Ginger, Bing and Pugsie in obsequious attendance, so I assumed the little dog must have mastered the art of the cat-flap. In fact, I suspected he now thought he *was* a cat, despite some obvious limitations in the jumping and climbing department.

I was careful to avoid afternoon tea, sneaking in late through the back door with Pye and Pugsie. None of us appeared to have been missed.

Chapter 32: Out of the Box

Knock, knock.
Who's there?
Chris.
Chris who?
Chris-tmas time is here again!

I changed into one of my few smart tops, a long, silky black tunic sprinkled with a smattering of silvery steel stars around the neckline, then went back into the kitchen to see if Mercy needed any help with dinner. But she had everything under control.

Tonight she was cooking a whole salmon, sealed into a foil parcel with butter and herbs, to be served with new potatoes, peas and asparagus.

We were to eat formally in the dining parlour, too, so out came the best silver from the sideboard – or best stainless steel, as Mercy put it.

'I think Randal said he was going to give Lacey a tour of the house after lunch,' I remarked. 'Did she get as far as the kitchen wing?'

'Oh, yes, dear, they had quite an exhaustive tour of

downstairs before they went out somewhere in the car, though I told them that they couldn't enter your sitting room or bedroom without your permission.'

'I don't mind really, except that there's a lot of my work lying around, so it looks messy.'

'I expect Lacey will want to see the rest of the house tomorrow,' she said, then went to summon everyone to the table, while I carried through the lordly dish of salmon, which had been neatly garnished with near-transparent circles of cucumber. I was careful to shut Pye in the kitchen with Pugsie, since he'd taken too much interest in the fish and I didn't want him harassing everyone while they ate.

When I told Lacey where Pugsie was and that he and Pye had been keeping me company at the mill that afternoon, she looked totally blank, so it was clear she'd forgotten about him entirely.

'You mean Pugsie and that evil cat—'

'Pye isn't evil,' I interrupted indignantly. 'And they've made up their quarrel now and are the best of friends,' I added, though that was a slight exaggeration, since Pye was merely tolerating the interloper.

'But if he got out of the house, he could have gone down to the road and got killed!' she said, as if it was our fault she'd forgotten to look after him.

'I don't think he could walk that far,' Silas said, looking up from his plate, which was so heavily loaded that I assumed salmon was a favourite and could even compete with his beloved ready-made dinners.

Lacey seemed to have a healthy appetite, too, though she was heavy on the salmon and vegetables and totally spurned the buttery new potatoes. I suppose avoiding carbs helps to keep your weight down, but so far I've never really had a problem with mine, apart from losing too much in prison. Normally I'm a reasonable size twelve, which is good enough for me.

'Let Pugsie back in, so he can have a little bit of this salmon,' she ordered me.

'Let him in yourself, if you think you can stop Pye coming in with him,' I rejoined. 'The kitchen door's over there.'

'We don't feed animals at the table,' Silas said shortly. 'And we certainly don't feed them on expensive fresh salmon!'

'Don't worry, Lacey, Pugsie ate his dinner long ago, when Pye had his,' Mercy said. 'Job went up to Little Mumming and got some of those dog dinners in small foil pots and a bag of biscuit, so he's fine.'

'Well . . . thank you,' she said, rather grudgingly. 'I usually bring his special food with me, because he has such a delicate little stomach.'

'So I noticed on the way up here,' Randal said darkly, and she gave him a look.

'I was tied up in a meeting with suppliers till late, so I had to rush to be ready in time for Randal to pick me up.'

Unfortunately, the idea of Lacey being tied up made me give a snort of laughter, though I quickly changed it into a cough.

'Sorry,' I apologised, eyes watering, 'something went down the wrong way.'

Randal's eyes narrowed suspiciously and I looked away from him quickly.

Mercy poured me some water, then turned back to Lacey.

'So, dear,' she said brightly, 'did you have a nice little run out in the countryside this afternoon?'

'I wanted to see my friend and her husband who live in Knutsford. We met halfway,' she said.

'How fortunate that one of your friends lives within easy driving distance,' Mercy said. 'And while you were out, one of Randal's friends, Jude Martland, rang to invite us all to lunch at Old Place on Sunday.'

'*Martland*?' repeated Lacey sharply.

'Yes, do you know him?'

'I've met a *Guy* Martland once or twice on the party circuit,' she said.

'That would be Jude's younger brother, but I don't know if he'll be up for the weekend or not. Jude and his wife live at Old Place in Little Mumming and they always have a large family lunch on a Sunday, which is great fun. I'm sure you'll enjoy it.'

'You never know quite who's going to be there, because they're very hospitable and Holly, Jude's wife, loves to cook,' Randal said. Then he added, frowning, 'I didn't know you'd met Guy Martland.'

Lacey shrugged. 'He just hangs out with one or two of my friends, sometimes.'

'Jude said you were always welcome to come to lunch too, Tabby,' Mercy told me. 'Though I did tell him that since Sunday was your day of rest, you might have other plans. Silas and I will go to the meeting first, of course, but you could come up to Little Mumming with Randal and Lacey and meet us there.'

That would be a jolly drive, I thought, before politely declining the invitation.

'Next time you visit us, Lacey, we'll invite the Martlands down here for lunch or dinner,' Mercy told her. 'I'm sure you'll get on so well and once you're living here it will be pleasant for you to have local friends. Randal was at school with Jude, though not in the same year, and he married a very nice girl. They have a baby boy now, too, a very joyful arrival.'

Lacey seemed bored by the turn of the conversation. 'Actually, when we're married I expect we'll divide our time between London and here,' she said. 'I'm sure Randal needn't be on site the whole time and *I'm* in two minds about whether to relocate my business here.'

'But when I'm managing Friendship Mill, I'll need to be here most of the time,' Randal said, before adding hopefully, 'Now you've seen the scale of the project, perhaps you'd even find the challenge of helping me to make the redevelopment a success more fun than running your own mail-order company?'

'What, give up my business? No way!' she said emphatically.

'Randal tells me your parents own a chain of shops and I think it's very enterprising of you to set up your own company at such a young age,' Mercy said. 'But there's lots of room in the mill buildings if you should wish to move the business up here.'

'I *was* surprised how much space there is,' Lacey admitted. 'But if I *were* to move my business here, I'd like the two big, light rooms behind the cracker workshop.'

'Impossible. I'm afraid that's where the museum will be,' Silas told her. 'And surely you will only need warehouse space for packing, which would be better located in one of the outbuildings?'

'I could sell to the public too,' she said. 'And anyway, you should close down the cracker factory and lay off all those geriatrics, because it's a dead loss. Use the space for something more lucrative.'

'Most of the workforce are younger than me,' Silas said, looking at her coldly.

'I suppose we do all seem old to you, dear,' Mercy said gently, 'but we don't feel it, or want to stop working, and we're determined to make the cracker factory a success.'

Lacey had stopped listening. 'If the cracker stuff was got rid of, I could have a shop front there by the entrance, in prime position,' she mused.

'What exactly is it that you're selling?' Mercy asked, and I could see from Randal's expression that this *wasn't* a question he'd wanted asked.

'Party supplies,' he said quickly. 'Everything you need, in one big box.'

'Oh, yes. I suppose that follows on from your parents' fancy goods shops,' Mercy said.

Lacey glanced defiantly at Randal. 'My parents own the All Thrills stores and *my* business is called Instant Orgy,' she announced.

Silas inadvertently swallowed a piece of salmon the wrong way and it was his turn to choke.

I gently patted him on the back while Mercy said faintly, 'Instant . . . *orgy*?'

'That's right, I supply everything you need for the orgy of your choice for two or more people – any number, any fantasy. There's S&M, Naughty Nurses, Transvestite – that's proving popular, though I think they just have an orgy of dressing up and trying on wigs and make-up – and I'm developing one or two other lines. I think my Bondage in a

Box will really pull in the *Fifty Shades* punters. People are surprisingly shy about shopping in person for what they want,' she added, matter-of-factly.

Mercy and Silas were both now staring at her as if she'd just confessed to a little light cannibalism when she felt like snacking.

'You're very . . . *businesslike* about such matters,' Mercy said.

'Lacey's parents never hid the nature of their own business from her, so naturally she doesn't see it as anything other than a way of making money,' Randal explained.

'It isn't,' Lacey said, shrugging. 'In fact, I find what people want silly and boring, but so long as they're prepared to pay for it, I'll supply it.'

Now I knew about her parents, I could see where she was coming from, but she seemed incapable of understanding that other people's reactions might be different to her own.

'I'm not sure replacing the cracker factory with a sex shop would draw in the visitors in quite the same way,' I suggested mildly.

'It certainly wouldn't draw in the *right* ones, because we want the mill to be a family venue for a day out,' Randal said. 'But there's plenty of room in the other buildings to house your mail-order operation, darling.'

'Not at Friendship Mill there isn't,' Mercy stated firmly. 'Not while I'm alive, at any rate. Your uncle Albert would have been horrified by the mere suggestion, Randal!'

'But times have changed, Mercy,' he pointed out. 'Look, I know this has come as a bit of a shock to you, but think it over, because I don't see the harm in Lacey basing herself in one of the outbuildings. For now, let's just take one thing at a time and concentrate on getting the mill ready to open.'

'I think you and I need to have a talk, Randal,' Lacey said ominously, her doe-eyes going all steely, and after dessert, which she spurned, he took her into the library.

By then she'd retrieved a reluctant Pugsie from the kitchen and was clasping him tightly in her arms. I could hear him snorting indignantly as they closed the door behind them.

'I thought she was a *nice* girl,' Mercy whispered to me, as if they might be able to hear us talking across the long length of the drawing room and through two inches of solid oak.

'She probably *is* a nice girl, just blasé about the whole selling-sex-aids thing. Clearly, it's just another way of making money to her.'

'Perhaps once they're married and she's living here, she'll learn our ways and become a true helpmeet for Randal,' she said hopefully.

'Perhaps she will,' I agreed, though I couldn't see Lacey as anyone's helpmeet, so I thought she'd better not hold her breath.

Chapter 33: Give Peace a Chance

Randal

'I did ask you not to rock the boat by telling Mercy about the sex shop stuff until she'd got to know you,' I said, once we were alone in the library.

'Are you saying there's something to be ashamed of in what my parents do for a living – or in what *I'm* selling?' she demanded, her blue eyes flashing.

'No, of course not, you know I don't mean that. It's just that Mercy, given her age and background, was bound to find it shocking and it'll take her time to adjust.'

'What century is she living in, for goodness' sake, the Victorian one?' she said scathingly. 'Do I take it that even if I'm allowed to run my business from her precious mill, it will be hidden away in some remote outbuilding?'

I looked at her, feeling a bit exasperated, if truth be told. 'There *are* no remote outbuildings; you'd still be in part of the mill. And I agree with her that an Instant Orgy shop in the main part of the mill wouldn't quite fit into the family ethos we're aiming for.'

'Whose side are you on?' she said bitterly. 'You're the

one who wants me to come and live in this godforsaken hole!'

'I do – and Mercy will soon get used to the idea,' I said, with more confidence than I felt. My aunt was infinitely adaptable to new ideas on most subjects, but now I'd seen her initial reaction to Lacey's announcement, I found it hard to picture the Instant Orgy sign over any door on the property . . . unless, perhaps, Mercy's dead body was lying in front of it with Lacey's stiletto footprints across it. And let's face it, I might resent not having inherited the place outright, but I was still fond of Mercy, who'd provided a home base for me after my parents were killed in a car accident.

Lacey's beautiful face was still stormy.

'Once she knows you, she'll love you as much as I do,' I assured her more gently. 'She just needs a little time.'

'I don't think Pugsie likes it here,' she said, stroking the wheezing creature's head.

'I don't know, he seems to have settled in very well, and lots of country walks would do him good. You have to admit he'd breathe better if he wasn't so overweight.'

'He's mummy's ickle roly-poly dumpling,' she said, kissing the dog's black nose with more passion that she'd ever shown to me, and I suppressed an unworthy pang of jealousy.

I was starting to realise I came a poor second in her affections . . . when she actually remembered the dog was there. And if it was out of sight and out of mind with Pugsie, might it also be the same with me? After all, I was going to be spending most of the next three or four months away on foreign trips.

'That horrible, vicious cat will have to go before we come back here again. I hate cats, anyway, and I can't have poor Pugsie terrorised.'

'Pugsie went for the cat first. It was just taken by surprise and defending itself,' I said, and she gave me a look.

'It scratched his nose!'

'But they seem to be getting on all right now,' I pointed out.

'I think that Tabby woman and her cat are both weird and I hope they're long gone before we're married, though I still won't want to live here all the time. It's not like how I imagined it would be.'

'What's the matter with it?' I said, surprised. 'I know it's not huge, but—'

'I thought you meant it wasn't a huge *stately home*, not that it wasn't a huge *house*. For a start, I expected it to have enough space for your old relatives to have apartments out of the way, so we didn't have to see them all the time.'

'I did tell you it was just an extended farm.'

'Yes, but you said it had a *moat*.'

She cast a disparaging look around the library, with its panelling and the painting of a severe-looking female Victorian Marwood over the fireplace. 'I'd have to make a lot of changes, even if I was just coming here for weekends. All this dark wood and the little rooms are oppressive.'

'Come on, Lacey, you can't call the drawing room or the kitchen oppressive – they're huge! And this library is a decent size, while the orangery off it could be made into a lovely garden room.'

'I'm not into gardening,' she said, as though I'd been trying to hand her a spade and a pair of secateurs.

'You haven't even seen all of the house yet, because you wanted to go out and meet your friend.'

'What I really needed was a drink,' she said. 'You might have warned me about that, so I could have brought my own.'

I decided not to try to explain why bringing her own alcohol would have offended Silas and Mercy. 'I go to the pub in the village sometimes when I'm here and meet Jude Martland, but I can manage fine without a drink for a couple of days if I have to.'

'Oh, so I'm an alcoholic now, too?'

'Of course not, darling,' I said, putting my arm round her, which she immediately angrily shrugged off. 'Look, tomorrow I'll show you the rest of the house and you can see there's lots of room. My bedroom and sitting room are over this wing, so when we're married you can get away a bit if you want to.'

'I suppose we'll need a chaperone to go round the bedrooms with us,' she said moodily.

'No, I don't think Mercy would go that far.'

'How about we buy a nice modern house somewhere nearby and divide our time between there and London, until you inherit?' she suggested, brightening at the thought.

I sighed. 'I love it here and I hoped you would, too, though I suppose it does seem odd starting married life in a house that belongs to someone else. But I'm sure Mercy would be happy to sit back and let you take over the reins of the housekeeping, if you wanted to.'

Actually, I wasn't sure Mercy would ever slow down and

take a back seat on *anything*, but Lacey wasn't interested anyway.

'Why would I want to do that?' she said blankly. 'I'd like her to move out and your uncle with her, but then I'd have to hire a housekeeper.'

'Lacey, try and give the place – and Silas and Mercy – a chance, will you? It's a long time till our wedding in the New Year and we can sort things out so everyone's happy by then,' I suggested. 'The mill will be open, I'll be managing it and I've already got Mercy's agreement that if the cracker business hasn't taken off by Christmas, we can change it to something more lucrative.'

'I suppose so,' she sighed reluctantly. 'But anyone in their right mind would have shut the cracker factory down and retired all those wrinklies long before now. It's ridiculous employing ex-cons anyway, especially having one of them living in the house. I wouldn't trust that Tabitha woman as far as I could throw her.'

'I admit when I found out I had my doubts about it, too, but I'm making sure she doesn't cheat my aunt in any way and she knows I've got my eye on her.'

'Your aunt seems to like her. You'd better make sure she doesn't worm her way into cutting you out of your inheritance.'

'She wouldn't do that. She has money of her own, though, that she can please herself what she does with, like providing for her ward, Liz.'

'Yet another person cluttering up the house,' Lacey said.

'She's at boarding school, so she's only here for part of the holidays. She stays with friends quite a bit,' I told her, but she looked unconvinced.

I hadn't expected Lacey's first visit to be like this, but I hoped by the New Year things would somehow have worked out, with a bit of give and take on all sides.

'I could do with a drink *now*,' Lacey said.

'You can have one tomorrow: tonight you'll just have to make do with coffee,' I told her firmly. 'And be nice to Mercy: she wants to love you, so just give her a chance!'

Chapter 34: On the Tiles

Q: Why are Christmas trees like bad knitters?
A: They keep losing their needles!

I breakfasted early with Mercy, who'd bounced back somewhat from the shocks and revelations of the previous evening.

'I'm sure Lacey – and probably Randal, too – think I'm very old-fashioned to have been shocked by how she makes her living, but I can assure you that my late husband would have been adamant that nothing like that should be associated with Friendship Mill,' she said, thickly spreading a slice of toast with lime marmalade to replenish all that energy she constantly burned off.

I was scraping a smidgeon of Marmite onto mine, a childhood pleasure recently rediscovered.

'I'm not shocked, particularly,' I said, 'though I was *surprised* – especially when she suggested opening a shop in the main part of the mill. She couldn't seem to see how inappropriate that would be for the sort of family venue we're aiming for.'

'But at least dear Randal did,' Mercy said. 'Of course, I

entirely understand and applaud Lacey's desire to continue to have her own business, but perhaps when she's thought it over, she could sell something less . . .' she struggled for the word and gave up, '. . . something with more general appeal, like children's party supplies.'

'I think that's already quite a crowded market. But she didn't really sound that keen on relocating it here anyway, did she? So perhaps she'll leave it in London with a manager in charge and commute up and down when she has to.'

'Yes . . . I suppose that would be one solution,' agreed Mercy doubtfully. 'Well, we'll just have to wait and see how things go on, but I'll be very glad when Randal has completed his current assignments and is living under this roof again, because I don't like to see him so thin. He's had no time for his digestion to recover since he was so dreadfully ill after that cruise, and he needs good home cooking.'

As if he'd heard the mention of food preparation, Pye, closely followed by Pugsie, came in through the cat-flap. This morning had been a repeat of the day before, with the little dog put out of Lacey's bedroom at dawn, for someone else to cope with. She was not an early riser. Mercy said she didn't eat breakfast and it had been after nine before she came down yesterday, which to her was halfway through the morning.

'And Bradley said that if Lacey's dog messed in his garden, he'd turn it into a pair of mittens,' I told her, remembering. 'Of course, he didn't mean it, but he's very proud of the knot gardens, isn't he? Always out there, snipping away.'

'Yes, he does keep them beautifully and, of course, after working on them for so long, he considers them his own,' she agreed. 'I'll get Randal to go out and check, after he's had his breakfast.'

I'd been about to volunteer, but this seemed an excellent plan to me.

'He should be down soon, so I'll put some bacon and eggs on for him. Then I'm going to Merchester again, for the Friend who gave us the sewing machines has obtained two more and I thought Randal and Lacey might like the opportunity to wander over the house on their own in my absence . . . so long as they don't disturb Silas. You could come with me and see your friend, if you wished?'

'I'd better not, because her husband has just come back from Dubai and it might be tricky since he's unreasonably jealous about her having friends, especially me.'

'Jealousy is a terrible thing,' Mercy said sympathetically.

'Job and Freda are going to Southport this morning, so I'm going with them, though we'll split up and do our own thing once we've got there.'

'That sounds fun,' she said. 'And if you should have time, there's a sewing shop there that quite often stocks old sewing machine needles and that kind of thing.'

'Write me a list with the address, and I'll see what I can do,' I promised.

Job, who had earlier prepared Silas's tray and taken it through, now returned with the remains and condescended to have a cup of coffee with us, brushing invisible coat-tails aside before sitting down.

'Mr Silas is as stiff as a board this morning,' he informed us. 'His pills are running low, too, so I have the prescription with me to get more in Southport.'

'Poor old Silas,' Mercy said sympathetically. 'Tabby says

she's going to Southport with you and Freda later, so I hope you have a lovely day.'

'Yes, and I believe you're coming to the Auld Christmas with everyone tonight too, Tabby, so we can properly celebrate,' he intoned in his usual fruitily melancholic way.

'Celebrate?' Mercy said.

'My untagging and the freedom to go out in the evening,' I explained. 'Everyone's going early for a pub meal, so I thought I'd join them, if you didn't mind my missing dinner?'

'No, of course not: the weekends are your own and you must do as you like in them,' she said. 'I'll do my best to get to know Lacey better since, if she's to marry Randal, we must learn to love one another.'

'Mr Silas said she was a brazen hussy,' remarked Job.

'Oh dear!' she said. 'But I'm sure he didn't mean it, he was just crotchety from the rheumatism.'

I could hear sounds of Randal's heavy footsteps approaching, so telling Job I'd be down at the garages by the mill shortly, I fled to my room to get ready.

I had to go back through the kitchen to get out, of course, and by then he was eating breakfast, fondly watched by his aunt. Pugsie was drooling on his feet, but Pye was ignoring him.

'Hi, Randal,' I said cheerily and he gave me that look of deep suspicion from under his thick, fair brows.

'Where are you off to so early?' he asked.

'Out,' I replied like a teenager and, taking the shopping list from Mercy, made my escape.

It was almost five when I got back, but Silas and Mercy were only just having tea, having delayed it because Randal and

Lacey had gone off again somewhere while Mercy was out and she'd waited for them to return.

She'd clearly pushed the boat out with tea, too, for there was an iced cake and thin, smoked salmon sandwiches in brown bread. Since she looked a little forlorn, I joined them and showed her the things I'd purchased from her list.

'And I came across this shoebox full of old sewing machine shuttles and spools in a junk shop, so I bought it.'

'Well done,' she enthused, examining my find. 'They're bound to come in useful.'

My appetite, sharpened by the Southport sea breezes, was up to the challenge of eating more than my share of the sandwiches, and Pye would have helped, if we'd let him – as would Pugsie, who seemed to have been forgotten by his mistress again.

I knew Randal and Lacey had finally returned, because his car was there when I set off for the pub later.

A light rain had begun to fall, so Phil went up in Bradley's car with Lillian and Joy, while I was a passenger with Freda, Job and Dorrie Bird in the estate.

Dinner at the Auld Christmas was a very excellent pot pie with buttered carrots, followed by raspberry jam roly-poly pudding and custard. I wasn't sure I'd be able to walk back to the car after that, in which case they'd have to roll me out, like a barrel.

By now I was starting to recognise some of the regular customers – not to mention Nancy Dagger's ancient father-in-law, Nick, who was usually seated in his antique hooded wooden chair before the fire.

We'd just begun a game of dominoes (Bradley cheats by

hiding them up his sleeves, so the others made him roll them up before we started), when Guy walked in, together with a very tall, heavy-set man and a woman with black hair, who Lillian and Joy told me were Guy's brother, Jude, and his wife, Holly.

'Mercy said they were all invited to Old Place for lunch tomorrow,' I said. 'She didn't think Guy was home this weekend, though.'

Of course, *I* might have known, had I bothered looking at his messages while I was in Southport, but I hadn't. I'd only turned the phone on briefly, to see if there was anything from Emma, which there hadn't been. I always worried when Des was home and she went quiet . . .

'Holly came up here from an agency to house-sit and look after the animals one Christmas and she and Jude got together,' Dorrie explained. 'Now they've got a little baby boy, though the poor lass had a couple of disappointments first. Still, all's well that ends well.'

'There are Martlands all over Little Mumming,' Joy said in her prim, upper class, cut-glass accent. I think she'd been doing it so long she couldn't talk any other way, though Lillian told me she was originally from Birmingham.

'There's Jude's aunt Becca at New Place, Mercy's friend – you've probably met her more than once already.'

I nodded.

'And Becca's brother, Noël, at the lodge, with his wife, Tilda – she was a TV cook years ago, they say.'

'I remember her cookery programmes. Black and white, they were,' confirmed Freda. 'But then that Fanny Cradock took over. She led that poor husband of hers a sad life.'

'Who, Tilda?' I asked, startled.

'No, Fanny Cradock,' replied Freda. 'It was "Johnnie do this" and "Johnnie do that".'

'Jude's niece stays with them a lot, too, because her parents work abroad . . . but she's away at boarding school like Liz,' Joy said. 'Only she'd be a year or so older.'

'I met her at the Pace-egging and she seems a nice girl,' I said.

'That Guy's trying to attract your attention,' Phil told me, putting down a tile.

I glanced across and Guy waved and made gestures at his glass. I shook my head and turned back to the game, suspecting that there had been some sneaky tile shuffling while my back was turned. It had quickly become clear that they were all at it.

Guy, unrebuffed, brought his drink across and sat down next to me on the end of the bench seat. 'Don't you ever answer your text messages?' he asked. 'I sent you a whole load earlier, because I wanted to see you while I was up.'

'No, but you're seeing me anyway,' I pointed out.

'But not alone. And presumably since you're out in the evening you've got rid of your tag, so that gives me much more scope . . .'

He didn't say for what, but his dark eyes, gleaming with laughter, were inches from mine . . . and so was the rest of him. His aftershave, subtle but pervasive, was trying to pull me into his force field.

Then Bradley called my attention back to the game and we finished that one and started another. Guy continued to buzz around me like a wasp, trying to get my attention. I think he was flirting, but it's not something I've had a lot of practice at.

'You're so beautiful, like a Red Indian princess,' he said, at one point.

'I'm not beautiful and I get my colouring from my father.'

'Who *was* your father?' he asked.

'An actor. He's dead now,' I said shortly. His family still didn't know a thing about me, and that's the way Mum had wanted it to be.

'What was he—' he began, then broke off with an exclamation. 'Good God, it's Lacey Bucknall – what's she doing here? And with Randal Hesketh, of all people!'

Lacey's red-gold hair seemed to flame in the dark, cavernous room and her short green dress clung to her figure like a second skin. She suddenly reminded me of Jessica Rabbit from a film I'd seen in prison.

'Do you know her?' Dorrie asked him, interested. 'Randal's brought her for the weekend to meet the family and see the place.'

'Now I come to think of it, Holly did say something about Randal getting engaged and that the Mote Farm lot were coming to lunch tomorrow,' he said, and then an unholy smile crept over his mobile face.

'Oh, don't tell me he's introduced *Lacey Bucknall* as his future bride to Mercy Marwood? I wish I could be a fly on the wall when she and old Silas find out what her parents do for a living – not to mention her own company.'

'What do you mean?' Lillian asked, puzzled. 'We know she's got a mail-order business that she might relocate to the mill when they're married, because we heard her say so when he brought her down to look round.'

'Her parents own the All Thrills sex shop chain,' he said.

'Bit downmarket, those,' sniffed Lillian.

'Well, you're the expert,' said Joy.

Lillian snapped, 'Oh yes, Little Miss Butter-wouldn't-melt, like you've never been in one!'

'I hate bloody women,' Bradley muttered morosely into his beer.

'Now, Brad, you know you don't mean that,' Dorrie told him severely. 'You'll only get depressed again if you start off down that track.'

'I'm a miserable sinner,' he said gloomily, 'but you and Lillian and Joy are all right, really.'

'Mercy knows all about it,' I told Guy. 'And Lacey can't help what her parents do for a living, can she?'

'Maybe not, but did she tell Mercy that her own mail-order company was called Instant Orgy? Sells sex party supplies.'

The others were dumbfounded by this news.

'I don't think that sounds at all the thing for Godsend,' Job intoned deeply and mournfully.

'I can see *you* knew,' Guy said to me, 'so presumably Mercy does, too? I bet she kicked up a fuss.'

'It was a bit of a shock and the dust is still settling,' I admitted.

He grinned again, maliciously, then got up with his drink and sauntered over to the bar. Lacey didn't seem that overjoyed to see him, eyeing him warily over her glass.

'Are we *ever* going to finish this game of dominoes?' grumbled Phil, and we turned back to it again. Bradley had definitely done something sneaky with the tiles while our attention was elsewhere.

There was a lot more concentrated slapping down of tiles, until Joy nudged me.

'That Guy's coming back again – but I bet it's not because

he wants to introduce you to his relatives. He may have his eye on you, but you're an ex-con like the rest of us and he's just after a bit of fun, you mark my words.'

'He'll have to find it with someone else, then,' I said. 'I'm not a fun kind of girl at the best of times and anyway, I'm not looking for romance.'

'Safer that way,' Brad agreed. 'Gardening and making crackers, that's all I want to do.'

'And cheating at dominoes,' Lillian said pointedly.

'Who, me? I never did,' he asserted virtuously.

Chapter 35: False Start

Randal

On the whole, it had been a trying day.

It had started off reasonably well, when Lacey found that my bedroom suite occupied the whole upstairs of the east wing, with a sitting room, bedroom and en suite bathroom. It had once been my uncle and aunt's, but on his death she'd decided that she'd like a smaller and cosier room and turned it over to me.

Lacey cheered up a bit and remarked that, like the rest of the house, the décor of the bedrooms needed dragging into the current century, but at least we had enough bathrooms, unlike a lot of old houses she'd visited.

'Though someone else is sharing *my* bathroom,' she added.

'That's probably Tabby, because it's the nearest to her rooms, just up the old backstairs.'

'Well, I don't like sharing one, especially with the help.'

'Tabby is Mercy's PA, so I don't think you can really describe her as the help,' I said mildly.

'She's an employee and an ex-prisoner, so she's not the type I really want to mix with socially, let alone having to share my bathroom with her,' she snapped, which reminded me of how she treated her long-suffering housekeeper, Maria.

'Mercy constantly invites all kinds of people to dinner, or to stay, so when we're married you'll just have to adjust to having random strangers from all walks of life around,' I told her a bit shortly, because this snobbish streak was not a side of Lacey that I found endearing.

'If you'd seen some of the ghastly places abroad I've had to put up with, you'd be grateful to have a bathroom at all,' I added. 'But if sharing one with Tabby really offends you, then Mercy's is just along the passage a bit and you could use that instead.'

Seeing I was looking cross she slipped her hand in my arm and smiled up at me beguilingly, her wonderful blue eyes glowing. 'I don't mean to be difficult, darling – and now we've seen the rest of the house, let's go out for a while, just you and me,' she coaxed.

Unfortunately, Lacey had insisted we head for a huge shopping mall her friend had told her about, where she could buy a particular handbag at a cut price. I don't know why she was so pleased about it, because it looked like a satchel to me. And those big retail outlets were hell on earth, so far as I was concerned.

Then Lacey wanted to stop on the way back for a drink and to call her friend to tell her about the handbag while her mobile still had a signal, so it was getting close to dinnertime when we got back.

She only belatedly remembered Pugsie when we were going up to change, but he was where I thought he would be: in the kitchen with Mercy, who was cooking.

'Something smells good,' I said, giving her a hug and kissing her cheek.

'Kedgeree – but I haven't spiced it up too much, because I know you're still trying to keep to a fairly bland diet,' she said, looking rosy and pleased.

'I'm a lot better, just still a bit cautious.'

Tabitha's big, black cat oozed through the flap and fixed me with those strange odd eyes. I blinked first.

'Sorry we didn't let you know we would be so late,' I apologised.

'That's all right, Randal. I know you young people like to get out and about, and Tabby kept us company at tea. She and Silas are fine-tuning the plans for the museum displays – the project has brought him quite out of himself!'

'Yes, she's become quite indispensable, hasn't she?' I said drily, but I was angry with myself, really: I should have been there, discussing the museum and the rest of the mill redevelopment, but instead I let Lacey lure me away to that blasted mall.

'Where is Tabby? Shouldn't she be giving you a hand with the cooking?'

Mercy looked surprised. 'She often does help me cook, but it's not part of her job and the weekends are entirely her own. But she's such a sweet, helpful girl that I forget she isn't part of the family.'

'I hope you'll soon feel the same way about Lacey,' I said, a bit stiffly.

'Oh, I'm sure I will,' she agreed. 'Such a beautiful girl, isn't she? And very enterprising, for someone so young.'

I thought we'd better avoid the discussion of Lacey's particular enterprise right then, so I asked, 'Can *I* do anything to help?'

'You could lay the table in the parlour for me. There'll be four of us, because Tabby will be out.'

'Oh? I expect she's making the most of having her tag off and her curfew removed.'

'It was most irksome for her, but she said it was wonderful being able to take a little walk in the dusk last night with her sweet kitty, and watch the bats flying.'

'I bet it was,' I said, and the sweet kitty gave me another of those looks.

At dinner Lacey put herself out to be charming to Mercy and Silas, and asked all kinds of questions about the history of the house, though then she blew it by glazing over with blatant boredom once Silas really got going on the subject.

He's not stupid, so he soon clammed up and then went back to his rooms afterwards, without waiting for coffee.

After that, it seemed like a good idea to remove Lacey from the scene for a bit, so we drove up to the Auld Christmas in Little Mumming, which had lots of old-world charm as well as good beer, though something loud and modern would probably have cheered Lacey up more.

It was full when we went in and the first person I spotted had to be Tabitha, playing dominoes at a table with some of the cracker factory workers – and sitting right next to her was Jude Martland's younger brother, Guy. He was leaning forward to whisper something intimately into her ear, but her face was just as secretive and shuttered as ever, under that heavy, dark fringe.

We found Jude and his wife, Holly, at the bar, so Guy had probably walked down from Old Place with them. I introduced Lacey and Jude gave her his usual lowering look under his heavy brows, which meant nothing; it was just his way. Holly smiled at Lacey and said they'd walked down for some air, since Becca had volunteered to listen out for the sleeping infant.

I wasn't sure I'd entrust anything non-equine to Becca Martland's care, but they seemed happy enough.

'Here's Guy,' Jude said. 'We weren't expecting him this weekend, but he keeps turning up like a bad penny.'

'I heard that,' Guy said darkly. 'Hi, Randal – and, Lacey, what a surprise! I wasn't expecting to see *you* here.'

'You know each other?' asked Holly.

'Everyone's bound to meet on the London party circuit at some point,' Lacey said unenthusiastically, so I deduced that she didn't like Guy much. She flashed her huge ring at him. 'Randal and I are engaged.'

'So I've been told – congratulations!'

'Thanks,' I said. 'We're going to be based up here when we're married – have you heard about the plans to redevelop Friendship Mill?'

'It's been mentioned, but I wasn't paying much attention,' he confessed, with a charming smile – charm just naturally ooze out of Guy, but you wouldn't want to trust him further than you could throw him. Maybe that was an asset in international banking.

'I should think your aunt is over the moon at the prospect of having you both living at Mote Farm . . . and presumably you'll be moving your business up here?' he added to Lacey, in what I could only think was a pointed way.

'Mercy's delighted, of course,' I told him repressively.

'I'm sure she is, and it'll be great having you around all the time,' Jude said. 'Won't it, Holly?'

'As to that, nothing's been decided yet,' Lacey said.

'No, I wouldn't have thought being stuck in the middle of Lancashire redeveloping a mill would be your kind of thing, Lacey,' Guy said. 'I don't see you as a clog-and-shawl kind of girl.'

'Well, you don't know me at all really, do you?' she said, and then seeming to lose interest in him, turned her shoulder and started asking Holly if she'd visited the shopping mall we'd been to.

Guy headed back to join Tabby and the others again, so it looked like she might be the draw that was making him spend so many weekends at Old Place recently. I hoped someone had warned her what he was like . . . I mean, not that I cared if she lost her heart to him and then got dumped, but it would upset Mercy, now Tabby had wormed her way so far into her affections.

Chapter 36: Charm Offensive

Q: Did you hear about the man who bought a paper shop?
A: It blew away.

'I don't think that fiancée of Randal's was pleased to see Guy, though he's certainly turning on the charm,' Dorrie said, critically observing the group at the bar. 'Maybe she's one of his past flings?'

'I don't *think* so,' I said, though the way he'd made a beeline for the beautiful Lacey the moment she'd appeared had brought home to me just how little his flirting meant. 'His name was mentioned at dinner last night, but she said she'd only met him once or twice in London.'

'Hey up, luv, he's on his way back,' she warned, nudging me with a sharp elbow.

Guy plumped himself down next to me, eyes sparkling wickedly, and I edged away slightly. He looked about as beautiful and trustworthy as a rattlesnake.

'Reading between the lines, I gather the new bride-to-be hasn't been an unmitigated success with Mercy and Silas so far?' he said, raising one dark eyebrow quizzically. 'But then, she and Randal are an unlikely pairing in the first place.'

'I don't see why, except that he's quite a bit older than her,' I said.

'There's the whole Quaker thing, too. His mother lapsed after she married, but enough's still rubbed off to give him a bit of a puritan edge, according to Jude. They're old friends.'

'I don't know either of them well enough to judge, but he can't be that much of a puritan, since he doesn't seem bothered by what line of business she's in,' I said.

'I used to know Lacey . . . *very* well,' he murmured, looking across at her under lowered lids. She glanced uneasily at him and then turned away and smiled up at Randal.

I hadn't known his stern face could soften like that and found myself hoping for his sake that things would work out, because it appeared Dorrie was right, and Lacey hadn't entirely told the truth about Guy.

'This is going to be entertaining! I think I'll be spending a lot more weekends up here,' Guy said. 'Which means you're going to see a lot more of me, too, you lucky girl! We should arrange to go out and have fun one evening, next time I'm up.'

'I don't do fun,' I said repressively, wishing now I'd never encouraged him by replying to one or two of his text messages. 'This is about as much excitement as I can take.'

'Come on, loosen up, Tabby!' he said, draping one arm along the settle behind me and leaning intimately close, which seemed to be his speciality. 'I could skip the family lunch tomorrow and we could go out together – how about that?'

'You told me your brother likes you to be there. And I'm working.'

'On a Sunday? I didn't have Mercy down as a slave driver.'

'She isn't, I'm going to work on one of my pictures – a papercut. I did tell you I was an artist, as well as Mercy's PA.'

'Did you?' he said vaguely. 'But you can do that any time, can't you?'

'No, and anyway, I *want* to do it tomorrow, whereas I don't want to go out with you.'

'Look, what if I get Holly to invite you to lunch?' he said, as if that was a prospect I couldn't possibly resist.

I shrugged. 'Mercy says I've got an open invitation to Sunday lunch anyway, so – no thanks.'

'I'd give up, lad,' Phil advised, leaning across the table, and I noticed that the others had packed up the dominoes and were getting ready to leave.

'We'll be off then,' Lillian said. 'Are you coming, Tabby, or staying here for a while?'

'Stay and I'll run you back later,' Guy offered. 'I drove down separately from Jude, because I knew Holly would want to get back soon. She was edgy about leaving the sprog.'

'Actually, they left ten minutes ago and Randal and Lacey went at the same time,' I told him and he spun round and looked at the bar where they'd been.

'Sneaky!' He looked disconcerted – and even more so when I got up, said goodnight and followed the others out.

But I didn't find it hard to resist his blandishments, especially not now I'd seen him turning the charm on Lacey, too.

The front of the house was in darkness, so I hoped everyone had gone to bed, though when I went round the side I could see that Mercy had kindly left the kitchen light on for me.

I let myself in – and found Randal there, with the revised plans of the mill and the architect's drawings of what the mezzanine café area might look like, spread out in front of him, weighed down with a plate of chocolate biscuits and a half-empty mug.

He looked up, his hazel eyes narrowing. 'You're back, then.'

'Like a bad penny,' I agreed, taking my jacket off and hanging it on the back of the door.

'I thought you and Guy Martland might be making a night of it – you looked pretty chummy at the Auld Christmas.'

'There is no "me and Guy Martland",' I said icily.

Pye, who had greeted me outside, but then lingered, stuck his head through the cat-flap, raked Randal with a narrow-eyed, disdainful stare, then decided to come in.

'Oh, look, there's your familiar,' he sighed. 'He was here when I arrived, but he gave me one look and then went out.'

'I don't think he likes you very much,' I told him.

'Pfft!' agreed Pye, going to his bowl and staring into it, as if he might really magic up some extra dinner.

'I expect he's picking that up from you,' he observed coldly.

'Except for your annoying assumption that I'm some kind of petty thief out to cheat Mercy, I feel entirely indifferent towards you,' I said.

'Then bring your indifference over here, and explain some of these changes to the plans since I last saw them,' he ordered.

'Like what?' I said, reluctantly drawing closer and peering over his shoulder and a long strand of my hair slithered into his cocoa.

'Sorry,' I said, fishing it out, 'I'll make you another.'

But somehow I ended up making some for us both and

showing him where the plans had simply had to be amended.

'It's sort of evolving organically as we go on,' I explained. 'Like here . . .' I pointed. 'Instead of blocking up the opening through from the cracker stockroom to the museum rooms, we had to fit a fire door, and now it seems we'll need to have a fire escape from the café level to the rear of the building, too. And the lift will have to go *here*, near the front, rather than where we'd originally put it, so there's enough room to turn a wheelchair easily.'

'Right,' he said, frowning, so I wasn't sure that he was entirely convinced. 'But I still think its rash of Mercy to do so much work before the planning permission's been granted.'

'She's certain she'll get it, but she said at least if she didn't she'd still have a much better workspace, producing amazing new kinds of crackers. Have you seen the women's toilets?' I added enthusiastically.

'Strangely enough, no,' he replied.

'No, I suppose not – but they're an absolute *palace*. Dorrie and the other women won't let the men use them while theirs are upgraded, so they're making the disabled toilet cubicle first and they can use that as a temporary measure.'

'There's a lot of money going into this – and if you and Mercy are wrong about the cracker-making bringing in visitors, we'll have wasted some of that.'

'We're not wrong,' I said positively. 'Visitors will love watching the crackers being made and then they'll want to buy some in the Christmas shop, along with lots of other things. It'll all be a big success.'

'*If* we get the planning permission.'

'I expect we will,' I said, then yawned and got up to wash

out the empty mugs. The end of my hair that had been in the cocoa had dried stiffly, so I rinsed it under the tap and wrung it out. I looked round to find him watching me, his expression unfathomable.

'Right, I'm off to bed. Pye, are you coming with me, or do you want to stay here and stare fixedly at Randal for a bit longer?'

'It's OK, I'm going,' he said, giving my cat an uneasy look and rising to his feet with such haste that he narrowly missed banging his head on the low light fitting over the kitchen table.

He was down early for breakfast, too – there seemed to be no getting away from him. But evidently he's not a morning person, because he didn't say very much, though he did look surprised when Pugsie followed Pye back in through the cat-flap.

'Lacey puts him out of her bedroom early every morning,' I explained, 'so I bring him down with me.'

'She has a live-in maid at home, who sees to him,' he said uncomfortably. 'I expect it's a habit.'

'We like the little doggy, don't we, Pye?' Mercy said, dividing a bacon rind between them impartially.

Pye gave one of his lost soul yowls, so I don't think he was in entire agreement.

'This place has become a madhouse,' Randal muttered.

I went to the Friends' Meeting that morning with Mercy, Silas, Job and Freda.

Randal and Lacey were driving up to Old Place before lunch to see Jude's studio – he was quite a well known sculptor – so Job dropped Silas and Mercy off there on our way back.

Mote Farm was wonderfully empty and quiet, apart from Pye *and* Pugsie, who'd been abandoned again.

I had a tuna sandwich for lunch, blandished into sharing some of it with Pye and Pugsie, but then a strangely restless feeling came over me and instead of working on my picture, I decided to go down to the factory and undercoat the second museum room.

Pye and Pugsie elected to come with me and Bing and Ginger appeared soon after we got there, but after a while watching paint dry must have palled on the two factory cats, who vanished again.

I was getting on well, singing quietly and whizzing the paint roller up and down the second wall, when a light, attractive male voice called, 'Tabby! Where are you?'

My heart sank into my Converse trainers, though I supposed it served me right for not locking the door behind me when I came in. But Phil and Bradley had been out by the garages, tinkering with bits of engine, so there hadn't seemed any need.

Guy popped his head into the doorway of the further room and spotted me through the archway. 'There you are! I thought you said you were going to paint pictures, not walls?'

'I don't paint pictures, I do papercuts, and I wasn't in the mood, so I thought I'd get on with this. These two rooms are going to be a museum about the family and cracker making, and I'm dying to get it finished so we can start to set it all out.'

'Fascinating!' he said, coming through and smiling at me, as if sure of his welcome.

'What are you doing here?' I asked, laying the wet brush down across the top of the tin. 'I thought you'd still be having lunch at Old Place.'

'I've had it, but I left them before they got to the coffee stage and now I'm on my way back to London.'

'Well, don't let me keep you,' I told him.

'Ah, but I didn't have to leave for London early, it was a cunning ruse to get a bit of time on my own with you,' he said, coming closer and then suddenly putting his arms around me.

'What on earth are you doing?' I demanded, and I'd have stepped back, except then I'd have been stuck to the wet wall like a bluebottle on flypaper. 'Let go, Guy!'

'But you look so cute with paint on your nose,' he said, smiling down at me. 'Mercy's just told me you're her Girl Friday, too – and a girl who'll do *anything* she's asked to is truly irresistible.'

He closed in for a kiss, but I pushed him away with more force than tact. 'Anything my *employer* wants.'

'How about anything *I* want,' he said huskily, undeterred. 'You're driving me mad and I don't think you even realise how attractive you are.'

'Oh, I do – I'm Mona Lisa and Marilyn Monroe all rolled into one,' I said sarcastically, ducking another attempted kiss, so that it fell on my cheek instead. 'Now, would you mind letting go of me? I want to get on.'

'Why don't you wash that paint off and come out with me for a couple of hours, instead?' he suggested. 'I know a nice, quiet out-of-the-way motel—'

'*Motel?*' I repeated, wondering if I'd heard him right – or even if I'd somehow managed to give him the impression I was that cheap!

'Yes, somewhere we can really get to know each other.' He gave me that confident smile.

'Oh, for goodness' sake, Guy – no means *no*,' I snapped and was just contemplating a spot of violence to release myself, when Pye solved the problem by sauntering over and deliberately swiping his claws into Guy's leg.

He yelled and this excited Pugsie so much that *he* joined in, too, darting at Guy's ankles and nipping them sharply.

Guy backed away, trying to fend him off. 'What the hell . . .?' he began angrily.

'That's Lacey's pug,' I told him, grinning. 'Good boy, Pugsie! And thank you, Pye,' I added. 'Nice claw-work!'

'Mrrow,' said Pye, then fluffing himself up to the size of a panther, he began to stalk after Guy, his odd eyes fixed on him in his most unnerving manner.

Guy picked up the broom that was leaning against the wall and prepared to defend himself.

'If you hurt my cat, I'll kill you,' I warned him seriously.

'I'm not going to hurt either of them, I just wanted to protect myself,' he protested. Then his eye fell on Ginger and Bing, who had now joined the others and he added nervously, 'Why are all the cats staring at me like that?'

'They think you're funny.'

'There's nothing funny about having your ankle ripped open by a monster cat!'

'Serves you right,' said Dorrie, and he swung round.

'How long have you been there?'

'Since the cat took a swing at you and I reckon you probably deserved it, luv,' she said. 'Tabby's a nice girl, not the sort you can mess with. That fool Phil shouldn't have told you she was in here on her own, but as soon as he let me know, I came right over.'

'Thank you, but I was all right, I can take care of myself,' I said.

'God, anyone would think I wanted to rape the woman, not take her out for a drink and get to know her better,' he said furiously.

Then he pulled up his trouser leg to reveal he was bleeding from deep claw marks, though Pugsie's little teeth didn't appear to have left a lasting impression.

'Bloody hell, I've been savaged!' he said, before rolling the trouser leg back down and regaining his temper with an obvious effort.

'Look, Tabby, I apologise, though I'm not sure exactly what for,' he said.

'And I'm sorry you got clawed, though it was your own fault,' I told him. 'Let me see you out.'

'If you can keep this menagerie in here with you, I'll see myself out,' he said shortly.

'Persistent, he is, but he'll be back, sniffing around, mark my words,' Dorrie remarked when he'd gone.

He'd spurned my offer to get the disinfectant from the first aid box and clean his wounds, so I hoped he didn't get blood poisoning.

I gave up on the painting after that and went back up to the house, and while Pugsie snored on my sitting-room hearth rug and Pye drowsed in his fur igloo, I began a papercut of Sleeping Beauty, a favourite theme.

This time she'd be tangled up on an island, surrounded by a shark-infested moat . . .

It was not an image likely to appeal to the greetings card market.

I worked on until Mercy tapped on the door when Randal and Lacey were about to leave, in search of Pugsie, though the little dog seemed more than reluctant to go.

When we'd waved the car off we had afternoon tea, just the three of us again – four if you counted Pye. Bliss.

Chapter 37: An Absolute Cracker

Q: What does the word minimum mean?
A: A very small mother!

Next day I received a bunch of velvety red roses, accompanied by a heart-shaped box of chocolates, which arrived at the house by courier.

They proved to be an expensive apology from Guy, though I was still unsure that he'd grasped quite what he'd done wrong.

The card said, 'Roses red and chocolates too – see, I really do love you!'

Mercy, who didn't know about our little tussle in the mill, was amused and started referring to Guy as 'your admirer,' though she also cautioned me that, joking aside, he had not always proved to be constant in his affections.

'I know, everyone keeps telling me about the time he ran off with his brother's fiancée, so I'm not taking him seriously.'

'I'm relieved to hear it . . . though I suppose even a leopard may change his spots, and this time he might be sincere,' she suggested, revealing herself to be a true romantic at heart.

'It would take more than a bunch of flowers, a box of

chocolates and a bit of bad verse to convince me of that,' I told her. 'Even if I wanted to be convinced, which I don't.'

Nor did I like the idea that Lacey and Guy appeared to have been a lot closer acquainted previously than she'd let on to Randal and Mercy . . .

However, sheer good manners made me walk down to the road later so I could text Guy and thank him for his gift. I added that I hoped his scratches had healed, but since I received a flurry of messages back, he evidently hadn't died of blood poisoning, so I deleted them unread.

I sent him one final one, saying that I expected I'd see him around, Little Mumming being a small place. (Though not, of course, if I saw him coming first.)

Then I went back and ate the chocolates.

During the ensuing days I found myself missing Pugsie, but not Randal, with his habit of glowering suspiciously at me, as if I might pop the family silver into my pocket if he didn't keep an eye on me.

Mercy told me he was returning briefly on his own the following week, before he jetted off to Vietnam, or wherever it was that was next on his schedule, so they could go and talk to the accountants and solicitors and get things onto a legal footing.

'We must make some decisions about the café design and installation, too, in case he's abroad when planning permission is passed,' she added.

'He was looking at the plans and drawings for the café in the kitchen, the evening before he left,' I said.

'Since he's going to invest some of his own money in the redevelopment, then it's only right that he becomes a director.

His moving to Mote Farm and managing the mill will be exactly what my husband would have wanted.'

Then she looked pensive. 'There's just the question of the location of Lacey's business to be resolved . . . but I'm praying about it and eventually I'm sure the way forward will become clear to all of us.'

I only hoped she was right.

Tons of gravel were delivered, tipped out with a loud, swooshing susurration of sound and then spread all over the newly extended car park, which had been edged with a split timber border to retain it.

The procedure produced clouds of dust, but the result looked very good. The three garages near the terrace were screened off with a trellis fence, so that in their free time Bradley and Phil could take their engines to pieces without an audience.

Everything still seemed chaotic inside the mill, but at least the finishing touches had been put to the newly revamped loos, including the sort of driers that blow your skin back like wrinkled gloves, though as Dorrie pointed out, most of them already *had* hands that looked like that.

After lots of trials and discussions, the designs for the first new ranges of crackers were decided, a rather more ambitious start than we'd at first envisaged. But the orders for the materials has gone off, so the die has been cast in more ways than one.

The chosen cracker designs were: Marwood's Luxury Victoriana, in a retro box based on one from the stockroom, containing gold and silver crowns and quality gifts;

Marwood's Magical, a revamped version of the existing ones, with simple magic tricks, plus a magic wand in every box; Marwood's Motoring (Bradley and Job came up with this idea) with wind-up thirties-style plastic racing cars, a fold-out racing course and a chequered flag – and then, the favourite among the workers, Marwood's Musical Crackers, filled with miniature mouth organs, ocarinas, kazoos and penny whistles.

There were also two kinds of small foil tree crackers, one brightly coloured and designed for children, filled with plastic toys like jumping frogs and monkeys that could hook onto things by one hand, while the adult one came in sophisticated silver and black and contained phone charms.

The stockroom was filling with cartons of the old design, so that there would be enough to fulfil all the current orders, but no more were being taken. There was a nervous sense of being on the edge of a venture that could sink or swim . . .

'I expect we'll sell less to some outlets, who like cheap and cheerful, but a lot more to those who are looking for something luxurious and a bit different,' I said encouragingly one day to the others, when I'd just made a totally perfect cracker in under five minutes for the first time.

'Even when money's been tight, people have still pushed the boat out with their Christmas crackers, going by the old catalogues I found in the stockroom,' I added.

'I'm sure you're right, dear,' Mercy agreed, stopping by my bench and examining my latest cracker with an expert eye.

'She'd better be,' Bradley said gloomily.

'Of course she's right,' Lillian told him. 'You can see how much prettier and more interesting all these new designs are, and it's not like they're more difficult to make, is it? Anyway, I like a bit of variety; those cheap ones are monotonous.'

'Lillian's right, a cracker's a cracker,' agreed Joy. 'Outer paper, cardboard tube, hat, novelty, snap and joke: roll them up, glue, tie, embellish, put them in a box – Bob's your uncle.'

It wasn't actually that simple – I'd got in a sticky mess with the glue gun several times while learning, and tying up the ends neatly was the really tricky bit, but all the others could do it in their sleep.

'I think they'll take off like a rocket and we'll end up having to hire extra staff,' predicted Arlene.

'It's possible, especially if we start to develop crackers for wedding favours and other celebrations eventually,' I agreed. 'But first things first!'

I went to another Quaker meeting with Silas and Mercy and I'm getting better at emptying my mind and waiting for something more than inspiration for a papercut to fill it.

And afterwards, I went up to Old Place with them for lunch, because Holly Martland rang me and said Mercy had told them all about my wonderful papercuts and they'd love to meet me.

I'd assumed they'd just included me in the general invitation before from kindness, or maybe prompting from Mercy, but now it seemed they really *did* want me to go. Mind you, I *still* wouldn't have, except that I knew Guy wasn't coming up this weekend.

At first sight, there seemed to be dozens of people at Old Place, which was a large and interesting house. Some looked slightly familiar, like Jude, Holly and Becca, but I was also introduced to Noël and Tilda from the lodge, and Old Nan and Henry, the retired vicar of the parish, who lived in the almshouses.

Then there was the baby, whose name was Hereward, but who was called Herrie. He was plump and very amicable, and was passed around the table like a parcel at a party, but without being unwrapped.

When he got to Old Nan she cooed over him and was reluctant to part with him again, even to eat her dinner. Afterwards, she said I was a bonnie lass, and almost tall and dark enough to be a Martland, which I took as a compliment.

Jude talked to me with interest about my papercuts and said I must go and see his studio, which was in a converted grain mill behind the lodge, and I told him how Mercy had promised me the workshop of my choice when they developed the studios at the mill.

I helped Holly carry out some coffee cups to the kitchen, where she said that Guy had mentioned he'd met me and then proceeded to give me the usual warning about his tricky little ways.

I was starting to think they could save themselves a lot of time and trouble by simply sticking a large sign on his back saying, 'Untrustworthy in Relationships'.

Anyway, her words were kindly meant, so I assured her I'd just come out of a disastrous engagement and the only thing I intended engaging in at the moment was my own work and helping Mercy make the mill a huge success.

While the cracker making was shut down for the May Bank Holiday, Mercy called in the professionals and had the workshop area freshly repainted in white and the grime of years cleaned from the long windows.

I popped in to see how it was looking on the Monday, while on my way for a walk up to Little Mumming, and found it finished, and Bradley and Phil pushing the racks of drawers and shelves back against the walls.

There was still an opaque ceiling of plastic sheeting overhead, which made it feel a bit like being in a cocoon, but I supposed that would have to stay to protect the workshop until the mezzanine floor had been completed.

When I got up to the village I sat and drew the church, the small row of quaint almshouses and the old humpbacked bridge over the rushing stream, then I had a cheese toastie for lunch in the Merry Kettle, before heading up to the top of Snowehill.

I remembered to turn my phone on when I was halfway there and found a couple of brief messages from Emma, saying things were OK and she would catch up with me after Des had left again. I also had a few missed calls from Luke Dee.

I wished my past would stay past and they'd all now leave me alone, but he rang yet again while I was sitting on the edge of the stone monument, eating a Mars bar and admiring the view down to Great Mumming on the other side.

'Hi, Luke,' I said with a weary sigh. 'What is it this time?'

But, of course, I'd half guessed already: he'd finally twigged that Kate was not actually living in Jeremy's granny flat, but in the house, and they were having a full-blown affair. I was only surprised he hadn't realised what was happening sooner, but he was such a dim bulb that I suspected that even now

Kate had arranged the accidental disclosure, because she'd decided Jeremy was a better marital prospect.

'I went over there to beg her to come home, but there was no answer from the flat or the house, so I went round the back to see if Jeremy was in the garden . . . and there they were, just the other side of the French doors, at it like rabbits!'

'Thank you for putting that graphic image into my head,' I said. 'But that doorbell didn't always ring, because the wiring was faulty.'

'You don't sound shocked?'

'That's because I'm not. Things looked more than a bit compromising when I called on my way here to try and find Pye. But I *am* surprised they were so careless, because I always thought she liked having both of you on a string, telling her how wonderful she was.'

He wasn't listening, self-absorbed as usual. 'It was a huge shock to me! And when I confronted them, she said I'd driven her into Jeremy's arms by accusing her of lying about you, so I might as well divorce her because she wasn't coming back.'

'I had a feeling it would all turn out to be my fault,' I said. 'What happened then? I mean, pretend I care what the three of you get up to any more.'

'Jeremy said he was sorry, he hadn't meant it to be this way and he hoped we could stay friends. And then I hit him,' he added.

'I can't say I blame you, really,' I said. 'Was that the end of it?'

'Pretty much, because Kate got hysterical and told me to leave, so I did . . . but if it wasn't for *you*, we'd still be together and none of this would have happened.'

'Look, face facts, Luke,' I told him wearily. 'Even if I had committed fraud, which I hadn't, Kate started the whole ball rolling by contacting that TV programme. No one forced her to do it, or to tell lies. You might like to ask yourself why she was so keen to incriminate me.'

There was a pause. 'You think she wanted you out of the way?'

'Hand the man a coconut,' I said sarcastically, and switched the phone off.

As I passed the almshouses on my way home, Old Nan appeared at one of the doors and beckoned me in, where she regaled me with shop-bought Chelsea buns, stewed tea and a lot of gossip about the Martlands, including the complete history of Guy's jealous relationship with his older brother and how it had only been when Holly came along that the breach was finally healed between them.

'But Guy was always a child who wanted what someone else had got, then threw it away the minute he had it,' she said acutely.

I don't suppose you spend a lifetime being a nanny without being able to put your finger on a child's character! I suspected he hadn't changed much.

Chapter 38: Give Me a Ring

Q: What did the beaver say to the tree?
A: Nice gnawing you!

On the morning of Randal's brief visit, I was down at the mill when he arrived and then he and Mercy were due to go and see the solicitor and accountant, so I knew they'd be out all day.

I thought I could put up with him at dinner, especially since he was flying off on Saturday to Vietnam, followed by another trip to Thailand, so wouldn't be back for ages.

This suited me, but I wondered how Lacey felt about seeing so little of her fiancée.

At the mill, the electricians had finished rewiring and putting new lights and sockets into the museum rooms, according to Silas's careful floor plan of where the lit displays would be placed, so I retouched the undercoat where it had been damaged, without getting any drips on the new floor.

The professional painters were coming in to apply the final coat of the soft, pale dove-grey chosen by Silas and Mercy, so other than waiting for window blinds to be fitted and the display boards and cabinets to be delivered, there wasn't much more for me to do in there.

Mercy had left me a long list of people to call and instructions to give to the various workmen, which I did, then I went on an errand to Great Mumming. Luckily she'd gone out in Randal's car, so I didn't have to outrage Job by taking the estate.

I made crackers all afternoon with the others (we were still completing the last orders for the old ones), until they clocked off at four and went home, but I could see that Randal's big car had returned and was parked at the garages near the house, so I turned down past Hope Terrace and went for a little walk along the lane at the bottom. I wanted to avoid any risk of having to be polite to him over an afternoon tea I didn't really want anyway.

I headed the other way for a change, right to the T-junction with the steep road up the hill to Little Mumming, where one of the rare buses was coming down, brakes squealing wearily as it reached the bottom.

There was a real seat at the roadside just there, a wooden bench weathered a shiny silver grey, and I sat on it to check my phone for messages. I hoped there'd be something more from Emma, and there was: she said Des was off to Qatar on the 11th and she'd ring me for a good catch-up after that.

I had no idea where Qatar was, but presumably they wanted structural engineers just as much as Dubai did.

There was nothing further from Luke, but to my surprise there were two messages from Jeremy! I couldn't think why *he* felt the need to try to involve me in his goings-on, too, but after hesitating for a few moments I opened them.

'*Ring me: I can never seem to get through on this number,*' said the first, while the second read, '*I urgently need to speak to you on a matter of great importance*.'

Importance to whom? I thought, and I couldn't imagine what he could think I needed to hear, but that urgent bit got me in the end and so I did call him back.

He answered at the third ring and I could hear a piano being strenuously thumped in the background, so he must have been giving a private lesson. 'Is that you at last, Tabby?' he snapped. 'Wait a minute, my pupil's just about to leave.'

There was a pause, during which I could hear his voice saying, 'That's the end of the lesson, Joshua. No, I realise your mother's not here yet, but she knows what time it finishes so you'll just have to wait on the doorstep for her, won't you?'

Then the door slammed and he was back.

'Bloody cheek some of these parents have, thinking I'm going to be a childminder, too,' he said. 'That woman's always dumping him here and coming back half an hour late.'

'Well, that's absolutely fascinating, Jeremy, but I didn't call you back to hear that. What did you want? You said it was important.'

'It is, and I'd have come over if you hadn't rung me back today.'

'Oh, you've missed me so much you just *had* to see me again?' I said sarcastically.

'No – it's my mother's ring I've just missed it and I want it back.'

'Your mother's ring?' I echoed blankly. Then the penny dropped. 'Do you mean my engagement ring?'

He'd presented me with the half-hoop of opals and pearls

instead of buying a new one, which at the time I'd thought was a slightly weird measure of his love for me, though later I realised he was just too tight to spend any money.

'Actually, it *wasn't* an engagement ring at all,' he asserted, to my complete astonishment. 'When I told you I wanted you to wear it, *you* were the one who jumped to the conclusion I was proposing.'

'Are you trying to say now that you weren't? But you told me you wanted us to be together for ever and you'd like me to wear your mother's ring, so I can't imagine how else I was meant to take that!'

'That's not exactly the same as asking you to marry me, is it?'

'I don't see how I could have interpreted it any other way, and we told everyone we were engaged, too. We even celebrated.'

'*You* told everyone and I just went along with it, because I didn't want to hurt your feelings.'

'How kind!' I said. 'Mind you, I did think an opal and pearl ring an odd choice, because it was too delicate to wear all the time. I was constantly taking it off, in case it got damaged.'

'I didn't notice it among your things when I was packing them up, though I suppose it could have been in that locked wooden box you're so secretive about,' he said, and I was so glad I'd always kept the key on my ring, so he hadn't been able to paw through the photographs and mementoes of my mother that I kept in there.

'I hope you weren't wearing it when you went to prison and it's gone missing,' he said sharply.

I cast my mind back. 'No, I'm sure I wasn't, because they

made a list of everything I had with me, including my watch and the things in my handbag, and the ring wasn't on it.'

'Then you *must* still have it.'

'Jeremy, after all this time I haven't the faintest idea where it is, but if I can find it you can have it, because *I* certainly don't want it any more,' I told him. 'But if it isn't among my things, then it must still be in the house.'

'Like where?' he demanded.

'I don't know – anywhere, I might have taken it off before I washed up, or done anything else that would damage it. Sometimes I put it in a vase,' I suggested helpfully.

'I'm sure I'd have noticed it by now, so I think you're just stalling, because you don't want to return it,' he said. 'But it's a valuable ring and if you don't come up with it quickly, I'm going to report you to the police for theft.'

'And I suppose Kate would back up your story, wouldn't she?' I said bitterly. 'Luke told me the penny's finally dropped about you two having an affair.'

'Leave Kate out of this,' he said, and rang off, leaving me feeling shaken, angry and worried.

I found the threat of the police terrified me, since I knew at first-hand how easily the innocent could be imprisoned, and now I had previous form there'd be even less chance that I'd be believed.

Lost in thought, I trudged back up the hill. Pye, who was sitting on the wall of the bridge over the moat like a weird heraldic beast, greeted me with a yowl of welcome. Then, seeming to sense that I was in need of comfort, he jumped onto my shoulders and wrapped himself around my neck like a strange fur cape.

I went round to the kitchen, which was mercifully empty,

and made for my rooms. There I ransacked my treasure box without finding any trace of the ring, before carefully sifting through everything else I owned, even checking the pockets of all my clothes.

The ring wasn't to be found.

I realised time had whizzed by while I was searching when Mercy called me into the kitchen for dinner.

'You look rather upset, my dear,' she said with concern as I took my place next to Silas, who was tucking a chequered linen napkin into the collar of his Tattersall shirt. 'Not bad news, I hope?'

Randal, who had evidently been helping her cook in my absence, put the last of the serving dishes on the table, removed a large blue and white striped apron and sat down opposite, fixing his dark hazel eyes on my face with his usual frown.

But despite his being there, I just had to tell someone what was on my mind and said, 'I've had a call from my ex-fiancé, Jeremy. He wanted the engagement ring back.'

'That seems a little curmudgeonly,' she exclaimed.

'It was an opal and pearl ring that belonged to his mother and now he says that when he gave it to me and told me he wanted us to be together for ever he wasn't proposing.'

'But under those circumstances, what else you were expected to think?'

'I don't hold with modern manners,' Silas interjected. 'Wait till you're wed before you live together, that's best.'

'With hindsight, I'm sure you're right,' I told him. 'But Jeremy certainly let me go on thinking we were engaged and talked about getting married, though he was always reluctant to set a date. Perhaps that's why.'

'Whether he meant it as an engagement ring or not, it does sound as if he *gave* it to you, rather than loaned it,' Randal said. 'I don't think he can expect you to give it back, though if it was his mother's perhaps it has sentimental value to him.'

'I didn't actually wear it much, because pearls and opals aren't the most durable stones for an engagement ring and I'd be more than happy to give it back . . . if only I knew where it was.'

'*Don't* you have it?' he asked, with another of the suspicious, searching stares he seemed to save just for me.

'I've no idea where it is. I hadn't even thought of it since I – since everything happened. Jeremy packed my stuff up himself, and I've been right through everything again, and it simply isn't there.'

'Where else might you have put it, dear?' asked Mercy.

'I could have taken it off while gardening, or washing up or something, but Jeremy said he'd have noticed if I'd left it lying about.'

'I can't see that you can do any more than you have, then,' Silas said.

'But he seems to be convinced I've got it and he threatened that if I didn't return it he'd report the theft to the police.' I shivered suddenly. 'I don't want to go to prison again!'

'No, no, dear, we won't let it come to that,' Mercy assured me.

'If you have witnesses who knew you were engaged and were shown that ring while your ex-fiancé was there, then I don't think he's got a case anyway,' Randal said, and I was just about to thank him gratefully when he spoiled it by continuing, 'I'd give it back if you know where it is, though.'

'I've just said I don't,' I replied indignantly, and he raised one fair, disbelieving eyebrow.

'I'll go through all my things yet again later, but that's all I *can* do, so I hope he doesn't follow through with his threat and turn up here.'

'You can leave me to deal with him if he does,' Mercy said firmly, and then the talk turned to the mill and what they'd been doing today, though I could see Randal would rather not discuss it in front of me.

He was even less keen that I was there when Mercy told him over the apple crumble and custard that she and Silas were both still troubled by the nature of Lacey's business interests.

'Not from any prudishness, because the physical love between two people who have committed their lives to each other in the sight of God is a beautiful thing,' she said, and I found my face colouring hotly as I inadvertently caught Randal's eye.

'But making a business out of sex is far removed from that and your uncle Albert would have been very averse to such a thing being based at Friendship Mill.'

'I'd be averse too,' Silas said, between greedy mouthfuls of crumble.

'I have to admit, it troubles me,' Mercy agreed.

'But times change and Lacey can't understand why you feel that way,' Randal said. 'She's already in two minds about whether she'd want to move up here now anyway, because I don't think she'd ever been further north than the Cotswolds and she found Lancashire a very long way from London.'

'It sounded like she was expecting a stately home like Chatsworth, too,' I said helpfully, and got another glare for my pains.

'I'm praying about it, Randal, and I'm going to ask for guidance at a Meeting,' Mercy said.

I don't think Randal was that keen on having such a personal subject revealed to the entire Meeting House of Friends, but he just said sarkily that perhaps she could let him know the outcome – if there was any.

After we'd had coffee in the drawing room, during which Pye tracked invisible creatures across the room, which seemed to unnerve Randal as much as it did me, he went out to see Jude Martland. I searched for the ring again, but drew a blank.

Then, assuming Jeremy still had the same email address, I went into the library and sent him a message telling him that I definitely hadn't got it and suggesting all the places in the house where I might have put it. It was a fairly long list, including a tin can in the garden shed and the pottery dish in the flat in which I kept the washing-up sponge I used for Pye's dinner bowls.

I felt a little reassured by what Randal had said, because I *could* produce oodles of witnesses to my being engaged to Jeremy, some of whom had admired the ring, which was distinctive enough to remember.

And although Randal himself might still think I had the ring, at least he didn't think I could be *prosecuted* for it!

Chapter 39: Sweet Liberty

Q: Who hides in the bakery at Christmas?
A: A mince spy!

Randal came down to the kitchen while I was cooking my breakfast – I'd forgotten he'd said he'd need to start back to London really early.

Despite his protests, I gave him my bacon and fried egg and cooked some more, and when I came back to the table I caught him feeding a bit of rind to Pye.

'Oh, you're friends now?' I asked, surprised.

'I wouldn't go that far, because the way he was looking at me, I was either going to give him the bacon voluntarily, or be mugged.'

'Mmmrow,' agreed Pye, licking his whiskers.

'Well, no more, because too much isn't good for him,' I said firmly.

'You tell him to leave me alone, then,' he said. 'And why isn't he after yours now?'

'Because he knows he won't get any from me, though Mercy is a soft touch, too.'

'I am *not* a soft touch – which you'll discover if ever you even put one foot out of line,' he said disagreeably, and then became entirely monosyllabic: he's really *not* a morning person.

Mercy and I waved him off on his journey (though only one of us felt any regret), and then I went to the library to check if Jeremy had answered my email. And he had: apparently he'd now searched the house with a fine-tooth comb, not to mention the garden shed and greenhouse, and the ring was nowhere to be found – presumably because *I* still had it.

Then there were more threats about reporting me to the police if I didn't return it, so I felt quite grateful to Randal for making me see how hollow they were.

I relayed this to Jeremy, then said the only other thing I could do was come to the house myself and search in all the places I might have put it, in case there was somewhere he hadn't tried.

There was no answer to that one at all, so I hoped that was the end of it.

On Saturday, still slightly softened by gratitude, I thought of poor Randal reluctantly winging his way across the world to Vietnam, Thailand and wherever else in that direction he had to go. I got most of my education from the nearest branch of the public library, and my geography was sketchy to say the least, but I knew it was a long flight.

I'd even less idea where Qatar was, but now that Des had finally left for his three-month stint there, I borrowed the car next day and met Emma and Marco at the Botanical Gardens in Merchester.

While Marco (who was carrying a tricorn hat under one

arm), was happily feeding the birds and guinea pigs in their pens, I asked Emma how she'd got on with persuading Des to go to Relate with her and she opened up about what had been happening at home.

'He's so clever, cutting and sarcastic when he's angry with me that it's hard to confront him in person,' she said. 'So I thought I'd write down what I wanted to say and email it to him, so he could read it on the way back and we could have a serious, calm discussion about it when he got home.'

'What did you put in the email?'

'Just what I've told you, really, about how hurtful I find his jealousy, especially his suspecting I might be seeing someone else. And I said that last time he was back, when he was snooping round checking up on me and even questioning Marco, was the final straw, so either we went to Relate and got some help, or we divorced.'

'How did he take that?'

'I was half afraid it might have made him even worse – and angrier,' she admitted. 'But actually, he was quiet and subdued when he got home and we had a long talk the same evening.'

'As in a *real* talk, not him ranting at you?' I said, and she nodded.

'He said he hated being away from me for such long periods of time, and that's what made him jealous about what I might be doing. So I said he should trust me, just as I trusted him – that's what real love is about.'

I nodded. 'I hope he saw how unreasonably he'd been behaving?'

'Well . . . not entirely, because when I said it was also

perfectly natural to have friends and socialise with other people too, he said I wasn't always wise in my friends.'

'Meaning me?'

'Yes, and I said you were totally innocent and would always be my best friend, so if he didn't like that, then he knew what he could do.'

'Bravo!' I applauded, and she grinned.

'I should have stood up to him a long time ago, not backed down when he turned on the temper and sarcasm. It's just . . . I never much liked angry confrontations and, he was so clever, the way he'd twist my words to put me in the wrong.'

She looked at Marco, who was having a long conversation with a golden pheasant through the netting of a pen, voicing both parts. 'I warned him that Marco was my responsibility, not his – and that I was never going to visit his horrible mother in her nursing home again, either. She hated me from the moment she met me, so it's pointless.'

'A total waste of time,' I agreed. 'So, are you going to Relate when he gets back next time?'

'I don't know – he said realising how I felt was a total wake-up call and he doesn't want to lose me, so things will be different. And he *was* much more like the Desmond I married after that, so maybe things might be OK now? He suggested we might feel closer while he's abroad if we talked every day on Skype, too.'

'Hmm,' I said doubtfully. 'I'm not too sure about that one, because it could be just another way of keeping daily tabs on you, couldn't it?'

'I don't know . . . I think I'll have to see how it goes. I did feel sorry for him when he said he got very lonely and that he'd had enough of being away so much, so perhaps he'd get a job in the UK after this, if he could find one that paid enough . . . Which will be OK if he really *does* change.'

I wasn't sure he would, but at least she had three months to think about things and see how it went.

Over lunch in the café, Marco, who was now wearing his tricorn and bowing a lot, because he was a musketeer, volunteered the information that he was glad Des – whom he'd never called Dad – had gone away.

'We're much happier when he isn't here, aren't we, Mummy?'

'But Des did quite a lot of things with you when he was home, like playing football in the park and taking you to the funfair in Southport,' said Emma.

'I don't like football and when I told him I'd rather go on the roundabout than the go-karts, he said I was a wuss.'

'Perhaps he'll get it right next time and ask you what *you* want to do?' I suggested.

'Or perhaps he won't come back at all,' Marco said cheerfully, and I could see he thought this was the best option. 'Mummy showed me Qatar on the world globe and it was right round the other side.'

As we moved through May, the whole mill was constantly chock-full of whistling, sawing, hammering, drilling workmen. Some days, it was practically standing room only.

Mercy, lively as a flea, was constantly bringing people around – whether from the council, or the planning department, or somewhere else, she didn't say, though some were shopfitters there to give estimates for creating the Christmas shop. Work on that and the café would begin the moment the planning permission came . . . if it ever did.

But as Mercy said, 'We'll crack on and get everything done that doesn't depend on it, but there's no point in fitting out the shop, putting in the lift or constructing the café area without permission to open to the public.'

'I think Randal will be totally amazed when he gets back and sees how much has been done already,' I told her. 'And we've even sussed out some possible staff,' I added, because Arlene had a friend with experience of managing a National Trust shop who'd love to run a Christmas one, and the daughter of one of Mercy's Quaker friends was interested in taking over the café as an organic wholefood enterprise, which sounded promising.

Meanwhile, cocooned by the partition wall and the plastic sheeting, the cracker makers worked on, finishing the last of the orders for the old-style crackers and then, as the new materials arrived, beginning to stockpile the new, ready for the orders we hoped would soon roll in . . .

Liz came home only briefly at half term, since she'd been on a school trip to Paris. She brought back presents – a scarf brightly patterned with fifties-style poodles for Mercy and one with black cats for me – but she said finding something Silas would like was impossible, so she'd simply got him a tin of Uncle Joe's Mint Balls at the local shop.

Mercy told her a little about Lacey's visit, but she guessed there was more to it, so as soon as we were alone, she asked me for the lowdown.

'I could see there was lots being held back,' she said, and added accusingly, 'and you didn't say very much about her in your emails, either!'

'No – well, it was all a bit difficult,' I said, but then, deciding she was more than mature enough to cope with the news of Lacey's business pursuits, revealed all, including that she and Randal had thought of relocating Instant Orgy to the mill after they were married.

'That's not at all the kind of thing Grandmother Mercy would like,' she said severely, before grinning like the teenager she was, and adding, 'It must have been quite funny when Lacey came out with the news that she sold sex party supplies!'

'It was a bit, and Lacey is genuinely baffled about why anyone should object. Randal understands, but of course he wants her to move up to Mote Farm, so he's all for her relocating her business here.'

'But if she's madly in love with Randal, wouldn't she want to help him with the mill, instead?'

'I think that's what he hoped, but clearly she likes her independence. In fact, when Mercy said she wasn't keen on having the business at the mill, Lacey went all huffy and started talking about leaving it where it was instead. She and Randal would have to divide their time between London and Godsend.'

'I don't think that would work, because it's a very long commute,' Liz said. Then she grinned again. 'Grandmother said Guy Martland sent you flowers and chocolates and wanted to court you, but you were a level-headed girl who wouldn't have your head turned by a handsome scapegrace. "Scapegrace" is a *great* word.'

'It describes him very well,' I agreed. 'He's persistent and can be charming – though he's not as irresistible as he thinks he is – but I've been warned he's not serious by practically everyone, including his own relatives.'

'Do you mind?' she asked.

'My pride took a little dent when I realised they were right, but then I'd done my best to put him off anyway. Pye is the only male I want in my life . . . large, vocal and bossy though he is. Now, who does that remind you of?'

'Randal,' she said, giggling.

Liz went back to school again and I think we all missed her, even grumpy old Silas. I began putting a bit more information into my emails to her and described in detail the following Sunday's Quaker meeting, when Mercy actually stood up and said she was troubled in her soul about the ethos of businesses selling sex aids and whether it could *possibly* be something she should allow on her premises.

There was a deep silence after she sat down that lasted for at least twenty minutes. Then a scholarly young man rose to his feet and said that sex within the loving relationship of marriage was of course a very good thing, but the exploitation of sex for gain might not be, which echoed what Mercy's first thoughts had been.

No one else said anything and soon afterwards we adjourned to the annexe for coffee and buns, where Mercy explained a little more about Lacey and the mail-order business, and said she would await heavenly guidance.

Quakers appeared to do a lot of thinking and waiting. Nobody expressed shock, surprise or even disapproval; it was just another matter to be turned over slowly in their minds until the correct answer dropped down, like manna from heaven.

Holly and Jude, with their baby, Herrie, had been invited to take early afternoon tea at Mote Farm. Mercy dug out an ancient wooden high chair, which had been fitted more recently with straps to make the little occupant secure.

Jude had an even healthier appetite than Silas and they competed for the last sandwiches. Pye, from a vantage point under a chair, watched in disgust as they vanished.

We'd brought an elderly gentleman back from the meeting with us and there was some confusion later, because Silas and Mercy each thought the other had invited him, but it turned out by teatime that he'd invited himself.

'Now, Christopher, of course we're delighted to have you, but did you let your daughter know where you were going?'

'I've no idea,' he replied sunnily, taking another iced finger roll, so Mercy went away to telephone.

When she returned she said, 'There was a slight panic, but everything's fine now and they'll collect you soon, Christopher.'

And luckily they arrived just as he was getting sleepy and insisting that he lived there and wanted to go to his bed.

Mercy, unfazed, said he was very forgetful, but always charming, and she'd have invited him anyway if she'd known he'd like to come. Then we took the baby to feed the ducks, before Jude and Holly took him home again. He was a delightful baby . . .

I'd tried to talk about having children to Jeremy once, but he'd said he saw enough of kids at school and the last thing he wanted was any of his own, *ever*.

I'd left it a bit late to get broody anyway, so I'd simply have to settle for a cottage full of cats.

Something exciting happened! By sheer chance I saw that Liberty, the famous London store, was to hold one of their open days, when the makers of all kinds of products could go and pitch to them. If they were successful, Liberty would stock their products.

It was to be in June, so I suggested to Mercy that she should book a slot and go down there with samples of our new crackers, and she did, but she wanted *me* to go with her!

I'd never been to London, unless you count changing trains there when I was on my way to the hospital to see my first fiancé, Robbie, after he was wounded. The thought of it was exciting but scary, though not as scary as having to accompany Mercy to the store.

She'd booked us rooms for a night at a small Quaker club near the British Museum, which was somewhere I'd always longed to visit, so she said if there was time we'd pop in.

Mercy suggested we didn't say anything to Randal at the moment, so as not to get his hopes up. That was OK by me since I wasn't in communication with him anyway, and also I don't think he had any hopes for the cracker factory in the first place.

He was to return to the UK at the end of the month and would bring Lacey here soon afterwards, by which time Mercy hoped God may have shown her the way forward on the Instant Orgy issue.

Unfortunately, opinions among her Quaker friends after the next meeting seemed divided, but Dorrie and Lillian said they didn't know what the fuss was about.

'It's only a bit of fun and people get their kicks in different ways,' Lillian said.

'That might be so, but some of those ways shouldn't be

encouraged,' replied Joy primly. 'What do you think, Tabitha?'

'It seems a tacky trade to me,' I said honestly, 'but I can't say I'm bothered by what people want to get up to, so long as no one is forcing anyone else to do things they don't want to.'

'Well, in *Fifty*—' Lillian began eagerly, but Joy cut her off quickly.

'Let's not even go there!' she snapped, and the subject was dropped.

Chapter 40: Missed Connections

Randal

Vietnam was interesting, mainly because it was a corner of the world I'd never visited before, but the hotel I went on to investigate in Thailand for my usual series was dubious in the extreme – and so was the food. I was careful, but still . . . I was glad to move on.

I was happy that the Vietnam trip wrapped up the *Gap Year Hells* segments, too, though on the whole, most of the disasters I'd found awaiting unwary students were likely to be caused by differences in culture and expectations. And after talking to many of the backpackers I'd met, I decided they seemed to blithely tumble, totally unharmed, from one danger to another.

I'd had intermittent web access, mostly via the ever-spreading internet cafés, and every time I managed to get a connection, Mercy bombarded me with updates about the mill, how helpful Tabby was being, what her Quaker Friends said about Lacey's business interests and much else besides, like a bothersome gnat.

After a long flight home and a missed connection I got

back to my flat in the middle of the night, feeling ill and exhausted, and crashed out to sleep, only to be shocked awake by Lacey several hours later, demanding to know why I hadn't called her.

'Sorry, darling,' I said contritely. 'I didn't get home till nearly one and I'm shattered.'

But even pleading jet lag didn't prevent her dragging me out to a nightclub that evening, though it was the last thing I wanted to do. It was one of her friend's birthday bash and I noticed, through waves of weariness, that in my absence Guy Martland appeared to have become a permanent member of her circle.

Everyone quickly got drunk and noisy, while I sat there quietly over a glass of tonic water, feeling as old as Methuselah and thinking that one minute Lacey was dead set on settling down and having a baby, as so many of her friends were doing, and the next she was a complete party girl and blowing hot and cold on the idea of leaving London at all.

Maybe the ten-year age difference was just way too much? Though then, that always seemed part of my attraction – she said I made her feel safe.

She didn't say what from. Herself, perhaps?

Suddenly, I longed to be back at Mote Farm, with its peaceful routine, good, wholesome cooking – *and* the irritating, sarcastic girl with the cool, lavender-grey eyes and silken curtain of darkest brown hair.

Chapter 41: Spats

Q: What's white and goes up?
A: A confused snowflake.

The first Saturday in June was a balmy sunny day, so that Mote Farm looked its magical best when Randal and Lacey arrived after lunch.

I'm sure both Mercy and I were shocked to see that Randal had lost yet more weight and also looked very tired. By then he'd been home for over a week, so you'd have expected him to have recovered from the long journey.

He seemed pleased to be back again, though, which was more than could be said for Lacey, who was bored and sulky from the moment she stepped out of the car, carrying Pugsie.

The second he saw where he was, he yapped imperatively and then began frantically wriggling, so Lacey put him down and he raced past us into the house, presumably to find his new best friend. I only hoped Pye was braced, ready and on his best behaviour . . .

'Lovely to see you again, dear,' Mercy said kindly, kissing Lacey's cheek. 'And I see you've brought Pugsie – such a funny little thing.'

'He's been a complete pain since the last time he came here,' Lacey said. 'He whined all the way home and then was miserable for days.'

'You're out a lot, so he probably gets lonely,' suggested Randal, following us into the house.

'I can't take him everywhere,' she snapped.

'You used to, when I first met you,' he pointed out.

She shrugged. 'It was a trend, only he got too heavy for the lovely leather bag I got to carry him in.'

It sounded as if Pugsie might have been a mere fashion accessory, for all the endearments I'd heard her lavish on him, and his day had waned.

I hoped for Randal's sake that *his* day wouldn't wane too, though I detected a hint of tension between them, as if they'd been arguing in the car.

I'd have preferred to slope off to the pub for one of Nancy Dagger's hotpot dinners and a game of dominoes with the others that evening, but Mercy asked me to join them and I didn't like to say no.

'I do find Lacey a little difficult to talk to, dear,' she'd explained earlier. 'So I'd be very grateful if you could step in if the conversation gets at all awkward. You could borrow my car if you'd still like to go up and join the others at the Auld Christmas afterwards?'

'Of course I'll stay if you want me to, though I don't think tact is my middle name, really,' I said doubtfully. I'd certainly not been tactful with Guy – though actually that didn't seem to have deterred him for long and he'd just texted me to say he was up this weekend and hoped to see me in the pub later.

And over dinner, I soon saw why Mercy had felt in need of support, because she announced to Randal and Lacey that she'd now consulted her Quaker Friends about the suitability of basing Lacey's business at Friendship Mill.

'I know, you emailed me,' Randal said shortly.

'Well, call me old-fashioned, but I couldn't be happy with it, especially knowing what my husband's opinion would have been.'

Lacey cast her a look of scorn, but Randal said levelly, 'I'm very sorry you feel that way, Mercy.'

'But all may still be most happily resolved,' Mercy told him eagerly. 'For luckily one of the Friends has a small industrial estate on the edge of Great Mumming and is currently constructing two new warehouse units on it. He has no objection to letting one of them to Lacey.'

She sat back and beamed at them both. 'There, wouldn't that be perfect?'

Lacey looked less than impressed. 'Big of him,' she said, 'but actually, since I've got great premises and a good manager and warehouse staff, I've decided I'm going to keep Instant Orgy where it is.'

'Lacey will keep her flat as a London base,' explained Randal rather wearily, so I thought I could guess what they'd been arguing about on the way up. 'I'll put mine on the market as soon as I've handed in my notice.'

'When we got engaged I thought we'd both sell our flats and buy a house somewhere nice, like Primrose Hill. Most of my friends live in London and I'm too young to be buried alive in the country the whole time,' Lacey said.

Mercy gave her a look of astonishment. 'But when you're married, you'll naturally want to be with Randal, won't you?'

'We've been going out together for ages and I've barely even seen him for the last few months. And he'll be off again to Australia at the end of next week!'

'I'm sorry, but that's the nature of my job – and *you* were the one who didn't want me to resign from it, so you can't have it both ways,' he told her, his jaw looking like squared-off granite and his lips compressing into a tight, thin line. There was *definitely* trouble brewing at t'mill!

'I didn't realise how many weeks you'd be away – or that even when you *were* home you'd be too tired to go anywhere,' she snapped back.

'But I don't think Randal has ever had time to fully recover his health after that illness he caught on a cruise,' Mercy said. 'He's usually full of energy.'

Silas, who had been a silent but disapproving listener during this conversation, now said pointedly that he would be glad when Randal was living at Mote Farm, but his expression when he glanced at Lacey showed very clearly that he didn't much care if *she* were there or not.

'Do tell Randal and Lacey about the advance orders we've had for the new crackers, while I clear the table and fetch the dessert,' I said brightly, springing up and clattering the dishes together.

'Oh, yes – and, Randal, we're going to pitch to Liberty's soon and who knows where that might lead?' Mercy exclaimed excitedly, so *that* cat was out of the bag.

Pugsie and Pye were in the kitchen looking hopeful, even though I'd fed them both before dinner and, unable to resist two pairs of beseeching eyes, I tossed them a few scraps.

Dessert was simple: small chilled ramekins of chocolate custard, which Mercy had showed me how to make earlier.

They were really simple and, once the top was sprinkled with a little grated dark chocolate, looked elegant. Lacey refused hers on the grounds that it looked fattening, so Silas ate it.

I offered to make the coffee before I went out and Mercy explained to the others that I was going up to the Auld Christmas.

'Oh, let's go too. At least it's something to do,' Lacey said, which I thought was rude, especially considering they'd only just got there and were leaving the next day.

But Mercy was understanding, as always. 'Yes, of course, do go if you feel like it! You won't want to sit with us oldies and you could give Tabby a lift.'

'OK,' agreed Randal, though I think *he* would have preferred to stay at home.

And *I'd* much rather have driven myself. But there was no help for it, so I said, 'A lift up would be great, but I'm meeting Freda, Job and some of the others, so I can come back with them.'

After a silently simmering trip up, it was a relief to leave Randal and Lacey at the bar and join the others at their usual table. Strangely, it appeared to be *my* round of drinks, but Phil volunteered to fetch them.

There was no sign of Guy, but just as I assumed he wasn't coming he walked in, looking his usual dark and elegant self, kissed Lacey on both cheeks, which she appeared to suffer rather than welcome, then brought his drink over to our table.

Being last one in, I was on the end of the bench seat and had to edge up so there was enough room for him to sit, much closer than I would have preferred. I hoped he wasn't getting the wrong idea again.

But then, I don't think he'd ever abandoned the wrong idea, because although I was trying to concentrate on the dominoes, he kept leaning over to whisper stupid things in my ear, like how adorable I looked and daft stuff like that.

I suppose it must all have looked fairly intimate, because I noticed Randal glancing our way and frowning, though it wouldn't have been any of his business even if I had succumbed to Guy's considerable charms.

But what I found even more disconcerting than Randal's glowers, was the way Lacey kept shifting round on her bar stool so *she* could see us, too – and whenever she did this, Guy stepped up the flirting.

I started to wonder if he was trying to make her jealous. He'd been out with her before, so perhaps now she was engaged to someone else he couldn't resist the thrill of the chase.

'Holly told me you went to Old Place for lunch when I wasn't there – so the least you can do is come tomorrow, when I am,' he said warmly down my ear.

'No, thank you, I've got other things to do,' I said firmly.

'Like what?'

'Mind your own business!' I told him, and he laughed and said I was a hard-hearted woman.

Then he added that he'd better be off and left, blowing a kiss to Lacey on the way out.

She looked less than enchanted by the gesture . . . and so did Randal.

Holly rang me early next morning and persuaded me to go to Old Place for lunch.

'Not because Guy has pestered me to ask you, though of course he has, but I just thought it would be nice to see you again. Perhaps Randal and his fiancée could give you a lift up?'

Mercy and Silas weren't going this time, because they were bringing guests back from the Meeting . . . and on the whole, I'd much rather have stayed with them and shared the delicious thick chicken and vegetable soup that Mercy had made yesterday.

But I liked Holly, so in the end I said I'd go.

Guy insisted on sitting next to me at lunch and was his usual flirtatious self, though he barely glanced at Lacey, so perhaps my suspicions that he'd been trying to make her jealous last night were mistaken.

Old Nan beckoned me over afterwards and said perhaps she'd been wrong to warn me about Guy, because the love of a good woman could be the making of him.

'I don't think I'm either that good, or up for the challenge,' I told her, and Randal, who was standing right behind her, gave me one of his best brooding looks, twitching his fair brows together in a formidable frown.

'Guy's very well off, you know. He works in a bank in London,' Old Nan said encouragingly.

'Are you selling my charms, Nan?' Guy said, handing her a glass of amber-coloured sherry. 'I'm young, solvent and single: what more could a woman want?'

'I can't imagine,' I said, then got up. 'Well, it's a lovely day, so I'm going to thank Holly for a wonderful lunch and then walk home.'

Randal had *definitely* been ear-wigging, because he said

bossily, 'You'd better wait, Tabby, and go back with us. We can't stay much longer because we're leaving for London this afternoon.'

'Thanks, but actually I'll enjoy the walk – but if I don't see you later, have a good trip,' I said.

'I'll walk with you, in case of bears, robbers or wolves,' Guy suggested, and wouldn't be dissuaded, though I was sure the only wolf in the area was him.

Randal's car slid past us as we walked down the drive, with Lacey, looking beautiful but sulky, in the passenger seat.

Chapter 42: Not Waving

Q: What's round and bad-tempered?
A: A vicious circle!

'Not even a wave from Lacey – I feel quite crushed,' Guy said as the car disappeared down the road. 'Especially since I've seen quite a bit of her lately on the London party circuit . . . though just as friends, of course.'

'She didn't look that friendly to me,' I said, 'but that's probably just as well, seeing as she's engaged to Randal.'

Guy laughed, accused me of jealousy and then tried to kiss me, which I'd half-expected, though not out on the open road, and he went all sulky when firmly rebuffed.

'I know you like me.'

'I do like you – I just don't *trust you.* So it's either be friends, or nothing. Take your pick.'

He grinned, as resilient as a rubber ball. 'I could just wear you down by sheer persistence.'

'That tactic hasn't worked so far, has it?' I said. 'And here's the pub, if you want to turn back now. I'm more than happy to walk down the track to Godsend without having to wrestle with you every other step.'

'I'll behave,' he promised, falling into step beside me.

'You'd better, or I'll set my cat on you again,' I threatened, and he laughed.

I thought he'd turn back once we got to the mill, but he said if he was going to have to hike all the way up to Little Mumming, then the least I could do was give him a cup of coffee first.

'You were the one who insisted on walking all the way down,' I pointed out, though I didn't suppose Mercy would mind my bringing him back.

As we crossed the bridge over the stream I saw that there was no sign of Randal's car, so he and Lacey must already have set out for London. But Mercy and Silas were standing near their garage, waving off the elderly couple who'd been there for lunch.

Their car, a venerable old Morris Traveller, wavered past us and negotiated the bridge cautiously, before vanishing down towards the road. Silas turned and began painfully hobbling back towards the house, though Mercy waited for us.

'Guy decided to walk back with me for some fresh air,' I explained when we got there, though I didn't add that things hadn't been as fresh as he'd hoped. 'He's going to have a cup of coffee before he goes back.'

'I think we could find him a little slice of cake, too,' Mercy said, beaming at him. 'I packed up a whole fruitcake for Randal to take back with him, but fortunately I made two and there's over half left of the cut one.'

'Wonderful – lead me to it!' Guy said.

'I think you have more visitors – here comes another car . . .' I said, and then faltered as a familiar Mercedes hatchback turned onto the gravel and crunched to a halt.

'Good heavens, Jeremy, what on earth are you doing here?' I exclaimed as he got out, followed by the even more unwelcome figure of Kate. 'In fact, how did you get this address?'

'I'm afraid I gave it to him when I collected your belongings, as your forwarding address,' said Mercy apologetically.

'I don't know why you're so surprised, because I said I'd come and get the ring if you didn't send it back,' Jeremy said belligerently.

Guy, puzzled, looked from one to the other of us.

I introduced him briefly. 'Guy, this is my ex-fiancé, Jeremy, and Kate, who is . . . well, let's leave it at that,' I said. 'I can't believe you've got the gall to turn up here, when I've already told you I haven't got the ring.'

'Which ring?' asked Guy, interested.

'A valuable old ring that used to belong to Jeremy's mother. She stole it,' Kate told him.

'Now, young lady, you're quite wrong there,' said Mercy firmly. 'Guy, the situation is that Jeremy is demanding his engagement ring back, but Tabby no longer has it.'

'She's stolen it,' insisted Kate.

'You *can't* steal your own engagement ring,' I pointed out.

'We were never engaged, I told you.' Jeremy said.

'Oh, don't be so stupid. We told everyone we were,' I said scathingly.

'So, where is this fabulous ring now?' asked Guy.

'I don't know. I hardly wore it because it was so fragile, so I probably took it off in Jeremy's house and put it somewhere. I've been right through all my belongings twice with no sign of it – and I wouldn't want to keep it even if I did find it!'

'Sez you!' Kate sneered.

Guy looked Jeremy up and down. 'I can't believe you've got the gall to demand your engagement ring back, but I *do* believe Tabby when she says she hasn't got it.'

'And she certainly isn't a thief, so your words are *very* ill-considered, and you should apologise,' Mercy put in severely.

'Let me search her room and then I might believe she hasn't got it,' Kate demanded.

'Who did you say this young woman was?' Mercy asked, fixing Kate with a colder gaze than I knew she was capable of.

'Kate Dee. She's the one who lied about my being involved in that scam and she's an old friend of Jeremy's. In fact, according to her husband, they're now more than friends, so I expect she wants the ring for herself. Is that right, Kate?'

'Leave Kate out of it,' Jeremy snapped. 'Luke's been totally unreasonable ever since you got at him with your lies, and now he and Kate are getting divorced.'

'That all sounds most unsavoury,' said Mercy distastefully. 'I think I'd like you both to go away now and not come back.'

'I'm not leaving without the ring,' Jeremy insisted stubbornly.

'I think you'd better change your mind, because you've definitely outstayed your welcome, and I don't want to have to change it for you,' Guy said pugnaciously, stepping forward and squaring up to him.

'I don't know who the hell *you* are, but I think you ought to keep your nose out of our business,' Jeremy told him.

'I'm a friend of Tabby's.'

'You didn't waste any time,' Kate said to me, and I think there was a trace of envy in her voice.

'Are you going, or do you need more persuasion?' asked Guy, and I thought he'd probably been watching too many action films.

'I'm going, but you haven't heard the last of this, Tabby!' Jeremy told me. He got in the car, quickly followed by Kate, and it roared off, scattering gravel.

'My hero!' I said to Guy and he grinned.

'Yes, indeed. That was such an unpleasant scene that I was grateful you were there,' agreed Mercy, and then added, as a harsh grating noise echoed up the valley, 'Oh dear, I believe they've taken the bridge too quickly and scraped their paint.'

By the time Guy finally left, Mercy was calling him her dear boy and she said, as we stacked the crockery from lunch into the dishwasher, that she thought he might be a reformed character.

'I'm sure he's put all his boyish indiscretions behind him now,' she added, and I decided not to disillusion her because Peter Pan was not about to grow up any time soon.

Then a diversion was caused by the rattle of the cat-flap and the belated appearance of Pye and Pugsie.

Mercy and I looked at each other.

'Oh dear,' I said. 'Lacey seems to have entirely forgotten Pugsie!'

Later, when Mercy rang Randal to tell him, it appeared that not only had Lacey forgotten Pugsie, but she didn't seem in any hurry to have him back.

Mercy offered to return him when we travelled down for our Liberty appointment, but apparently that wasn't convenient to her, so he had to stay here and literally dog poor Pye's footsteps for the foreseeable future.

I was both excited and nervous when we set out for London with our overnight bags and the cracker samples, which looked so wonderful I didn't know how Liberty would be able to resist them.

Job drove us to the station and Freda was to keep an eye on Pye and Pugsie till we got back.

Once we'd dropped our bags off at the club, which was actually not at all grand, but like a little hotel in a Georgian square, Mercy was still brimming with energy, so we walked round to the British Museum.

It was just as wonderful as I thought it would be and Mercy finally had to tear me away so we could meet Guy for dinner. He'd insisted on taking us out when he'd heard about our plans.

He'd chosen a small but excellent Italian restaurant and behaved so charmingly to Mercy that I started to think *she* might be the one in danger of losing her heart to him.

We breakfasted at the club in a communal sort of way next morning, all seated round a long table, then took ourselves and our precious cracker samples in a taxi to Liberty.

The black and white store front looked exactly the same as it did on their website – and totally unlike the nearby modern shops. We joined a queue of others on the same mission as ourselves entering a side door . . . and emerged a couple of hours later with an order!

They'd like to try the Victoriana crackers, but with a Liberty twist to the display box; the adult tree crackers in black and white foil, and Marwood's Magical Crackers just as they were.

When we arrived home that evening, exhausted (or at least, I was, Mercy wasn't flagging much) and exhilarated, to a welcome party of Silas, Pye and Pugsie, we felt like triumphant heroines returning from battle.

Arlene soon had samples of the special Liberty display boxes to send down to them for approval and there was quite a buzz of new energy in the workshop.

Production had by now entirely switched to the new designs anyway, which we were stockpiling as fast as we could make them, before we had to begin on the Liberty special order.

It was just as well that I'd now mastered cracker making, because the way orders were pouring in, things were only likely to get busier!

Mercy was keeping Randal, now somewhere in Australia, in the loop with what was happening by way of emails, though I expect at least half of them instead exhorted him to eat well and look after himself.

And he'd be back all too soon, like a boomerang.

Emma and Marco paid another visit, this time to see over the cracker factory while it was relatively quiet on a Saturday, though some of the workmen were still around.

None of the cracker makers were there, though, so I showed Marco and Emma how to make one myself and then they had a go. Their first attempts were a lot neater than mine, especially Emma's. I thought she was a natural at it.

When we came out, we decided to walk up into the woods

a bit, to where there's a little shingle beach by the stream and Marco played quite happily while we sat on a handy nearby log.

I asked her how the daily Skype chats with Desmond, in Qatar were working out.

'They're a total pain: he expects me to be home and ready to talk to him at the same time every day, and when I'm not, he's angry.'

'I thought it might just turn into another way of controlling you,' I said.

'You were right, because despite what he promised when he was home, he still wants to know what I do every moment of every day, and now he can ask me face to face.'

She looked pensive. 'He says there's a possibility he'll get a year's contract after this and then *we* could go out and live in Qatar too.'

'Would you want to move to Qatar for a year?' I asked, startled.

'Not really. I wouldn't be able to work over there, and Marco would have to fit into a new school, which might not be that easy, though I expect there's an International School.'

She looked at him affectionately as he scooped some kind of water creature up in his cupped hands and examined it carefully, before letting it go again.

Today he was back in the ruff, but I don't think he was anyone in particular, he just liked wearing it.

'I'm trying not to think about it – maybe the year's contract won't happen,' she said.

Back at the house we went into my sitting room, where Marco told Pye and Pugsie all about his theatre group's coming performance of *Alice in Wonderland*, in which he was to play the White Rabbit, while Emma and I were discussing the pop-up illustrations I was working on for our joint book project.

She was fine-tuning the words of the story to go with them, so the whole thing should soon start to come together . . . as long as she didn't vanish to Qatar for a year!

Life wouldn't be the same without her, or Marco, who entertained Silas and Mercy over tea by acting out part of his White Rabbit role.

Oh, my ears and whiskers!

Chapter 43: Christmas Every Day

Q: What's the best Christmas present in the world?
A: A broken drum: you just can't beat it!

By the time Randal finally returned from Australia, the Liberty designs had been approved, the order confirmed and the cracker team were working flat out – and me too, when I wasn't running round on errands for Mercy.

It's odd that summer should be the peak time for making Christmas crackers, but so it is, and once the Christmas shop opened we'd have a seasonal feel to the place all year round.

When Mercy phoned her dear boy, to make sure he had arrived home safe and well, he told her that he felt fine, but he'd advise anyone bungee jumping in the Antipodes not to go for the cheapest option.

She was not entirely convinced about his health, but she'd be able to see for herself the following weekend – and the planning permission was finally passed on the day before he arrived, so we had something to celebrate!

* * *

This time Randal was alone, because apparently Lacey had gone to a friend's wedding in Cornwall and was staying down there for a few days.

This seemed to make him extra morose, which wasn't helped by his not being able to get in touch with her.

'The phone reception must be as bad as here, or she's let her mobile run down and forgotten the charger,' he said, coming back into the drawing room from yet another failed attempt to contact his beloved.

'Or she simply switched it off because she was enjoying herself so much she didn't want to be bothered?' I suggested brightly, and he gave me a glare.

'Here,' I said, handing him a glass of ginger beer and we clinked glasses with Silas and Mercy to toast the passing of the planning permission and the future success of the enterprise.

'*Now* can I have a decent cup of tea and something to eat?' asked Silas grumpily, so I passed him the plate of sandwiches. Since the time we'd tried out a Mexican taco recipe on him, he's been very suspicious and now had a tendency to lift the top off and inspect the contents, but on this occasion all he found was egg mayonnaise, or ham and mustard.

'Did Lacey say anything about Pugsie, last time you spoke?' asked Mercy. 'I thought perhaps she might want you to take him back.'

'No, she didn't mention him, and to be honest, I'd forgotten he was up here, too,' he confessed, bending to stroke the little pug, who wriggled ecstatically. 'Do you mind keeping him a bit longer, if I still haven't spoken to Lacey before I set off back to London tomorrow? I've got work to do before I fly out to India, so I can't have him.'

'No, he isn't any trouble at all. In fact, he's company for Pye, isn't he, pussums?' she said.

'Ppfft!' Pye said disgustedly and stalked off back to the kitchen.

Randal's mind was clearly still elsewhere. 'Lacey wanted me to go to this wedding with her, but I didn't know either the bride or groom, and anyway, I needed to come up here and settle a few details about the café before I go off on my next trip – the last long-haul one.'

'I'm so glad, dear. India, did I hear you say?' Mercy asked.

'Yes, and Nepal, but I'm still waiting for the final itinerary. Filming two programmes back to back has made for difficult scheduling.'

'We'll be so happy when you've finished your programmes and are home for good,' Mercy said. 'And we have some more good news for you: Liberty is going to feature Marwood's crackers in their Christmas window display.'

'I'd love to go and see it,' I said wistfully, 'but I should think we'll be really busy in November, finishing off the last cracker orders for delivery before Christmas.'

'Yes, orders are positively rolling in now, Randal, and it's all thanks to dear Tabby,' Mercy said. 'Her enthusiasm and artistic eye have been invaluable.'

'I haven't had *that* much input, really,' I said modestly, 'it's been more of a team effort.'

'No, I think Mercy's right and it's your fresh eye that's turned things around,' he said to my complete surprise, but then he spoiled the moment by adding, 'That museum's not going to be worth the space it's occupying, though.'

'You wait and see!' Silas said, grumpily.

'Yes, the proof of the pudding will be in the eating,' Mercy told him, and then they went into the library to spread out the plans for the mezzanine area of the mill and decide on a whole lot of details about the seating and kitchen areas.

I don't know why designer's interior sketches all look like space-age walkways, dotted with impossibly slender and elegant people.

I left them to it and went to my sitting room to work on a pop-up page for the book, collecting Pye, and another glass of delicious ginger beer from the fridge on the way.

We had roast duck for dinner and since I'd never cooked one before, I helped with that. In fact, I had to put it in the oven, because it takes ages and Mercy and Randal had taken the plans and gone down to the mill.

She'd left the times written on the back of an old envelope, though: it went in for half an hour on a high setting, then the oven was turned right down and that was it, for about three hours.

Mercy came back in time to roast the potatoes in the fat, while I set the table and then Randal neatly quartered the cooked duck with a large pair of chicken shears.

Over dinner, Randal and Mercy were still full of their plans for the café and the second phase of the development, but Silas was more interested in the fact that he could now get on with finishing the museum.

His rheumatism seemed to be playing him up tonight and he retired to his rooms after dinner, while Randal vanished into the library, presumably to try Lacey's mobile again.

He came back with a brow like a thundercloud, so I assumed he'd had no luck.

'*You* still here?' he said to me, sounding surprised.

'No, I'm a hologram,' I said tartly. 'Do you want me to go away?'

'No, of course he doesn't, dear – do you, Randal?' Mercy asked.

'I thought she'd have gone to the pub,' Randal explained. 'Don't you usually do that on a Saturday, Tabby?'

'I've been to the pub a few times, but it's hardly a habit and I don't always go in the evening, either, because Nancy Dagger does a mean Sunday lunch.'

'I've heard she's a good cook,' Mercy said.

'Your cooking is much better,' I said loyally, and she blushed.

'I thought you went there to meet up with Guy Martland,' Randal said, eyeing me closely. 'Jude says he's suddenly wanted to spend more time with the family since you arrived.'

'Now I come to think of it, didn't you tell me Guy said he'd be up again this weekend, Tabby?' said Mercy.

'I've never met Guy anywhere intentionally,' I said coldly to Randal. 'But he did text me that he'd be up this weekend – and then sent me another to say something had come up and he wouldn't.'

And now I came to think of it, his messages had suddenly dried up, just like Lacey's. Maybe someone had cut the wires between the frozen north and the south of England?

'You *seemed* very friendly, especially letting him walk you home from Old Place,' Randal said, still looking at me narrowly, though I don't know why he was so interested in whether I was having a fling with Guy or not.

'I did *not* let him, I simply couldn't stop him,' I said, with dignity.

'It's just as well that he did walk you home, given what

happened,' Mercy said brightly and then, to my complete embarrassment, described the scene with Jeremy and Kate.

'Guy was quite the hero, then,' he said sardonically, then asked me curiously, 'What did you do with the ring?'

'Nothing!' I said indignantly. 'I haven't got it.'

'Tabby can't remember seeing it since she went to prison,' Mercy said. 'Still, I expect that unpleasant young man she was engaged to will find it somewhere about his house eventually.'

'Let's hope he does, because I certainly don't want my relatives exposed to any more scenes like that,' he said pointedly.

'I didn't know he was going to turn up – especially with Kate,' I snapped back. 'And *Guy* totally believed me about the ring!'

'I don't think Guy's as black as he's been painted,' Mercy said. 'Perhaps he did do a few silly things when he was younger, but he's probably ready to settle down now and I'm sure he's got his eye on Tabby.'

'Then he'd better cast his eye somewhere else,' I said firmly.

'Lacey doesn't like Guy very much,' Randal said. 'But he's friends with some of the people she knows, so she can't avoid him all the time. She said someone should warn you not to get involved with him, because he's a love-rat.'

'I think it's most unkind to call the poor boy any kind of rat,' Mercy protested, then changed the subject by dropping the bombshell that she intended to leave me, Silas and Arlene in charge of the mill at the start of Liz's school summer holidays, while she took her back to Malawi to visit her relations.

She'd already told me, but Randal's jaw dropped.

'*What*? I thought you weren't going to fly long-haul any more?'

'No, I only said I wasn't going to *work* abroad, though this may well be my last trip.'

'But . . . you can't possibly leave Tabby in charge!'

'She won't be managing everything alone, but sharing the responsibility with Arlene and Silas,' Mercy reminded him.

'She'll still be in a position of trust – and I don't think that's a good idea,' he said stubbornly.

'Randal, you really must try to overcome these unworthy prejudices against Tabby, who has truly proved her worth.'

'Thank you for your trust,' I said to her sincerely. 'And we'll all do our utmost to keep things going while you're away.'

'I'll only be gone a couple of weeks, anyway,' she said, 'and I'll always be contactable by email, if nothing else.'

Randal was still eyeing me uncertainly. 'I'll go over the books when I return from India,' he warned me.

'You can check the books and count the crackers till the cows come home, but you won't find anything wrong,' I said.

Feeling I'd had enough of Randal for one evening I wished them good night, but I didn't go to my rooms. Instead, followed by Pye, I let myself out of the kitchen door and wandered through the dark scented knot gardens, with their herbs and rosemary and the sharp tang of box. It was very soothing and totally quiet, except for the occasional hoot of an owl.

I was sitting on the bottom step of the terrace just above the moat when Pye hissed warningly.

'Ill met by moonlight, Titania. There's no sneaking up on you, when your familiar's about,' said Randal's gravelly voice.

'Did you *want* to sneak up on me?' I asked. 'Push me into the moat, perhaps? Only I can swim, so that would be pointless.'

'No, I don't think you're allowed to dunk witches any more,' he said, and then, uninvited, lowered his large frame down next to me.

'Hello, Pye. Are you speaking to me now? What if I promise you a bacon rind in the morning?'

Pye's milky eye seemed to glow eerily. 'Mmrow?' he said, quite mildly, before getting up and sauntering off.

'His allegiance *can* be bought, but only temporarily,' I told him.

'You seem very attached to each other.'

'He was my mother's cat, too . . . which makes him the last living link between us.'

There was a silence while we both regarded the chewed-silver-penny moon, reflected on the moat's surface.

Then he said, 'I trust Charlie Clancy's opinion – he's rarely wrong in his judgement of character – but . . . sometimes I wonder if you were quite as guilty as he thought you were.'

'Gee, thanks, I'll treasure those words for ever,' I said.

'And other times, I think you're a sharp little witch trying to pull the wool over all our eyes,' he said, ignoring that. 'On the make – only I just haven't figured out how yet.'

'I'm going to run off with the entire Marwood's luxury cracker stock and sell it on the street,' I said scathingly. 'Don't be daft. The only money that passes through my hands that isn't earned from my greetings card illustrations, or my wages, is the cash Mercy gives me when I run errands for her. She'll tell you that I always give her the receipts *and* the change.'

'I expect she would, because you've certainly got her under your spell,' he said, turning his head to look at me. The moon silvered his hair, but made mysterious dark pools of his eyes. He put his hand under my chin and pushed it up, bending to stare into my face, as if he could find what he wanted to know written there. He was so close that our breath met and mingled . . . and then our lips touched, fleetingly.

He sprang away and rose in one lithe movement, as if the contact had seared him, and strode off without another word.

'Weird!' I murmured, shaken and staring after him.

'Ppft!' agreed Pye, materialising from the shadows.

Chapter 44: Snowed Under

Q: What do you get when you cross a snowman with a vampire?
A: Frost bite!

If anything, Randal was even more monosyllabic than usual in the morning, so I began to think that maybe last night's fleeting kiss hadn't actually happened. Or at any rate, was accidental, because it had been the merest brush of the lips . . . so it was odd that I could still feel that momentary pressure.

My eyes met his dark hazel ones as he sat at the kitchen table and I looked away again quickly, turning my back so he couldn't see that I was blushing. He was probably comparing my dark ordinariness with Lacey's alabaster skin and red-gold hair, which would light up the room like a bright flame.

Or it would have, if she'd come with him and ever got up for breakfast.

Mercy, who was buttering toast with a lavish hand, told me that Randal had offered to drive her and Silas to the Quaker meeting, but I left long before them, in Mercy's car, because I'd arranged to spend the day with Emma.

It was Marco's birthday and he'd decided on a fancy dress party at home for his six closest friends, mostly from his theatre group, so I'd been roped in to help. I had a tin full of iced fairy cakes as my contribution, and Marco's present – a very realistic-looking broadsword, helmet and breastplate, which had reminded me of the suit of armour in the drawing room.

I got back by late afternoon, having had an exhausting but pleasurable time, and bearing two paper napkin-wrapped pieces of cake, which Marco insisted I bring back for Silas and Mercy.

And I hadn't told even Emma about the kiss, because I was now convinced that Randal had merely misjudged the distance between us and the contact wasn't intentional . . .

He'd long since left for London and Mote Farm had sunk back into its usual air of quiet enchantment, with the two elderly siblings cosily having tea together in the drawing room, while Pye tracked the movements of the Invisible Ones and Pugsie snored.

While Randal was winging off to yet more exotic locations, here at Godsend, with the planning permission finally in place, the activity at the mill ratcheted up several gears.

The mezzanine floor was being strengthened before the café was fitted out and the interior of the Christmas shop completed. Arlene and I had spent many happy hours designing the layout and sourcing the stock and I was slowly rediscovering my love of Christmas to the point that I was now becoming evangelical about it.

'We need to totally immerse visitors in the Christmas

experience the minute they walk through the door, starting with the right background music,' I said to Arlene.

'What, have carols or Christmas pop songs playing?' she asked doubtfully.

'Actually, I was thinking more of some kind of electronic mood music, with jingle bells, tinkling noises like icicles falling off windowsills and a sound like an icy wind blowing through snowy pine trees . . .'

Arlene looked totally blank.

'Something like you find on those stands of CDs in garden centres.'

'Oh, I know,' she said, enlightened. 'I've got one for meditation, all trickling water and bamboo wind chimes. One of my eldest son's friends might be able to come up with something like that, if you want me to ask him.'

'Great,' I enthused, making a note. 'And since we're already going to stock those wooden incense burners shaped like nutcracker figures, we can light one or two of them every day, so the whole mill will smell seasonal.'

'Yes, that should get them in the mood for buying lots of lovely glass baubles and tree toppers, and all the rest of it,' Arlene agreed.

'Not to mention realistic fake trees, scented fir cones, tinsel, snow, traditional stocking fillers, door wreaths, cards, tags, gift-wrap, cribs, snow globes . . . and perhaps even chocolate tree decorations,' I said.

'There's a chocolate maker over in Sticklepond who might do special ones just for us,' suggested Arlene. 'Though they'd be very expensive, I expect.'

'Expensive is OK as long as they're really individual, because we want to stock things you can't get anywhere else.

What about sourcing some unusual Scandinavian decorations and maybe those funny little trolls they have in Norway?'

'I'll have a look on the internet,' she promised. '*And* the shop will have a huge display of Marwood's crackers, too. The new ones do look much prettier and more special than the old.'

'It's a pity you can't post them because of the snaps, or we'd probably do a great mail-order business through the website,' I said regretfully.

'I think the cracker workshop's more than busy enough now, anyway,' she pointed out, 'what with all the orders for the new crackers to fulfil and the Liberty ones to complete and pack off in good time.'

'Freda and Job have offered to work for a couple of hours each afternoon, because a bit of extra cash would be welcome,' I told her. 'And I'm putting in time making them, when I'm not running around after Mercy and being sent off on errands to buy things, or pick up yet more old sewing machines.'

'Silas got me to confirm the order for the museum display cases and extra signage yesterday,' she said. 'He's bound to want you to help with that, too.'

'I don't mind; it'll be fun. And eventually there'll be more staff anyway, what with the shop and café, so perhaps they'll take on extra cracker makers too.'

'We'll need proper cleaners,' Arlene suggested. 'Bradley pushing a broom around the floor from time to time isn't going to cut the mustard when the mill is open to the public, is it?'

'It's OK, Mercy's already sorted that angle out. Dolly Mops do business cleaning as well as domestic, so she's going to give them the contract.'

Arlene looked down at the drawings of the shop interior again. 'What's going in this empty space at the back?'

'Father Christmas's grotto. He'll have to be there from mid-November onwards, but the rest of the time we'll just hang a notice on the door saying he's gone on holiday to Lapland and if they pop their Christmas lists in the special postbox, he'll read them when he gets back.'

'I'm starting to feel all nostalgic and Christmassy myself now,' Arlene said. 'It's going to be lovely.'

'I just hope we'll have enough to keep the visitors amused until the gallery and craft workshops are opened,' I said.

'Oh, I think so. When the visitors have seen the mill, they can always go for a walk up the footpath in the woods, or use the picnic area,' she said. 'I wonder how long it will be before we'll open the first phase.'

I don't know – Mercy would like to wait till Randal can be here all the time. He's off abroad again at the moment.'

'Where's he gone this time?'

'India and Nepal, he said. Sounds wonderful to me, but I think he's had enough, so I suppose even world travel palls after a while.'

'We haven't seen a lot of that Lacey, have we?'

'No, and she seems to have totally abandoned any idea of moving her business up here.'

'So long as she doesn't abandon Randal, too,' Arlene said with a grin. 'He's totally besotted with her; you could see that, though she's so beautiful it's hardly surprising.'

'She is,' I agreed, though actually I'd thought at times Randal had looked a little impatient – even cross – with his lovely bride-to-be.

I shrugged. 'I expect they'll work out their differences. I'm more worried about Mercy going off to Malawi with Liz and leaving us to cope!'

'We'll manage, and we can email her if we need to ask anything,' she assured me. 'It was always OK when she was away before.'

'Yes, but now there's so much more going on and decisions that need to be made daily!'

'It'll be fine,' she said soothingly.

And she was quite right, because it was – exhilarating, exhausting, hugely busy, often challenging and a real roller-coaster ride – but we did it!

Chapter 45: Guilt-Edged

Randal

It was the day after I got back to London before I could get hold of Lacey and she said she'd forgotten her phone charger and her battery went dead . . . though of course that didn't mean she couldn't have called me from a landline, or someone else's phone, as I pointed out.

Then I remembered Tabby's suggestion that she'd been having so much fun she'd just turned her phone off and asked her if she still wanted to marry me.

'Of course I do, darling!' she cried, opening her blue eyes wide, like a startled Disney doe. 'It's just that I don't want to leave London and move to Godsend right now, because I need just a *little* more fun before we settle down and have a family. But I absolutely adore the way you make me feel so *safe*.'

She came over and wound her arms around my neck in a rare, spontaneous gesture of affection, but it didn't have quite its usual effect on me.

'But we've had all this out, Lacey: I'm going to be managing the mill site and I'll need to be up there all the time, at least for the first few months – and anyway, I want to move back, because I've had enough of London.'

She untwined her arms and pouted. 'I think you're very selfish – it's all about what *you* want.'

'I suppose I did spring it on you, but I thought you'd like the idea. You kept saying you'd like to have a house in the country.'

'Yes, for weekends and holidays! At heart, I'm a London girl and now I've seen Mote Farm I know I don't want to be stuck up there all year round – I'd go mad.'

'Couldn't you just give Mote Farm a bit more of a chance?'

'That's not going to be easy, with your family looking down their noses at me as if I'm selling something dirty.'

'It's not really like that,' I protested. 'But . . . we seem to have reached a bit of an impasse, don't we?'

She shrugged. 'Not really – my business base can be here and yours up there and we'll divide our time between them.'

'Perhaps when we've got a family you'll feel differently about spending more time up in Lancashire?' I suggested, and she softened a bit and said perhaps she might.

She promised to visit Mote Farm with me again after my next trip abroad and I expected we could work things out . . . I tended to forget how much younger than me she was, so maybe I just needed to give her more time.

I asked Charlie to show me the secret film footage he took of Tabby at the Champers&Chocs warehouse when she was showing him round, and he was right: she looked totally shifty and guilty.

'It's clear she knows what's going on,' he said.

'You're right, though that's not the same as playing an active part in the scam, is it?'

'But she was the one packing up those "special orders" in the evenings and being paid wads of cash – and both her friend and her boss implicated her.'

'Wasn't she supposed to be having an affair with her boss, too, even though he was years older and no oil painting?'

Charlie shrugged. 'People never fail to surprise me. Still, it doesn't really matter any more, does it, so long as she's going straight now?'

'*If* she is, because it's a worry when she's working for someone as trusting as Mercy and has the free run of the house and mill.'

'Oh, Mercy's no fool when it comes to character,' he said. 'She likes me, so that shows you!'

Then he asked me how the beautiful Lacey was and I said, 'Dragging me to every nightclub in London whenever I'm between assignments – and she's got severe cold feet about moving to Lancashire. Never get engaged to someone ten years younger than yourself,' I added darkly, but that might have been the beer talking.

It was hell being in India and trying to work, when more than half my mind was worrying about what was happening at the mill, once Mercy and Liz had flown out to Malawi.

It was such a critical stage in the development, and leaving everything in the hands of Silas, who'd hardly been a success at keeping an eye on it in the past, a secretary (however efficient) and an ex-con I didn't quite trust was hardly likely to make me feel any better about it.

Emails flew between Godsend, Malawi and wherever I

could find an internet connection and I could always tell when Tabby was the one emailing, because she had a distinctly acerbic edge.

And I really didn't want to think about Tabby at all since that evening in the garden, because I still had absolutely no idea what had come over me! In fact, I was starting to wonder if Tabitha Coombs might actually be a witch. Or maybe that kiss never happened at all, because at breakfast next morning Tabby seemed totally unconcerned.

And Lacey seemed totally unconcerned about me too, because she rarely answered my messages and when I phoned a couple of times in desperation, she was either sleeping or out.

Chapter 46: Picture Perfect

Q: How do snails keep their shells shiny?
A: Snail varnish!

Silas had taken on a new lease of life after buying a golf buggy! Jude Martland's uncle Noël had one and suggested it, and it was a great idea, because now he could whiz down to the mill and home again whenever he felt like it, even on his bad days.

It was a top-of-the-range super-duper one, too, since he was not short of money, and Job had taken to polishing it lovingly whenever he buffed up the estate car.

While Randal was away we'd been having quite an acerbic and enjoyable exchange of emails about the final décor of the café on the mezzanine floor. He appeared unable to grasp the principle of simple Shaker style, which we'd agreed would suit the mill best, and instead indulged in an orgy of rustic gingham. Arlene and I had changed the order – or rather, I had, because she was afraid of him.

But as his trip wore on, his messages became terser, with longer intervals between them, and I started to wonder if he was feeling ill again. When I broached it with Mercy she said she had been wondering the same thing, so she emailed and asked him directly and he said he'd found eating plain bland food almost impossible on this trip and a local doctor thought he might be starting an ulcer.

I hoped not, because it wasn't likely to do his temper any good, so I did a quick internet search (or a slow one, really, because the connection takes for ever here) on what he might safely eat in India and Nepal, and emailed it to him.

He snapped one right back, saying I should use my time to do my own job, not give him unwanted advice and sounded so much more like himself that I sent him an attachment showing the lovely, simple white china I'd picked out for the café, along with six smiley emoticons. I thought that might finish him off.

He certainly went silent for over a week and then he was back to the terse one-liners, so he was no fun to play with any more.

He was scheduled to return to the UK just before Liz and Mercy got back from Malawi, and I wondered if he'd hotfoot it straight up here to check that I hadn't stolen any crackers.

At the very least, I expected him to ring and grill me the moment his plane touched down. But he didn't . . . and then, a day or two later, the phone rang just as I got in from the mill and a voice asked to speak to Mercy.

'Tell her it's Charlie Clancy,' he added.

'I know, I recognised your voice straight away,' I said. 'This is Tabitha Coombs.'

'Oh God,' he said, sounding embarrassed. 'I'd forgotten you were living there! But I really *do* need to speak to Mercy – it's about Randal.'

'She's still in Malawi and not due back for a couple of days,' I said. 'Is Randal . . . all right? I mean, we'd been emailing and I think his digestion was giving him hell again. He said he might be getting an ulcer.'

'Oh, he told you he wasn't so good?' he said, sounding relieved. 'I went round to see him last night and he was feeling so crummy he'd struggled to file his copy. Then he went white as a sheet and keeled over, so when he came round, I made him go to A&E.'

'Is he all right?' I demanded. 'What did they say?'

'They did a load of tests but didn't find anything very wrong, so they thought it was mostly exhaustion and told him to rest up and eat a bland diet for a couple of weeks. But he's always been so fit and I've never seen him in this state before. His doctor's signed him off work for a fortnight but really he needs a bit of TLC and I'm off up to Scotland.'

'Where's Lacey?' I asked, though I couldn't really imagine her doing the Florence Nightingale stuff.

'She went off on holiday with her chums to St Lucia for a fortnight the day before Randal got back, apparently. He was a bit miffed about it.'

How odd, I suddenly thought: in one of his recent messages Guy had said he was going on holiday, too . . . but it was surely a coincidence?

'Randal could come home,' I suggested. 'I'll look after him till Mercy gets back. Perhaps you could drop him off here on your way up to Scotland?'

'Not unless he's wearing a parachute, because I'm flying. And anyway, he must have forgotten Mercy was still away, because he's already on his way. He insisted he was fine to drive himself and you know what he's like when he makes his mind up about something. I couldn't stop him.'

'Mercy and Liz *were* going to be back today, but then they changed their tickets so they could go to a wedding. Still, it's OK, I'll go and make his bed up and think of something bland to give him for dinner.'

'Great,' Charlie said, sounding relieved. 'Well, I'd better be off, then and – well, sorry.'

'What for? Palming a ratty invalid on me or being the instrument of my downfall?'

'Both,' he said, sounding amused, and rang off.

I'd never been right into Randal's apartments. Mercy had merely opened the door when she first gave me a tour of Mote Farm and I'd just looked in at a small but pleasantly sunny sitting room, with a glimpse through an open door of a bedroom beyond.

The team of Dolly Mops cleaners who came every week had the place gleaming and dust free and his bed, a huge four-poster with curly columns at each corner, was already freshly made up.

I wasn't sure quite how ill he'd be feeling when he got back, but I turned down the corner of the quilt and plumped up the pillows, in case he wanted to go to bed straight away.

It was only as I turned away that I was stopped in my tracks by the sight of one of my own papercut pictures on the wall opposite: there was no mistaking it, for it was of Mum seated like Boudicca in a chariot-like wheelchair among a Sleeping Beauty tangle of thorns.

For a moment I was stirred by a maelstrom of feelings and memories: the renewed sadness that my lovely, free-spirited mother was no longer there; my first gallery exhibition, when

I'd been filled with happiness and excitement at the future that suddenly seemed to be within my reach . . . and then Charlie, and the appalling sequence of events that followed, orchestrated by Kate.

I wiped my eyes, filled Randal's bedside carafe with cold water and then went downstairs to tell Silas what was happening.

Charlie had been quite right and Randal shouldn't have driven himself up, because he had enough trouble getting out of the car and standing. He looked so pale and drawn that Silas took one look and ordered him up to bed.

And he must have felt ill, because he went. Luckily Job was by the garages giving the estate car a long, loving slow polish, so he brought in the bags and took them up.

When he returned, he reported that Randal had gone to bed and said he didn't want anything to eat or drink, only to be left in peace and he'd be fine in the morning.

'But in my opinion, Tabitha, he has that nasty flu that's going round and you should call in the doctor,' Job said gloomily. 'He admitted he felt dizzy and he's alternating between hot and cold. I'll pop back again later and see if he wants any assistance,' he added, and I was grateful, because I couldn't see Randal letting me tuck him up for the night, let alone anything else, and climbing stairs was beyond Silas.

But anyway, Silas and I decided to do what Job had advised, to be on the safe side, and called the doctor out. I filled him in about Randal's recent health issues and trip to the hospital and then took him upstairs to see the patient.

Randal was sweating so heavily that his dark blond hair stuck to his forehead and his eyes were shadowed and vague, but he still had enough fight left in him to be furious that I'd called out the doctor without asking him.

'It's this really virulent strain of flu, all right,' the doctor said when he came back down. 'I've told him to rest in bed and I'll give you something he can take to get his temperature down. Lots of liquids, but he's probably not going to feel hungry for a day or two.'

Then he checked that Silas had had a flu vaccination, which he had, and left.

I hadn't had one but, evidently, I'd just have to take my chances.

'I don't want anything to eat tonight, just leave me in peace,' Randal said, eyeing me belligerently when I returned after seeing the doctor off.

'Good, because I was only going to offer you chicken soup anyway. I made it as soon as Charlie told me you were on the way, and some fresh lemonade to Mercy's recipe, which will do you good. I'll bring some of both up shortly. And Job will pop in again later to make you comfortable for the night.'

'He needn't bother,' snapped Randal. It was fast becoming clear that he was going to be the patient from hell.

He seemed worse later, but I managed to persuade him to drink some of my very excellent soup and a little lemonade to wash down the capsules the doctor had left for him.

Pugsie and Pye, probably curious as to why I was in this part of the house, had followed me up and Pye jumped on the bed and stared down at Randal.

'Go away,' he said weakly.

'Mmrow,' Pye said, helpfully head-butting him, as if to encourage him to get up.

Pugsie tried and failed to jump up on the bed too and then, showing more intelligence than I'd previously given him credit for, used the low wooden chest at the end as a step.

He had to be dissuaded from licking Randal to death, but finally settled down next to him.

'Are you going to keep Randal company?' I asked him.

'I don't want him,' Randal protested, but I left him there anyway, though Pye followed me out.

There's nothing quite so comforting as the presence of a pet when you're ill, is there?

Job came back later as he'd promised and reported that Randal was now very feverish, but he'd taken another dose of the medicine and he hoped that would bring his temperature down.

Silas had gone to his rooms by then, so I locked up the house for the night and then tiptoed up and peeped in at Randal. Job had left a dim lamp on and he seemed to be restlessly asleep . . .

I took Pugsie downstairs, so he and Pye could go outside while I got into my pyjamas and dressing gown, then went back up again, because there was no way I was leaving Randal alone that night.

I spent most of it dozing on a small Victorian day bed in the sitting room, and when I heard him muttering I went in to check his pulse, which was racing.

'Hot,' he said, half-opening his unfocused eyes, so I wiped

his face with a cold, wet flannel and then got some more medicine and a bit of lemonade down him before he went back to sleep again.

The next time I tiptoed in to check, he woke up as I laid my hand gently on his hot forehead and grabbed my wrist.

'Lacey, where have you been?' he demanded urgently.

'It's not Lacey,' I said gently, 'just relax and go to sleep, Randal. You're not very well.'

His eyes narrowed as if trying to bring me into focus. 'It's the witch. You've put a spell on me, haven't you?' he said, his grip on my wrist tightening. He'd tossed aside the coverlet and his unbuttoned pyjama top revealed an admirably muscular chest, considering how underweight he was. I overbalanced and found myself briefly clasped to it, before his grip on me loosened.

'Yes, and this nice cold lemonade is the cure,' I told him, slightly breathlessly, but he was off again with the restless muttering.

I was in two minds whether to call the doctor out again, but finally he quietened and dropped off to sleep and I sat there as the night slowly turned to morning and the birds began to sing.

Chapter 47: True Lovers' Knots

Q: What are the wettest animals in the world?
A: *Reindeer!*

Next morning, Job arrived early to see to Randal and came back downstairs saying he thought he'd turned a corner in the night and should now quickly improve, though it hadn't done anything for his temper.

No great surprise there, then.

I chopped a soft-boiled egg up in a mug and when I presented it to Randal with a spoon and two toast soldiers, he gave the tray a look of disgust and said he felt about six again.

He was pale and there were interesting blue shadows under his eyes, but at least, thanks to the super-efficient Job's ministrations, he was washed, shaved and as much in his right mind as he'd ever been.

I expect Pugsie, who'd clearly cast himself in the role of Devoted Companion as soon as he was let back upstairs, got most of the egg and toast once my back was turned.

In the afternoon, after demonstrating to his own satisfaction that his legs wouldn't hold him, Randal demanded when I took him a cup of tea that I stay and give him an account of everything that had been happening at the mill.

'I've got things to do,' I protested, but he was adamant, so I sat down and started to list what we'd done, making my voice deliberately monotonous when I saw his eyelids looking heavy.

He fell suddenly and deeply asleep halfway through my description of the unusual chocolate tree decorations I'd discussed with the chocolatier in Sticklepond.

I looked at him, lying there like a fallen and rather ruggedly handsome giant in a fairy tale, and I simply couldn't resist it: I went and fetched my sketchbook.

By the time Mercy and Liz arrived home Randal was well on the mend, though his temper wasn't. He'd insisted on coming downstairs earlier and getting underfoot in the kitchen while I was baking a welcome-home chocolate fudge cake, to one of the recipes Mercy had taught me.

It was good to see them home, though of course Mercy immediately began to fuss over Randal. I noticed he accepted her ministrations with much better grace than he had mine.

'Well, I'm glad you're getting better, though I'm sure you shouldn't be up yet,' she told him. 'And isn't it sweet, the way Pugsie has attached himself to you?'

'He thinks he's a cat,' he responded. 'That demonic beast of Tabby's has brainwashed him.'

'Pye isn't demonic!' I said indignantly. 'But I think you're right about Pugsie thinking he's a cat.'

'He and Pye both stalk ghosts in the drawing room – you should have seen them when we were having tea,' he said. 'The place is a madhouse!'

'There are no ghosts here, they're just playing a little game,' she assured him cheerfully. 'Now, what could you fancy for dinner?'

'Anything except chicken soup. I've practically grown feathers and wings.'

'There's gratitude for you,' I said, 'and it was all you could do to keep that down for ages. But there's shepherd's pie for dinner tonight. Silas fancied it.'

'I can see you've been a bad patient, Randal, but Tabby's looked after you very well,' Mercy told him. 'I don't suppose a little of the pie will do you any harm, but perhaps I should make you a plain rice pudding for dessert?'

Later she asked me if I'd seen anything of the Martlands and I said I'd been to have coffee with Holly one day and then she'd shown me Jude's sculpture studio, which I'd found fascinating.

I noticed that no one asked after Lacey or, indeed, even mentioned her name, though she must have been on Randal's mind, or he wouldn't have assumed I was her when he was feverish.

There'd been no more messages from Guy since he'd gone on holiday, either. The silence was deafening.

Liz tried Randal's patience to the utmost by practising her future-doctor skills on him, but then luckily went off to spend a couple of weeks in France with her friend Maisie's family at their *gîte* before his already frazzled temper could get the better of him.

Persuaded by Mercy, Randal handed in his notice, though of course he'd have to go back to London to work it out when he was well enough.

But he looked stronger with every passing day and was soon champing at the bit to go and personally check on things at the mill – and probably check the accounts as well, just in case I'd been fiddling them – so finally Silas drove him down there in the new golf buggy. Pugsie went too, wedged between them on the seat.

Of course, after that first visit we had some lively discussions over the dinner table about the changes that I'd made in his absence, but I was certain my decisions had all been good ones and gave as good as I got, especially about his misguided attempt to turn the café into Gingham Central. Mercy backed me up.

He did admit that Silas's museum was starting to look really interesting, but that might have been because he'd fallen for the super golf buggy and wanted to borrow it.

Lacey returned from her holiday and spoke to Randal several times at length on the phone, but she didn't exactly rush up to see him and smooth his fevered brow. He said some problem had come up with her business while she was away, so she'd had to sort that out first. I expect they'd sent the wrong kind of cable ties for the Bondage Box, or something.

When she did finally appear, it was with Guy in tow!

'Darling, how are you?' she said, rushing over to kiss Randal. But he held her off and said, looking at Guy with a frown, 'What's *he* doing here?'

'Oh, Guy insisted on driving me up, because he was coming to spend the weekend at Old Place anyway,' she said.

'That was kind of you, Guy,' said Mercy.

'Not at all,' he replied, with one of his charming smiles.

'But I can't stay, I've only popped in to give Tabby a little present I brought her back from my hols, to show her I was thinking of her.'

'What, for *me*?' I said, taking the small bubble-wrapped parcel he was offering me.

At exactly the same moment, Randal, his eyes narrowing, demanded, 'Were you in St Lucia, too?'

'Yes. Pity you couldn't make it,' he said casually. 'Lovely island and we had a great time. Tabby, do you like your present?'

It was a tiny oil painting, perhaps only four inches by three, of minute dark figures on a long white stretch of beach. I adored it.

'It's lovely!' I exclaimed, wondering if he really *had* been thinking of me while he was away, though his present attentions seemed aimed at annoying Lacey, because her face went all tight and she turned back to Randal and told him how much she'd missed him.

Guy suggested before he left that he and I, and Randal and Lacey, met up in the pub later, but Mercy pointed out that Randal still wasn't fit to go out yet and anyway, she'd hoped for a quiet family party that evening.

Mercy had already asked me to be there for dinner and after the last few days I was exhausted anyway, especially now Randal had begun firing off questions and commands at me as if I was *his* PA and not Mercy's, so I turned Guy down, too.

Lacey suddenly exclaimed that she'd left her Ray-Ban sunglasses in the car and darted out after Guy, but she wasn't carrying them when she came back.

'Must be in my handbag, after all,' she said with a small

laugh and I saw Randal look at her with the sort of suspicious, narrow-eyed gaze he usually reserved for me.

Pugsie had made himself scarce the moment Lacey arrived, so I expect he thought she'd dognap him, but he couldn't stay away from his new hero for long and was soon hanging round Randal's feet, wanting to be picked up.

Randal looked pale, interesting and romantic at dinner, so I wasn't surprised when Lacey began an all-out charm offensive and was all over him like treacle. I don't think I could have been charming if my life depended on it, especially to Randal, who was still sniping at me over Gingham-gate.

Lacey's charm seemed to work on him, though, and he'd just started to mellow slightly when Mercy asked her whether she intended taking Pugsie away when she left. 'Because he's attached himself to Randal while he's been ill – so sweet.'

'Actually, one of my friends said she'd like him, so I was going to give him to her, but you can have him if you want him, Randal.'

'I intended getting a dog when I was here permanently, but not a ridiculous creature like Pugsie,' he said, but I knew he'd grown fond of him, even if they did make an incongruous pair.

'Oh, good, that's settled then,' Mercy said. 'Dear little Pye will be pleased his friend is staying, too.'

Frankly, I thought Pye was profoundly relieved that Pugsie now spent much of his days shadowing Randal, because he'd been cramping his style.

Mercy and Silas went off to the meeting next morning, but I'd been reluctantly deputed by Randal to take a clearly bored

Lacey down to the mill and show her the big changes that had been happening.

And actually, once we were there, her business head took over and she made some intelligent comments about what we'd been doing.

'And getting that order from Liberty was impressive, so I suppose you might make a go of the cracker business after all. I still think that museum's a waste of good space, though.'

'So does Randal,' I said. 'Do you think you might move your own business to this area, after all?' I added, seeing she was opening up a bit.

'No, I'll leave it where it is. Once the mill is up and running, there's no reason why we can't divide our time between here and London. I'm not quite ready to bury myself in the middle of nowhere and vegetate yet.'

Then she looked at me with narrowed blue eyes and said, 'I hope you're not thinking Guy's serious about you, because he's not. You're just an amusement.'

'I'd grasped that he wasn't the serious kind, even before everyone warned me about him. But he knows I'm only interested in being friends and he's accepted that.'

'Has he? He was flirting with you yesterday . . . though actually, that was more to make me jealous.'

'Yes, that's what I thought,' I agreed.

'Well, I hope Randal didn't notice. He doesn't know I used to go out with Guy.'

'Did you really? I'd never have guessed,' I said, but the sarcasm went over her head.

'It was a few years ago and I thought we were serious. But then I found out he was seeing someone else – his brother's girlfriend – so of course I dumped him.'

'Yes, I'd heard about that, though he did Jude a favour really, because Holly is *lovely*.'

But Lacey wasn't interested in Holly. 'Of course, Guy came running back to me eventually, but I told him where to go.'

She looked pensive.

'And then you met Randal and fell in love with him?' I suggested.

'Yeees,' she agreed slowly. 'I mean, he's just as attractive in a different way, and being older he seemed so safe and dependable.'

She frowned, which was not something I'd advise her to keep doing, if she didn't want to end up Botoxing her forehead rigid on a fortnightly basis.

'All my friends were getting married about then and having babies and I felt left out and ready to settle down . . . and he seemed perfect husband material. Only now I think I'd like another year or two of fun first. There's plenty of time for all that.'

'I suppose there is,' I said, feeling suddenly sad, because seeing Holly's little boy had stirred up maternal feelings I didn't even know I possessed.

'Anyway, I just thought I'd warn you that Guy means nothing with his flirting, in case you got your hopes up.'

'That was kind of you,' I said, though I thought it was more a case of her warning me off, because she didn't want anyone else to get him. 'But really, my only ambitions are to have a small home of my own and work from a studio at the mill.'

She gave me a searching look from those amazingly bright blue eyes, then said it sounded boring as hell to her, but each to their own.

'But maybe when Randal and I are married, it won't be so tedious coming up here for weekends and holidays because I can invite lots of my friends, too. We'll have some fun and put a bit of life into the old dump.'

That sounded ominous: Mercy was very hospitable, but it hardly sounded like the kind of fun she and Silas would join in with! I'd hate to see the magical peace and tranquillity of the farm destroyed, too, but I suppose it would all be up to Randal.

She made me swear not to tell him about her previous relationship with Guy.

'But why not just tell him yourself? After all, it was a long time ago and before you met him.'

'I would have, if I'd realised Guy's family lived practically next door to Randal's. Telling him now would be difficult and maybe he'd start imagining things.'

I thought he probably already was a bit suspicious, but I didn't say anything and we went back up to the house to find the others had come home again.

After lunch, Guy came to pick Lacey up and take her back to London, but this time he didn't come into the house, just hooted his horn.

When we'd waved them off, Randal, looking distinctly grim, turned and headed back up to his rooms. Pugsie was under his arm, but I expect he'd forgotten he'd picked him up to keep him from getting under everyone's feet.

Chapter 48: Santa's Little Helper

Q: How did the human cannonball lose his job?
A: He got fired!

Until he went back to London to work out his notice, Randal spent every day at the mill, which was hardly the quiet rest that the doctor had prescribed.

I told him there was no point in checking the accounts. 'Arlene and I can only order things from firms Marwood's already have an account with, unless Mercy or you authorise them.'

'I didn't really think you'd been cooking the books,' he said to my surprise. 'You still puzzle me, but I can see now that you're genuinely fond of Mercy and wouldn't do anything that might hurt her.'

'I wouldn't, and I'm fond of Silas, too. It's been fun working with him on the museum.'

And after that conversation the air seemed to clear a little. We still argued, of course, but in a more amicable, bickering kind of way and Mercy commented that she was glad we were getting on so well.

'Once Randal is permanently based here, we will all be

able to work as one big, happy team,' she added, but I thought: not if Lacey has anything to do with it!

Guy had resumed the flirty messages, though they were less frequent, but I didn't need Lacey's warning to know the value of this renewed interest . . . though the painting had showed another side to him, since obviously he'd not only thought of me while off enjoying himself with Randal's fiancée, but chosen a gift I'd love.

He was full of contradictions.

Ceddie Lathom, my former prison visitor, came to stay a night on his way up to the Lake District to see friends and it was lovely to see him again.

'My dear, you're positively blooming,' he said, beaming at me much as Mercy did, and then kissing my cheek.

'It was a wonderful day for me when you directed my attention to Tabby,' Mercy told him. 'She's literally been a godsend for Godsend!'

'I knew at once she was what you needed,' he said. 'And where is Randal?'

'He went down to the mill, because they've begun fitting out the new café, but he'll back shortly,' she said.

He was, too, but though he greeted the visitor in a friendly way he then turned and snapped at me: 'Where did you vanish to earlier? I wanted you. You're the one who changed all the orders, so you might at least be there!'

'Mercy needed me to help her arrange the shipping on the next sewing machine consignment,' I said, 'and I can't be in two places at once.'

'I see that Randal can't do without Tabitha, either,' said

Ceddie, twinkling. 'And you told me they'd become engaged, Mercy? Bless you both!'

'Oh, no,' I said quickly as Randal's expression became even more thunderous. 'Randal *is* engaged, but to someone else.'

'Silly me,' said Ceddie. 'Who is the lucky girl?'

'She's called Lacey Bucknall and very beautiful, Ceddie,' Mercy told him. 'They're to have a January wedding.'

'Beauty is as beauty does,' Silas said darkly, so Lacey's sporadic attempts to charm him during her last visit hadn't entirely won him over.

Emma went quiet, once Des returned from Qatar, though she did manage to give me a ring one day and said he still seemed to be making more effort to be less jealous, but he insisted that she and Marco fly out to Qatar at half term, because he was definitely going to be offered that year-long contract after the next one, and he wanted her to move there.

'So are you going?'

'I told him it was a long way to travel just for half term, but I gave in in the end. I suppose it's only fair to have a look at the place and he says there's a good international school Marco could go to, so I'd better check that out . . .'

Emma sounded troubled, but said we'd have a good catch-up when Des had flown off again. I wished he'd migrate permanently.

There seemed to be an endless demand for structural engineers in far-flung places, but he'd been involved in a lot of prestigious projects, so I suppose he was good at what he did, even if not brilliant at being a husband.

* * *

The first couple of times that Randal visited Mote Farm I'd been happy to see the back of him, but now when he returned to London to work out his notice, the house felt strangely empty . . . not to mention the mill, where he'd seemed to be everywhere at once.

For the next few weeks, however, he travelled back up again at every opportunity he got, though Lacey didn't reappear . . . and nor did Guy, though he continued sending me occasional messages despite my even more infrequent replies.

I sincerely hoped Lacey had been telling the truth and there was nothing going on between them now . . . for Randal's sake. I found, for all his abrupt bossy ways, I didn't really want to see him hurt.

Liz was home again for the last of the summer holidays and had been helping Mercy, so I was free to spend long hours making crackers with the others for the ever-increasing orders.

The next year should be easier, because we'd be producing the new designs from January onwards, so it wouldn't be an unusually late rush to get them out there.

Which was good, because I'd had little time to do any of my own work, other than the occasional greetings card design and lots of sketches. I was starting to long for the day when I had my studio and the opportunity to develop my work in different directions . . .

Liz saw my drawing of Randal when she was looking through my sketchbook one evening and she said she'd never seen him looking quite that peaceful and relaxed.

'No, it was only because he was unconscious,' I told her.

She grinned but said she thought we made a great team, while Lacey, who she hadn't met yet, sounded exactly the wrong kind of girl for Randal. I wasn't entirely sure what she meant by that.

As always, I missed her when she went back to school for the autumn term.

Summer had flown by and though it hadn't been entirely all work and no play, since Mercy was a great one for organising impromptu picnics to the open-air riverside Lido over in the village of Sticklepond on hot days, it had certainly been exhausting – and as we moved ever closer to the day we'd open the mill to the public, which Mercy had decreed should be held on the last Saturday in September, it was only likely to get more so!

Randal finished work and came back up, though at some point in the future when things were less frantic, he'd have to empty and sell his flat.

His presence took a lot of weight from my shoulders; he seemed to have regained his health and his energy in one mighty bound.

It was due to Mercy Marwood's magical cooking, I was convinced of it.

The Liberty special order was finally completed and dispatched, and the workers settled down to turning out the new crackers like clockwork Santa's elves.

Speaking of which, at Emma's suggestion I'd commissioned the couple who ran Marco's theatre group to make Santa's grotto. It would look like a cottage with a snowy roof and, inside, Santa would sit in front of a fireplace hung with Christmas stockings and receive the children.

It was basically two stage backdrops really, so it seemed

the most economical way of doing it. They came and installed it and helped with the finishing touches, too: drifts of fake snow lining the path and the branches of the little fir trees around it.

Randal, who'd been inclined to take umbrage that I'd gone ahead and sorted this while he and Mercy were away, had to admit it was perfect . . . as was the Christmas shop.

Suzanne, Arlene's friend, had taken charge of that and was unpacking the stock and setting up the displays. And the background electronic tape created by the friend of one of Arlene's sons sounded wonderfully atmospheric.

Silas and I arranged the items in the cabinets in the museum rooms, which were now lined with information boards illustrated with blown-up family photographs evocative of the Victorian era. It was everything we'd hoped it would be: the story of a benevolent Quaker dynasty, trying to keep the local families in work and living above the poverty line.

I caught Randal in there having a good look and he said, 'You're quite the little Quaker yourself now, aren't you? Going to meetings and helping Silas . . .'

'I don't go to the meetings regularly yet, I'm just an attender, but the more I find out about the Quaker ethos and history, like the way they always considered men and women equal and were involved in the abolition of slavery, the more I like it. It's a very all-embracing and relaxing religion.'

'I suppose it is,' he agreed, and then went back to overseeing the fitting out of the new staff room.

He now had his own desk in the office, since the small back photocopying room has been knocked through into the main area, but he was seldom to be found sitting at it.

He constantly snapped his orders at me or demanded my help as if he'd again forgotten I was Mercy's PA, not his, but then, sometimes he did remember and thank me. But I didn't mind anyway, since I felt we were now all one big team working towards the same goal.

Occasionally he came up to the pub with us in the evening and, if Jude wasn't around, played a mean game of dominoes.

By then the mill opening day was so close and there was so much for Randal to do that he'd been down to see Lacey only once and there was certainly no sign of her wanting to come up here and get involved in what we were doing.

And neither had there been any sighting of Guy, so either I'd entirely lost what little allure I had, or he had other fish to fry . . . and I hoped in the latter case it wasn't a bronze beauty called Lacey.

Chapter 49: On the Case

Q: What did Adam say on the day before Christmas?
A: *It's Christmas, Eve!*

Jeremy had been totally silent since his abortive visit so I hoped he'd given up and I could finally put the past behind me and forget about him . . .

But then one day Arlene came into the museum, where I was buffing up the old printing press to black and gold gleaming perfection, and announced, 'Someone's looking for you, Tabby.'

And there was Luke Dee, looking thin, tense and pale – but then, he always *had* reminded me of an anaemic tapeworm. I don't think he noticed Randal, who I'd roped in to move the hand press and who was now adjusting a badly angled light in one of the display cabinets.

'I went up to the house and some cleaning woman said you might be here,' he said.

'Well, as you see, I am, but I can't imagine what you want this time,' I said, feeling exasperated. 'Did you know Kate and Jeremy had the gall to turn up a few weeks ago, demanding that stupid ring – which I haven't got, by the way. I've no idea where it is.'

'Yes, but I don't care about that,' he said. 'It's Kate. She thinks I'm going to let her walk all over me when we divorce and take half the house – which my parents gave us the deposit for – plus everything else of any value in it, including the car!'

'Well, I'm sure I'm very sorry, Luke, but it really has nothing to do with me and—'

'But it has,' he interrupted. 'When I told her she'd have to fight me through the courts before I'd give her anything I wasn't forced to, she was livid.'

'Hell hath no fury like a tapeworm scorned,' I said, but he wasn't listening.

'When she'd gone I packed up all her stuff and dumped it on Jeremy's drive and she came out and totally lost it. She said she didn't know why she'd married me in the first place, but I was too stupid to realise she'd been having an affair with Jeremy all along.'

'So was I,' I said.

'She said she'd realised what she was letting go and luckily she knew a way of getting rid of you, and then basically admitted she'd lied about your involvement in that scam so she could have Jeremy to herself.'

'I'd sort of worked that out actually, Luke,' I said. 'It took me a while, but I got there.'

He stared at me. 'But – aren't you *furious*? I mean, you went to prison because of her lies!'

'I *was*, but now I've moved on – or I'm trying to, if you lot would only leave me alone!'

'I thought we could go to the police and I'd tell them what I know.'

'Luke,' I said patiently, 'I can see you'd like to get back at her by getting her into trouble, but I'm not going to be part of it.'

'But you must want justice? She ruined your life, just like she's ruining mine.'

'No, she hasn't. In fact, she did me a good turn, because I love living here and I never want to leave.'

'But – you could clear your name.'

I sighed wearily. '*I* always knew I was innocent and nothing will erase the time I spent in prison. It would be just my word against hers, too – so no, I don't want to take it further. But thanks for telling me.'

He didn't give up that easily, but in the end, frustrated and still angry, flounced out.

I said over my shoulder, 'You can come out now, Randal,' and he appeared from behind the big central showcase.

'That was a bit awkward,' he said. 'He was well into it before I realised what he was saying, or I'd have left.'

Then he grasped my shoulders and held me at arm's length, looking down at me and frowning. 'So – you really weren't involved in that scam?'

'No, *nor* having an affair with my boss.'

'I never really believed the affair part of it anyway,' he said, 'but once I'd got to know you a bit, I asked Charlie if he was sure you were guilty of the scam. And I'm sorry,' he added.

'That's OK: as I said to Luke, it's all turned out for the best.'

'I really mean it – I am sorry, Tabby.'

I looked up at him and our eyes met and held . . . His were deep, green-flecked and mysterious as mountain tarns . . .

His hands tightened on my shoulders and we drew closer, just as we had that night in the garden . . . and then Mercy's voice, calling my name, broke the spell of the moment and we stepped quickly apart. Or maybe Randal stepped away and I was the only one touched by the magic?

I only knew that, unlike Guy, I'd have let him kiss me, forgetting all about Lacey and my dreams of cosy singledom.

Randal must have told Charlie Clancy what Luke had said, because he turned up on Saturday, when Emma and Marco were visiting, to apologise in person.

I accepted his apology and told him I'd looked so guilty on the film that I didn't really blame him. Then Mercy predictably invited him to stay to tea with us.

Emma had been inclined at first to cold-shoulder the man who had caused her best friend to go to prison, but was won over once he started playing with Marco, enacting duels with invisible swords, up and down the wide staircase in the hall.

In fact, it turned into a really fun afternoon, with even Randal joining in. I didn't know he could do fun: he'd kept it pretty quiet till that moment.

Charlie seemed increasingly smitten with Emma as the afternoon wore on, to the point where he could hardly take his eyes off her . . . not that it was likely to get him anywhere, because she was still determined to fly out to Qatar at half term and give her marriage a chance.

Mercy invited Emma, Marco and Charlie to the opening day of the mill: but by then she had invited *everyone*!

There was one desperate last scramble to have everything ready on the morning the mill was to open, but finally the staff were in place, the pine and incense smell of Christmas was spicing the air and the faint jingling of bells and whistling of snowy breezes was drifting through the building.

Lillian and Joy were poised at a table behind one of the viewing windows ready to demonstrate their cracker-making skills and the sign at the bottom of the steps to the café had been turned round to read 'Open'.

There was quite a crowd waiting outside for the moment when Mercy, beaming and rosy with happiness, cut the ribbon across the door and welcomed everyone to Friendship Mill. Most of the inhabitants of Little Mumming seemed to be there: all the Martlands, including Guy, Old Nan, the elderly vicar, Henry, and even Nancy Dagger and her father-in-law, Nick. And of course the cracker workforce and Arlene and her family, too.

The adverts Randal had placed in the local papers appeared to have brought in people from much further afield, as well.

Or perhaps it was the lure of today's free tea, coffee, cold drinks and cakes in the café, which would be served till eleven thirty, after which the lunch service would start. Bluebell Lyon, who was running it, was going to serve coffee, lunch, cakes and afternoon tea till she closed at three every day, except our closing days, Sunday and Monday. Mercy had put her foot down about Sunday opening and wouldn't be budged.

'That's archaic,' sniffed Lacey, when she had finally made her appearance about an hour after the opening ceremony and been handed a leaflet about the mill on the way in.

She'd been dropped off by Guy so late the previous evening that everyone but Randal, who waited up for her, had gone to bed. Then we'd all had to come down to the mill early, so we hadn't seen her till now.

Randal was troubleshooting any glitches that came up, Mercy was giving the older Martlands tea and cakes upstairs, Silas had stationed himself in the museum and I was to relieve the two cracker-making demonstrators when they felt like a break, so Lacey was left to amuse herself.

Or rather, let Guy amuse her, because I saw them together in the café a little later, heads together and talking like a pair of conspirators – or maybe arguing like a pair of conspirators, because Lacey looked cross. One day the wind would change and her pretty face would stay that way.

The day passed in a blur and so did what seemed like an endless stream of people. They lingered at the viewing windows and over the museum displays, bought oodles of stuff in the shop and cleaned out all the hot lunch dishes in the café and most of the cakes.

'Success beyond our wildest dreams!' said Mercy, smiling happily once the last visitors had gone, the tills had been cashed up in the office and all the staff departed for home. The café closed earlier, of course, to allow time for cleaning the kitchens, but the agency would be sending in a team to take care of the rest of the building early on Monday morning.

'Yes – and you must be exhausted,' Randal said. 'Silas went back home in the buggy soon after lunch.'

'Oh, no, I've spent lots of time sitting in the café talking to friends – and even total strangers,' she said cheerfully, 'but perhaps I should leave you two to lock up and go back to the house, because of getting dinner ready, though when Lacey said earlier that she had a headache and was going back to lie down, I asked her to pop the casserole into a slow oven if she felt better later.'

This seemed an unusually domestic scenario for the glamorous Lacey.

'My God, Lacey!' exclaimed Randal. 'I'd forgotten she was here, it's all been so frantically busy. When did you see her, Mercy?'

'Definitely after lunch,' she said vaguely.

'Yes, I caught a glimpse of her heading out, about two,' I agreed, but didn't add that the glimpse had included Guy.

'Then I'm sure she's back at the house and I hope her headache has gone,' Mercy said kindly, though as Silas had wickedly said to me earlier, Lacey was as much use as a chocolate teapot.

Randal and I went round the building checking that all was secure before setting the new alarm and leaving. The shadows were dark and thick in the valley and there was a hint of damp wood smoke in the chilly air to remind us that autumn was well on the way.

'I feel so shattered I'm not sure my legs will get me up the hill,' I confessed. 'I don't know where Mercy gets her energy from.'

'She's always been a little dynamo,' he said with the attractive grin I'd seen all too rarely. He took my arm. 'Come on: we'll have to help each other up.'

But then his hand suddenly dropped away as Lacey walked round the corner of the building from the direction of the track to Little Mumming, snuggled up in her fake yak coat and Ugg boots. We were surprised, but she looked quite taken aback.

'What are you doing out here?' exclaimed Randal. 'We thought you must have gone back to the house.'

'I did, but then I needed some fresh air.'

‘Isn’t it a bit late in the day and too cold for that? And Mercy thought you were going to put dinner in the oven for her.’

‘I’m not really into all that domestic stuff,’ Lacey said, as if he’d suggested she clean the loos and dust the banisters.

‘I’m not sure any more exactly what kind of thing you *are* into,’ he said. ‘But going for country walks on your own on chilly evenings hasn’t seemed to be one of them till now.’

‘You don’t know everything about me,’ she snapped.

‘It certainly appears to be that way,’ he said.

I started to feel embarrassed: if they were going to have an argument, I’d so much rather not be there.

‘I’ll see you back at the house,’ I said, and dashed off before they could come with me.

Let them sort out their own differences and if, as I suspected, she’d been with Guy, then probably Randal suspected too, by now.

Pye and Pugsie met me at the bridge: they’d sensibly avoided the noise and activity surrounding the mill today, and even Ginger and Bing had only emerged from hiding after the last visitor had gone.

Relations between the happy couple at dinner seemed a little strained, though Lacey was doing her best to win Randal round.

She followed me into the kitchen later when I went to make the coffee, but not to help: it seemed I’d been selected for the role of confidante.

‘I suppose you guessed I’d been with Guy this afternoon?’ she said, leaning against the fridge, her pretty face dissatisfied.

'Yes – and I don't think I was the only one.'

'If you mean Randal, I can twist him round my little finger whenever I want to,' she said, though so far as I could see, the twisting hadn't seemed to be getting the desired results this time.

Then she said she'd got engaged to Randal because he was Mr Right, but she still had a weakness for Guy. 'Randal's attractive but . . . I don't know . . . he leaves me cold, really . . . while Guy just *does* it for me.'

'Too much information,' I said, but between the two men, how on earth could she think Guy was more attractive than Randal?

'What are you going to do?' I asked.

'Oh, Guy's not serious, he'd just dump me again the minute he'd got me back,' she said impatiently. 'I'll settle for Randal: he's a safe bet and once we're married I'll make sure that things round here are run to suit me – starting with stocking that empty cellar downstairs. I'm dying for a drink!'

'Is it fair to marry Randal when he'd be second best?' I asked.

'Of course – Randal's mad about me,' she said confidently.

He was certainly mad: he walked in just then and demanded to know if we were having coffee tonight or not, but the effect was slightly spoiled by the tiny pug dog tucked under one arm.

Chapter 50: Fireworks

Q: What did the snowman say to the blizzard?
A: It's been ice snowing you!

The mill being closed on Sunday and Monday at least gave us a chance to recover and prepare to do it all over again on Tuesday, albeit without the bells and whistles – *or* the arguments.

I went to the Quaker meeting with Mercy and Silas and I felt so vacant with tiredness that I thought my mind would be wide open to Higher Thoughts. But instead, an image of Randal's face kept filling it, looking down at me the way he had after Luke's visit, as if I was a problem that had to be solved.

While we were out, he and Lacey had gone off somewhere in the car and came back again on better terms, so she must have been right about being able to twist him round her little finger and had convinced him she wasn't in the least interested in Guy. It was unfortunate that Guy had to come and collect her for the journey back to London after lunch, slightly undoing her work.

Randal took her small suitcase out and stood talking to

Guy for a few minutes. His back was turned, so I couldn't see his face, but his stance didn't look exactly friendly.

Perhaps Randal hadn't been entirely convinced by whatever line Lacey had spun him after all, because he turned restless when we'd had dinner and said he needed some fresh air, then invited me to walk up to the Auld Christmas with him.

'Yes, do go, I'm sure a walk will do you both good,' Mercy said, and found us a large torch to light our journey home.

Randal spent the whole walk in brooding silence, so I might as well not have been there, though he did cheer up when we found Jude and Holly had utilised their Sunday abundance of babysitters again to pop to the pub for an hour.

Randal wasn't as silent on the way home, taking me by surprise by asking me whether Lacey had ever mentioned Guy.

'Only she's so beautiful that he can't seem to resist flirting with her, even though she doesn't encourage him at all. And I'm afraid after I found out he'd also been on that holiday to St Lucia, I may have jumped to conclusions a bit . . . I even thought she'd been meeting him in the woods yesterday, when she was only having a walk to clear her headache!'

'She hasn't said a lot about him to me, only that she doesn't like him very much and she knows his flirting is just a game,' I said carefully.

'Yes, that's what she told me and pointed out that he flirts just as much with you.'

'I suppose he does, though *I* don't encourage him either,' I said.

‘I still didn’t like seeing Guy picking her up earlier . . . but she says she’ll drive herself up in future.’

If she comes up, I thought and Randal’s mind must have been heading in the same direction, because he added ruefully: ‘You know, I hadn’t realised she was such a town girl until her first visit here. I thought she’d love it as much as I do, but she was disappointed. I think she’d got the mad idea that the Marwoods were landed gentry with a huge pile in the country.’

‘But it’s a beautiful old house!’ I exclaimed. ‘I don’t know how anyone could want to live anywhere else.’

He turned his head and looked at me, his face clear enough in the moonlight, even though his eyes were unfathomable pools of darkness.

‘Of course, *I* intend moving out before your wedding day,’ I told him hastily, in case he thought he was stuck with me as a lodger for ever. ‘Lillian says I can always have her spare room, until I can afford to rent somewhere.’

That rare smile appeared, softening the hard lines of his face. ‘You don’t have to move out for me: I’ve got used to having you around now. A bit like Pugsie,’ he added.

‘Gee, thanks,’ I said, but in my heart I knew I wouldn’t be able to bear living in the same house when he and Lacey were married, especially if she kept telling me things I’d rather not know!

That was assuming that she would go through with the wedding in the end. She’d probably never had to choose between her head and her heart before, and there was no certainty that *Guy* had a heart, so perhaps better a Randal in the hand than a Guy in the bush, as it were.

* * *

The mill reopened on the Tuesday morning and once the initial teething troubles of the first few days were solved, it began to run smoothly.

Soon I could divide my time between making crackers and running errands for Mercy, though of course Randal was inclined to yell for me whenever he needed another pair of hands, or even just a sounding board for his thoughts.

On the whole, he and I were now oddly companionable, probably because we had a common interest in the mill. Since that first time we walked up to the pub together we'd done it again a couple of times, when the weather was fine, and either had a quiet drink or joined the cracker workers if any of them were there. I loved being out in the dusk, though I wouldn't have walked back through those woods on my own in the dark, even though I knew no wolves were about, not even Guy.

I have no idea how Pye knows when I'm coming back, on these occasions, but he and Pugsie always met us at the bridge over the stream and we'd all head home up the hill together.

But there were no more confidences during these walks – and come to think of it, no more visits from Guy. It made it blatantly obvious to me, at least, that he'd only bothered coming up here recently because of Lacey, but perhaps that hadn't occurred to Randal.

He went down to London for a couple of days when things at the mill were slightly less hectic, in order to start the process of putting his flat on the market, and came back complaining that Lacey had dragged him to some minor celebrity's birthday bash and he'd never met a more vacuous set of people in his life.

I bet he was the life and soul of the party.

When we were alone together in the kitchen later he told me that Lacey seemed to be cold-shouldering Guy now, so when she'd said she really didn't like him, she must have meant it.

I could only hope she'd come to her senses and realised she really did love Randal after all and wasn't going to risk losing him by playing with fire.

Liz went skiing with the school at half term. I'm sure Emma would have preferred to have spent her and Marco's break doing that rather than having to go out to Qatar because when she got back and we met up so she could tell me about it I could see she'd already made up her mind that she and Marco weren't going to live there.

'It's way too hot, for a start, and though I'd be able to drive there and go about on my own, I still think I'd find it a bit restrictive and claustrophobic,' she told me. 'I took Marco to see the International School and they give the children a great education . . . but I'm not sure how well he would fit in and he'd miss all the after-school things he does, too, like his drama classes.'

'Did you tell Des?'

'Nooo . . .' she said pensively. 'He thinks it's wonderful out there and of course he'd just love having me under his eye all the time, with no one else I knew around!'

'So what will you do?'

'I thought perhaps if he takes the contract, we could fly out for some of the school holidays,' she said. 'That could be a compromise. But I'll leave it a bit before suggesting it.'

'But you'll have to tell him before he actually *signs* a new contract.'

'I know, and I will, but I'm not looking forward to it.'

To divert her mind a bit I told her everything Lacey had confided in me about her and Guy, including how she felt about Randal.

'And it's so unfair to him, because she's obviously still in love with Guy, she just doesn't think he's serious – which is probably right – while Randal is good, solid husband material, so she's going to settle for him. Only he's worth *so* much more than Guy and he shouldn't have to be second best.'

'Oooh,' she said, looking at me wide-eyed, 'you've fallen for Randal yourself, haven't you?'

'Don't be silly,' I said, going pink. 'We argue all the time and he's only just stopped thinking I'm cooking the books and stealing the silver.'

'I don't see what that's got to do with it,' she said stubbornly.

Trust your best friend to guess the one thing you'd like to keep hidden!

'I do find him attractive, though I've no idea why,' I confessed. 'He's bossy and keeps trying to order me about. And he's never going to look at me when he's engaged to someone as stunning as Lacey.'

'I'll have to take your word for it, because I haven't seen the woman,' she said. 'She sounds a pain to me, though. Maybe you should save him from her?'

'I couldn't if I tried,' I said.

While Lacey didn't come back to visit, she rang Randal constantly and he probably saw her on the quick trips he made down there, coming back each time with a car full of stuff he wanted to keep from his flat. Luckily there was plenty of space in the attic rooms for him to stash it in till he had time to sort it out.

He had some nice paintings, though: he asked me to go up to his sitting room and help decide where to hang them, but I noticed mine was still in his bedroom.

All the cracker orders needed to be completed and delivered by the end of November, so we were flat out in the workshop. I didn't know about the others, but I dreamed nightly that I was tangled in tartan foil and bound with red ribbon.

I'd almost entirely lost my snap.

Everything went swimmingly until the weekend after Guy Fawkes Night, when the Little Mumming bonfire was to take place on the green.

Freda had told me that they all always watched the fireworks from the pub window, which was cosier but not as exciting, so Randal offered to drive me up there.

'I've been once or twice and they collect wood for weeks, so it's a good blaze. Nancy Dagger brews up her famous wassail for the occasion, too.'

'Oh, yes, someone told me they drink that at the Twelfth Night Revels, another local annual event I'd love to watch.'

'Well, you'll be able to, though if the weather is icy the steep hill up to Little Mumming tends to get too dangerous to drive on, so you'd have to walk.'

'I could walk up to see the bonfire, if you didn't really want to go,' I offered. 'I can get a lift back from the pub afterwards, with one of the others.'

'No, that's OK,' he said, 'I'd like to go.'

* * *

And the bonfire *was* spectacular, though the wassail, a drink served hot from what looked remarkably like a cauldron, was perhaps an acquired taste . . . and it was a cold night, so I attempted to acquire it in the hope it might warm me up. It didn't taste that alcoholic . . .

'Perhaps I should have sobered you up with coffee in the pub before taking you home,' Randal said, sounding amused and putting a steadying hand under one of my elbows as we made our way along the grass verge back to the car. So many people were there that he'd had to park it on the edge of the village, in the gateway to a field.

'I'm not drunk – my head is clear as crystal,' I said indignantly. 'It's just that my feet keep wandering about. I try to put them one in front of the other, but it's not really happening.'

'Oh, well, at least Mercy and Silas will have gone to bed and you'll be sober by morning, so they won't blame me for letting you drink the wassail.'

'It didn't taste very alcoholic,' I said.

'It's surprising – and I suspect people sneak more spirits into it as the evening progresses.'

'I had a bag of roast chestnuts, that should have soaked it up a bit,' I complained. 'There was someone selling them outside the British Museum when I went down with Mercy,' I added inconsequentially.

'Yes, I've seen a chestnut-seller there too, and it always seemed a bit Dickensian,' he said. 'Did you buy any?'

'No, because we were going to have dinner with Guy,' I said, and in the moonlight I saw his face go all shuttered.

'I don't want you to be another of Guy's victims and

end up with a broken heart,' he said. 'You've heard what he's like.'

'I won't be, because I never took him seriously from the moment I met him, and he knows that. Any flirting with me is just because he's running on his default setting.'

'I'm glad to hear it, because you deserve someone better than that and—'

He broke off and grabbed me as I went headlong over an unfriendly tussock of grass.

'Got you,' he said, holding me upright with a firm grip while I got my unruly legs under control.

'Who do I deserve?' I heard my voice saying as I looked up at him . . . and then, I'm not sure how it happened, but we were suddenly kissing like it was going out of fashion and I'm sure I saw fireworks going off, even though they'd long since finished.

'Oh *hell*!' Randal said finally, pulling away and sounding unflatteringly horrified. 'Sorry, I didn't intend doing that.'

'It's OK, I know it didn't mean anything – that wassail should have a health warning on it,' I said shakily. 'Let's forget it – and here's the car,' I added brightly, though I fumbled the seatbelt fastening when I'd got in.

He was silent on the short drive back, and then went straight upstairs, without having a mug of cocoa in the kitchen with me, as he generally did when we'd been to the pub together.

Next morning I discovered he'd vanished like a thief in the night, leaving a note for Mercy saying he'd had to go down to London, but he'd be back tomorrow. We weren't sure what time he'd left, so it was unclear if he meant to be back today, Sunday, or tomorrow, when we were supposed to be fine-tuning the plans for the second phase of the development.

'Never mind – perhaps he was really missing Lacey and that's what made him go off so suddenly,' Mercy suggested.

'Ppft!' said Pye disgustedly, and poor Pugsie looked forlorn, as he always did now whenever Randal was away.

Chapter 51: True Lies

Randal

I think I was running away from my feelings, more than anything else – for try as I might, there was something subtly bewitching about Tabby that kept drawing me into doing things I didn't intend to in the least . . . things I certainly shouldn't even be tempted to do, seeing I was supposed to be in love with Lacey.

And Lacey had been so sweet and forgiving about my unfounded jealousy – or so I thought, until I checked my phone later that morning and found an anonymous message, telling me that she and Guy had been a lot more than just good friends before she met me . . .

'Yes, we were going out together, but it was *years* before I met you!' Lacey confessed.

'Then why on earth didn't you tell me?' I demanded. 'In fact, you let me think you didn't even know him very well.'

'But I didn't *lie* to you,' she said earnestly. 'I mean, you didn't ask me if I'd ever been out with him, and anyway, he dumped me so it was true when I said I didn't even like him, let alone take his flirting seriously!'

'I suppose all your friends knew and I'm the only one who didn't?'

She shrugged. 'It was ages ago and I hadn't seen much of him till recently, when he started hanging out at the same places again.'

I was feeling . . . I don't know, sort of deceived. But then, my conscience wasn't quite clear either now.

'I'll drive myself up to Godsend next time,' she promised. 'It just seemed silly not to get a lift with Guy when he was going to Little Mumming anyway, even though I didn't enjoy being cooped up in his car with him.'

'But he only seems to visit Old Place when you're at Mote Farm for the weekend,' I pointed out, jealousy rearing its ugly head again.

'It's a coincidence. He was chasing Tabby, but I think he's lost interest. I'm not surprised, because she doesn't make the best of herself. She should do something with that hair, for a start.'

'What's the matter with it?' I said, surprised, because I rather liked Tabby's curtain of long, cocoa-brown hair and the fringe that framed her face, set with those all-too-enchanting lilac-grey eyes . . .

'It's boring,' she said pettishly. 'But let's not talk about Tabby, darling.'

'I wasn't; you brought her up.'

I looked at her, young, beautiful and more than a little devious, and instead of going all gooey, as I admit was the effect she usually had on me, I just felt exasperated.

'Lacey, I don't think things are really working out between

us, do you?' I asked suddenly. 'I mean, we have such different tastes and want different things out of life. We can't even agree on where we want to live!'

'But – we can work all that out,' she said, and then added, staring at me with wide eyes filling with reproachful tears, 'Don't you love me any more?'

'Of course I love you,' I said uncomfortably. 'I just thought you might have changed your mind, or wanted to postpone the wedding for a bit.'

'But I've got my dress and everything,' Lacey said, as if that was the clincher. Then she swore she still loved me and, goodness knew, I couldn't stand being cried at, even when I was sure the waterworks were being turned on for effect.

The upshot was that we agreed that she was to come and spend Christmas at Mote Farm, so we could have more time together and work things out.

Or not, as the case may be . . .

Chapter 52: Daggers Drawn

Q: How did Scrooge win the football game?
A: The Ghost of Christmas passed!

Randal came back from London both tense and terse, so I assumed that things hadn't gone too well between him and Lacey, until he announced to Mercy that she wanted to spend Christmas with us.

'How wonderful!' Mercy said, clapping her hands. She was still convinced that there was a lot of good in Lacey, though if it was true I thought she might need to start fracking to find it.

'Yes, isn't it just? Lacey suggested it,' he said gloomily, though you'd have thought he'd have been pleased about it.

'We'll show her a proper family Christmas and get the chance to really know one another – it will be so much fun,' she said, though personally I thought that sounded like a recipe for disaster . . . and I was starting to think more like Scrooge by the minute.

For a moment I even contemplated going to Blackpool for Christmas and New Year with the cracker workers, rather than watch Lacey do any more of the twisting-Randal-round-her-little-finger stuff, but I didn't think I could stand all the bingo and karaoke.

'Tabby's been helping me to make the Christmas cake,' Mercy told him. That had been fun and involved soaking the dried fruit overnight first in most of the contents of the small bottle of brandy kept in the cupboard with the other baking supplies.

'Well, speaking of Christmas,' Randal said (though actually, we speak of Christmas just about every day, so it wasn't exactly a novel topic), 'I walked round to Liberty's and they'd just done their windows, so I took pictures of our crackers.'

He showed us on his iPad and very splendid they looked, too. They'd made a giant cracker in the same colours and suspended it, broken in two, so that our sparkly new Marwood's crackers seemed to be spilling out of it.

Friendship Mill now had its own Facebook page and Twitter account, and Randal put the pictures on there next day. Not that we needed any extra publicity, for the closer we got to Christmas, the more visitors we got, so that at peak times the place was practically bursting at the seams.

With all that was going on, very soon Randal and I were back on our old footing again, with him snapping orders at me as he organised the rewiring and redecoration of the upstairs room, which was to be the new gallery, displaying the work of the artists in residence – when he had anyone in residence.

You could access the gallery from the café level, where the lift was, but there were stairs down, too, which brought you out by the workshop I'd earmarked for myself. And between bouts of cracker-making and helping Mercy in the office, or with whatever else she wanted me to do, not to mention being at Randal's beck and call, I'd sometimes sneak into my workshop and gaze out of the back window at the trees . . . And if the sketches I made for future papercuts at the weekends showed variations on the theme of a male Sleeping Beauty, with a suspiciously bronze-haired beauty hacking her way towards him, I blamed my subconscious – *and* Lacey, who seemed to be constantly ringing Randal, as if to bind him to her firmly with words of a love I only hoped was true.

We'd advertised for a Santa, and Nick Dagger from the Auld Christmas had been hired. He was very ancient, but insisted he was up to the job and that it would make a nice change of scene from the pub.

'And I've got me own white beard and hair and a pair of black wellies,' he'd pointed out, which for Mercy at least seemed to be the clincher. Randal was more doubtful, but said if Santa couldn't stand the pace, then we'd have to draft Job into doing it instead, though I suspected that his deep and mournfully fruity voice would frighten the poor little mites to death.

After a drought of messages from Guy, there was a sudden flurry: he was coming up the following weekend *especially* to see me, he said, to which I replied that he should pull the other one, it had bells on it.

Then he said I had the wrong idea and he had something he wanted to talk to me about, which had an ominously familiar ring to it.

I only hoped he wasn't going to confide anything I really didn't want to hear, like everyone else had seemed to do lately!

He was driving up late on Friday night and going back the next evening, so we would have to meet on Saturday, but that was impossible: the mill was way too busy now we were getting closer to Christmas and Santa was arriving in his grotto that day, too, so I couldn't just go waltzing off.

In the end he wore me down, though, and I agreed to meet him in the woods behind the mill at nine, before we opened.

Guy was sitting on a log in the clearing near the pebble beach at the stream's edge and his handsome, mobile face looked so unusually serious that I wondered what on earth he was going to say.

He certainly surprised me, because it seemed that the wolf had a heart, after all, and had lost it to Lacey.

'I love the woman, but she doesn't believe me,' he said bitterly.

'Well, you must have heard about the man who cried wolf once too often?' I said, and he gave a wry grin.

'But I really do mean it this time! I realised I loved her when I heard she'd got engaged to Randal, of all people.'

'But that's all part of the pattern, isn't it? You always seem to want the girls who're engaged to other men,' I pointed out helpfully.

'I wanted you and *you* weren't engaged to anyone.'

'I know – I'm *so* flattered,' I said sarcastically.

'Randal warned me off Lacey. He does a very good veiled threat with menace, does Randal,' he said.

'Yes, I can imagine.'

'Now Lacey's told me not to go near her any more, she doesn't even want me around,' he said. 'She had a big scene with Randal when he found out she hadn't told him we used to go out together. He was tipped off by an anonymous message.'

'Oh, I wonder who that was from,' I said drily.

He raised one dark eyebrow. 'They didn't seem exactly like a marriage made in heaven, so I thought it might just cause enough of a bust-up to derail the engagement. But no, she says she's definitely marrying him and she's even spending Christmas here with the family.'

'I know, and we're all *delirious* with pleasure at the prospect,' I said.

'Look, I really am serious about this,' Guy insisted. 'But I don't know what I can do to convince her I love her.'

'You'll have to find some way of *showing* her you mean it, then. And I don't mean the caveman stuff you tried on with me in the mill,' I added.

'Like what?' he asked, looking blank.

'I can't imagine, short of eloping with her,' I said, 'and if ever there was a man less likely to head for Gretna Green, it's you.'

I rose, hoping my decent black trousers weren't green with moss from the log.

'It's getting on towards opening time, so I'd better get down to the mill. Santa's arriving early and I want to see him settled before the children start to form a disorderly queue.'

He got up too and said, 'I'll walk you down, but I won't go in because I'm too afraid of Randal.'

I think he was only half joking.

'Sorry I couldn't be more help,' I said.

'No, actually you've been really helpful,' he replied, giving me a hug and kiss that took me by surprise. 'You've given me lots to think about!'

He strolled off up into the trees and I turned and carried on down to the mill, where I appeared to have given Randal something to think about too. He was staring up at me from the stockroom loading bay with a face like a thundercloud and then he turned round and went back in, slamming the doors behind him.

Mercy had already taken charge of Father Christmas and installed him in a comfortable chair in his grotto, with a sack of toys nearby. He made a very good Santa because, as well as looking the part, he had a high, piping, elven laugh and said the same thing to every child: What would they like for Christmas and had they been good? And then he would listen carefully before saying he'd see what he could do.

'Eh, I've seen you in the pub and you're a strapping lass! Would you like to sit on my knee, too?' he said, when I went in to tell him Lillian had volunteered to bring him some lunch, which he intended eating in his grotto with the door shut, the curtains drawn and a 'Santa has gone down the chimney but will be back in half an hour' sign.

I thought he was being a bit ambitious and would probably crumble under my weight, but apparently he had better luck with Lillian. When she didn't come back from delivering his lunch and it was almost time for the cracker-making demonstration, Joy went to find her and said she was cuddled up in the armchair with Santa, sharing his sandwich.

Just as well we'd drawn the curtains . . .

'Lillian's had her eye on Nick Dagger for ages.'

'Isn't he a lot older than she is?' I asked.

'Yes, but he's well off and he's got his own cottage by the pub,' she said. 'She thinks it might be better to be an old man's darling, but I expect she'll find out she's mistaken,' she added, with prim relish.

Randal was avoiding me and when we finally met over the dinner table he didn't mention seeing me with Guy – not that it was any of his business who I walked in the woods with, anyway. I just hoped he hadn't got the wrong idea about that kiss, even if *that* wasn't any of his business either . . . though what I'd discussed with Guy certainly was.

'You were out early this morning, dear,' Mercy said. 'You'd already had breakfast, fed Pugsie and Pye and gone when I came down.'

'Tabby was having a little tryst with Guy in the woods,' Randal told her.

'Really? Is he paying you attentions again, dear?'

'No, it wasn't a romantic tryst, he just wanted to chat to me.'

'A strange hour and place for a little chat,' Randal said. 'A *friendly* little chat.'

I gave him a chilly look, but it didn't stop him following me into the kitchen later and warning me not to get involved again with Guy.

'I wasn't involved with him in the first place,' I told him coldly.

'When I was in London, I found out that Lacey was involved with him – but ages before she met me,' he said, frowning. Then he looked consideringly at me. 'That didn't surprise you, did it? Did Guy tell you?'

'Actually, Lacey did, some time ago,' I said.

He was still looking at me. 'Someone sent me an anonymous message telling me about it.'

'Well, it wasn't me. Why would I want to drive you apart?'

'No reason at all,' he snapped, slamming down the tray he was holding and walking out, though he had to reopen the door to let Pugsie through when he started yapping.

'I understand nothing about anyone,' I said to Pye.

'Mrrow,' he agreed.

After that, Randal seemed to throw himself into his work even more and so did I, until the very last of the Christmas cracker orders were sent out and the workshop could resume a more leisurely pace.

I did tell Emma all about Guy's visit next time I saw her and she said the situation sounded impossible, but she thought Christmas should prove interesting, though maybe not in a good way.

Then she added that she wasn't sure how good hers would be, come to that, since Des would be home for it and had already signed a new contract for a year without first asking her if she *wanted* to move out there.

'So then I said it would be better if we stayed here and flew out for the school holidays and now he's furious, though I'm sure he thinks he can get me to change my mind at Christmas.'

'And will he?'

'No way,' she said with determination.

The busy days passed quickly and suddenly we were poised on the edge of December and the slippery slide down to the festive season. Despite everything, I felt as excited as I had when I was a small girl, wondering what Father Christmas would bring me.

Had I been naughty or nice? I think the jury was still out on that one.

When Liz returned from school for the holidays, she shared my excitement and together we fetched down the decorations from the attics and spent a happy afternoon adorning the large pine tree that Randal had set up in the corner of the drawing room.

He said Pye's ghosts would just have to walk through it and then, after hanging around criticising our efforts at decoration, helped festoon the ceiling with paper garlands and balloons.

Freda ordered up a huge supermarket Christmas food shop and filled the fridge, larder, freezer and cupboards, while Mercy, Liz and I baked up a storm of mince pies and stollen.

Liz was to be an elf, so that she could help Santa and earn some extra pocket money. We'd already ordered her a costume and she looked very fetching in green, with silvery bells.

A small padded envelope was awaiting me one evening when I went home after the mill shut.

There was no one other than Emma who might send me a present and I hadn't ordered anything, but when I ripped open the envelope out fell a small sealed plastic bag and a note. The dried-out and crumbly grunge in the bag looked disgusting, and embedded in it I could see a small section of gold studded with what might once have been shining opals and pearls.

I snatched up the note that had fallen out of the envelope with it, which explained that the enclosed had been in the Lost Property box at the cat rescue centre ever since Pye had passed it into his litter tray upon arrival. A kennel maid had spotted it and popped it into the bag, but hadn't thought it of any value and they'd forgotten about it till now.

'Are you so greedy you swallow rings whole with your dinner?' I asked Pye, and he made one of his silent grimaces at me, possibly in apology.

When I told the others at dinner what had happened, Mercy said how fortunate it was that it had turned up and was I going to send it to Jeremy?

'Yes, though it looks in such a state I'm not sure how pleased he's going to be,' I said. 'But never mind, at least he'll have it back and realise I was telling the truth.'

'Do you want me to help you try and clean it a bit first?' asked Liz.

'No, he can do that himself.'

'A truly crappy present,' Randal commented, his face straight, so I didn't know if he was joking or not, though Liz giggled.

'Really, Randal,' Mercy said indulgently.

* * *

Something came over me and I couldn't resist it: I made a special red tartan foil cracker and enclosed the letter and the plastic goodie bag in it, before posting it to Jeremy.

Off with a bang.

I didn't add a message of my own, because it spoke for itself, really.

Chapter 53: Advent

Q: What must you know to be an auctioneer?
A: Lots.

Lacey, who had up to now kept Randal warm by frequent phone calls, suddenly fell silent on the day she was supposed to travel to Godsend to spend Christmas with us.

When she didn't arrive by evening, he started to get worried and phoned her flat.

'There's only her housekeeper there,' he reported, coming back with a face like thunder. 'But she left a message for me: "Tell Randal if he calls that I'm not coming for Christmas after all."'

'Short and to the point,' I said, and he gave me a glare.

'Could she have been called to her parents' house?' suggested Mercy. 'Perhaps one of them is ill?'

'I thought of that and rang them, but they didn't seem concerned – they said she was so impulsive she'd probably decided to go and stay with some of her friends, instead.'

'I suppose she might,' I said. 'It certainly sounds as if she suddenly changed her mind about coming here.'

'It seems I'm never going to meet this mysterious Lacey,' Liz complained.

'You're not missing anything,' Silas told her.

Randal looked exasperated. 'It was her idea to come for Christmas in the first place, so I don't know what she's playing at! And what am I supposed to think of that message?'

'There might be a good reason she dashed off like that, Randal. I'm sure she'll let us know where she is tomorrow and explain everything,' Mercy said gently.

'She'd better,' he said.

But there was no explanation – no more messages at all. Randal was both angry and concerned, until her parents passed on the news that they'd had a brief text from her saying she was having a lovely time, though she didn't say where. After that, Randal was just angry.

We'd long since stopped expecting Lacey to call and explain herself when the phone rang after dinner one evening. We all looked at each other and then Randal got up and went into the library, grim-faced.

But to my surprise he came back and said the call was for me. It was Emma, sounding so distressed it took me a few moments to get the gist of what she was saying.

'Des got back this morning and we argued about living in Qatar. He insisted we were going and that he even hoped we might make our home out there, in which case we'd send Marco back to boarding school when he'd turned eight. I said: over my dead body!'

'And then you said he actually *hit* you?'

'Not right then: it was later, after my neighbour's son dropped in to see if my kitchen tap was all right. The washer went yesterday and I hadn't got one, so I popped next door to see if he could fix it. He's an apprentice plumber.'

'Don't tell me Des was jealous of him?'

'Oh yes, and he's only about twenty; I'm almost old enough to be his mother! You wouldn't believe the things he accused me of and then . . . well, he lost his rag totally and back-handed me and I went flying. His signet ring's caught my face, too. I look a bit of a mess.'

'Where is he now – and more importantly, where are you and Marco?'

'We got away in my car. By sheer good luck, his mother's nursing home called just after he'd hit me, because she has pneumonia and he needed to get over there fast. It's the kindest thing she's ever done for me,' she added. 'He locked me in and took the keys and my car keys, too. Only of course, I have spares and keep a back door key in the dresser drawer, so I could get out.'

'Where are you now, then?'

'Parked in Sticklepond, near the church. I woke Marco up and we just tossed a few things into bags and left. He's got his headphones on at the moment, listening to a book . . . but I'm sure he heard what was going on earlier. I don't know what to do and the rain's torrential,' she added desperately.

'You'd better come straight here and we'll think what to do next. But you'll need to be careful, because Job says there's flooding on the bottom road.'

'Won't Mercy won't mind us just turning up at this time of night?'

'I'm positive she won't, and I'll go and tell her now. Drive carefully.'

Randal had vanished when I went back to the drawing room, probably in a huff that it hadn't been a call from Lacey.

'Poor thing!' said Mercy when I told the others about Emma and Marco's imminent arrival and the reason for it. 'Of course they must come and stay here and for as long as they want to.'

'She was already in Sticklepond when she rang, so she should be here very soon,' I said. 'Twenty minutes, at most.'

'Then, Liz, do go and stand by the front door and look out for the headlights turning in by the garages.'

'If I put on my mac and take the big golf umbrella, I could help them in with their things?' she suggested, calm as always. 'If they had time to pack, that is.'

'I'm not sure what they've got. I don't think Emma lingered long enough to pack properly.'

'The Blue Room is always made up for unexpected visitors, dear,' Mercy said to me. 'Perhaps they could share that just for tonight and Marco might like to move into the adjoining small room tomorrow.'

'That would be wonderful, thank you,' I said gratefully.

I gave Emma a hug when she arrived – I'd never seen her look quite so distraught and poor Marco was the quietest I'd ever known him. Their luggage seemed to be Emma's handbag, a backpack stuffed with soft toys and several bulging bin sacks.

'I'm so glad you've come, my dears,' Mercy said welcomingly. 'I'll let Liz and Tabby show you to your room and by the time you come down again I'll have hot soup ready to warm you both up.'

'I can stay tonight?' Emma said hopefully.

'Of course: you're very welcome to stay for as long as you want to,' Mercy assured her. 'Isn't she, Silas?'

'What?' he muttered, waking up with a start, then opened his eyes wide and said, 'All these people coming and going lately – the place was a haven of peace and now it's turned into bedlam.'

'I thought you were dead,' Marco said, sounding relieved. 'You looked dead and I couldn't see you breathing. That's a pretty good sign.'

Silas said, 'Well as you see, I'm not. Are you both coming to stay for Christmas? I'd sooner have you than that brass-haired hussy of Randal's.'

'I suspect that might be ex-brass-haired hussy of Randal's,' I said, or at least, I *hoped* it was.

When I took them up to the Blue Room, Emma said, 'It's so kind of Mrs Marwood to let us stay here tonight. I wasn't thinking straight when I phoned you. Really, I suppose we should have found a women's refuge or something . . . but I didn't want to involve the police . . . and who'd have thought it would have come to this?'

She sobbed and Marco looked worried. 'Don't cry, Mummy. I like it here. Am I going to sleep in that big bed?'

'We both are,' she said, blinking back tears. 'Just for tonight, at least.'

'For as long as you want. Mercy invites all kinds of random strangers to stay here, so she'd be perfectly happy to have you stay over Christmas. And Randal's fiancée isn't coming after all, so there's loads of room.'

'I'll take Marco downstairs now,' Liz suggested, dumping the bags by the door, 'and you can come down when you're ready. Come on, Marco.'

When they'd gone, Emma said, 'Goodness knows what I've got in those bags. I told Marco to pack his favourite things while I went round the house with the bin bags tossing in clothes and shoes and stuff. I knew it would take Des twenty minutes just to get to the nursing home, so even if it was a false alarm and he turned back again, we'd have a good hour to pack and get away, but I wasn't thinking straight.'

She went over and looked in one of the bags. 'I seem to have swept half the contents of the bathroom into here, but at least my make-up's in there, too.'

'All is not lost, then,' I said, and she gave a weak smile.

I stowed away what there was in the wardrobe and drawers while she brushed her hair, dried her eyes and sponged off the small cut on her cheek.

'Come on. You'll feel better after a drink and some hot soup,' I said.

Marco was already drinking his from a china beaker, watched by Pye and Pugsie, who seemed in favour of the new arrivals.

Randal had reappeared and clearly had been updated on the situation, because he said hello when Emma came down, but barely glanced at her bruised and cut cheek.

'I hope you don't mind our being here,' she said to him timidly.

'Oh, it's always been open house at Mote Farm,' he said. 'Goodness knows who else Mercy's invited for Christmas and forgotten about.'

'Only Ceddie. And your friend Charlie.'

'What? Charlie's coming?' he said, looking astonished.

'Didn't I mention it? It was when he rang a week or so ago to talk to you and while we were waiting for you to come in, we had a little chat. His parents are in New Zealand visiting his sister and he was going to stay in his flat alone, so of course I insisted he come here.'

'Well, let's hope he brings a canoe, unless this rain stops,' Randal said. 'The ground's soaked up as much as it can take.'

Marco was bathed and put to bed with his soft toys around him, and Emma, exhausted by tension and trauma, soon followed.

'Mercy's so kind, but I can't stay here imposing on her for ever,' she said as I made sure she had everything she needed. 'I suppose I should have rung the police really and had him arrested for assault, but I just wanted to snatch Marco up and run.'

'Let's worry about it tomorrow, because things always seem better in daylight,' I suggested.

When I went downstairs, Mercy and Silas had gone to bed and Randal was locking up.

'I've put everything in the dishwasher,' he said. 'And don't look so worried,' he added, 'your friend and her little boy are safe here and welcome to stay as long as they want to.' Then he smiled, said goodnight and went upstairs.

I don't know why that little bit of kindness should bring tears to my eyes, but it did.

And it was a very watery night, because when I was tucked up in bed, the hissing waterfall roar of the seemingly endless rain carried on into my dreams.

Chapter 54: Box of Delights

Q: Why don't ducks tell jokes when they're flying?
A: Because they'd quack up!

All that emotion must have worn Emma out, because she and Marco had only just come down when Randal, Liz and I were leaving for the mill. At least it had finally stopped raining.

Emma looked much better and Marco had certainly got his bounce back.

It was going to be another busy day, but Mercy said she had baking and other things to do at the house and would bring Emma and Marco down later, to visit Santa.

'You and Randal are so efficient, you don't really need me there all the time now. I'll see you later and we'll bring you some stollen.'

I'd just taken Father Christmas a cup of tea and a mince pie to sustain him when it was Marco's turn to go in. I couldn't resist lingering to listen.

First Marco asked Santa what it was like living in Lapland most of the time, which was clearly a curveball Nick hadn't prepared for, because he took a moment or two before he replied.

'Eh, it's a grand place if you like snow and reindeer,' he said finally.

'Your elf is very big,' Marco said. 'I thought elves were little tiny things.'

'They're magic, so they can appear big or small,' Emma said quickly.

'And she looks like Liz,' he said, undeterred.

'I get told that all the time,' the elf said gravely. 'Now, tell Santa what you'd like for Christmas and then the other children can have their turn.'

'I'd like lots of books about history. I like history. And a big box of dressing-up clothes.'

'Ho, ho, ho,' Santa said, looking slightly baffled, and then his elf handed Marco a present and ushered him out, to Nick's evident relief.

The gift was from the shop's Christmas stocking range and was a Mr Potato Head, something I'd had as a child. Mercy promised they'd go right back to the house and find Marco a lovely big potato, but Emma stayed for a while.

'It was lucky I remembered to put all Marco's presents from under the tree into a bag when we were leaving, but I forgot the stocking fillers, because they were hidden in the wardrobe.'

'There are plenty more in the Christmas shop,' I assured her. 'And maybe we might pop up to the village store, because Oriel Comfort stocks all kinds of little gifts and I'm sure I saw a jar of sugar mice in there last week, too.'

'That sounds great – and luckily I did get him one or two books, though not the box of costumes he asked Santa for . . . and Mercy seems to be taking it for granted I'll be staying right over Christmas.'

'Of course you must, and now horrible Lacey has taken herself off somewhere and I've got you and Marco here instead, I'm expecting it to be a whole lot more fun!'

'I have an idea,' said Mercy later, when Marco was in bed and Liz had told her what he'd said to Santa. 'There are two or three trunkfuls of old clothes in one of the attic rooms and I'm sure there's a tin toy box up there too, so you could fill it with anything you think he might like to dress up in. Then he'll get everything he asked for!'

'He'd love that more than anything else,' Emma said gratefully and, together with Liz, we went to see what we could find – and had to come back and fetch Randal to carry down the green tin trunk, filled with all kinds of treasures: a plume of feathers, a red velvet fez with a tassel, a Victorian beaded cape, an embroidered waistcoat, a tawny velvet mantle with a silk lining and a fur muff.

'He's going to love these,' Emma said.

'We can hide it in my room and you can wrap it up and put it under the tree with his other presents tomorrow,' I said, and Randal took it through for me.

'Randal's very kind, isn't he? Emma said.

'He has his moments,' I admitted.

Chapter 55: Hasty Pudding

Q: What's the best thing to put into a Christmas cake?
A: Your teeth!

It being the last Saturday before Christmas the next day, the mill was likely to be even busier so Randal and I went down there early.

Mercy planned to drive Emma and Marco up to the village shop in Little Mumming, to find a few more things for Marco's Christmas stocking – or rather, Emma would find them, while Mercy diverted Marco by showing him the interesting stained-glass windows in the small church.

At Friendship Mill the tills jingled faster than sleigh bells all day, so that Randal and I were completely shattered but happy when we finally locked up and went up to the house.

On my way through the kitchen to change I found everyone gathered around a large mixing bowl on the kitchen table, including Ceddie, who'd been collected from the railway station earlier by Job. Liz and Marco were eating mixed dried fruit straight from the jar and Emma was sitting with Pugsie on her knee and Pye draped along the back of the chair like a fur headrest. He'd always liked her.

'I'm just about to finish stirring a really hasty Christmas pudding,' Mercy said. 'I can't imagine how I forgot! Of course, it should have been made weeks ago, but it will be just as nice, you'll see. You must stir it and make a wish, Tabby – we all have.'

'There are lots of silver things in it,' Marco told me gravely. 'They're wrapped in greaseproof paper so we can find them easily.'

'Good idea, because it wouldn't be lucky if you broke a tooth on one,' I said. 'I'll just take my coat off and wash my hands. Randal's changing; I expect he'll be down in a minute.'

In fact, he was quicker than me and had already taken his turn when I got back, so I took the big wooden spoon and stirred, closing my eyes.

What should I wish for – a place of my own? But I hated the idea of leaving Mote Farm!

For love . . .?

Then my inner voice whispered, *I want to stay here with Randal at Mote Farm for ever!*

I stirred again quickly and added a second wish. *Let Lacey be safe, but don't let her ever come back here.*

Randal, Ceddie and I went to the Quaker meeting next morning with Silas and Mercy and no one said a word for the whole hour: it was very peaceful.

When we got home we found Charlie had arrived, along with a hamper of Fortnum and Mason's goodies to add to our already overflowing food stocks.

I found myself pleased to see him and he was soon proving useful, since he seemed happy to play endless games and playact with Marco. He wasn't just doing it because he wanted to please Emma, either . . . though I think he did and he went out of his way to clown about and make her laugh, so I thought Randal had probably told him why she was staying with us.

After lunch we went for a walk and you could feel the air growing chillier by the minute, so that the cold snap that was predicted for Christmas might actually be on its way.

Emma checked her mobile when there was a signal, half expecting a stream of messages – even apologies – from Des, but the only one was from her neighbour, asking her to ring back, which she did.

It seemed that she'd spoken to Des the morning after Emma had left, when he was loading bags into his car, and he'd said he was going to his sister's in Scotland till he flew back to Qatar after Christmas.

'And then she looked through the cottage windows, because there'd been a lot of crashing noises the night before,' Emma said. 'And it looks like he's trashed the place.'

'Oh, no!' I said. 'That's so petty and spiteful.'

'I think I'll just try and forget about it till after Christmas, since Mercy says she'd love us to stay till then,' Emma said. 'I'll be able to face it, then. And start divorce proceedings,' she added.

'Attagirl, and I've got holidays due, so I'll come and help you clear up the house,' promised Charlie.

'We'll all go, because the mill will be closed till New Year after tomorrow morning,' Randal said. 'We don't usually open on a Monday, it's just because it's so close to Christmas and we're closing at noon.'

'There you are,' I said to Emma, 'your very own clean-up taskforce!'

* * *

Freda, Job and the others set off for Blackpool in a minibus just after nine.

'Don't forget Ginger and Bing!' had been Lillian's parting shot, because I'd promised I'd go down and feed them every day while they were away. I'd written it at the top of the kitchen chalkboard to remind myself.

Randal opened the doors of the mill at ten, as usual, but there wasn't exactly a rush, because by now the ice freezing over the flooded roads was starting to make travelling treacherous.

And of course, though the lights were on in the cracker-making factory, no one was home.

When I took Santa and his elf cups of tea later, there were no queues of children and Santa seemed to be telling Liz possibly dubious anecdotes about his life as a boy in Little Mumming, but I thought his Lancashire accent was a bit too broad for her to follow everything he said.

Then I went through to what would be my workshop in the adjoining building. The floorboards were now back down and the channels, where the new electricity points had been put in, plastered over. It was more or less ready for the final touches that would turn it into my very own little studio and I couldn't wait . . .

I was still dreaming in there when Randal came to find me. 'It's almost one, you know! We didn't have a visitor for the last hour, so I let everyone go early and I've already cashed up. I've even fed the cats.'

I shivered. 'Sorry, I hadn't realised how long I've been in here – or quite how cold I am until now.' I looked at him and added, 'It's been a huge success, hasn't it?'

'Yes, all of it – including the museum. I was entirely wrong about that *and* about you, and I'll happily eat my words.' Then he gave me his rare and attractive smile. 'Come on.'

As we passed through the mill it seemed so dark, empty and echoing, though it still smelled of Christmas. The large tree twinkled in the entrance lobby until Randal switched it off as we left, locking the door behind us.

'It seems mean leaving Ginger and Bing alone,' I said.

'They'll be warm enough and fine here; they're used to being factory cats.'

'Actually, I think when Lillian's here, they often spend their evenings with her. They must miss her when she's away.'

'Perhaps Pye will invite them to the house then,' Randal said drily. 'He seems to have assumed the role of lord of the manor.'

'He is lording it a bit,' I admitted.

'A *bit*? He seems to do exactly what he wants around here – like you,' he added, and a large, fat white feathery snowflake fell from the sky like a heavenly message and landed on my nose.

Christmas Eve dawned bright, cold and snowy – pretty, if you didn't have to travel anywhere, which we didn't. We had enough food and drink to sustain a siege and nothing to do but eat, drink and enjoy ourselves. And already our disparate group had jelled into a happy family party, all helping where they could with whatever needed doing and making their own amusements.

After breakfast, Randal came into the library just as I was opening an email from Jeremy. There was no subject, but I thought I could guess: and when I read it I was quite right.

'This is priceless,' I said to Randal. 'Jeremy and Kate have finally pulled the cracker!'

'Which cracker?' he asked, puzzled.

'The one I sent them. I put the bag from the cat rescue centre in it.'

'You're a wicked woman,' he said, though a smile twitched the corner of his mouth.

'That's what Jeremy says. And that it's hugely valuable and I'll have to replace it, because it's been permanently damaged on its transit through Pye.'

'I'll permanently damage him, if he tries to pursue that avenue,' Randal promised.

'Do you want to see if there's anything from Lacey before I turn it off?' I asked.

'I'm sure there won't be, but I did think I might check her Facebook page.'

'You're on Facebook?'

'Lacey persuaded me, but I've hardly used it.'

He took my place and after a few minutes got Lacey's page up and scrolled down. Then he gasped.

'My God, Tabby, just look at these pictures – she's only gone and got married, and you'll never guess who to!'

'Guy?' I said, looking over his shoulder at a succession of photographs of the happy couple – in a wedding chapel in Las Vegas. 'Elvis helps us tie the knot' was my favourite.

'Well, I told him he'd need to do something impressive to convince her he really loved her and he's certainly done that.'

He turned to look at me. 'I might have known this was your doing.'

'It was when we met in the woods – he told me he loved

her but she didn't trust him any more, which was hardly surprising and . . . I'm so sorry, Randal.'

'What for?'

'Sowing the seed of the idea in his head, so that Lacey left you.'

'I thought when I saw you in the woods with Guy that day that he'd got round you and was going to break your heart . . .' he said. Then he stood up and smiled. 'Those pictures are the best Christmas present ever!'

'They are?'

He pulled me into his arms. 'I've been wanting to kiss you properly for weeks,' he said, and suited the action to the words.

When we eventually emerged and told the others what had happened to Lacey, Silas said, 'Hurray! I think that deserves a toast – break out the ginger beer.'

'Really, Silas,' said Mercy, then added gently to Randal, 'I'm so sorry, but she wasn't the right girl for you, dear boy.'

'I'd come to that conclusion myself,' he said cheerfully, and went to get the ginger beer.

The rest of the day passed happily: the snow still fell slowly and softly onto the icy roads and little except gritters and the occasional hardy four-wheel-drive vehicle passed on the lane at the bottom of the hill.

The ducks walked about on the moat and quacked mournfully for food, but they did have an open bit of water under the bridge to swim about in when this palled.

After lunch we left Mercy, Silas and Ceddie in the drawing room listening to a Christmas carol concert on the radio and went sledging on the sloping field below the house, till Marco got so tired Charlie had to carry him piggyback up the hill home, where we all thawed out over hot tea, mince pies and the Christmas cake I'd helped Mercy to bake.

It was a strangely old-fashioned but enjoyable Christmas Eve and after dinner we played traditional board games from a vintage compendium we found in the library, till an excited Marco was finally put to bed by Emma.

But all evening my eyes had constantly been drawn to Randal's, and when this happened, we both smiled, as if we shared a secret.

He hadn't said anything when he kissed me, so I didn't know where we were heading, but I was sure in my own heart that I loved him.

I said so to Pye when I was getting ready for bed and sang him a snatch of 'I'm in Love with a Wonderful Guy'.

'Pfft!' he said, but I knew he was getting quite fond of Randal . . . so long as he kept the bacon rinds coming.

Chapter 56: The Big Picture

Randal

I felt . . . I didn't know how to describe it – exalted, perhaps? It was as if I'd found the final piece to complete the jigsaw of my life, after wasting time trying to hammer a piece from an entirely different one into it.

Tabby had already woven herself into my life – and into Mercy and Silas's hearts, too.

'Mercy,' I said, drawing her aside when Tabby and Liz had gone into the kitchen, 'I've got something to ask you.'

And when I'd explained, she beamed. 'Leave it to me – and Silas.'

'Silas?' I echoed, but she'd already bustled off on her mission.

Chapter 57: Crowned

I woke early to a world muffled in snow and opened the door to the passage so Pye could go out into the garden if he wanted to, while I got ready.

I'd just dressed and was brushing my hair when I heard the sitting-room door open again and a moment later, Pugsie trotted in, wearing a big blue bow.

Or rather, it *wasn't* a bow, but a large cracker, attached to his collar with ribbon.

Pye followed him in looking ruffled and pulling faces. I kneeled down.

'What's that, Pugsie, is it for me?'

It had already slipped round by his ear, so I undid the bow and took it off . . . and then looked up to find Randal standing there, his fair hair ruffled and his dark hazel eyes bright. There were a set of scratches across the back of his hand.

'Please tell me you weren't mad enough to try to tie a cracker round Pye's neck first?' I begged.

He nodded. 'But I gave that idea up fairly fast. Pugsie was much more accommodating.'

He bent and hauled me to my feet.

'Do you need someone to help you pull that cracker?' he asked.

'Wait a minute,' I said, getting a firm grip on the end . . . and then, with a bang, out popped a small box and inside it – a large single diamond ring, simple and beautiful.

'Where on earth did you get this?' I gasped.

'Silas. The girl he wanted to marry chose someone else before he could ask her and he said he'd like you to have it – for ever.'

He unrolled a lilac tissue-paper crown and gravely set it on my head. 'I want you to marry me.'

The ring slid onto my finger as if it was made for me – and my arms went around Randal's neck and pulled his head down towards mine.

'I love you, Randal Hesketh,' I said.

'Good, because you're already Queen of Christmas and queen of my heart,' he said, then lovingly kissed me till my crown fell off with a papery rustle.

'Pfft!' said Pye, and stalked out.

Q: Who is Santa married to?

A: Mary Christmas!

Recipes

Mercy's Citrus Crush

This simple version of lemonade is a refreshing drink on a hot day. It makes a large jug, but double or triple the quantities if you need to. I have used the American cup measure, where one cup equals half a pint, but so long as you use the same cup measure for all the ingredients, it will be fine.

Ingredients

3 unwaxed lemons and 1 lime
1 cup of sugar (granulated or caster)
3 cups of cold water

Method

Wash and dry the lemons and lime.

Zest one lemon and one lime and put the zest in a saucepan.

Add all the sugar and one cup of the water.

Bring to a gentle simmer and continue to cook gently for

about five minutes. (Don't let it boil.) The water will go a pale yellowy colour. Take it off the heat.

Squeeze all the lemons and the lime and put the juice through a strainer into a large jug along with the contents of the saucepan.

Stir in the remaining two cups of cold water.

When it is cold, cover and keep in the fridge. Good served over ice in tall glasses. You can also make a larger quantity straight into a punch bowl.

An Igloo Christmas Cake

This is a fun Christmas cake, which you can make with the traditional mixture, as a sponge cake or, as here, a fruitcake.

I used one half of a big Christmas pudding mould as a cake tin, but half a ball-shaped cake mould or even an oven-proof glass bowl would do. This quantity of mix will fill a cake tin about seven or eight inches across but my mould is slightly smaller, so I had a little left. I made the excess into small cakes in a muffin tin.

Ingredients

6oz/175g softened butter
6oz/175g caster sugar
4 beaten eggs
8oz/225g self-raising flour
14oz/400g mixed dried fruit with peel
1 tablespoon golden syrup
Zest of an orange or lemon (optional)

To cover

Apricot jam
Roll-out marzipan
Roll-out fondant icing
A large circular cake board or plate

Method

Preheat the oven to 325F°/170C°/gas mark 3. Grease and then line with greaseproof paper whatever mould you are using.

In a large mixing bowl beat the butter and sugar together for a couple of minutes and then add in all the other ingredients and stir well until blended.

Put it into the tin and, although this fruitcake won't rise a huge amount, remember to leave about an inch for this. Smooth the top.

Put the cake in the oven and after an hour, loosely cover the top with foil to stop the edges catching. If you are using a small mould, start to test whether it is cooked after an hour and a half – the skewer will come out clean if it is ready. A larger cake will take about two hours.

When cooked, let it cool a little and then turn it onto a wire rack and remove the paper. Don't worry about any imperfections – the icing will cover those!

When totally cold you can store it in an airtight container until you are ready to ice it.

To ice
Warm a little apricot jam in the microwave on a low heat for a minute or two and then brush it liberally all over the cake.

On a flat surface, roll out the marzipan into a large circle (it will have to cover the whole dome of the cake) using icing sugar to stop it sticking to the board and rolling pin.

Drape over the cake and mould it round the edges, then trim off the excess. From the bits left, make a little tunnel entrance to the igloo and push it onto the front.

Put the cake onto the board or large plate.

Now, roll out the fondant icing in the same way and then cover the whole cake, the entrance tunnel and the cake board, so the igloo looks as if it is surrounded by snow, as it should be! Smooth it into shape – if you dust your fingertips with icing sugar you can polish out any lumps and bumps in the icing.

For the finishing touches, draw in the 'blocks of ice' that form the igloo. I also added two Eskimo figures and a Santa on the roof to mine.

Coconut Pyramids

These are a long-time favourite of mine and very easy to make. I have a special plastic cone mould, but you can just shape them by hand. The recipe makes about twenty bite-sized ones, or ten big ones.

Ingredients

2 large egg whites
4oz/110g caster sugar
7oz/200g desiccated coconut
Glacé cherries for the top, if liked. (Use a quarter or half for each, depending on the size of the pyramids you're making.)

Method

Preheat the oven to 170C°/325F°/gas mark 3.

Line a baking tray with baking paper.

In a mixing bowl, beat the egg whites until frothy (but not stiff) and then add the sugar. Beat gently till it dissolves and then stir in the coconut.

Then either press the mixture very firmly into your mould and turn each one out onto the baking tray, or, using damp hands, form the mixture into pyramids.

If you are using cherries, place a piece onto the top of each one.

Bake until they are slightly golden and firm, which takes about 25 minutes. Remove and let them cool on a wire rack.

When cold, store in an airtight container.